snapshots

snapshots

william norris

riverhead books
a member of Penguin Putnam Inc.
New York 2001

This book is a work of fiction. Names, characters, places, and incidents either are the product of the author's imagination or are used fictitiously, and any resemblance to actual persons, living or dead, business establishments, events, or locales is entirely coincidental.

Riverhead Books
a member of
Penguin Putnam Inc.
375 Hudson Street
New York, NY 10014

Library of Congress Cataloging-in-Publication Data

Norris, William, date.
  Snapshots : a novel / by William Norris.
    p. cm.
  ISBN 1-57322-183-X
   1. New Jersey—Fiction.   I. Title.
  PS3614.O77 S63   2001   2001019725
  813'.6—dc21

Printed in the United States of America

10 9 8 7 6 5 4 3 2 1

This book is printed on acid-free paper. ∞

Book design by Marysarah Quinn

acknowledgments

I am lucky to have a circle of remarkable and talented friends who do work that inspires and delights me. If I have neglected to mention someone here, be assured the slight is not intentional.

Thanks are due first to Joan Weimer, a remarkable teacher who made me believe this was possible many years ago. Mary LaChapelle's kind and astute readings of many, many drafts provided guidance both on the page and in life. I am also fortunate to have studied with Susan Thames—who went above and beyond the call of duty for this book— and I am luckier still to call her my friend. I am indebted to Kris Malone-Grossman and Dawn Williams for both their friendship and the time they took to read and respond to the manuscript.

I owe thanks to my family, especially my sister Kerry and my mother, for their support. I cannot measure the depth of my regard for all of you.

Lisa Bankoff's work on my behalf, not to mention her enthusiasm for this book from the moment it landed on her desk, is deeply appreciated. I could not ask for a better advocate. In addition, I owe thanks to Patrick Price for all the unheralded work he has done for me. It has not gone unnoticed. Thanks are also due to all at Riverhead, but especially Wendy Carlton, whose thoughtful editorial suggestions and comments allowed me to craft a better book, and Venetia van Kuffeler, who fielded my phone calls and handled my questions with aplomb and grace.

Finally, I am blessed to share my life with Asia Friedman, who reads me first, curbs my propensity for unnecessary apostrophes and is the best reason I've found yet for getting out of bed in the morning.

For Mary Norris, for many reasons.

1 9 9 7

The mother, always an early riser, finds it difficult to sleep much past six as she grows older. This day, Christmas Eve morning, she is up once again with the seabirds; their songs melding with the creaks and moans of this old beach house, winterized, finally, for these retirement years. Careful not to wake her still slumbering husband, she stretches her limbs, eases to a sitting position, slowly gets to her feet. This effort, she thinks, is what it is to be old.

Half a world away, Sean, the only son, hails a black cab in a London already empty for Christmas. "Heathrow Terminal Four," he tells the driver. He settles back to watch the city shrink down into suburbs as the cab shoots out the M1. Molly, the woman he loves, the woman who he still cannot believe loves him, left earlier, bound for her own family in Ireland. She'll join him in a few days, her seventh or eighth trip over now, and he knows he'll find himself marveling at how much he feels like a tourist when he's in New Jersey with her. Because this city is home now, except at Christmas and those days of July and August when the heat creeps to eighty, the BBC weathermen complain of "scorchers," and he longs for the humid Jersey Shore summers leavened by that breeze off the water.

Nora, the baby, the only sibling with her mother's fondness for the morning, wakes alone in her small country house. She reaches across the bed for Eve, then remembers Eve has left to visit her parents for the holiday, parents who won't let Nora into their home. Nora climbs from bed, lets Hound out back, her tail whipping fiercely as she darts towards the woods. She perks coffee, pours a cup, dons thick corduroys, a sweater, a vest. Heads out onto her deck, surveys the small, quietly eroding mountains heading out into Pennsylvania. Her breath circles the steam pouring from her mug, and though she wishes Eve had not flown back to Indiana at this, her favorite time of year, she thinks to herself, this life, my life, is good. Fingers to her lips, she blows a shrill whistle for the dog, then turns towards the house and a shower. Soon she will drive out to Newark Airport and collect Sean before turning south towards the beach for this holiday she loves.

It's 8:30 a.m. when Kate, the eldest, is startled into consciousness by the buzzer on her clock radio. Around the edges of the minor hangover left by her teachers' pre-Christmas break cocktail party, she recalls her dream and lingers for a moment in that color-and-light filled memory.

She was a girl again, in a scene lifted from the canvases of one of the Impressionists she used to love. The mirage of one too many Tanqueray martinis lingers on the back of her tongue. The shower in the master bath is running, her husband Brian has a half day in the office today. Kate stands with her mother's effort, believes she is too young to feel so old, walks into the steamy bathroom. Last night's med sits on the counter like an accusation. She picks it up, holds it closely in front of her face as if she's trying to search the future out in a saucer full of tea leaves, then wells some spit in her mouth and coats her throat with its chalk.

The father wakes. Checks the digital clock, squints, can't make out the big, red numbers. "God-damn it," he mumbles as he scratches around the books stacked on the night stand for his glasses. Slipping them on, he sees the steady clear numbers: 8:47. He tries to edge back into un-consciousness, but finds it impossible. In the old days, he would have rolled over, found sleep again, and snored until noon or later. But today, he gives up the struggle. For a moment, he lies still in the bed, hoping against reason for sleep to return. Gradually, he becomes aware of the catalog of his body's complaints. His left elbow burning tautly with tendinitis, a stiff ache in his lower back as he heaves himself into a sit-ting position, his knees, both surgically reconstructed long ago, throb-bing with arthritis, a reliable predictor of a storm on the way. It is only really now, at moments like this one, that he confronts the specter of his aging. What has happened, he thinks, to my body? How have I got-ten this brittle, this old?

Patty, second born, wakes last to the first sounds of life on her West Village block. Delivery trucks move through the streets, bringing crates of liquor and cartons of catsup to the trendy bistros and hanging-on dives still lingering on the margins, even here, in the gentrification capital of New York. She hears grates going up, cabs with squealing brakes, the street cleaners. No, there are no street cleaners today, alternate side rules have been suspended for the holiday, but the man at the corner newsstand hawks the *News* and the *Post,* letting the *Times* speak for itself, and the Salvation Army Santa is already out ringing his bell.

Nora sits in her truck, letting it warm up, pops a Country Gentleman tape into the deck, and thrills as she always does to the way a good bluegrass band can send shivers of longing down your back just by wringing a fiddle around a banjo while the guitars hold the melody. She uses her car phone to call her service, leaves the number for a twenty-four-hour large-animal emergency clinic in case any of her regular farms need a vet while she's away. She switches off her beeper and tosses it into the glove box, reaches across to open the passenger door and calls Hound. The dog races from the yard, zigging and zagging, nose to the air, and leaps into her place in the truck. Nora pops the clutch and rolls off down the country roads towards Interstate 78, keeping time on the steering wheel, eager to be driving. Eager to greet her brother who comes home too little for her taste now that they've found themselves close through letters and transatlantic visits. She hopes they can have a night out here before he wings back, a night where he'll cook stew, the rough peasant food he loves, but doesn't often make because London's fine diners crave the trendy lightness of seared tuna. A night with just him and Eve and Molly, a solid dinner, and the pleasure of their company.

When she'd found Eve, when they'd met near the end of college, Sean had been the first one she'd told. Called him in London, forgetting the time difference and waking him in her exuberance. He'd asked finally, cutting through her chatter, "What's going on Nora?" Before she could weigh her response with the careful words she'd been using since going off to school, she'd blurted it out, "I think I'm in love." And though she was worried then that the discussion would go down a disastrous route, that the bond they'd formed since leaving home, the closeness they'd gained by growing up and away, would suffer, he replied exactly the right way. "What's her name?"

The mother cleans in preparation for the chaos of her children flocking to her hearth. She dusts and vacuums. Mops and shines. She lingers as she goes along the rows of photographs chronicling the passage of what she sees now is her life. Her and the father before the children, carefree on the deck of some sailboat. Drinks in hand, cigarettes held casually before they were truly bad for you. She does not really remember these people. This woman. Her. So thin, hair long and bleached blonde, a face untouched by wrinkles save for deep smile lines around the eyes. And that man she's leaning against, a handsome rake, something almost dangerous in the Black Irish blue eyes and thick, ebony hair. Where is the hint of the round potbelly that comes later, his silences? And these children? The class portraits with gap teeth, bangs and freckles. Group shots from vacations. A shot of all four kids on the end of the jetty, Kate and Sean looking seaward, Nora and Patty crouched over a tide pool. Good moments, these photos. But where, she wonders, is Kate's trouble, or the wandering impulse that's taken Sean, her boy, halfway around the world? Where is the hint that Nora would grow into someone whose life could change her mother's whole value system, where are the clues that Patty would cut them out, exile them to the margins of her life?

Patty lingers in bed, surprised to be alone for a moment, reaching across the duvet to find just space, then recalls leaving that East Village bar early, before closing. She remembers draining her club soda just as the sea glass blue bottle of Bombay Sapphire began to whisper, "Just one won't hurt." Remembers waving good-bye to the old friends from medical school who'd be staying in the City for the holiday, remembers almost turning around and going back in for a quick one. But also the clearheaded walk home, New York sparkling with Christmas lights, the air brittle, her own breath sharp. During that walk, hands jammed into the pocket of her coat, she remembered other walks home from that same bar, stopping in doorways to fumble with whomever she'd picked up that night. Remembers stopping and thinking, Christ, I'm too old for that shit.

She gets up, still amazed to find morning bearable when it isn't marred by a thumping head or queasy belly, and grinds the beans for her coffee. Sitting in her sun-drenched eat-in kitchen, just for a moment, she dreads going home. Dreads it because of the years she has lost with them, the years where they saw her as she wanted them to see her. Dreads it because now, when she turns down a gin and tonic or glass of wine, when she sticks to fruit juice or club soda, they will ask her, "Why?" And with that question hanging in the air, she'll be forced to admit, to them, to that family who has seen her only in the flattering light she herself has cast, that she, Patricia Elizabeth Mahoney, has flaws. That she has made mistakes, caused damage to herself and to them and that, now, she may have need, for the first time in a long time, of their help and support. Now, she may need their forgiveness.

The father putters, flicks on The Weather Channel to ease his quiet fear of storms over the Atlantic downing his son's plane. There has been talk of a bit of snow, his knees ache, and his thoughts are on Nor'easter gales and wings icing, but the smooth anchor eases his worry, predicts the storm will hold off until that night when his son is safely arrived. This son he loves but does not understand. His son who has chosen a life of spices and food, who never excelled at the sports that came so naturally to him, but who will sit with him now over a glass of fine Bordeaux and talk of Billie versus Ella or how to grow different herbs in the garden the father has kept since giving up work. My children, he thinks, are people I don't really know. He is surprised by this, this drifting, because he is not sure when it happened. One day they were there and he was sure of them. Then suddenly they were grown, different, their own persons. Of course, there was Kate and her trouble, and that perhaps is the marker. The thing that energized Patty, his favorite, into the path of her success, that pushed Sean to grow up, into their clashing for a time, and Nora? Nora, his baby girl who he might pass on the street because she's frozen in his mind at six. A tomboy climbing trees and riding horses. This woman comes to visit now, calls herself Nora, and he can see that girl in there, faintly, but when did she grow so poised? How is it she looks at that Eve so softly?

But mostly, he wonders about his son. How he wanted a son. Wanted father-son games of catch and day games at Yankee Stadium, the chance to repair some of the wreckage strewn about by his own father. When his Liz swelled with their second child, he dreamt of drowsy August afternoons with Pat, Jr. casting for snapper blues, of coaching Little League or Pop Warner. The signs were good. That second baby was riding low, his kind mother-in-law whispered to him in the eighth month, "Low means a boy." And didn't he already have a daughter? So when the doctor slapped his back, told him, "A healthy baby girl," he cut his losses, had her christened Patricia Elizabeth after him and the mother, and put his dreams into her, made her his favorite. When Sean appeared four years later, he tried, but the boy wasn't the son he had dreamt about. He realizes now, he gave up. Later, he tried to make up for it, tried to build a relationship when his son was grown into a man. But as he waits for all his children to come home, he remembers the bitter stain of his own father's violence, and thinks, I tried to do everything right, to be a real father to my son. I see him twice a year, we speak on the phone, but if I answer when he calls, the phone always goes quickly to Liz, his letters are addressed to her. I don't know my boy, he thinks, and I don't even know if he likes me.

. . .

A British Air 747 soars over the North Atlantic bound for Newark International Airport, and Sean eases his seat-back from the upright position. The plane is packed with holiday travelers and he feels more claustrophobic than usual. Flying is unnatural, he thinks, and signals a passing attendant for a Bushmills on ice. He's not looking forward to the meal. Too much time with only the best food necessitates the slight blurring of whisky to stimulate his appetite for airline food, and coming home from this distance leaves him anxious. Although things never really change, he alone can see how things are subtly different. The way you can see a puppy growing if you visit only at intervals, he's the only one aware of how old his parents are growing, of how much age works in six-month intervals. His mother abruptly gone totally gray, the sagging folds grown seemingly overnight on his father's neck. And in his sisters too: the dark rings deepening and blending into Patty's eyes, Kate looking more and more like the middle-aged schoolteacher she is, Nora's sureness in her body, the ease with which she leans against Eve on the beach-house porch swing.

There is mourning as well, a sadness for the way time has passed and changed them. When he sees them, when they all gather together, he cannot help but be reminded of what and who he's lost. As a small boy, Patty took him under her wing. Though he can't remember it, their mother likes to talk of how Patty insisted on reading him his bedtime story when she could barely read herself. He does remember how she would play with him as they got older, how when he first got to high school, she showed him the ropes, how as a senior, she bestowed on him a bit of cool. But it was also during that shared year in high school that she pushed him away for good. When she first put up her walls, when she started to divide her life into compartments. When on the surface she was still straight-A Patty, the achiever, but underneath she was drinking and fucking herself to numbness. He tried to ask her, to talk, but she put him into the box called "family," and he was cut out from all she didn't want him to know. And of course, Kate. When he'd drifted from Patty, floundering, at fourteen, fifteen, they suddenly found themselves friends. Almost overnight, he went from being a pest to a confidant, someone who could sit with her for hours and talk about everything or about nothing. Kate took him seriously, and when she came in on a Friday or Saturday night, she'd shake him awake and they'd sneak back out, hop into her fishbowl-shaped Pacer and drive to the Broadway Diner. The air filled with smoke from their cigarettes, his Camel Lights, her Dunhills, Van Morrison and Sinatra from the personal jukebox tacked to the wall over their table, and the manic thrust of conversation. Now, of course, it's different. And though he knows it's for the best, knows the pills are necessary, he is still saddened by how something so small, just mixtures of powders, can change so much.

Kate believes she can feel the medication at work as she wraps the expensive presents she'll cart down to the beach later. Fancies she can feel the world dulling just a bit from the excitement she felt waking from her wonderful dream, what was it again? She welcomes the dulling. It makes things easy. It makes this suburb easy, this big house easy, it makes Brian's perfect, boring love easy. Then, briefly, she hates herself for accepting blandness. Coping is not living, she thinks. But she banishes that thought easily enough on the crest of her pills, and goes back to wrapping, humming "Silent Night" under her breath.

It is brisk but not frigid in New York and Patty elects to walk uptown, bundled in her long leather coat and cashmere scarf, to Penn Station and her train. Walking, she'll have the time to gather her thoughts and ready herself for the face she must present to her family. Before locking her apartment and heading out, she calls her office, reassures herself that her calendar is cleared through the New Year, that her partners will cover should any of her little patients get the flu or an earache over the holidays, and tucks her sponsor's phone number into her wallet. Walking up Broadway even under the burden of her luggage, her Channel 13 tote bag, and shopping bag full of wrapped gifts, she still finds New York thrilling. Thrilling still, after all these years. These years of Barnard and NYU medical school, her internship and residency at Mt. Sinai, the challenge of her practice. Her life has been this city, revolving around its choices and rhythms, and as she picks her way through the crowds of last-minute shoppers, she feels at home amongst the strangers.

She pushes past the station and pauses in a sea of people to take in the decadence of the Macy's Christmas windows. The flow of pedestrians swirls around her, taking about as much notice of her as a stream takes of the rocks that alter its course. No eyes flicker off her face with recognition, not one of these rushing people stops short to offer a surprised hello or Merry Christmas. She's jostled by a man in an overcoat who clutches a trial bag like the one her father used to carry to work, and as he grunts something that might be "Excuse me," she suddenly realizes—I am alone. Realizes with harsh clarity that the years of gin, of dividing her life into facets, her surgical removal of lovers when they got too close, have left her totally, bitterly alone. All the times she dodged and deflected her brother or sisters when they caught some oblique angle of the truths of her life and came to her concerned and questioning have rendered her anonymous, another face in the millions of faces here.

The mother checks her watch, anxiously, waiting. Sean is roughly halfway across the ocean, Nora should be rolling towards the airport, Patty catching her train, Kate waiting for Brian, loading the car. Her brood, coming home. The tree is trimmed, the presents wrapped, the plum cake, from her mother's recipe, found in the attic during the renovations, waits for its turn in the oven. It is a surprise just for Kate, a reminder of childhood. The mother remembers other Christmases when the children woke her and Pat too early. Just a few hours after all the wrapping and assembling were finished, four of them, jumping on the bed, calling, "Santa *came*! Get up!"

And, in her memory, those days are pure. If she thinks hard, she can remember troubles; fretting over money back when they were just starting out, Sean and Nora always at each other's throats, but it was mild, they were her children, and she knew them. Knew their minds and the thin swaths of their bodies in the bath. Knew their pleasures and their fears. Could soothe or control them with a glance, a word, the right snack. Now, there is pride in what they have become, a sense of achievement, but she worries. Is Kate rigorous with her meds? Is Sean okay halfway around the world? She has the unyielding sense that Patty is never happy, not with her professional success, not with her life. The feeling that Patty is alone, that Patty is too much like her father, substituting the pages of books, hours at the office, an affinity for the bottle for people. And, her baby, her Nora. Seeing her with Eve, the mother, of a different generation and way of thinking, can not help but think on roads she left untraveled. Seeing them together, she grows contemplative, until Pat asks, "What's wrong?" and she shakes off her distress because she loves him, them, and because, of course, she is the mother.

Clouds move into the New York Metropolitan area, the wind picks up, swirling gusts of road salt into tiny funnels. The mercury in thermometers around the tri-state area slowly begins to ease downward.

Nora pulls her truck into the short-term parking lot, tucks the parking ticket into her sun visor, and clips the leash onto Hound. Getting out of the truck, she zips her jacket against the wind and flips her collar up. She is fond of the cold, the way it breathes new life into older horses who find themselves frisky, snorting and bucking like yearlings under shaggy winter coats. Walking towards the terminal, the dog presses against her legs. The commotion of a holiday airport, these smells of exhaust and jet fuel are threatening, and Hound nuzzles Nora's hand for reassurance. Nora pats her and walks straight inside without hesitation. Her dog goes everywhere she does, and she has found if she moves with authority, people will rarely stop her. She makes her way to the waiting area just outside Customs, settles in an uncomfortable chair, the dog resting its head on her lap.

Sitting there, the closest thing she has to a child nestled next to her, Nora thinks of her mother. Thinks how hard she's tried to welcome Eve into the family, seeing how with effort she treats her with the same sort of love she treats Kate's husband or Sean's Molly. Knows how hard it must be, how a lifetime of Catholic dogma and years of expectations clash with what her mother sees when Nora and Eve visit. And she has seen a sadness overwhelm her mother. Caught her mother watching as she and Eve take their turn preparing dinner on summer weekends or cuddle on the porch swing after dark. In those moments, a small part of her still wishes she were somehow different, wishes she were able to come home with a man on her arm and a baby in tow instead of Hound. But then her mother comes out to the porch, kisses them both goodnight on the tops of their heads, makes Eve feel she too is her daughter, and Nora wonders about the source of her grief, something the mother keeps locked down tight, and she wishes that they could talk about whatever it is, but she doesn't know how to ask. So she just hugs her for a moment longer than necessary, and the next morning, her mother is herself again, full of laughter and in charge, and they sit in the kitchen while whoever else is in the house snoozes, and they talk over coffee about nothing in particular.

The father holes himself up in the bedroom, banishing the mother. He puts some Art Tatum on the small boombox CD player he keeps in there and goes into his closet, pulling out the gifts he's bought for the mother. He wraps them with no small measure of anxiety—he frequently gets things wrong with gifts. He tries, hard, phoning Nora or Patty to ask their opinions, but for every success, for every gift the mother opens and turns to him with pure gratitude and love on her face, there are two or three failures. The gifts his children see and raise their eyes at each other from across the room. Warming to his task as he wraps, he grows confident. These are all perfect, he thinks, just right this year, just right.

Kate greets Brian at their front door with bags packed and gifts ready for the trip. She's always surprised by how happy he is to see her, how his face softens from whatever crisis work has leveled on his mind, how he takes her into his arms, strongly, confidently. How safe he makes her feel. He deserves better, she thinks, I do not deserve this love. But, she has it, and at these moments, she counts her blessings, and is thankful for the pills and what they have given her. In other moments though, solitary moments when she's forgotten or neglected her meds, when the sharp green of a single blade of grass recalls something in her head the way a snatch of forgotten music or the smell of particular foods can conjure ghosts, she remembers how it used to be. How she used to crave jug wine and smoke, dusky saxophones, and falling naked onto drop sheets until she and her man were sweaty and coated with paint like warriors. At those moments, she thinks of calling Sean and telling him, "I'm back." Thinks of running off someplace again, of doing anything to escape. But as she rushes to the bathroom, resolved to empty the pill bottles, watch the meds swirl in a spiral down the drain, she realizes exactly what it is she would lose. Remembers the bad times, thinks of the scars marring her legs, thinks of how Brian loves her so much, how he's done everything right those few times she has gone off, how he's rescued her from herself, and how he's earned her love. She unscrews the lids, pours herself a glass of water from the tap, and takes her pills.

She and Brian load the trunk, settle into the soft leather seats. As they head for the Parkway, the radio weatherman relays a winter storm warning for that night, and the news anchor muses on the possibility of a white Christmas before spinning that holiday classic. Kate covers Brian's hand on the gear shift, and raises her voice with Bing's.

Patty boards her New Jersey Transit train, finds an empty bench seat and spreads her bags beside her. She pulls a new novel from her tote bag, feels its heft in her hands for a moment, the hefty pleasure only hardbacks bring, before cracking it open and delving into the world it promises. The train lurches from the station, underground until they hit Newark, and when the conductor comes by, she barely notices. She just hands him her ticket, her eyes still on the page. Her father suggested this book, and she hopes to be well into it before she gets home. Hopes to sit with him the way she alone can and speak of what she's found in its syntax and language.

Pausing in her reading, she wonders if maybe things can be different now. If she can find a way to bring Sean and Kate and Nora back into her life. Daydreaming, she remembers Nora coming to New York for some veterinary seminar a few years ago. Sitting in Patty's living room, sharing a bottle of wine, Nora told her a story about one of her early memories, a day out on their grandfather's sailboat. Nora was maybe five years old and Patty lifted her up as the boat tacked into a gale out on the bay. "I was petrified at first," Nora said, "but I closed my eyes and leaned into the wind, and learned something about trust." That night, sitting there in the apartment, they were quiet for a while, then Nora said, "But you know, it's getting hard to trust a shadow."

Her legs cramping on the commuter train, her mind spinning over the years, remembering slights both real and imagined. Thinking, I had reasons, reasons for everything, Patty stands and considers walking through the train, searching for a bar car. Thinks with sharp longing of the tart brine of gin. But she sits again, because as comforting as gin sounds now, even though she still remembers how beautiful the dew forming on the sides of a cocktail glass can be, as dull and flat as she sometimes feels without the company of booze, she doesn't really want to go to any of the places all those drinks took her. Not again. Picking her book back up, she reads.

Sean's flight touches down at Newark. He releases a breath he hadn't realized he'd been holding and joins the other passengers in applauding the safe flight, the perfect landing. The plane taxis slowly towards the gate, Sean gathers his things from under the seat, and when the seatbelt light is off, he gets his gifts from the overhead compartment, and joins the slogging procession off the plane and into the terminal. The woman stamping passports wishes him "Merry Christmas and Welcome Home." With barely a wait, his suitcase comes around on the carousel and he's waved through Customs without a second glance. Coming out into the terminal proper he is struck for a moment by the voices. He hasn't heard this much New York and New Jersey in the air for a long while and the tones jar against an ear tuned to the cadences of Britain. Scanning the waiting faces, he spots Nora, Nora and Hound. Sees Nora's face break into a smile, sees her wave, catches the dog's tail whipping, caught up in Nora's excitement. "Nora," he says, pulling her into a hug. "Merry Christmas, favorite brother," she says. "Where's Eve?" "Indiana. They don't think her father's going to see another Christmas. She told me to send you her love. When's Mol get in?" "The thirtieth."

Walking to the car, Sean remembers the moment he realized about Nora, years of little things falling into place. She was just eighteen, he'd come home from culinary school for summer break, met her out at a party in the woods, and found her raving drunk, crying. A story had come out, his rage rising at the boy, a high school God that year, a three-sport letterman. A drunk boy, who'd led her away into the trees after Nora's best friend had gone off to reconcile with her ex-boyfriend. A boy who'd forced her, not reckoning on her fierce sense of self-preservation, not reckoning she'd fight back. When Sean got to the party the boy was bragging about getting some from Nora Mahoney. Sean had never hit anyone before, not a stranger, but he did some damage—the jock was drunk, and Sean had a thick tree branch that felt more natural swinging than a baseball bat ever had. And as he drove Nora round and round the small town of their childhood, fueling up on take-out coffee, just driving and letting her talk, she'd cried at one point, "I only went off with that fucker because Kath left me alone."

He knew then, but little things over her college years made him certain. Her books, her careful wording, the avoidance of pronouns. He wanted her to tell him, but he didn't pry, just hinted around the subject when he felt he could. When she called him finally, gushing across the ocean about falling in love, he decided not to give her a chance to evade this time. "What's her name?" She told him about Eve, told him first, and when she and Eve came to visit that summer after they graduated, he'd never seen Nora more easy with herself, never seen her so complete.

The mother cooks. Places the plum cake into the preheated oven. Rolls out the dough for stuffed bread, layers the fillings, artichoke hearts and Romano, pepperoni and mozzarella, slivers of Portobello and Brie, and rolls the loaves back up. Separates an egg, coats the dough with the whites, thinking of Sean. Thinking of the pleasure he gets from the feel of food under his hands, of the nurturing impulse she's passed to him, the impulse to nourish. She is happy, when he's here, to turn over her kitchen to him, to watch him dice and chop and baste. To join him and Nora in a quiet glass of wine while food cooks, filling the house with the scent of meals she can only imagine creating.

She taught him to cook, the basics she learned from her mother. But suddenly he zoomed past her, found his calling in the subtle flavor of leeks and the rush of garlic, and now when he visits, he teaches her. When he is back in England, and she misses him harshly, she'll dig through the recipes he left her, squinting at the cramped angles of his handwriting, remembering the little tricks and techniques gleaned from her son, and she'll produce an exquisite meal, almost as good as Sean's, and toast him silently with a glass of wine from her husband's cellar.

Her husband. A good-natured man, quiet, they seem well matched. She supposes they are, they complement each other, her booming laugh and tendency to fret matched by his contemplation. Cooking, she is reminded of the exuberant rush of their courtship, meeting down here all those summers ago. He was a young man standing in a group of other young men, all in faded jeans slung low on their hips, tight white T-shirts and beat-to-hell motorcycle boots. They were all trying so hard to look tough, squinting through Lucky Strike smoke, but those blue eyes surrounded by thick lashes were really something else with that black hair. His face almost looked delicate when his guard was down. She remembers thinking as they leaned on the railing and looked out at the water, he almost looks like a girl.

She flirted shamelessly, teasing, as they walked along together, separated from his friends and hers by an island of her banter. Maybe she was a little mean at first, and those blue eyes twisted into confusion and then pain, and she felt as if her air was leaving her, so she put her arm around his waist and her fingers brushed the top of a Penguin paperback sticking out of his back pocket; she left her arm there, and after a moment he put his arm around her waist, and they settled into a comfortable gait as they walked along.

Thirty-seven years later, she thinks, we at least still have that comfort.

.   .   .

Patty's train rolls along the coast, coming close to the town where she'll switch to the local train that will carry her to the station a short walk from the beach house. Her book, more than halfway finished, is face-down on her legs; she's caught now in the view. There is the occasional flash of the water between buildings as the train slugs southward, and she realizes she's excited. Excited to see her family, excited for this holiday to come. For tonight with just the six of them, with few surprises between them, with years of routine to fall back on.

We'll have dinner, she thinks, and at some point, after the catching-up, the coming-home awkwardness gone, we'll start to remember things—good, funny things. When the four children have gathered in one place, under the right circumstances, the stories flow, they all remember the same things. Even though they can never know one another the way they did as children, she thinks, despite the ways we've drifted and collided over the years, we are still linked. When we were little, when we were all under the same roof, she thinks, when we were kids, we were mostly happy.

The father loads the CD changer in the living room, filling the first seven slots with his favorite jazz discs, Dave Brubeck, Miles, Coltrane, Billie, Ella, Sarah, Lester Young, then three Christmas records in deference to the season. He goes to the cellar, thinks with pride, I have a wine cellar, my own wine cellar, then mulls his choices for a while. Selects a nice Sauvignon Blanc from Washington State and a crisp Pinot Grigio for Nora, Patty and his wife who favor whites. For the rest of the family, he picks a light, dry Pinot Noir, a very old, woody Bordeaux he'd been saving for something special, and a peppery Zinfandel he is eager to try. Upstairs, he puts the whites in the refrigerator to chill, and opens the reds, giving them air before the time comes to pour. He turns the volume up on the stereo, comes into the kitchen and takes his wife, flour coating her hands, into his arms and for a moment they dance to some jazzy swing, dipping and twirling.

For a moment, he feels young again, feels his first flush of love from all those years ago and he marvels at his luck.

He could not have predicted his life. Could not have said thirty years ago, coming from his home, "I will be married, a retired lawyer, have four kids who turned out well enough, enough money." He could not have said, "In thirty years, I'll consider myself lucky."

The sky is nearing black as the day gets later and storm clouds gather, obscuring the high, flat sun and any early rising stars. The wind bowing the arms of trees with steady gusts is cold, bone-cold from the north. Way up, in the highest reaches of the sky, snow crystals form, making their way down, for now, as flurries.

The song on the CD player ends, the mother leans on the father for the briefest of moments, comfortable the way she always is with him. But, she shoos him out of the kitchen, "I'm getting flour all over you." When he is gone, she washes her hands, goes to the old rotary phone on the kitchen wall, fits her fingers into the sockets on the dial and turns them quickly in a number that flows from her fingertips. Her best friend, from childhood through today, is out. The machine plays its greeting, and after the beep, she says, "Anna, it's Liz. Calling to wish you and Jack a Merry Christmas. Love you." Placing the phone back in the cradle, she stands for a moment, before shaking her head briskly. Turning back to the food on the counter, she thinks, Now where was I?

Kate's watch beep-beeps, a reminder to pop a pill, just as Brian finishes parallel parking in front of the beach house. She silences the watch without looking, doesn't reach for her purse. Brian glances at her. "After we get inside," she says. "After we get inside." They gather their things from the trunk, bound up the porch, arm in arm, and crash

open the door. "Merry Christmas!" Kate calls, "Are we first?" The father comes from the living room, shakes Brian's hand, hugs his eldest.
"Merry Christmas. Merry Christmas." The mother is there. When the
father releases his hug, she pulls Kate to her, hugs her with a mother's
fierce hug, then pushes back, still gripping Kate's arms, searching her
face. "How's everything?" the mother asks, looking in Kate's eyes, wanting them to be bright, fearing they are bright. "Fine. I'm behaving
myself," Kate answers. For a moment they are still, until Kate catches a
hint of the smell wafting in from the kitchen. Struggling, she tries to
place it, then realizes. "Nana's plum cake! You found the recipe?"

A med goes untaken.

The father bustles, pours drinks, asks Brian about his job. Walks with
him into the living room where they talk, closely, in the language they
share, the language of corporate law. The father likes this young man,
likes that he is serious about his work. And when Brian asks him, as he
always makes it a point to ask, his opinion on some case or point of law,
the father leans back in his chair, sips his drink and gesturing with his
hands the way he once did around conference tables and occasionally
courtrooms, he reaches into the depths of his knowledge and tells Brian
things Brian already knows. And though on some level the father knows
Brian is being polite with his queries, lingering on the law, the sane, orderly law that follows the same rules and procedures year after year, re-
lieves the father and makes him comfortable in his own home, where
he sometimes feels misplaced. As he sits with his son-in-law, the father
thinks, Kate is lucky to have found him, something solid to hook on to.

The New Jersey Transit train pulls into Bradley Beach, Patty gathers her
things, steps onto the platform. She's startled by the snow. Dry, light

snow, gusting in heavy swirls through the air, not sticking, not yet, to coarse winter grass or road. As she walks down Main Street, crosses the bridge into the town of her destination, makes a right and then a left, the big front porch of the old beach house comes into view, and she thinks, A God-damned white Christmas.

Nora wheels her truck onto Fourth Avenue, the windshield wipers brushing away the lightly falling snow. Hound, picking up on the slower speeds, the more frequent turns, or just the feelings of the two humans bracketing her in the truck, barks once, and thump, thump goes her tail against the seat. After the dreary first leg of the trip from the airport, the swamp gas stench of the refineries along the Turnpike, the raft of cars rushing by at eighty, ninety miles an hour, the desolate industrial waste of northeast New Jersey, Sean is heartened by the quiet, the slight whiff of salt coming into the truck over the toasted air seeping from the heater vents. He wants to ask Nora to keep driving for a moment, to cruise past the house and down to the beach so that he can glimpse the ocean, so that he can feel, as he didn't feel at the airport, that he is home. But, there is Patty trudging up the steps to the porch. He rolls down his window, yells, "Patricia Elizabeth!" Nora toots the horn. Patty puts down her bundle, waves, waits for Nora to jiggle the truck into a spot on the street, for Sean and Nora and Hound to spill out of its doors. Waits for the hugs. "Favorite brother," she says, "Baby sister. Merry Christmas."

The mother feels that tinge somewhere in the back of her head or corner of her heart that alerts her to her children, pulls back the curtains by the door, and sees them, her three youngest children, grown, her children, adults, her children. They come to the door, chatting, laughing, and she flings it open, pulls them to her, all three at once, then one at time. Wishes Merry Christmases. She gives Sean a long look, scanning up and down. Is he too thin? Whispers as she embraces him, "Welcome home." Asks Nora, "Where's Evelyn?" "She had to go home." The father is there suddenly, and though he's eager to see them all, glad to have all four children safe under his roof, he can not quite quelch his relief at finding Nora alone.

So, they are arrived, the family gathered around the hearth. The father takes drink orders. "Red wine?" Sean asks, knowing the bottles have been opened for hours. "I'll take white," Nora chimes in. "Club soda?" asks Patty. The father, pouring out Nora's glass of wine, stops and turns. Nora tries to catch Sean's eye, but he's staring at Patty. Kate, coming in from the living room says what's on the tips of all their tongues, "What? You know that's zero proof, right?" "I've stopped drinking," Patty says. The mother, thinking, Now is not the time, comes over, steers Patty to the kitchen, saying, "Club soda coming up."

Wine is drunk, the chatter is constant, full of old jokes, bad puns. Dinner is served. Over stuffed breads and a platter of medium-rare filets, braised new potatoes, tender asparagus shoots in lemon butter, and under the influence of a couple of bottles of excellent wine and a refilled glass of club soda, bridges form across the distances of geography and age that separate them. Sean, so far away from their day-to-days, tells them little stories of his life in London: jokes about kitchen disasters, the sauce one of the other sous-chefs made with sugar in place of salt, the restaurant owner's clumsy daughter filling in as a disastrous waitress. When they ask about Molly, he fills them in, his face softening the way it does when he sleeps.

Patty, pride in her work evident in the quiet, sure tones of her voice, tells stories about her little patients, broken but mendable mostly. The father and Brian swap war stories of depositions and discovery motions, a bawdy joke about a judge they both know. Kate and the mother, listening to Patty talk of her children, steer some talk around to education, and the pediatrician and two teachers agree it's surprising how little parents know of their children. Hound begs plaintively at Nora's feet, looking for scraps, and Nora scratches her ears, telling a funny story about a customer who had a prize mare and his wife go into labor on the same afternoon.

All through this eating and talking, though the memories of the bad times or things are there, close by, for all of them, they've agreed, without voicing it, that tonight will be a night of rosy remembering. So, they tell stories they all know. Nora, at seven, with the pussy-willow buds up her nose and up the old family dog's nose as well. Sean, at five, bursting into the house from kindergarten after seeing a movie about Martin Luther King, "Mommy, Mommy, we learned about the king of the black people in school today!" Kate's grade-school art teacher calling home and complaining that ten-year-old Kate had accused him of, and he quoted, "Ignorance of history and Impressionism" in front of a roomful of fifth-graders when he called a Monet a Manet. Patty, age twelve, right after Nana died, asking the old, dogmatic, asthmatic Father Anthony to prove the existence of God or she was leaving the church and never going back. They tell stories like these. Stories all families have, the spiritual knickknacks of a shared past, and through the telling, the family is reunited.

When they are stuffed and lazy in their chairs, they all help clear and as they stack pans and load the dishwasher, Sean whispers his compliments to the chef. Because he knows his saying it matters more than anyone else saying it, because she looks more like a grandmother than a mother now, he tells her, "Great food, Ma, great food."

As they sit with coffee in the living room, Sean realizes he's still itching to see the ocean. To see that great expanse of water leading off forever that separates him from here. He asks, "Anyone want to walk down to the beach?" The mother and father demure. Shaking her head and taking her husband's hand, the mother says, "Too cold for us." But his sisters and Brian agree. Yes, let's go for a walk. They bundle up, wrap on scarves and pull on gloves, and they walk. Kate hand in hand with Brian, Patty and Sean just a bit behind, then Nora with Hound clipped to a leash. Sean loops his arm through Patty's, "So, no booze?" She puts her head on his shoulder, "Yeah. Got to be too much." "That's good, then?" he asks her and she smiles to herself at the British inflection in his voice and answers, "Fingers crossed."

As they cross Ocean Avenue and come up on the boardwalk, they go, without speaking, down to the sand and head for the jetty guarding the inlet. Walking out in the bitter cold, they hear snowflakes hissing into the waves. The tide is too high, the wind too strong for them to get all the way to the end under the foghorn. But they can get about halfway out, and as they turn and stare back at the land, Nora asks, "Anyone have smokes?" They're all supposed to have quit, but Kate pulls a pack from her pocket, "I thought we might need these." Sean fishes out an old Zippo lighter from inside his jacket and manages to get one cigarette lit in the wind, then uses the cherry end to light three more. Brian declines.

Nora, her gloved hand rubbing Hound's ear, looks over at Kate leaning back into Brian's chest, occasionally raising the cigarette to her lips, and thinks of heading back to the house and phoning Eve before bed.

Patty watches them all, wanting a drink and thrilled she's not taken one.

Sean, looking at the sea crashing around the rocks, the red and green lights blinking through the snow out on the channel marker buoy, thinks, Of all the places I've been, this spot right here is my favorite.

When Mol gets here, I'm going to ask Mom for Nana's old engagement ring, and we'll walk out here together, and I'll ask.

Kate, aware of the bulk of Brian behind her, the reassuring heft of him, but drawn also to the deep shades of gray and green all around her, feels torn. Feels she would like to capture this scene somehow with paint and small horsehair brushes. Feels anxious about the missed meds. She knows that even though tonight the flushing of drugs from her system feels like a promise, that if she keeps not taking them, it becomes a curse. And though something in them keeps her from being able to translate what she sees to something on canvas for others to see, and though that knowledge breaks part of her spirit, the feel of those strong arms around her waist is triumphing again, and she knows she'll take a pill just before she goes to bed.

It's too cold to stay out for long and they decide, flipping their butts into the swells, that they should get back. In the house, the whole family sits together again in the living room, lights off, a fire burning, the tree glowing under its curtain of white bulbs. Through the windows, they can see the snow drifting down, see the layers forming on the window ledges. Nora and Sean chat quietly together. Patty curls on the floor at her father's feet, speaking to him of books, her work. Kate and Brian lean on one another, Kate's gaze misty under the influence of too much wine, two missed meds. Sean catches her eye, sees the fire, usually suppressed, starting to kindle and raises his glass to her. The mother, sleepy with a crystal tumbler of Bailey's, waits for midnight, hums the carols playing on the stereo.

The clock lurches towards Christmas Day. Two blocks away, the bell in St. Elizabeth's steeple tower begins the twelve chimes for midnight.

They all look up at each other expectantly. There is one last ritual before they go to bed, one last thing before sleep, before Nora wakes them
too early on Christmas morning as she has done for years, for decades,
before the gluttonous morning of frenzied opening, the drive farther
down the coast to gather with uncles and cousins, before this day is
over. One gift each, opened before bed on Christmas Eve. One gift and
they know what is inside. It is a thing they know and cherish; a tradi-
tion that when the time comes, the children will pass to their children.
The mother leaves for a moment, and comes back with an armful of
boxes, "Christmas PJs!" The father, hoping he has guessed right with a
long flannel shift, pulls a box from under the tree, hands it to the
mother, says, "Christmas PJs."

When the opening is done, when the boxes are shoved aside and the
wrapping stuffed into the trash, when Christmas Eve feels over for the
mother, she and the father turn in. The mother wishes for a moment
she was not so old, wishes she could stay awake with her children for
the few hours they will all stay awake, refilling their glasses until the
Bailey's is gone, smoking the cigarettes they all claim not to smoke anymore. But she heads to bed, kissing them each in turn, wishing them
pleasant dreams. As she takes the father's hand to head upstairs, she
thinks with surprise, Even with everything that's happened, the mistakes we've made, even with any regrets, we're going to be okay.

Brian turns in soon after, leaving the four Mahoney children alone in
a dark room with three glasses of Irish cream and one club soda. In
the flickering light of an aging fire, with faces occasionally lit as they
drag furtively on smokes, hoping the cracked window is sucking the
smell out into the snowy night, here, in this room, old wounds are
scarred over, slights have been forgotten, the distances between them

crossed as best they can. On this Christmas Eve, as adults, the four Mahoney children are together without doubts or misgivings. Together the way it was when they were children, together the way they were before anything had ever happened that made them know they were separate.

1 9 9 2

Sean is hot. Working three pans at once, flipping a julienned vegetable medley in a thin coating of citrus-infused olive oil with his left hand, folding a handful of fresh porcini mushrooms into a delicate cream sauce with his right, keeping an eye on the tuna steak searing on the back burner. Sweat runs down from under the brim of his stiff, white paper hat, sauce smears and meat juice from knife wipes stain his kitchen whites. The head chef, bulky from years of careful tasting, leans back against the wall, sipping his after-work cognac. The hairy spill of his gut pokes from under his neat-as-a-pin dress uniform as he watches the young American work. Sean pours a pool of brandy onto his mushrooms, angles the skillet so the liquor catches and rears back from the flame. Lowering the heat under the sauce, he grabs the handle of the pan with the tuna and barely registers another burn to his heat-numbed fingertips. He flips the fish onto his cutting surface, quickly cuts the deep rose-hued flesh into thin strips with a couple of pivots of his chef's knife, arranges the slices in a precarious pyramid on a large round plate, scatters his julienne mixture around the tuna, dribbles a touch of the citrus oil over everything, and slides the plate into the pick-up window. Turning back to his mushrooms, he tosses in some fresh fettuccini with a few deft flips of his wrist, pours everything into a shallow bowl, quickly slices a grilled Portobello into thin strips, arranges it in a fan shape on top of the pasta, and slides the dish next to the tuna. He pops his hand briskly on top of the little bell, slaps down the ticket next to the plate, calls "Order up" in his gruff kitchen voice.

Nora reclines against one of the old oak trees that, along with the stoic, stone buildings, tag this suburban Philadelphia campus as a place of serious inquiry. An Organic Chemistry text open in front of her, a backpack festooned with political buttons—HATE IS NOT A FAMILY VALUE, KEEP YOUR LAWS OFF MY BODY, JERRY BROWN '92—sits agape at her feet. All around her women, her classmates, walk in groups or pairs, sit like her against trees, with books propped open on knees, lie together on blankets in shorts and men's tank-top undershirts, soaking up the afternoon sun of one of the first spring days whispering of summer. She's not really studying, the day is too wonderful to absorb anymore Organic, but she's got lab at 4:20, and she feels some sort of academic obligation to at least glance over the work before she has to leave this afternoon and meet her lab partner. Shading her eyes against the sun with her hand, she watches Bryn Mawr begin to take on its weekend persona as Friday afternoon classes let out. All these shades of women, the preppy in pearls and penny loafers, the hippie-chicks with flowing, brightly patterned Guatemalan skirts, the radicals with shaved heads, clunky boots and army shorts. Her attention is drawn repeatedly to a girl, a woman she corrects herself, a hundred yards away using a knotted rope to play tug-of-war with a short-coated, brown-and-black mottled puppy. The little hound dog–looking thing's guttural play growls are audible, and her mistress is unselfconsciously laughing and scampering with the dog, her chin-length, angled black hair swinging in front of her face, the muscles in her legs and arms moving with athletic ease under her shorts and T-shirt. She's a stone-cold babe, Nora thinks, and she loves her dog.

The mother bustles around the beach-house kitchen, sweeping a closed-up house's winter of dust into swirls that cloud the sunbeams dancing through the newly opened windows. She can hear her friend Anna clomping around on the porch's roof with the hammer, prying the boards off the last of the windows. They both called in sick, taking what the mother calls a "mental health day," and drove down the Parkway to open the house for the season. This work is a labor of love. The house left to her by her parents feels purely her own now, and this is one of the last years it will be necessary to throw it open at the first sustained breath of spring. This autumn or next, a troop of workmen will descend, making the necessary adjustments so the house can withstand the blows of winter occupied. So that when she retires from teaching and her husband hangs up his trial bag for good, they can live here. Every year, opening the house leaves her both nostalgic and refreshed. She's done this since she was a teenager and helped her parents with what she saw then as a chore. The day is almost religious in its details—the careful examination of the foundation and exterior, solemnly checking for any winter damage, then the celebratory removal of the window-boards, tapping the hammer lightly on all four corners of each window frame to loosen them from a winter's worth of mooring. Uncovering the furniture in the house, dragging the hammock and wicker furniture from the basement to the backyard, turning the water back on with a gurgle of pipes and hosing everything down before arranging things in their customary spots on the front porch. Dusting and mopping exposed surfaces, helping this casual, worn house come alive again. Filling it with light, replacing the cooped-up funeral smell with a mixture of sea air and lemon cleanser.

Patty puts the flourish of her signature on an Amoxicillin scrip for a little boy with an ear infection and a haggard-looking mother kept awake for hours last night. Her writing hand trembles just slightly. "Make sure he finishes the prescription," she says, handing the paper to his mother. "Three times a day, with food. He should feel better in a day or two, and you can send him to school on Monday." Ruffling the little boy's hair, she pulls a Blow Pop from the pocket of her white coat, and hands it to her suddenly more animated patient. "You're gonna pull through this time, big guy." She follows the boy and his mother, her last scheduled appointment of the day, out into the lobby, and says her good-byes. "Anything else today?" she asks the receptionist. "Just Miss Hathaway over there." The woman tilts her chin in the direction of the waiting area where a fifteen-year-old girl Patty has treated since joining this practice earlier in the year is nervously leafing through a back issue of *Cosmopolitan*. "What's the complaint?" Her response is heavy with measured gravity; they both know what this means, "She won't tell me. Only said she wanted to talk with you. Said it couldn't wait for a scheduled appointment. The other docs all left for the weekend." "Christ," Patty says. "All right. Get her chart for me, room three, then you can head home. I'll close everything up." She walks over to the waiting area, "Well, Mary-Ann, I can fit you in, come on."

Kate stands on the platform of Hoboken's PATH station, waiting for one of the ten-minute-spaced trains to carry her under the Hudson and into the City. Sinking onto one of the benches, she is relieved to be here, on time. It had been a rush to catch the Morris & Essex Line train from Summit, she'd been a bit late getting out of school, couldn't find a parking space for the Volvo. She's not really looking forward to the evening. Dinner out with Brian and a show would be nice, but they're being joined by prospective clients, a rising star from the in-house legal department at some drug company and his wife. Someone who had been on *Law Review* with Brian, but not someone he hung out with, not someone from the group of future lawyers she had met over pitchers of beer after class. She hopes the wife will be interesting at least, hopes they can find something to talk about while Brian and the husband delicately *talk shop*. Brian subtly wooing, for just a fraction of the evening. She knows landing this account would be a coup, could be the leap that pushes him over the last hurdle into the finish area of partnership. And she wants to do her best for him, to sparkle, charm the lawyer and delight his wife. But it was a long fucking day at work, and if she's going to make the trek into the City, she'd like to do it on her terms; she certainly has no desire to see *Les Miz* for the third time, and as the 33rd Street–bound PATH train clambers into the station, she wonders what would happen if she just didn't show up, if she got off the train at Christopher Street. If she exited downtown, walked the streets she once walked in high school, in art school, would any of it look the same?

The father hits the SEND button on his car phone as he waits on one of the lights that line the two-lane road connecting his law firm with the exclusive country club where the partners share a corporate membership. "Riker, Thames, Silber, LaChapelle, & Abrahms," the receptionist chirps into his ear, and he responds, wishing he could remember this woman's name, but no longer able to keep track of the rotating cast of receptionists, "Hi. It's Pat Mahoney. Can I have Michael Barnes, please." "Certainly, Mr. Mahoney. One moment." The young associate who has been doing most of his work these days picks up quickly. "Nice work on the D&B brief, Michael. I made a few changes. Get the corrections from Suzanne and have the copies ready to send out by lunch on Monday." Across the line, static filled and crackly, the reply, "Thank you, Sir. Consider it done." The father knows Michael won't actually be doing the copying and the binding, someone in the mail room will be taking care of that. But he knows Michael, one of the best young lawyers in the office, ambitious and courteous, will key in the changes himself on his own network terminal, telling his secretary to go on home. It's Friday. And he knows, dimly remembering his own days responding to similar requests, that Michael will stay late tonight or come in over the weekend, sacrificing any plans he might have in order to get the job finished. It's the nature of the beast, the father thinks, trying to feel guilty. But the gates to the Club loom ahead, it's a wonderful spring afternoon, his wife is down at the beach, and he's going to get in at least nine holes before dark.

Nora watches as the puppy wins, breaks away from the girl and runs in Nora's direction, her owner fast on its heels. But the dog is wily, weaving from side to side, throwing the human off balance, until it's right up on Nora's lap. Dropping the rope, the puppy buries its head in Nora's backpack, its little nose twitching at the scent of napkin-wrapped dining-hall cookies. She pulls the puppy from her bag and it scrambles up her chest to lick her face. Nora's face crinkles with laughter, the sheer joy of playing with an animal in the animal-deprived college setting releasing some childlike force upon her. Her features, normally closed these days, are open and lively when the dog's mistress plops on the ground next to her, "Hound, damn it, have some manners. Sorry. I just got her yesterday and she doesn't listen like she should. I'm Eve." Nora takes the proffered hand as the dog moves between them, tail wagging, tongue licking, "No problem. Good girl. Nora," she replies, thinking all the while, Why don't I know you, and why the hell do I have lab in fifteen minutes, and where will I find you again, and Jesus, what a body.

Eve leans back, resting her head on a pillow of gnarly exposed roots, shirt riding up to expose a lean swath of belly, and Nora fights to tear her gaze away, scratching the dog's tummy as it rolls over at her feet, setting one of its hind legs to thumping in the air. She isn't very good at this. She's had her flings, drunken one-nighters her first year after dancing all sweaty in Philly bars, ambiguous shade-drawn Sunday afternoons and the odd week-long relationship cut short because of the hours Nora needs to spend boning up on her Chemistry or Biology. Hours when the students in the other departments, what Nora thinks of as the less-rigorous disciplines, are free. While she hasn't been around the block, Nora has strolled down to the corner, checked out the view, and headed home. She's dedicated her free time to the political and cerebral, riding buses to demonstrations or marches, searching the Women's Studies shelves in the school bookstore. *She hasn't had time for this.*

But Eve is watching her, unflinching, from her reclining perch, saying over Nora's thoughts, "She seems to like you." "She might not if she knew I was going to vet school in the fall." "A vet, really? Maybe you could help me with her?" This coming with a slight shift in tone of voice, could she be flirting? Nora wonders. Trying to match that tone, turning to meet that direct gaze, "I think I'd like that." Eve smiles then, skin around her eyes crinkling, as she glides into a sitting position, hugs her knees and says, "Good. Me too."

A long moment, quiet, with just the two of them looking at one another, perhaps both feeling suddenly a bit shy, is broken by excited puppy barks. Hound, back end stuck way up in the air, crouched down in front, has her rope toy again and has lost patience with these humans. And with that barking, Nora glances at her watch. "Shit," she says, "I've got class. I gotta go." Eve rouses herself, stands, and offers two hands down to the still sitting Nora. Taking them, she pulls herself to her feet, but her legs won't turn and carry her in the direction of her destination. Her mouth won't form the words, "See you." They stand there, hands nestled together, and Nora thinks, gazing on this person, Who are you? Eve breaks the reverie, asks softly, "You have a pen in that bag?" Nodding, Nora unclasps her fingers, reaches down, grabs a Bic ballpoint, hands it to her. "Your number?" And Nora recites the seven digits as Eve scratches them onto her own forearm, caps the pen and hands it back. "I'll call you." She clips a leash on Hound, and starts to walk away, Nora watching her as she goes, her vision filled with this departure, obscuring everything else on campus; other students, sunlight, traffic out on the road, the looming lab work. Only when Eve turns, giving a final, brief wave, does the spell lift. Only then does Nora check her watch again and see she's almost late. Only then does she start off in the direction of the Chemistry Lab where the work, as long as she is careful about her procedure, should hold no surprises.

Sean is just finishing his cleaning duties when Molly, the Irish head waitress, last on tonight, backs into the kitchen, scrapes the scraps from that last order of pasta and tuna into the trash and stacks the plates next to the dish machine. Heading back onto the floor, she calls over her shoulder, "The last of them Sean. I'll be bringing your whisky shortly." He hops up on the counter, watching the Kenyan dishwasher and a couple of Cockney line cooks finish their stations.

This job was considered a plum offer from the perspective of cooking school—a Michelin-starred London restaurant, under a chef whose name had begun to seep out of the food world and into the public consciousness. From the start, he's been saddled with the hot, dirty work while his boss harasses the wait staff and bellows orders at him from the cool side of the line, never touching food after he's set his menu for the night, and wandering out into the dining room in his clean, pressed whites to accept praise for dishes he hasn't touched. But at the end of the night, he polishes off his cognac, heaves himself out of the kitchen, always saying the same thing as he goes, "Bon! A demain, Sean."

For the few months he's been here, living in a tiny fifth-floor flat with coin-fed gas and electric, a kitchen that's just a nook with a two-burner stove and half fridge, and a bathroom he shares with two other tenants, he hasn't done much more than work and explore the city alone on his day off, a current issue of *Time Out* and a secondhand *Rough Guide* tucked into his bag.

He likes this city. When he landed, the first thought that popped into his jet-lagged brain as he pulled his luggage off the conveyor was, "Thank God I'm home." He'd barely slept on the flight over, and at first, he attributed the feeling to weariness. How else to explain arriving, a stranger, no place to live except for a Bayswater hotel where a reserved room would be his for a week, and feeling as if he'd straggled into his own house after weeks of traveling? But, waiting to clear Customs, fumbling with the small stack of paperwork that granted him leave to stay and work in the United Kingdom, the feeling didn't lift. It settled in during the cab ride to the hotel and buoyed him all through his search for a flat and his rough first weeks on the job. It has only intensified.

He knows it is not just excitement. He knows it's not just being in a city—whenever he's spent too many hours in New York, his molars ache from grinding—but that it's *this* city. It's the neighborhoods like the one he calls home, still carrying the ghosts of the small towns they were before London swallowed them up. It's being able to shop for food without ever stepping into a supermarket. It's the local butchers, fishmongers and veg stands. It's the landlord of his local who starts him a pint of stout before he asks. It's the way the city rewards walking and a sentimental affection for riding on the top of double-decker buses. Of course, he knew none of this that first early morning at Heathrow, and perhaps it was just that the future looked, at that moment, laden with possibility.

He has one complaint. There hasn't yet been time to make any real friends. He sometimes goes out with the waitresses for a tipple in some Soho spot with a late license, and he's developing the young expat's concealed scorn for loud groups of American tourists or college juniors abroad bellowing in the West End pubs. He thinks he's blending in now, that but for the cut of his clothes or the timbre of his voice, he would be unrecognizable as an American. He's becoming a Londoner.

Molly comes back into the kitchen bearing two lowball glasses of Powers' on ice, her bow tie dangling from her unbuttoned tuxedo collar. She hands him one and hops up next to him on the counter. He's got a killer crush on this girl, this tiny woman with the whisky and cigarette-scarred Derry brogue. His first few nights, as he was learning the ins and outs of the kitchen, as he was screwing up orders, his timing off, the recipes and storage locations unfamiliar to him, she had helped him out, not showing any anger when he screwed up her tables, bringing him a whisky after close. "What's this?" he asked the first night, thinking it must be a single malt like those favored by his father, but finding the taste altogether more smooth. "Don't tell me you're called Sean Mahoney, and you've never drank whisky?" "Well, Scotch, Jack Daniel's." "Bah. It's time you sampled the Irish."

Sitting there, leg to leg, and feeling the stresses of the night seep from his limbs with each sip of Powers', he wonders if she might be the thing he ventured to London to find. She leaves him slightly stunned. That mass of black curls, a remnant of an ancient Spanish invasion of her home island, paired with eyes that shift from gray to blue to almost green, all set against the almost translucent skin peculiar to certain Irish clans. He senses too the taut energy of her body moving under the stiff cloak of the wait-staff tuxedo. Could she be the next one, the next woman who will turn into his best friend, his confidante? First there had been his sisters, moving from Patty to Kate, then Amy-Beth, his first lover, all of them leaving him eventually. All of them leaving, so far. Sitting there he thinks, How do you spend your days?

"Good night?" he asks as she pulls free the chopsticks that hold her hair up, shaking those curls loose, obscuring the skin on her neck. "Not bad, the new girl's a cunt." He's still not used to hearing that word, not used to immediately translating it into "bitch" or "pain in the ass," but he's learning, and any discomfort passes quickly. "She'll be fine once she gets sorted. You want to go for a drink?" "I don't fancy Soho tonight." Disappointed, not wanting to show it, he says, "All right, maybe tomorrow?" "There's a good band playing at a club near my place, traditional music. Fancy coming to Finsbury Park?" Buoyed, alert to the possibilities of "near my place," he's down off the counter, "Let's get changed."

Roughly 11:30 p.m., Greenwich Mean Time, pubs closed down, barmaids mopping down bar tops, shooing lingering punters outside. In the reliable London spring, fog rises from the Thames, softening the lights strung along the Embankment. A drizzle threatens, but the sky holds its tongue for now. Across the Atlantic, along the Northeastern seaboard of the United States, daylight lingers for a moment longer than it did yesterday, the early evening hours holding the warmth of a glorious day. Most people are off the job, children are home from school. Good restaurants have no reservations left, movie theaters are expecting sell-out crowds, teenage babysitters are booked. It's a beautiful Friday night, winter shed, and people are itching to shake off their cocoons.

The mother leans her broom against the wall in a corner of the kitchen, and calls, "Anna? Almost done?" Anna who spent most of that first summer with her down here, the year they were thirteen and her father bought the house. Anna who has known this house as long as she has. She slams through the front door, sweat stains on her T-shirt, dirt streaks on her forehead, and flops onto a kitchen chair. "Finished. I can't believe this might be the last time." The mother pads across the kitchen to the refrigerator, pulls two cans of Schlitz from a six-pack resting lonely on the otherwise bare shelves, and in what has become the crowning moment of these ceremonies over the years, she cracks both cans open, slides a cheap beer across the table to her friend, "Cheers." They both take a swallow of the beer they drank when it was still illegal for them to drink, the beer the two of them have reserved, by mutual unspoken agreement, for this day only. It is beer with a taste charitably defined as pedestrian, a beer they don't even like, a beer, to be honest, they didn't even like back then. But today, after the hours of work, it's as refreshing and wonderful as the dry white wines her husband carefully buys for her by the case after perusing his subscription copies of *Wine Spectator*. Anna clinks her can against the mother's, and using a childhood nickname, says, "Cheers, Lizbreath."

The mother always feels a twinge of guilt about now because she hasn't included her family, hasn't asked her husband or badgered her children into helping with this task. She is guilty of carving out a space that only has room for two, and she knows she would refuse their help if any of them offered. But the guilt is quickly subsumed by pleasure as she and Anna each drain the first Schlitz of the night because the rest of the evening is also planned. Dinner out at a fish restaurant along Shark River with an outdoor deck that always opens about the same time she opens the house. An inexpensive place, the huge portions always fresh off the boats from the Belmar fishing fleet, served up without fanfare on paper plates. A bring-your-own-bottle sort of place, where they'll finish the beer before moving on to a cheap bottle of Chardonnay her husband would frown at. After dinner, they'll walk back over the Main Street drawbridge, and if the air is still balmy, they may walk past the street that fronts this house and head down to the boardwalk. They'll sit on one of the benches, scanning the waves and chatting before heading back to the house and turning in for the night, together in the same bed, wrapped in nightgowns and curled under quilts. A slumber party for the little piece of their friendship that still lets them believe they are little girls.

.   .   .

Patty lingers for a moment in her office, the girl waiting for her in the examining room. After a second glance through her phone messages, she decides they all can wait. The receptionist calls, "Have a good weekend!" as she leaves the office. Patty picks up the phone and dials the number of her man-friend of the moment, and at the prompting of an automated voice-mail voice, leaves a message at the tone, "It's me. About quarter to six, I've got a teen pregnancy to confirm, unscheduled. I may be a bit late getting downtown. Wait for me."

She puts her game face back on as she walks down the hall, takes a deep breath outside the closed door, then swings it open, all business. "Well Ms. Hathaway, what seems to be the trouble?" This girl, Patty's experience of her limited to a case of the flu, a strep throat, a sprained ankle from a basketball injury, sits quiet, perched on the edge of the examining table, eyes focused on her swinging feet. "Mary-Ann?" The girl's voice, cold, calculating, "You won't tell my mother?" A murky ethical matter, the patient is a minor, but here, with the relatively liberal laws of New York State at her disposal, she feels she can agree. "I shouldn't have to, I don't think." And, looking Patty right in the eye now, without embarrassment or self-pity, "I'm late. Three weeks. I did a home test; I need an abortion."

Efficiently, matching the tone of her patient, Patty conducts her exam, and when she has at last drawn the blood that will confirm what they both already know, she feels the need to talk with Mary-Ann, to find out what has allowed her to get to this point. It angers her, the way these girls, a handful each year, all the products of Upper East Side privilege, can be so damn careless.

"How long have you been sexually active, Mary-Ann?" "A few months. I love my boyfriend." "You know you should be using condoms. For more than just pregnancy protection." "We always do." "Did it break?" A moment's pause, and then the girl decides, as most of them do, to spill her guts, to tell their doctor what they haven't told anyone, not their parents, not their best friends. "It wasn't him. I went to Palm Beach with my family for Easter break, I met this college guy at a party on the beach. I was drunk." There's almost a note of pride in her voice, a note Patty hears only because she once sang similar tunes herself, and she knows that below the anguish, outside the tough choices this girl will face in the next week or so, she is, somewhere, chomping at the bit to get on with her life. To suck down booze or sip on joints, to go to bed with whomever she damn well pleases, to take risks with her body to mark it as a thing of her own, a thing she alone has dominion over. And though her professional obligation requires a chat about the risks of unprotected sexual activity in the wake of that unique modern pandemic and the effects of alcohol on a still-developing body, she feels her admiration for this girl growing as they talk. As she gives her little lecture, she learns that Mary-Ann Hathaway is a top student at her prep school, a starter on the varsity basketball team as a sophomore, a volunteer downtown at Housing Works on weekends, and Patty decides that this girl is different. The other ones, the dissemblers and outright liars, the scared children of the City's rich, never show her any spunk. That note of pride never pops into their voices as they sing their sob stories, and she gives them their referrals to another discreet neighborhood doctor with contempt. This one is a lot like me she thinks as they conclude their talk, Patty telling her the results of the blood test should be in Monday afternoon, and they can set up an appointment for her abortion then. This one will have learned a lesson, she won't get caught out again, won't have to ask for help. This one is a survivor.

In the theater district around Times Square, Kate bustles up 44th Street towards an Italian restaurant with a solid reputation and family-style portions bordering on the absurd. Ducking into the doorway, the crowd three-deep around the bar, she searches the suit backs knoodling over cocktails for the line of Brian's shoulders, the tilt of his head.

There he is, huddled in conversation with another suit as they wait on their wives. Brian spots her as she approaches the high, round cocktail table, stands, gives her a quick, businesslike peck on the side of her lips, makes introductions, "Tim, Kate, Kate, Tim." A handshake, and she's told that Tim's wife, Joan, is on her way downtown from her job at the Whitney, she should arrive in just a few moments. Kate leaves them for the bar and orders a Sapphire and tonic over the din. She squeezes her lime wedge into the sparkling mixture, swirls everything with her swizzle stick, takes a fortifying sip. The Whitney, she thinks, the Goddamned Whitney. The building once the summation of her ambitions, its odd-year Biennial show the apex of her younger self's dreams. She has, despite the vanishing of her own drive and talent, tried to keep up. She goes to exhibits; reads the expensive glossy magazines that chart *the art world*. She still loves to look, still, somewhere, longs to feel connected to that place, even as a tourist. Walking back to the table, she searches her brain for what she's heard or read about what's what at the Whitney these days. And as she sips her drink, half listening to Brian and Tim talk about their law school days, it comes to her, she can lead with an inquiry on Charles Ray—will he be included in next year's Biennial show?—and take things from there.

Suddenly there is one of those impossibly thin, stylish, altogether New York women standing beside them, and Tim is greeting her, making introductions, grabbing her a Campari and something from the bar, lighting the Dunhill cigarette she pulls from a silver case. Their table is ready, thank God, and as they head in that direction, Kate and Joan make small talk, feeling each other out, each taking in the surface of what they see and despairing. This could be a very long night indeed, the two of them appear to have nothing in common, and neither has much interest in the delicate negotiations to be carried out by their spouses. But as they settle into their banquet, Kate broaches the subject of the Whitney, asks her rehearsed question about Ray, confides that his work tends to leave her cold, and Joan, surprised this suburban teacher has any idea about art, confesses, "I find Ray altogether too obvious, but as a fund-raiser my opinion on the work shown is not particularly valued, and the word is he'll have some sort of sculpture in next year's Biennial."

So, the men select their wine, pick the large platters of food they will share before leaving for the theater, and relieved their wives are occupying one another, talk the business that is the real reason for this expense-account evening. Over their low voices, Kate and Joan talk animatedly about the art scene, Kate bumming a cigarette from Joan, finding common ground on some work they love, sheepishly expressing their preference for dead artists over many of those working today. The antipasto arrives and as they pause to load up their plates, Kate thinks, Well I'll be damned. I'm having a good time.

In the middle of the 9th fairway, a par four dogleg left, dusk descending, the father stands by his ball, trying to measure the distance to the pin in the remaining light. He selects a seven iron from his bag, takes his stance, waggles his feet, wiggles the club. Taking a deep breath, keeping his head still, he slowly draws the club back, torso quiet, weight coiling around his hips. A slight pause at the apex of his swing, then the turn towards the downstroke. He savors the solid thwack of the ball, the ineffable pleasure of a well-struck golf shot, the ball rising quickly, then softly dropping to the green. This has been a good round. Playing alone, not having to make conversation with another member or one of his regular playing partners. Moving at his own pace. Alone with his thoughts.

Nothing could be better than this he thinks as he shoulders his bag and moves off towards the green. As he has grown older, the nest empty, his children seeming to do well on their own, he's come to treasure those moments of each day that are his and his alone. Those hours when he isn't working, when he isn't doing something that requires other people's personalities or voices, have become his talismans of the perfect life. As he grows older he's come to treasure silence; he's begun to cut back on his working hours, spending more time just sitting with a book, working on building wine cellars in the basements of both houses or driving off for solo weekend outings to one of those towns along the Delaware River with their country inns, antique shops and developing vineyards whose output gets better each year despite the odds of climate and location.

On the green now, he pulls the pin and walks around the line of his putt, setting it up. Knocking this one in will give him his best round of the new season, a solid 42 for nine holes, and he doesn't want to miss. Settling over the ball, his stroke smooth, he raps the ball right into the center of the cup, loving the sound of its rattle as it settles into the plastic base. Plucking the ball free, replacing the pin, and shouldering his bag again, he heads towards the locker room, wondering what he'll do with the rest of his night.

A free night, without his wife. And while just a few years ago that possibility would have been fraught with either temptation or a queasy anxiousness at their growing distance from one another, he thinks they are at a new place now. A place where they can run on different tracks for lengths of time, knowing that those tracks will intersect somewhere, sooner rather than later. And in those intersections the simple strength of their long bond, the trueness of their affection and friendship will carry the day. She is the only real friend I have he thinks, stowing his clubs in his locker and heading for the shower, and we're strong because we have been tested.

As Nora and her lab partner, a woman she's worked with for four years but knows absolutely nothing about, clean their workstation, Nora apologizes, "Sorry. My concentration was shitty today." "Don't sweat it, happens to all of us." But it hasn't happened to Nora. She's been adept at losing herself in work, adept at locking herself away in the refuge of carefully attended details, the demand for precision in her class work spilling over into her life. She believed she preferred things that way.

Her models, her family, taught her things. The youngest, looking up at them, she'd sampled of all their approaches and decided her own way—quiet, keeping things to herself—was best. Sean, always open, too eager to give all of himself, had suffered for it, and Nora had decided not to leave herself vulnerable to that. Kate, in her suburb with her Volvo and husband, her dreams abandoned long ago, gives her the shivers. She seems content, but Nora can remember the restlessness of her oldest sister, the years when they called her Katy-did because Kate always had done something. Looking at her now, docile, relentlessly normal, Nora can't help but wonder what happened to that girl who was willing to toss the family into turmoil to preserve herself. Can't help but see that giving up means losing part of yourself.

Her parents she doesn't understand, not a whit. Her mother and Aunt Anna, a Boston Marriage if she's ever seen one, the inscrutable distance of her father—what is it that keeps the two of them linked? And Patty, with her careless disregard for others and herself. Patty's example led to a night Nora can't quite distance herself from, a night by the river that still troubles her sleep. She doesn't blame her sister, but she can't help dwelling on how Patty's easy survival in the face of her carelessness had blinded Nora to the danger of that evening.

There is, of course, another reason for keeping her cards folded in close to her chest. She believes *they don't know.* She's certain that telling them is impossible, they would reject her, cast her aside, her mother retreating to the teachings of the Church, her father ignoring it entirely, her sisters pretending to be fine, but calling her even less. And, Sean. Sean might be okay, but she can never be sure, and she doesn't want to risk it. Doesn't want to jeopardize their newfound closeness.

The clean-up is nearly finished, her lab partner packing up her bag, the other students filing out into the night, and Nora is bursting with her afternoon encounter. She says, desperate to confide in someone, "Sorry again. I met someone this afternoon." Her lab partner, curious, asks, "Really, who?" And Nora, Nora who doesn't tell anyone anything, is gushing as she goes out the door. "Eve Something. She's got this dog, a puppy, and these arms. Listen to me." Oddly, to Nora's mind at least, her lab partner knows Eve, a bit, and as they walk along the faux gas lamp–lit paths, she fills Nora in. "I know her. Hot. She plays guitar in some band. A Lit major. Works a few nights in the library and runs around with a few people in the theater crowd and a few of the Lit magazine people." Reaching the point where they'll part ways, each heading to their own off-campus apartments, Nora slows under one of those carefully spaced lights. "Thanks. For the lab, for filling me in." "Don't worry about it. Just get your head together for next week, okay? Free radicals fuck me up. Oh, and by the way, she's single."

After walking the few blocks to her apartment, she checks her mail, finds a missive from Sean, and trudges up the stairs. Her never-home roommate is out. Nora wanders into the living room, the answering-machine light blinking red in the dark, and hoping against hope, thinking, What the hell is wrong with me, she pushes PLAY and flops onto the couch. Beep. The machine voice, *2:30 p.m.,* her honor's thesis advisor, "Nora, Phil Mundo, I've been looking over the latest draft, and I've got a couple of sourcing questions, but the work is just getting stronger." Beep. *6:27 p.m.,* "Hey. It's Eve. From this afternoon. Hound asked me to call. I told her you wouldn't be home yet, but she just sort of cocked her head to the side and raised those ears up. I'll be in The Pub around eight-thirty. I'm saving a stool for you."

It's just a bit before eight, she should call Dr. Mundo at home, work through those sourcing concerns tonight, she should stay in, *she's got studying to do.* But as she pulls her backpack to her feet and roots around for her thesis notes, she thinks, The hell with it. Checking her watch, still not quite eight o'clock. Not wanting to seem too eager, she decides to shower, take her time, get to the bar a bit late. Padding into the bathroom, turning the taps, peeling off her clothes and stepping under the spray, she is surprised to hear herself singing some radio-friendly pop tune. And those off-key notes bouncing off the acoustic amplification of her shower stall, sound, to her, absolutely perfect.

Sean sits on a couch pockmarked with cigarette burns, two half-empty pints of Guinness, several empty glasses and an overflowing ashtray on the table in front of him. Molly's wedged in next to him, using Rizla papers and the dregs of a Golden Virginia pouch to roll each of them a cigarette. This pub is packed, full of exiles from a neighboring island, nodding their heads as the fiddle and guitar lurch into a reel behind the propulsion of a frantic bodhrán. The old man charged with collecting empty glasses dances nimbly in the cramped space between tables, stacking pints one on top of the other in a tower. Molly seals both smokes with her tongue, strikes a wooden match, lights them up, and hands one to Sean. A woman comes over to Molly, leans in by her head and says something Sean can't quite make out. Molly laughs, bitterly Sean thinks, shakes her head no, and motioning for the woman to lean over again, says something of her own. As the woman wanders off, Sean wonders what the hell is going on, this is the third or fourth person to come by and whisper to Molly. Leaning over, his lips right up against her ear so she can hear over the din, attempting to create a confidence of his own, "They're good. Very good." She looks at him, says, "They are" without leaning in before turning back to the stage and watching for a moment. The reel winds up, the tenor with the beard and the guitar announces a short break, and as the hum of conversation rises to fill the vacuum left by the absence of music, Molly turns back to him. "The bloke with the beard is my brother. I'm just after breaking it off with the fiddle player." The tone of her voice shifts to bitter, "Amicable as they say." "I'm sorry." "Don't be. I'm not." She pauses, her eyes shifting away from him and her voice suddenly hesitant, "And you?" "Me?" "Anyone pining for you in America?" "Hardly."

In the brief second that follows, there is a mutual awareness that their workplace flirtations have suddenly taken on a different tone.

With just those nuggets of knowledge, something has shifted, changing the view slightly. And as their brains work to process the details of the new landscape, her fingers brush his hand and linger there for just a shade too long, but before he can react, twine his fingers into hers, her brother is sweeping down on their table, plopping down on the couch with them, bellowing, "Molly O'Brien, you should be off at home, sleeping a virtuous sleep, not cavorting in some public house with a man of dubious origin."

Sean watches as she smiles a broad, open smile, the skin around those eyes crinkling, her tiny hand balling into a fist and moving with surprising force at her brother's arm, "And you should know you were a half-step off on that last reel. Timothy O'Brien, Sean Mahoney and vice versa." Sean reaches across Molly to shake hands, "Nice to meet you. It sounded fine to me." "You as well. I'm afraid she's right on the reel. I've misjudged the amount of Guinness necessary tonight. You're the new chef, then? My sister doesn't know many Americans." "I am, sous-chef." Turning back to his sister, he jerks his head towards the bar where the fiddle player is gazing into a small glass of whisky, "Walk carefully around Finn tonight, he's fully pissed and treading the line between maudlin and violent. I'm not up to judging which way he'll fall."

The other members of the band are straggling up to the makeshift stage, checking to make sure they're still in tune. "I'm off then. Sean, a pleasure. Mol, 'Foggy Dew' is our closer, will you sing?" "I shouldn't tonight. Finn." "We've had a chat about it, should be all right. With you on whistle, he hangs in the back in any case." "I'll see." "Right then. Ta." As he lumbers off towards the stage, Molly leans in a bit closer to Sean, "My big brother," she says, simply, as if there's no need for further comment. "He seems nice." "He is. I moved in with him after Finn. A bit strange to be back in that. . . . Do you have brothers?" "Three sisters. Two older, one younger." "Ha! I'm the third of four as well, the rest boys. Tim and I are here. Seamus, the baby, in Dublin, and Joseph, the eldest, off in New York." Before Sean can answer, the band launches into "Dueling Banjos" from *Deliverance,* the mandolin player and Tim trading the licks. "This is for you," Molly whispers in Sean's ear, "They haven't done it in ages."

The band works faster and faster, upping the tension of the music to a point where the crowd whoops and hollers in the silences. Sean is listening, half caught in the music, but also actively aware of an answering pressure as his leg brushes up against Molly's under the table. Suddenly the band stops, and in perfect four-part harmony, breaks into another song. Their matched voices rise without accompaniment, "When I was an itty, bitty baby, my mamma would rock my in my cradle, in them old, cotton fields back home. . . ."

Sean drums his fingers on the table, feels Molly's weight come up against him with slightly more force as she shifts to see the stage better, and as she turns her head around to look at him, he ventures to place that drumming hand around her waist to hold her in place against him. She covers his hand with her own and leans on him, "Glad you like it."

The mother, leaning back in her chair with her coffee and gazing out on the tidal pull of the Shark River inlet, feels at peace. The dinner, as it always is here, was wonderful. Anna's company, as always, a warm and pleasant thing. Anna's been talking about her husband, complaining that since his early retirement he's been underfoot too much, rooting around the house for projects, generally making her nuts. But able to make the complaints with a laugh, not really upset, marveling at the turns their life has taken. The waitress comes by with their check and coffee refills and Anna says, "Enough about Jack and me. How are my nieces and nephew?" "Oh, fine, I guess. Sean's working hard over there. I miss him. Kate's settled, no trouble in a long time. I haven't spoken to Patty in ages, but she calls Pat and he seems to think she's fine. She's never given us any worry, but she drinks." Laughing, Anna nods towards the empty wine bottle on the table, "We all do." "I know, but it's different. She hides things well." "And my God-daughter? Still tearing it up in Philadelphia?" The mother smiles, but her voice is hollow, "Dean's List after Dean's List. Cornell in the fall." These two women have been friends for too long for Anna not to hear the emptiness in her voice, "Liz, what is it?" "I saw her on TV last week." "For what?" "On the Channel 10 news from Philadelphia, at a protest." "Well, good. We did a couple of those ourselves back in the day." "An AIDS thing." "Okay." "Something called a kiss-in. She was kissing a woman."

A few weeks prior. The mother comes home to the big empty house after work and clicks on the television for some noise. The five o'clock news from one of the Philadelphia affiliates fills the screen and the cheering noise of protestors draws her attention from her fistful of junk-mail, catalogues and bills. Outside the Liberty Bell, a throng of people carry signs starkly marked with bold black on white lettering. They chant, men holding hands with men, women with women. In a sudden silence, they turn to one another, the men to the men, the women to the women, and the screen fills with a panning image of kisses. It cannot last more than a few seconds. But for the mother, whose thoughts on the issue at hand are complex, whose religious and cultural background have conditioned her to be repelled by what she's seeing, but who finds herself thinking these young men and women are incredibly brave, whose sense of justice and fairness is stronger than her religious convictions, the moment seems to last for hours. Something she can't name is stirred by the images on the screen, she feels somehow triumphant for these people.

As the kisses break and the noise of a joyful, defiant cheer moves through the crowd, the camera comes to rest on a pretty young woman linked arm in arm with two other young women, her ebullient face lifted towards the sky, and the mother finds herself thinking, I know her. Out of context, it takes her a moment to place the face, a moment to recognize her youngest daughter. To realize that some news editor had chosen her child to punctuate their coverage of the protest. She stares at the television as the news breaks for commercials.

Uncomprehending, she clicks off the television and sits in the quiet for a long while, trying to piece together what she's seen. She picks up the phone and dials Nora's number three different times, hanging up before it can ring.

As she thinks about it, it begins to make sense. Scanning the years, there were no high school sweethearts, no reports of college boyfriends, no thirteen-year-old phase of shirtless rock musicians gracing her bedroom walls. No condoms peeking from a carelessly left-open purse or birth control dial in her sock drawer. Her assumption had always been that Nora was the cautious one, perhaps more romantic and old-fashioned in her leanings than her sisters. That Nora was waiting, for marriage maybe, or simply for the right guy to come along. Summoning a reserve of her good humor, she thinks, We all know what happens when you assume.

But as she sits there, waiting for Pat to get home, spinning with her thoughts, she feels herself growing angry. Why hasn't she told us? What must she think of us? Was one of those girls her girlfriend? How can she exclude us from her life like this?

The mechanical whirring of the automatic garage-door opener breaks her reverie. Rising from her perch, she flips on lights, decides not to share this information with her husband just yet. When he comes in, she's in front of the open fridge door, scanning the contents for the makings of their dinner for two. They settle down in front of the television with their books after supper, and she is careful to make sure they watch only the New York affiliates. But the image of her daughter's face triumphantly raised at the close of that story lingers on the margins of her thoughts all night.

This night, Anna looks at her steadily from across the table, "You're okay with that, right?" "I'm trying to be. Why hasn't she told me?" "Oh, Liz, give her time. I know that girl. She'll tell you." Trying to shift the subject, Anna continues, "How'd she look on television?" No answer comes immediately, the mother rooting around in her internal thesaurus and coming up short of a description for the look on Nora's face. A fierce, proud, beautiful look she hadn't seen since Nora was little and she scored a goal in a Saturday afternoon soccer game or climbed the biggest tree in the yard. "Liz?" "I was going to say proud, but I think—I think radiant. Or maybe, she looked just like herself, only more."

.   .   .

Night falls in earnest on the New York–Philadelphia corridor. Far enough from the lights of the two metropolises, the sky is clear, the predictable pattern of the stars starkly drawn, the moon barely an orange razor edge, waning. Early diners are on coffee and dessert, plopping American Express cards down into tip trays. In the cities, the hot night spots are starting to fill up, bartenders shaking liquor and mixers with ice and straining drinks into chilled cocktail glasses, cocktail waitresses bustling through impossible gaps wielding trays loaded down with Cosmopolitans and martinis. In London, all but the most diehard late-night spots are closing up, clumps of people slouch drunkenly around Trafalgar Square, waiting on the hopeless night buses. In the outer reaches of the city, everything is quiet, shut up for a few more hours, save the odd kabob shop or fish and chips take-away serving late-night cravings.

The pub is momentarily silent as the last whistle notes of "Foggy Dew" fade into silence, then Sean joins the spirited clapping and foot stamping, the crowded room begging for just one more. But the request is denied by Molly's suddenly bashful "Thank you" into the microphone, the whistle passed off to her brother, and the lights up to full.

Sean, mildly drunk, stunned by the beauty of Molly's voice, the despair lurking in the sparse whistle tones and drum beats of the tune, feels on the verge of tears. Maudlin and mildly drunk, suspecting he might be falling in love, with Molly, with music, he thinks, with the peculiar pride and self-deception of those who bear Celtic surnames in America, *I'm Irish, damn it.*

She flops back in next to him, cheeks still flushed with what? Excitement? Nervousness? Picks up the dregs of the pint she left behind, tosses back the warmish beer. "You were great," he says. "Nonsense," she replies, "I've learned to sing only if the crowd is Irish and it's coming up on last orders. Give us a fag?" He fumbles in his pockets and produces his pack of Silk Cuts, pulls one out, hands it to her, gets the wooden match lit, watches her drag, exhale and relax back into the battered sofa.

The punters are slowly making their way to the door, the crowd thinning down, the barmaids briskly washing empties and stacking them back on the racks around the taps. Sean drains the last of his Guinness and begins to wonder, What now? He glances over at Molly, puffing on the last bit of the cigarette, her face showing something, but he can't decipher what. She's not as close to him on the couch as she was before she stood to sing, and though he wouldn't trade having heard her voice, he wants her body back against his. Wishes that he could determine how, exactly, they'd landed in that position so that he could work them back into it now in a way that seemed neither desperate nor one-sided. "Fancy a walk?" she breaks into his thoughts, "I'm not quite ready for sleep." "Sure." "Be right back."

Briskly, she moves towards where the band is packing up their instruments, pulls her brother into a brief conference, gives him a quick hug and a peck on the cheek, and is starting back towards him. "Right," she says, "Shall we?"

Outside, the street is empty of traffic, bits of paper trash billowing down the deserted road, shops all shuttered and dark. She seems to have a destination in mind, and they start off in silence, walking very close to one another, coats open against the air, seemingly more brisk after the warmth of the pub. Walking very close to one another, their fingers brush occasionally, until, a few blocks later, they lace their hands together as they walk along. This part of the city is unfamiliar to Sean, it's as off the beaten track as his own neighborhood. He has no idea where he is or how and when he'll get home with the Underground closed and no sign of a black cab anywhere, but between the beer and the pressure of her hand in his, he doesn't care.

As if she's reading his thoughts, she breaks their silence, "Where do you live again?" "Kilburn Park. Why?" "Curiosity mostly. It's not far from here." They walk on a bit further until she suddenly stops at a corner, he half turns so he's facing her as she releases a long sighing breath.

He touches a finger to her cheek, "What?" Her voice cracking some, "Oh, Sean Mahoney. I like you." "That's bad?" "No," she answers, smiling now, "that's good. The timing, Finn and I just over, is piss poor."

Half elation, half despair, all amplified by Guinness, and no vocabulary to comfort or seduce that wouldn't be half a mistake. So he takes her in his arms, just a hint of sex in the close embrace. And she gives in to it, gives him some of her weight, rests her head on his shoulder. After a time, she stands back and takes both his hands. "Right," she says, snuffling.

"I should find my way home," he says with barely the hint of a question. "Probably," she says, "there's a mini-cab place open all night down the road a piece." Nodding over her shoulder, "I live here." They stand as they are for a moment longer, taking one another in with the dim aid of street lamps and left-on porch lights. "Goodnight, Molly O'Brien," Sean says finally. "Goodnight, Sean Mahoney." This is the moment of the gamble, the moment when he could lean his face into hers, and she could meet him, or turn slightly and offer her cheek. She meets him, and the kiss is brief and tender and holds a tentative promise of something deeper and more animal on some other night. The beginning and end of a night's sexual congress, it feels whole in itself, and for now, it is enough.

He gives her hand a quick squeeze, walks a few steps backwards down the street towards the mini-cabs. They both wave, and she turns, going up the steps to her building, fumbling in her pockets for her keys.

On the ride home to his empty flat, he watches the roads they travel, piecing together the maze of the city that connects his home to hers and whistles fragments of Irish melodies under his breath.

Patty curses the traffic under her breath as her cab idles on Fifth Avenue somewhere in the Twenties. Rooting in her tote bag, she pulls free an airline bottle of Tanqueray, cracks the top and takes a few settling sips from its little mouth. All day she relished the knowledge that she had this small comfort waiting for whenever she needed it. But it's gone too quickly. She's only at Washington Square, she's an hour late, and the cabbie is turning right, edging towards the snarl of MacDougal Street. "I said Mercer between Houston and Prince. You're going the wrong fucking way." The squeal of breaks and the blare of several million horns ring in Patty's head. She just wants to get to the bar, where her boy should be waiting, where she can get her next drink.

"Lady, you can get out right here," the cab driver is saying. "You don't like the way I drive, you walk or you get someone else." "Just drive," she says, the horns still blaring from the traffic backed up behind them. "No. Five fifteen. Get out." "Please drive," the chorus of horns, rising in a crescendo, a cacophony of flats and sharps, running up and down her spinal cord. "Five dollars, fifteen cents. Get out." "Jesus fuck-ing Christ almighty. You want five bucks you cab-driving piece of shit?" she says, digging her wallet from her bag, flinging a five and a sin-gle through the partition. "Keep the fucking change," she backs out into the street, gathering her things, screaming at the top of her lungs through the open door, "You fucking jackass. If you knew the fuck-ing city, you'd know how to get to goddamned Mercer Street and you—." Her harangue broken as the cab pulls away, the door swinging shut as the driver banks a left onto MacDougal, she's left standing in the middle of Washington Square North as the light on Fifth changes again, and the traffic starts to surge in her direction. Scurrying out of the street, she starts to cut through the park, dodging the whispering dealers, "Smoke, smoke, crack, smoke?" and then briskly, along Fourth to Mercer, her anger mellowing but still simmering as she dashes across Houston against the light.

The less privileged are already lined up outside the bar, begging a chance to get in, to rub shoulders with the City's trendy and famous. Bustling up to the burly doorman, his serious face opening into a smile as she approaches, "Hey Jer," she says, going up on tiptoe to accept the buss on her cheeks. "Doctor Patty," he unclips the rope, and motions her inside, "The man's been waiting inside for a couple of cocktails now."

Inside, the hum of conversation and something jazzy on the stereo soothe her mood. She spies her boy at the bar, chatting with a down-town type she vaguely knows, a performance artist she thinks, and why isn't he mooning over his Bourbon, waiting for me? So, she takes her time, leaning in to get another kiss on the cheek from the woman working behind the bar, and watching with satisfaction as she sets to work with shaker and ice, the blue bottle of gin, a quick dash of ver-mouth. The martini glass waits on the bar top, filled with ice and soda water, its skin growing frosty as the bartender shakes vigorously. She dumps the ice and soda, grabs a twist, and runs it around the broad rim of that glass. After straining the liquor, she twists the twist, plops it into the gin and takes Patty's twenty.

Patty leans down over the bar and takes the first sip without lifting the glass. She feels the gin working its way down her throat, into her belly, spreading out into her veins, making her sane and steady. God, she thinks, I was a bitch to that cab driver. Another slurp without lifting the glass and she's downed a third of the drink. Her hands are rocks as she plucks her cocktail from the bar, leaving behind her usual generous tip to assure prompt refills and a warm welcome at the door.

He still hasn't seen me she thinks as she moves forward towards her guy. She likes this one. He's been around for a few weeks, a carpen-ter/set designer with gentle, calloused hands and an easygoing manner. He hasn't gone all needy and desperate, hasn't paged her with numbers to spell out "hello." She sidles up next to him, carefully puts her mar-tini on the bar, and wraps her arms around his waist, "Tommy," she drawls, "you waited. Good boy. Sorry I'm late." He swings around, and his hand touches her cheek as a counterpoint to a kiss that makes her want to drag him someplace dark and quiet. "Patty," he grins, "this is Angelica, she's doing a one-woman thing we're doing the design for. Angelica, Patty." She couldn't care less about Angelica, but she's nothing if not charming and polite, and she takes the proffered hand before turning back to reach for her martini. Somehow it's gotten low, and before she turns to join their conversation, she catches the bartender's eye, tips her finger towards her glass and drains what's left as a replacement is mixed for her.

Kate, Brian, Tim and Joan hail a cab in Times Square, deciding over dinner to bag *Les Miz,* they've all seen it, and have an after-dinner cocktail someplace downtown. The account has been secured, Brian's work is done, Kate really likes Joan, Tim seems okay, and after the wine, everyone is a bit mellow, the company easy. Tim gives an address in Soho and the car lurches down Broadway, the meter ticking in the background as they chat.

Traffic snarls around Union Square for a few minutes, then shoots down Broadway again, the sidewalks packed with NYU students, people clutching guitar cases. Some of the stores are still here, the stores Kate used to browse in during her high school days when she'd cut school and take the train into the City. Shakespeare and Company gated and dark, the Antique Boutique. Just west in the park, old men playing chess, the dog run, jugglers by the fountain, Rastas hawking weed. In the dark, nothing much seems to have changed, it still makes her feel alive. These streets still fill her with a rush of energy and exuberance.

Turning right on Houston, then left on Mercer, the cab cuts over to the curb in front of a signless spot, a small crowd gathered in front of a grim-faced doorman. We're not going to get in here, she thinks. But Tim is paying the driver, she's sliding out, taking Brian's arm and Joan is already speaking to the doorman. The rope is unclipped and they're waved inside, as someone on line is saying Madonna was here just the other night. But she's past them and into the vestibule, where someone solicitous is taking their coats. It's all dark wood and candlelight, crowded but not packed tight, the music low enough so it doesn't crush the hum of conversation. Looking around she's starting to feel hopelessly unhip, all these sleek people, a scatter of faces she recognizes from movies and magazine covers. Joan, satisfied, leaning against the leather of the banquette where they've been seated, taking everything in, Brian and Tim, at ease, chatting, back on their law school days.

"Where are we?" she asks. "It's a new place. I did an event here for the museum just before they opened officially," Joan nods her head towards the back of the room, "Nan Goldin's over there in the corner." Their drinks arrive in heavy, dewy glassware, and as she lifts hers to her lips, Kate thinks, stealing a peek at the famous photographer with the bottle of mineral water in front of her, This could have been my life. I shouldn't feel like a misfit here.

Nora pushes into the din of the college bar after having her license scrutinized and her right hand stamped by the guy at the door. She scans the room. Equipment for a band is set up on the makeshift stage and there's Eve, sitting with a group of people, three girls she's seen around campus, a couple of skinny, flannel-clad guys with long hair and goatees, her back to an empty bar stool.

Nora makes her way over, plops down on the stool, and the motion attracts the attention of the little group. Eve turns, saying before she can see who's joined them, "Sorry. This seat's take—" But her eyes light on Nora and she finishes, "Hey! You made it. This is Jen, Colleen, Jason, Rich and Beth. Everyone, Nora." They do the nice-to-meet-you thing, and as Nora turns to grab the attention of the bartender, Eve leans in close to her, squeezing her arm, "Glad you're here."

Turning back to the group with a mug of draft Bud in hand, Nora asks, "There's a band tonight?" "Them," Eve says, nodding at her friends, "I'm opening though. I didn't want to tell you on the phone." "Why?" "Was afraid you wouldn't show." Nora looks at her, takes her in again, as if her memory from earlier may have been distorted by some trick of the sun, some optical illusion wrought by the beautiful

spring afternoon. "Not a chance," she says, loving the way Eve is blush-
ing a little now, bowing her head to conceal the color rising on her
neck, loving the small dimples that corner her smile. "Not a chance."

The bartender comes over, says, "You're up" to Eve, and she whispers, "Wish me luck," to Nora before crossing over to the stage, shouldering an acoustic guitar, strumming a few chords, adjusting a couple
of tuning pegs, the volume on her amp. Tilting the mike towards her
face, she says, "I'm Eve Kimble," and gets a smattering of clapping from
around the bar. She starts strumming the intro to her first song, full of
staccato energy, dancing a bit behind the confines of the guitar, before
coming to rest right in front of the mike, pausing for a beat, and belt-
ing out the first words in a smoky alto that grabs Nora's stomach.

The father wraps aluminum foil around the last three slices of the pizza
he picked up on the way home and tosses them in the freezer. He de-
liberates for a moment between another beer and a glass of wine from
the bottle they opened the previous night. Deciding on the wine, he
releases the fancy pressure system he bought to keep open bottles fresh
for several days, listens to the satisfying pop as the seal is broken, almost
like the celebratory pop of a champagne bottle. Turning to the glass
ware cabinet over the small sink, he reaches for a white glass from the
hanging rack and pours himself a glass three-quarters full. Padding into
his study, he flops down on the couch, rests the glass on a coaster sitting ready on the end table, grabs his book, opens to the marked page
and tries to read.

He can't concentrate. Words swim, sentences transpose themselves,
he passes over the same paragraph seven or eight times before thinking, Bear down. But the story won't arrange itself. Words that had
seemed so vital when he first cracked this volume last night before bed,
words that gave him that childlike thrill of *just one more chapter* as he
fought sleep, now seem flat and unreal.

Glancing around the softly lit sanctuary of his study, he fumbles for

the vocabulary of his emotions. He sees the warm glow on the paneling. The eight-by-tens of the family, of vacation scenery, a few of just
birds (a family joke, his film always peppered with the greeting-card
shot of the wheeling gull or the bloated, resting pelican) framed and
hung by Liz. He's never thought about these pictures before, they were
just there, and now, he wonders, Why? A reminder? Something to
point out to him that there are lives and places outside these four walls
that are important to him, that there are people dependent on him?

Rising, he grabs his glass and walks around the room. Looks closely
at the shots, his children and Liz, a shot of Sean and him from just before Sean left for London. The two of them on the back of a boat, wine
glasses in hand, sunset in the background. There was a letter from Sean
in the mail today. Addressed to Liz, it sits unopened on the kitchen
counter with her other mail. There will be a few words for him in
there, "Send Dad my love" or "Tell Dad that the wine reps say Provence
should be outstanding this year." But no letters for him and him alone.
In the photo, there on the back of a boat belonging to an old family
friend, they look the best of friends. Does the picture lie?

Moving to the other shots, his favorite of Nora, maybe five or six
years old, in the "V" of the old maple tree, the leaves blowing orange
and red around her, her corduroys and velour shirt contrasting in burgundy and dark green. This is the way he still sees her in his mind, all
shaggy bangs and buck teeth, cheeks dusted with freckles, her face
open in uncomplicated joy as she waves from her perch. Another. Kate
and Patty, before. On the beach, leaning against one another, Patty's
head buried in some book, Kate absently sucking on a plum and staring into the distance.

The house is deathly quiet. He longs for the bursting of the furnace
as it comes to life, any noise to break into his train of thoughts. He feels
. . . what? Moving around the room, sipping on his glass of Sauvignon
Blanc, regarding the faces of his family on the wall, he feels, with a sudden clarity, that he is fifty-two years old and unsatisfied with his own
company. That even though he craves his own time, he is who he is be-

cause of them. Without them, without the people on these walls, what does he have? In a quiet house, surrounded by things he is supposed to love and enjoy, with all the lovely solitude he could ask for, he is lonely.

The mother and Anna sit on one of the benches lining the boardwalk, watching the waves, shivering slightly against the ocean breeze. They don't speak but the draw and fade of the restless tide leaves a steady rumble in the air. In a few short weeks the boardwalk will be filled at this hour, preppy families out strolling after dinner during their week at the Shore, summer teens darting underneath the old dance pavilion to sneak beers and steal kisses. But, tonight they're alone. There has been too much to drink as there always is on this night, and the heavy subject of their after-dinner conversation turns in their thoughts. The mother is aware of Anna's shoulder pressing against hers, and the vast sweep of the deserted beach filling her view gives her too much space for thought. It is difficult to focus. The beach, the beer, the bottle of wine.

The mother tries to imagine what they would look like to someone strolling by their bench. Trying to see them, two women in their late forties, comfortable enough with one another to sit in silence and give some of their weight to the other. We would look like lovers the mother thinks, lovers with the gift of a long history together.

And there is love there. A love different and more fierce than the love she has for Pat. And though she touches Anna, hugs her and kisses her good-bye and hello, sits like this from time to time, she's never thought of their love as a love expressed in the physical. Never thought of Anna in terms of desire. What's the difference, she wonders, the difference between Nora and myself? If she loves some woman, the mother thinks, and I love this woman, is the difference just sex? Turning to look at her lifelong friend, taking in the sweep of her profile as she contemplates the night herself, the mother thinks, yes, she is beautiful. The long salt-and-pepper hair, those eyes deep-set and mahogany brown, the shallow lines etched in her face by the passing of each year. So what is it, she asks herself, what is it that has kept us from turning those chaste kisses of friends into something more? And what would it be like to give in to this sudden curiosity? Staring at her friend now, wondering, the mother decides it would be unbearable. Unbearable if it was good because of the regret of all of those years missed. And unbearable if it was not good because the guilt of cheating on Pat would be crushing, but more because of the knowledge that there was something, at last, that they could not share.

Anna turns to her, looks at her curiously for a moment, smiling shyly, "What?" she asks. "Nothing," the mother says, "just thinking." "Yes. Me too." Anna stands then and offers her hand. "Come on Liz, it's fucking freezing all of a sudden. Let's go home." Taking the proffered hand, the mother rises and they start back towards the freshly scrubbed and opened house, walking slowly, holding hands.

Patty surreptitiously squeezes the knee of a guy, an Ed, who has joined their little group. No one seems to know him, his face all dark stubble and the glint of the steel pushed through his eyebrow, his tongue, his nose. Tom is quiet across the table, his disapproving, "Another?" as round after round turned into at least one too many earning him exile from Patty's sphere, at least temporarily. And Patty is voluble, her tongue thickened to the margins of slurring, the group hanging on her words as she regales them with med-school stories and legends of the odd and inconceivable ways in which people find themselves ill or injured, saving her favorite for last. A poor woman from the Lower East Side, come into the emergency room with something green sprouting from between her legs, "I got this from an intern who swears he was there. They removed a potato end, all the eyes sprouting. Can you believe that shit? She used it for birth control, like a sponge."

Gratified by their laughter, the center of attention, she sees her glass is low. Signals for another. "Patty," Tom says, softly, but serious. "Yes?" coldly. "I think it's time to head home." "Go ahead then." She is conscious of the eyes riveted on them around the table. Angelica, slightly predatory, stalking the approaching carcass of this relationship, the pierced and shadowy Ed with his firm thigh and bemused expression. But she stares at Tom, a visual dare from across the table. "Fine," he says, draining his Maker's, pushing back from the table and angrily slamming through the crowd and out the door. A few seconds pass in silence, and Angelica is on her feet, "I guess I'll head out too," and slipping away.

Patty turns her gaze full on to Ed, moves her hand a bit further up his leg, feels the tin of lip balm wedged into the pocket of his 501s, traces its outline with her fingertip. "Are you going to stay and drink with me?" Noncommittal, cool, he looks at the beer bottle with the slightly frayed, picked-at label, "I've got a full beer and I wouldn't want to waste it." Her new drink arrives in front of her, she picks the full cocktail glass up quickly, sloshing some contents down the edges and around her fingers clutching the stem, laughing, "Alcohol abuse." This draws a slight smile from Ed, and she takes a long satisfied drought of the bone-dry, ice-cold gin. They drink steadily and quietly for a few minutes, Patty's hand absently on his leg, moving a bit more boldly from time to time, thinking, I'm in control, a light brush across the strain in his pants, I'm in charge.

He finishes his beer. She downs the last of her gin. Their faces turn to one another and she darts a quick kiss across his lips, touches her tongue to the beer-tanged protrusion in his mouth and pulls back. But his left hand reaches out and grasps her neck, pulls her in again. Her lips mash against his and his hand is twisting her hair, pulling it taut, his teeth biting at her lip. Faint alarm bells toll but Ed is standing, saying, "I've gotta go to the head. We'll split when I get back," and she just nods, says, "Yes," unable to imagine going home alone, not as drunk as she suddenly feels, not tonight.

Desperately maudlin while he's gone, thinking, So lonely to go home alone, she digs out a compact from her purse, checks her reflection in the cool light of the bar. If she had any objectivity, if she were looking at a patient, she'd think the face in the glass looked like hell. Pasty, booze-bloated features, the dark rims around her eyes losing their makeup concealment. If the light were better and she could look in the glass with any honesty, she'd see the tiny capillaries bursting free in her cheeks and nose, her literal gin blossoms, and think, Alcoholic. But all she can think is, Fucking Tom, I'll fucking show him.

Suddenly he's back and she's being guided through the crowd, his fingers snug on her elbow. On the way to the door, she thinks she hears a familiar voice—"Patty?"—from a woman sitting at a nearby table. She turns her head to get a look, thinks she sees Kate of all people, tries to spin off and see who it is there, but the hand is guiding her so firmly and she's out the door, in a taxi and on her way. Wherever.

Brian's back was to the woman, but Kate is sure that was Patty, looking like hell, stumbling drunk and being pushed towards the door by some seedy guy. So surprised she blurted her name out, her companions turning towards her, Brian glancing over his shoulder as the man and what might have been her sister disappear through the door. "Sorry," Kate says. "That woman looked an awful lot like my sister."

Their round of drinks is nearly finished, Brian checks his watch. They need to get on their way if they're going to catch the next train from Hoboken. The tab is settled, they're outside, exchanging good-bye pleasantries with Tim and Joan, cabs are hailed and Brian orders their cab driver to the Christopher Street PATH station. All the scenery flashing past them is a blur now; she's distracted and exhausted. It couldn't have been Patty. The coincidence would be too much. She leans her head against Brian, leans into the comfort of his shoulder and enveloping arm. Brian's pleased with the evening, "Thanks hon, you helped a lot." "Don't mention it. Christ, I'm sleepy." "We'll be home soon."

. . .

Nora snuggles against Eve on the ratty, secondhand couch in Nora's apartment. The credits run on a rented movie. After Eve finished playing, they talked in the corner of the bar for a while, feeling each other out, small talk, and Nora kept thinking, She's perfect. She's wonderful. The conversation grew deeper, their fingertips touching, but the other band began to play and they were too loud. After a few songs, Nora, brave, leaned over and shouted, "You want to rent a movie or something?"

So they'd left, stopped off at the video store, browsed the shelves for a title they both hadn't seen yet. Back in Nora's living room, they snuggled closer as the film progressed, each half focused on the screen and half on where the other's body lay in relation to her own. Nora all nervous and clenched in her stomach. In the black and white glare of the credits, they finally kiss. No awkwardness, no clicking of teeth or clumsy hands, a sure fine thing that mirrors the way their bodies lock together on the couch. But as their touches grow more bold, their pleasures more specific, Eve pulls away.

Nora brushes her hand through her hair, sitting back, "What?" she asks, tentatively. "I'm sorry. Hound. She needs to be walked." "Are you sure that's it?" She leaps on Nora, those muscles working in her arms to roll Nora on her back, and she kisses her again, briefly, fiercely. "I'm sure. But she needs to go out." "Okay."

Nora watches as Eve pulls on her Docs, laces them, stands. She walks her to the door, and they clutch in an embrace, Eve burying her face in Nora's neck. "I don't want to go," Eve says. And Nora has a solution, "Come back." "What?" "Go get Hound, clip on her leash, walk her over here." The simplicity, the obviousness of the idea, seems to stun Eve for a moment, they've discovered they only live ten blocks apart, and she laughs, "Twenty minutes," planting a kiss on Nora's nose and running down the stairs.

When she's gone, Nora clicks off the TV and hits the REWIND button on the VCR. Restless, she prowls the apartment, the swell of her desire mellowing but not abating. *She wants to tell someone.* Wants to pick up the phone and call someone. But, who?

On the dining-room table that unopened letter from Sean draws her. She slits open the envelope, pulls the fragile blue leaves from inside and reads the tale of his crush on some Irish waitress. Before she can think, she's picking up the phone and punching in country and city codes and the phone is ringing and ringing. Sean's sleep-muffled voice picks up with a groggy, "Hello?" "Oh Jesus. Sorry. I forgot the time thing." "Nora?" "Yes. I'm sorry, I'll hang—" "What's going on, Nora?" "Sean, I think I'm in love." As soon as the words are out, she realizes her mistake right away, realizes she's going to have to lie, dissemble, and she doesn't want to, not now. But in the slightly hollow timbre of the transatlantic connection, his voice more awake now, she hears, "What's her name?"

She's floored. He knows, and she'll have to find out how, but in the mean time she's too excited and starts chattering, "Eve. And Sean, she's great." The conversation, her monologue really, goes on for a while; she hears his voice going sleepy again when he puts a word in edgewise, "Sean, are you with me?" "I'm here, but I just got in a little while ago and I've got to get up in a few hours and cook." "I'm sorry I woke you, I had to tell someone." "It's okay. Talk to you soon, all right? There's a letter—" "—Came today, I'll write you. 'Night." "'Night. Love you, sis, and thank you." "For what?" "For telling me." "Goodnight favorite brother, love you." "Only brother. Bye." She listens to the silence on the line for a moment before the apartment explodes with the noise of her buzzer and she hangs up and pushes the door button and Eve's clomp and the scuffle of puppy paws come up the stairs towards her.

Lying prone on the couch in his study, the father listens to the spectral sounds of the empty house around him, the random creaks of an old house settling, the scrape of a tree limb in need of pruning against a storm-window pane. He's tried counting sheep, tried warm milk laced with honey, tried a shot of brandy. But, he still can't stop *thinking*. Finally, he'd rifled through the bathroom medicine chest, but in this house there are no sleeping pills, not even of the over-the-counter variety. An ancient bottle of NyQuil, its rim crusted with deep green deposits, was the closest thing he could find. He slugged back a double dose and returned to his couch. Now, his clarity begins to suffer, he can't follow the train of his thoughts. He can feel sleep pressing in on him, and he chases it, working too hard at it. But in spite of everything, the NyQuil coupled with wine, warm milk and brandy is triumphing over his racing brain. Muddled, he drifts into sleep.

Muddled, her mind swimming in gin, Patty is dimly aware of occasional flashes of pain, brief moments of pleasure. Something in her welcomes the hurt, its bite reestablishing her connection with the room, making her aware of the grit in the dirty mattress pushing into her back. She's somewhere on the Lower East Side, she couldn't follow the cab's turns beyond Ludlow Street, and that guy is here, nipping at her flesh, rough with his fingers, his naked body tense as he hovers above her.

She's not protesting, not even in those fleeting moments of lucidity. When they first arrived, and he'd pushed her onto the bed, ripping at her clothes, she'd played along, drunkenly asking, "So you like it rough?"

She does not. Not generally, and never to this extent. Somewhere from the depths of the gin, she realizes, This is not what I want, this is not what I had in mind. Somewhere, she realizes she is not in control.

She just wants this over. Wants it done. But she's in and out, unable when she's awake to raise the strength to protest, get up and leave. Awake again, she feels him inside of her, thrusting quickly, raising bruises on the inside of her legs, an ache radiating outward from her labia. No condom, she thinks, he's not wearing a condom. He rests his weight on her and she's out again.

When she's back, he's dressing, not looking her way, her body bruised, her blood coursing 80 proof, and she can't seem to move. But she manages to ask, unbearably sad about the thought of being left alone, "Where are you going?" He doesn't answer, she's vaguely aware of his seepage pooling between her legs, but as he strides out the door, he turns on her with malice, "I'm positive, you slut."

Several hours will pass before she wakes fully, daylight seeping through the grimy windows. Gradually, it will come back to her, and the panic will set in. She'll look around and find nothing but this dirty bed in the apartment, no power to the light switch, roaches scurrying, rat shit and crack vials. She'll realize that this is an abandoned building; there will be no way to trace the guy.

Later the next morning, she'll go into the office and draw her own blood. For a couple of days, she'll move in a fog of worry. When that first test comes back negative, she'll have six months of late-night, lying-awake anxiety until she can be certain. This time she's ended up with just the bruises and the nightmares. This time she gleans that first sliver of knowledge, It's the drinking, Patty. It's the drinking.

But all that will come later, for now, she's blissfully, dreamlessly, asleep without awareness of the real danger of her situation. And though she will pass the rest of the night unmolested, she will not feel lucky when she wakes.

1992. The family scattered, living separate lives, but connected still. The patterns they form as their lives unfold link them together. They may be in or out of touch, they may hide things from one another, but if and when it all comes out, they will have the dubious comfort of recognition.

1 9 8 8

Nora drops her car into second gear, eases around a corner, and flicks the volume on the classic rock station louder as she puts the pedal down. Driving with the exuberance of a person who hasn't been driving long, who still revels in the feel of power under her feet, she works the gears with enthusiasm, watching the tachometer, up shifting to third at thirty, fourth at forty-five, and slamming the gearshift home to fifth as she cruises past fifty-five. She's driving too fast for this street, singing along, at ease. She'll swing by the pizzeria where her friend Kathleen works after school, pick her up and tool around for a while before heading out to the woods for a long-planned beer blast. Late May, high school graduation is just around the corner, her acceptance letter from Bryn Mawr is tucked in the corner of the mirror in her room. In just a few short months, she's out of here, on her own, away from all this, away from the rumor and innuendo that have nipped at her heels for the last couple of years. She pops in the cigarette lighter, tucks a Marlboro Light into the corner of her mouth, and drums her fingers on the steering wheel, keeping time with the radio, "Philadelphia freedom . . ."

Sean loads the last suitcase into his car, his chef's pouch filled with knives and basters on the front passenger seat. The term's over, and he's heading home. He sits on the porch of the two-family house he's been sharing for the year and waits for his summer sublet to arrive. Itching to get on the road, he's eager for the drive through the beautiful Hudson Valley, the hills freshly alive again, past the towers of New York City, the wasteland of northeast Jersey, and out to his parents' house. He'll spend a few weeks there before starting his "out-termship" down at the beach, cooking nights in a seafood restaurant and living the whole time, the entire summer, down at the shore house.

Patty slumps in a chair in the physician's lounge at Mt. Sinai, her shift just ended. In this grueling time of thirty-six hours on and thirty-six off, she's becoming overwhelmed by fatigue. Near the end of this shift, she'd lost a patient who'd come onto the Pediatric Oncology ward about the same time she started her residency. A little boy, a seven-year-old boy with leukemia who withstood chemotherapy, never complaining about the neck catheter, never protesting the pricks and prods. His skinny, sharp features losing their angles from the Prednisone. When things were slow, Patty sometimes sat and read to him, and when he'd drifted off to sleep, she'd trace her fingers over the dome of his scalp and pray for a miracle. I'm a doctor now, she thinks, and there was nothing more to be done. It was a mercy. But, as she spins the dial that opens her locker and reaches for her street clothes, she remembers his coltish body, his indignation when he lost the strength to walk up and down the hall pushing his IV. She remembers his mother sitting with him and helping with the homework sent over from his school, the normal domestic scene somehow prevailing over the hospital noise of intercom codes and pages. She thinks of him asking her, "Dr. Mahoney, when can I play soccer again?" and she wonders, Why are the sickest children the most beautiful?

Changed now, and gathering her things to head out, she thinks, Jesus, I need a drink.

The father, last in the office for no good reason, thinks with pleasure about Kate's upcoming wedding party down at the beach. He's not had his entire family in one place for quite some time. With just Nora at home now, and even Nora grown up into someone who doesn't need him anymore, he's been spending more and more time working. He doesn't have to—the years of grinding out seventy and eighty billable hours a week are over, he's been a partner for over a decade. He has as-sociates working for him, doing the long, dull work. But when a young attorney comes to him with a question, when he's sitting in the con-ference room with a client depending on him, when he fills in the billing sheets that assign monetary worth to his day, he feels needed. At home, that once-noisy house is subsumed in quiet. It's grown gradu-ally, this silence, as the children have left for their own lives. When they were younger, and his return from work each night required the me-diation of some dispute between brother and sister or child and mother, he longed to come home to a quiet dinner with his wife, to have the time and the inclination to sit with her as they had during those long-ago years before the children, talking and reading. But even the mother, caught up in the plans for Kate's wedding, has been lost to him lately. He has no work that's pressing, nothing that's keeping him in his chair after hours; he can't see any reason to go home. Standing up, slipping on his suit jacket, and patting his pockets for car keys, he says aloud to himself, "Fuck it."

. . .

Kate steps out of St. Anne's basement arm in arm with her fiancé. They're finally done with the absurd pre-Cana ritual the Church requires before marriage, and she has evil thoughts in her head. She looks up at Brian, "What do you say we go out for a nice dinner, then back to my place where we can violate several of the Sexuality in Marriage rules?" Brian looks down at her, with his face curled into the warm grin that first drew her attention, "Sounds good to me." Just then, the vague insistent tone of the alarm on Kate's watch goes off with a steady beeping. She reaches under her sleeve and silences the watch without looking, rummages in her purse, produces a bottle of water and a pill case. She doesn't miss a stride as she washes her pill down and stows everything back in her bag. There's no thought of not taking the med, but she catches a trace of relief on Brian's face and her pleasure in him briefly turns to disgust as she thinks, Without these fucking pills, this son of a bitch can't handle me.

The mother, rummaging in the file folder filled with the details for Kate's wedding, is satisfied that everything is just about complete. The church reserved, the reception arranged and paid for, the band hired, flowers ordered, invitations sent, acceptances and regretful declines coming in, dresses and tuxes fitted and ordered. She's just made the reservations for the rehearsal dinner, after a long consultation with Brian's mother, and she thinks with satisfaction, That is a job well done. She picks up the phone and dials Kate's apartment, gets the machine and leaves a message letting her know things are ready. She glances at her watch, sees that it's after seven and thinks, Sean should be on his way. She realizes too that her husband is late, again, and she is angry with him. Angry with him for working these long hours now, when the need for long hours has abated, and angry for the way he's been around the house lately. Distant, slipping away to his study after dinner with a beer and his book. She cannot remember the last time she talked with him, talked with him about things that weren't about the minutiae of running a family: bills, vacations, what the children were up to these days. She can't remember the last time they spoke as friends.

The high sun of spring slants below the lines of trees dotting the foothills of the Appalachian chain. The light, an unearthly shine through fresh leaves, glances off car windshields as drivers mount hills or turn curves; sun-screens are flipped down quickly, sunglasses groped for in glove compartments. In window-filled rooms of houses, cats and dogs search out sun-warmed spots and television pictures are obscured by glare. As the sun sinks, the temperature barely dips, the mercury holding near sixty-eight degrees, and school kids running home to dinner are reminded that the freedom of summer vacation looms just over the horizon.

Nora and Kathleen cruise the rural roads just outside the grasping reach of suburbia, sharing a joint, speaking about the night to come, about the tangled lives they share as high school seniors. Kathleen has just broken up with her boyfriend of two years, he's started fucking some sophomore slut, and she hopes that prick won't be out tonight. "If he shows up with that little bitch," she growls, "I'm going to knock his ass out." Nora squinting against the setting sun, thinking of how she held Kathleen while she cried over Kenny last week, thinking about the delicate strength of Kathleen's spine under her hands as she stroked and patted her friend's back, just nods her head as Kathleen raves. They ride in silence for a while and Kathleen turns her head to stare out the window. When Nora pokes her so she can pass the joint, Kathleen asks, "Still not going to the prom?" "Nope." Kathleen drags until her finger tips are singed, pinches out the roach and plops it into the ashtray. "If you don't go," she says, "people will say it's true." Nora thinks of the scribbled words on the high school girls' room wall—Muff Muncher Mahoney—"I just don't like any of the asshole guys we go to school with." But, she's thinking, It is true and I'd go to the prom with you.

High now, heads bobbing to the music, Kathleen reaches over to turn up the stereo, and they sing along as the Eagles fade into Zeppelin into Floyd, those songs of a previous generation that just won't disappear. They drive without agenda, through the twisty back roads, Nora's hand steady on the stick shift. Drive with light heads, not talking, and when they come up over Solberg Hill and the little single-prop plane airport comes into view, Nora glances over at Kathleen, sees her neck blending into her collarbone just above the edge of her tank top. She remembers a night, six, seven years ago. She'd been here with Kathleen and her parents at the annual hot air balloon festival. Sticky-faced from lingering cotton candy and funnel cake, she'd gone back to Kathleen's house to spend the night.

In the pink dusk of Kathleen's canopy bed, lying together under the sheets, their late-night talk turned to boys and bases and practicing. She remembers how, starting that night and going on until they started high school, she learned just exactly what desire meant. And now, now she wants to tell Kathleen—she's ready to tell someone, and if not Kathleen, then who? But she's too scared, she'll let it wait, build up a couple beers worth of courage, tell her it is true, and I learned the truth with you. Glancing again at the base of Kathleen's neck, she thinks with lustful clarity, I want to kiss her right there.

The father, stuck in creeping highway traffic, impatiently jabs at the buttons on his car stereo, flipping from the classical station, to jazz, to all news all the time, to NPR and back again. His heart thumps a bit, his stomach is queasy. He realizes he wants a cigarette, badly, then remembers he quit years ago. The traffic reporter on 1010 WINS reports New Jersey highways backed up because of sun glare. Exasperated, he cuts over to the right-hand lane and gets off at the next exit, thinking, I'll find a back way. He finds himself in an old factory town, Main Street mostly boarded up with the factory gone now, only the taverns and barely hanging on businesses remaining. He hasn't been this way in years, not since they completed the highway, and he is startled to see strip clubs sprouted up on several corners. Waiting for a light, he reads the marquees of competing clubs on opposite sides of Main Street. "Happy Hour 5–8, Over Thirty Girls, Lap Dances, VIP Room!" and "Hot Tub Shows, Go-Go Rama, Private Dances!" I could use a beer he thinks, and when the light turns green, he cuts the wheel and swings into the parking lot of "Happy Hour 5–8," looks around to be sure there's no one he knows on the street, and darts inside.

Kate and Brian sit at a table in one of the overpriced, moderately good, Italian restaurants that dot the New York suburban corridor. Kate slugs back a Tanqueray and tonic, savoring the slightly bitter liquid on the back of her tongue, thinking of her mother and the smell of the ocean. Remembering childhood cocktail parties down at the beach when she came out to the porch in her nightgown, unable to sleep, and saw for a moment the forbidden world where adults ceased to be parents. There was her mother in tank top and shorts out on the front porch, shoes kicked off hours before, legs curled under her on the chaise. She'd be leaning her head back and laughing or fingering her earrings as she listened to the stories of her friends. She looked beautiful in those dusky moments, the brine of the beach wafting across the blocks, mixing with cigarette smoke and citronella. Kate hung on the borders of the porch, hands touching the bumpy plaster of the walls, bare toes curling around the rough edges of the wood floor, just watching. Finally her mother saw her there, came over, and was changed from a woman at a party back into the mother. She ruffled Kate's hair and gave her a sip of her gin and tonic before guiding her back to bed and sitting with her, rubbing her back until she was sleeping and suddenly, before Kate knew it, it was morning.

Patty comes up from the 6 train into the growing dark around Astor Place. She walks east towards her apartment and the atmosphere crumbles around her. The junkies in the tenement doors know her by now. "Hey Doc!" they call after her, "My arm hurts. Can I get a house call?" She keeps her head down, ignoring them tonight, until she reaches Avenue B, her street. She's walking, and thoughts of that pale, dead boy bump in her head against the thought, There is no room for this now, I am a doctor. On the corner of Seventh and B, her favorite bar beckons, and though she is weary, though her bones call out for a cup of tea and crisp sheets and the vacuum of sleep, she pushes inside for a quick one, maybe a laugh with the bartender who knows her by now. Then, I'll go home, she thinks, get some sleep and not worry about hospitals or working or dead kids for the next couple of days.

Sean pushes his little car past seventy as he heads down the Major Deegan Expressway. The hatchback grumbles at this treatment, shuddering slightly, revving too fast for its four-cylinder engine. Sean just turns the radio louder and drives. He's itching to get home, he has plans to meet Nora later down by the river, for this party that's become an annual event. Everyone back from college for the summer, this year's seniors ready to head away for the first time, and, of course, Amy-Beth back in town for a few weeks.

They've gone their separate ways now, she in the City, stalking the downtown galleries, still snapping photos, spending hours in the darkroom, the eggplant Manic Panic in her hair glowing under red lights. And Sean, upstate, cooking in the hospital glow of CIA's classroom kitchens, learning presentation, the subtle hints of flavor found in small bits of fennel. They still talk, each the only high school friend really in touch with the other. And though they've both had others, flings and the odd relationship that lasts for six months, a year, there's still a spark there. Sean comes down to the City on a Friday night, she puts other friends on hold and they go for a cheap dinner at Dojo. There is, of course, some awkwardness at first. They fumble around that part of the conversation, relearning each other, and without their noting the change, maybe after the second glass of rough red wine is finished, the ground is familiar again, and they are charting familiar terrain.

They might hit some bars then, they might not. But by the night's end, they're back in Amy-Beth's studio, soft music on her stereo, pianos or classical guitar. And though it wasn't what they had planned, though Amy might be with an actor she met at some opening she crashed or Sean might be seeing a classmate, they're crushed together in her single bed, lying there under the pretext of sleep. Though they may not have planned it, they make love in the way only two people who learned what they like from each other can. Their sex is flavored with history and regret, and when they wake in the morning, before Sean has to catch a train back to Poughkeepsie, they're shy with one another, parting with just a hug after Sean whips up omelets or French toast in her tiny kitchen.

It's the same when they're both back in Jersey, mingling with people they don't really know anymore. At those summer parties, drinking in New Brunswick or beach-town bars with fake Maine driver's licenses, they greet people they never liked all that much with hugs or high-fives and "How's school?" And by last call or party's end, there are Sean and Amy-Beth, leaving together, not quite touching, and whoever is driving that night cuts the engine at the top of the other's driveway, and they make out and fog the windows. Then, for a little while, they get to remember the good part about being seventeen without any of the bullshit.

· · ·

The father sits at the corner of the bar in the dimly lit, dingy strip club in a failing town. On stage a woman, A girl really, the father thinks, gyrates halfheartedly to some rock tune that grates on his nerves. He hasn't been in one of these places since his own bachelor party, and he feels detached as he watches the girl dance. Watches her drop her bikini top, cover her breasts with her hands in a lame imitation of coyness, then tug sharply on her nipples, drawing blood into them, hardening them. Suddenly, she's swinging on the pole, bending backwards from the waist, catching the father's eyes with her own, rubbing her tongue over her lips. The father thinks, She must be Nora's age, and shifts in his seat as he feels himself stiffen.

She's off the pole now, bending from the waist to look at the father through her legs. She raises her finger to her lips as if to say, "Shhh," then pulls her G-string aside, showing the father all of her ass, her close-cropped strip of pubic hair. I'm a dirty old man, the father thinks, aware of his dick pressing through the flap of his boxers and rubbing on the brushed wool of his suit pants. The song ends, she climbs off the stage and walks straight towards the father, holding his eyes. She loosens his tie as she leans over the bar in front of him, then presses her breasts together, and he realizes she wants him to put a bill in there. He reaches for a single from the stack on the bar, folds it in half and tries to place it where she's suggested without touching her too much, but she grabs his hand and rubs his palm across her nipple. He half wants to get up now, drain his beer and be on his way, his transaction completed, but he sits transfixed as she bends over in front of him, rubbing her hands around the backs of her thighs, her buttocks, dipping a finger inside the G-string and raising it to her lips. Suddenly her leg is on the bar, she's stroking her barely covered crotch, and raising and lowering the waistband of that skimpy undergarment. The father realizes she wants another bill, and he tries to just slip it gingerly under the hem, but she snaps it closed, trapping his hand, and rubbing his fingers into the fleshy part of her upper thigh. When she leans over, runs her hands up and down his tie and asks, "Would you like a lap dance?" he wants to say, "No, thank you." Wants to get up and leave, go home, kiss his wife, see his son who should be there about now, but all he can think about is the feel of that firm, young thigh. "Yes," he says, "I'd like that."

The sun is set; the season's first lightning bugs appear, blinking on and off. Couples heading out to dinner or to an early movie at the Mall remind each other to turn on headlights. The air is fresh, the scent of mud and early-blooming cherry and misplaced Magnolia trees mingling with the clipped grass of the season's first lawn mowings. Early arriving June bugs and moths bat against porch lights. Barbecues are filled with coals, drenched with lighter fluid. Little League games are called because of darkness, and the teams, both winners and losers, head to Hid-E-Ho or Phil's Pizza for post-game treats. In New York, midtown is battened down for the night and downtown is just starting to thump. Down in a clearing by the Raritan River, the people in charge of procuring the beer for this year's spring party lug kegs, coolers and tubs of ice from the parking area up to the party site.

The mother waits. By her calculations, Sean should arrive at any moment, and her husband, she thinks as she checks her watch without really registering the time, should have been home by now. She walks from room to room, flipping on lights, turning them off again. In the big antique living-room mirror, she sees a flash and turns her attention to her reflection. The woman in the glass looks older than she feels, heavier. The reflection shows a woman in the throes of middle age, hair specked with flecks of gray, cropped short and permed tightly, folds of flesh slowly sinking off her cheeks, the skin a bit leathery from too many summers in the sun. Smile lines are etched deeply around her eyes, and more subtly, the tight nicks of worry have been etched around her mouth. The mother pulls the skin tight around her eyes, tries to imagine her hair longer, in a bob or skimming down her back in thick, straight lines as it did when she was young, and she can't quite. Can't quite find the hint of her younger self anywhere in that reflection, and she wonders where she went, wonders how her life has turned her into this middle-aged woman.

I've not done a bad job, she thinks. In all the ways the world can sabotage a family; the pitfalls of divorce, juvenile delinquency, unemployment, child abuse, late-night phone calls of arrest or tragedy, adultery; in all those ways, I've been fortunate. Looking back, she can even smile about Kate now, a rueful smile, but yes, in the mirror her lips are turned up, because Kate seems to have found her way. Engaged to be married, to a lawyer like her father, and working, like her mother, as a teacher. If someone had told her, even five years ago, that Kate would end up okay, she would have prayed they were right, but she wouldn't have believed. She still half waits for the other shoe to drop, but as each day passes, she's allowing herself the comfort of growing confidence.

Patty, she thinks, I've never had to worry about. That girl is driven. And if she doesn't see her enough these days, if she doesn't call to share her life, well, she's busy, and she's always been a private person. And Sean. Sean she has never seen more happy. Her skinny boy nearly grown into a man. A man who's begun to step out of the shadow of always trying to please his father, who is living his life for himself. She's surprised sometimes by how gentle he is with the children of her nieces and nephews. Surprised too when she catches him in conversation with one of his sisters at Christmas or Thanksgiving, and sees him listening, really listening, his fingers worrying the earring his father quietly seethes about. He has so much of her own nature in him; might he someday wake, as she has, with his children grown and gone, and a spouse so quiet by habit that he will feel alone in the same room with her? Might he wake one day and find he's listening to nothing?

The phone rings before she can add Nora to her catalogue, and as she steps away from the mirror, she wonders, How can things have turned out so well—nearly thirty years of marriage, my kids all doing okay; how can things have turned out so God-damned well, after everything, and still I'm feeling uneasy?

Patty sits at the bar in a dark tavern known only by its address, talking to the bartender and glancing at herself in the mirror over the liquor shelves. She still likes what she sees. Her look now more respectable than it once was, spiky hair grown out into a shoulder-length cut she can pull back when she works, tasteful makeup, her clothes—that hospital doctor's prerogative, casual but neat, so she looks comfortable but competent under the white coat. That one quick drink has morphed into three down and the fourth in front of her. After the third, the bartender put the upside-down shot glass in front of her, signaling the next round on the house, and how could she refuse a buy-back?

She is in that fearless place, when her buzz makes her cocky and invincible, and she has the experience to know she should slow herself, pace the drinks, because this good time can too easily slip through her fingers and toss her into that other place of blackouts and weeping. That place where she dials people on the phone she hasn't spoken to in years because of something, anything they may have done to offend her and rants and raves like some lunatic. She knows if she doesn't pace herself, the gin will control her. And while she can barely admit how much she enjoys ceding her control to something else, it's early still for that. She has the experience to know if she lets it slip now, she'll wake later tonight, feel her hangover setting in, and to stave off that moment, find another drink.

At this hour the place isn't too crowded, the grungy bartender leans against the beer cooler and chats with her. She thinks he's pretty, in an East Village sort of way, even if he is short, and she sips her gin. Not even for an instant does she think about that dead little boy.

.   .   .

Kate and Brian sit and chat over after-dinner coffee. She tells him of her day, recounts the story of Paul Medina, aged seven, who'd asked her to marry him. Again. There was also Angela Giolitti, also seven, who apparently learned the many and varied derivations of the word "fuck" on the bus and is having trouble with the suggestion that the word, in all its grammatical splendor, is not appropriate in a first-grade class-room. He listens to all of this, takes the stories of her day as a little gift, laughs with her, and the talk turns to their own, hypothetical, children to come.

More than one, less than four. He's always wanted a brother or sis-ter, believes that spawning an only child is cruel in a world where friends can be scarce. She, though she loves both her sisters and her brother, thinks more than three is too many, that maybe they'd be closer if there were fewer of them. There should be at least two years between each child, but not more than four. Too close together and they'll fight for years, like Nora and Sean, but too far apart, like her and Nora, and they won't know one another, the rope that connects them will be too loose.

Sitting there, at a mostly cleared table, heady with the excitement and fear of their impending union, Kate watches Brian's smile as he lowers his coffee cup and remembers their first meeting. They'd been paired together on a group project in a history class at Rutgers during her first year there after leaving art school. When she was rootless and unsteady, just out of the hospital. Stable, medically, but still not con-vinced she was doing the right thing. Her paints and easels stowed up in her parent's attic. No one she felt she could be with, no one who knew this new person she was becoming.

And then here was this boy, obviously smart, but wearing some ab-surdly striped Land's End rugby shirt. He took control of their pres-entation, guided things, but he listened to her. Really listened, the way she remembered her mother listening when she was a little girl and ex-cited or upset. On that last night of working together, her overhead slides creatively illuminating the text of their project, everything ready for the presentation the following morning at ten, he'd asked if she'd like to go for a beer. And in the quiet of one of the small bars off College Avenue, the three-dollar draft pitcher between them, a bowl of peanuts they cracked and ate without looking, they'd talked of other things. She told him about giving up art school to get a degree in education. He was full of fire about law school, not to follow the corporate route, but to be a public advocate. He was serious that night when he'd said, "Ralph Nader is my hero." Equally serious, she'd replied, "Yeah, but the Corvair was a bitchin' car." He studied her grave face for a moment, but she couldn't quite hide the laughter in her eyes. His face slowly curled into a grin, and he burst out laughing, and they laughed together until they were both in tears, and Kate felt alive for the first time in months. Alive because she realized she was having a good time with this guy, rugby shirt and all. Alive because they were connecting. Alive because she, Kate Mahoney, hadn't gotten a reaction like that from anyone in a long time.

That was a while ago, before the crush of his law-school loans killed dreams of anything other than a big firm with a good salary. But he still listens that same way, she can still go deadpan and make him laugh, and she loves curling up against him on the couch after work.

When the check is paid and they're walking out into the lot to drive to her apartment for the night, she takes his hand. Leaning into him, she's aware he is not what she once wanted. Nothing here speaks of grand passion. She is about to pledge the rest of her life to a man who still wears rugby shirts, but she knows too that his arms will always be safe and is aware that his temperament suits him to rescuing should she need it. She is comfortable with him. Yes, she thinks, life with this guy is going to be all right.

Nora and Kathleen pull into the clearing that sits before the trail head leading into the woods where generations of this town's teenagers have gathered to drink and be merry. The makeshift lot, not visible to the prying eyes of passing motorists and cops, is half full already with the cast-off cars and pickups of high school and college kids, and over the sound of the river they can almost make out the hum of a party just getting under way. As they walk down the trail, the canopy of trees grows thicker, blocking out the thin illumination of late-spring's dusk, and Kathleen grabs Nora's hand when she stumbles over a root, and, beginning to skip, they chant an old childhood rhyme together, "Ceci, my playmate, come out and play with me, and bring your dollies three."

Stoned, they skip down the path together, hand in hand, Kathleen free with her affection for her friend, her personality growing brighter the way it always does when a party is in the offing. Stoned, Nora feels as if they're floating down the dark path. She can hear the sounds of the early arrivals as they get closer, a bright, "Hot damn!" the signature phrase of their class's handsome preppie hero, Princeton-bound Doug Kenworthy, state wrestling champ, third in the class. Stoned, Nora really only notices the slim pressure of Kathleen's fingers against her own, and she wants to feel those fingers, heavy with desire, dragging down her sides and over her hips.

They come out into the small field, and the fire's already burning, the kegs and coolers iced, clusters of friends gathered in conversation. Later, the couples will form, people pairing off and heading into the woods alone, but for now, this is an event for groups. Kathleen is greeted warmly by everyone—she has that rarest of high school skills, social mobility. And, of course, the recent breakup, where she's clearly the wronged party, has earned sympathy from many, as well as the eager glances of boys hoping to snag her on the rebound. Nora, they're not sure how to handle. She's Kathleen's best friend, and she's accepted because of that simple fact. But she keeps to herself, has a certain reserve that puts them off. Good at sports, she's the leading scorer on the girls' soccer team, but not the captain. And she's never gone out with anyone. She's been asked, but she always declines, politely, and on those nights when they don't go out in groups, when she doesn't tag along with Kathleen to some event, when Kathleen *has a date,* she mostly stays in by herself.

No one is quite sure how to handle her, so behind her back they snicker, call her a dyke, Muff Muncher Mahoney. But not when Kathleen is around, Kathleen doesn't stand for that sort of thing. And so tonight, as Nora follows Kathleen from group to group, sucking on a solo cup of keg beer, she is greeted, if not warmly, then cordially.

Sean pulls into the driveway of the family home, gathers his things from the front seat, leaving his suitcase until later, and walks around the garage to the kitchen door. He sees his mother sitting at the breakfast nook, talking on the phone with animation, gesturing, laughing. His father's Caddy isn't in the driveway. Nora's little Bronco II is missing from its spot as well; she must be out in the woods already. The family dog hears him first and comes tearing into the kitchen, barking furiously and sliding on the linoleum until she realizes it's Sean who has broached her territory. Then her tail starts to whip; she's jumping a little, even in her old age, nuzzling and licking at his hands. "Down. Good girl," he ruffles her ears.

His mother looks up as he comes in, her smile full of both welcome and relief. She points at the phone and holds up her right index finger. "Sean just walked in," she says, "I will. I'll see you tomorrow for lunch then? Great. Love you too, Anna. Bye-bye." Hanging up the phone, she pulls Sean into a hug, then steps back, looking him over, searching out any changes since his last visit. "Where's everyone?" he asks. "Nora's out for the night. She said you were meeting up with her later. Your father's not back from work yet." "Trial coming up?" "Who knows. You know how his hours go."

Sean, thinking of things his father missed when he was growing up—school plays, choir concerts, soccer games—knows. "How's Aunt Anna?" he asks. The mother's face brightens, her thoughts off the father for a moment, moving to the woman she has known her whole life—her childhood sleep-over friend, her crush confidante, her Trenton Teacher's College roommate, her maid of honor, her colleague in the school district, the person she would have given the care of her children in the event of a tragedy—"She's good," the mother says. "She told me to send you her love."

Sean is starving; he'd driven without stopping. "What do you want to do for dinner?" he asks. "I was going to wait for your father, but it's after eight and he's on his own now. Do you want to order some Chinese?" "I don't feel like going to pick it up. Do you have anything in the house? I'll cook if you clean-up." "Poke around the fridge. See what you can do."

So he digs and comes up with a can of chopped plum tomatoes, a head of garlic, some fresh basil from the plant on the windowsill, an eggplant going soft in the refrigerator crisper, bottles of dried oregano and rosemary, some olive oil. He sets his materials in a row on the counter, gets his heavy chef's knife from his bag of tricks and sets to work, separating the garlic into a handful of cloves and mincing. He skins and chops the eggplant, tears the basil into shreds. The mother, seeing his choices, pulls a bottle of Chianti from the rack on the dining-room hutch and maneuvers around him in the kitchen to open the bottle, pour out two glasses. She prefers white, but knows he likes red, and he is just home.

As he works, putting the old iron skillet on a medium flame, and gently sautéing the garlic and eggplant, they sip wine and she asks him about school. "It's good," he says, "Tough. Outside of the cooking, the stuff on nutrition, on flash points of oil, on menu creation, on hygiene and health department code. Some of that's too much like science." The mother grimaces, remembering sitting with him, trying to help him decipher high school chemistry and physics, "Doing okay?" "Yeah, we help each other out with that stuff."

He pours the tomatoes into the pan, lets them sizzle for a moment, lowers the heat a bit. Adds his spices and herbs, cracks some fresh pepper over the pan, tosses in a hint of salt and stirs. The scent filling the kitchen, garlic and tomato, eggplant and fresh basil, is like the Sunday afternoons of the mother's childhood in Newark, walking around her neighborhood on sauce-making day for the Italian blocks, and she can't remember the last time someone cooked for her. "Everything going okay for the wedding?" Sean asks. "Just about set. Still getting the tent arranged for the backyard down at the shore. Other than that, it's done." "Patty got off that day, right?" "So she says." "I met her in the city a few weeks ago when I went in to interview for that job I didn't get." Stirring, he reaches for the bottle of wine without looking, adds a healthy dollop, finds a cover that fits and lowers the heat a bit more. "She looked like hell," he adds. Not really worried, the mother answers, "She works too much."

She does, Sean thinks, but that's not really it. They met for brunch a good twenty-four hours after she'd finished one of her thirty-six on shifts, and it wasn't the fatigue smudges rimming her eyes that bothered him. She was showered and clean, but when he hugged her, he caught the specific scent of gin, not on her breath, but coming from her body. And she didn't really eat, just some coffee and toast and a half pack of Marlboros. It wasn't that she was hungover, not exactly, it was that she didn't mention it, like she always felt like that in the morning. As if morning for Patty equaled feeling sick, every morning, and he wasn't sure what knowing that meant, and he knew if he brought it up, she'd just lie. So he let it be. Going over to the fridge to pull out a head of lettuce, the shaker of cheap Parmesan cheese, grabbing a loaf of Italian bread from on top, he decides to let it be again and doesn't tell the mother. Doesn't tell her because there are secrets siblings keep for one another, even if they think the parents might know anyway, and why bring it up if he's not sure?

The father sits in a deep, red velour chair, his arms at his sides, the music throbbing in his head as, "I'm Tyna," she'd told him, gyrates in front of him. Up against him now, she squats some and rubs her thighs across his knees. She pushes his legs tightly together, straddles him and pushes her skimpily covered crotch against his hard-on, rubbing back and forth. Leaning in, she places her lips to his ear, bites with the tiniest of bites and says, "For another twenty, this dance can get even closer." He slips his hand into his back pocket, pulls out his wallet, fishes out two twenties and hands them to her. "Double your pleasure," she says, "I like that." She grabs the bikini top from the table beside them, wraps it around his neck, and pushes his face between her breasts. "No touching," she coos when she feels his arms start to come up, nodding at the burly man in the shadows, "Frankie doesn't like it if you touch." Grinding her crotch into his leg, just above his knee, brushing her hair across his face in time with the drums, she works a couple of fingers between the buttons on his oxford shirt and plays with his chest hair. Moving in closer, she pushes her G-string onto his thigh, and concealed by the shadows of her body from the bouncer, she strokes him through his trousers, gripping him tightly, then moving away.

The first song ends, but his second twenty gives him another three and a half minutes or so, and the DJ cues some sultry R&B. The dancer stands and turns, showing off her ass, the cloth of the G-string pushed askew, the stubble from where she's shaved her pubic thatch just visible this close up. She spreads the father's legs wide, lowers herself onto his lap again, backwards now, and bends from the waist, pushing her ass against his dick and grinding. The father is close to the edge, and against his will he grinds back. Tyna feels him, drops a hand between her legs and rubs him down by his balls. The father strains, pushing harder now, wanting only to get off.

The song ends. The dancer gives one last push against him and stands up, all business. "We can go for another twenty," she says, "or for fifty we can go into one of the phone fantasy booths." Suddenly disgusted, with himself, with Tyna, the father says, "I don't think so." "Suit yourself," she fastens her bikini top around her breasts and heads back to the bar, "Bye." He gathers his suit jacket, slips it on and heads for the door. Before leaving, he stops in the men's room, steps up to the urinal, unzips, and with four quick strokes, takes care of his problem.

Patty sits at the bar with the grungy bartender, his shift over, the night crew on. One quick drink morphed into five down, the sixth in front of her. She thinks he is pretty, more pretty than he was a couple of hours ago. She is lingering on the far margins of that fearless place of being drunk, her buzz still making her cocky, but there is something maudlin creeping into the edges of her vision. In the fog of five and a half extra-dry gin martinis on the rocks with a twist, she keeps spinning her thoughts back to a pale blond boy, lying in a hospital bed, not moving, the machines around him clicked off, their pumping sounds silent, the LED indicators dark. His mother sitting there in the room, quiet too, just looking at him. "I'm a doctor now," she slurs at her new bartender friend. "And it was a mercy, but I don't want to talk about that. Tell me about you."

Sipping her gin on the rocks, she half listens to him talk about his band, but is focused on the thin wisps of chest hair poking out from the top of his wife-beater T-shirt. He thinks she's cute, in a slumming professional sort of way. Drunk too, and if he plays his cards right, he just might get laid. So he's saying something about them sounding like the Buzzcocks, but with a jazz-trained lead guitarist, and that they're playing later that week at the Knitting Factory. Not headlining, they go on at nine, and she reaches over and twirls that little wisp of hair into a tight twist. She pulls harder, trying to hurt him just a touch. Looking into his eyes, she wants to see if they change expression, if his speech falters maybe. See if he gets the message that she doesn't give a rat's fat ass about his fucking band.

What she wants is to feel alive beneath this curtain of gin, feel alive to spite the death that took that little boy. She twists his little wisp tighter, "You know what the oncology guys call cancer treatment? Slash and burn. Slash and fucking burn."

He raises his own hand and stills her fingers, leaving her holding the hair, but keeping her from pulling. He strokes her fingertips, calculating, "Shhh," he says. "It's all right. It's gonna be okay." She looks down again, sees his hand holding hers, decides she likes his thick, drummer forearms. Putting her drink on the bar, she uses her other hand to stroke his stubble-bumpy cheek. "You're sweet," she says. "So, so sweet." But she's thinking, If this stupid fucker doesn't kiss me now, right this fucking minute, I'm going to finish this drink, have another, and then who knows what.

Calculating, he disengages her fingers, brings her hands together in front of his face in the shape of a schoolgirl's prayer and lightly sucks her two index fingertips just inside his lips, tasting the lingering latex dust around the tips of her short clipped nails. Gin tears pool in her eyes, "So sweet." "We can go down to the stock room and talk in private if you want." "Yes," she says, "let's." He signals one of the night-shift bartenders, leans over the bar and whispers something into his ear. The night-shift bartender grabs a key ring from over the register and tosses it to him with a laugh. He stands. Patty follows, unsteady but not yet stumbling. Follows him to a padlocked door between the antiseptic and piss smells coming from the men's and ladies' rooms. He uses one of the keys from the ring, plops the Master Lock into his back pocket, and pulls open the door, "After you." In the dim light, Patty can just make out stairs, and she steps down one and turns around to see him pull the door shut. One step down from him, their height is even, and she can just make out his face in the dim. She leans in and kisses him on the mouth, scraping her tongue across his teeth, tasting the stale bread taste of old beer, the cold tang of his fillings.

Kate and Brian cuddle on the couch, half watching the Friday-night movie, half necking the way people who've developed a routine for lovemaking will kiss before getting down to the serious rituals that they both know will bring them pleasure. She wants to enjoy this, wants to abandon herself to the sensations his fingers and tongue can give her. *She wants to want this.* But there's no real desire there. Only flashes of interest on her part, startling, but passing. She can't remember the last time she came. It's the meds, a side effect, one she barely touches on when she debates their merits, their disappointments.

But she wants Brian to enjoy it, tells herself that giving him pleasure is her pleasure, and she feigns enthusiasm, hoping by pretending she'll actually find it.

The mother eats dinner with Sean at the breakfast nook in the kitchen of the family house. There's Italian bread warmed in the oven, lightly drizzled with olive oil, and covered with spoonfuls of cooked tomato, eggplant and spices. A simple salad of lettuce, Parmesan, cracked pepper, finely diced raw garlic, virgin olive oil and balsamic vinegar. A decent Italian red wine. The food is good, but with each bite, she grows more and more angry with her husband. Angry and worried. It's damn near nine o'clock and the son of a bitch still isn't home yet, and she called his office and he wasn't there, and the car phone isn't on, and just where the hell is he?

Men, she thinks, looking at Sean and hoping the generalization isn't really the case, are too much trouble. They finish their food, pour out a bit more wine and chat amiably over the dirty plates for a time. Sean checks the kitchen clock, thinks he should get going. He's thankful he won't have to drive; he can cut through the backyard to the woods, take the long, well-worn path to the clearing, about half an hour or so in the dark, on a route he's walked most of his life. The mother sees him worrying over the time, "Go ahead. Don't wait for your father. You'll see him tomorrow. Don't miss the party." "But, Ma . . . " "Go."

He helps her clear, loads the dishwasher, stacks the pan and wine glasses next to the sink and watches her plug the drain, pour in too much soap and run the hot water. "Go," she says. "Have a good time." He slips into his spring coat with a gesture like shrugging his shoulders, kisses her on the cheek on his way through the kitchen to the back door, "See you tomorrow." "'Night," she says, her hands soapy in the sink.

She listens to the door click shut as she scrubs the skillet with a scouring pad, crumbling the old Brillo against the pan. She lets the pan sink to the bottom of the sink, and stands there for a moment with her hands in soapy water, thinking, Damn, damn, damn. With sudden resolve, she twists on the tap, rinses her hands clean, dries them with the dishtowel, dials Anna back.

She picks up on the third ring. "Hey sweetheart, it's Elizabeth." "What's wrong?" "Nothing, really, it's just that Pat's not home yet, and I can't find him." "I'm sure it's nothing. Just men." "Except Jack." "He has his days, you know that. The other night he was flirting with this waitress over at La Cucina in Somerville. I mean she was beautiful, but he was so bad at it, it was pathetic. I was sort of pissed off and I went to the ladies, and was walking past the wait station, and our waitress was cracking up a waiter and two busboys, doing Jack, 'Would a luffly lady like yourself go for the veal piccata or the osso buco on a spring night like tonight?' You know how he gets sort of an English accent when he has a couple of drinks in him?"

The mother is laughing now. Laughing because she is speaking with someone who takes pleasure in just making conversation with her, pleasure from trying to make her feel better. She wraps the cord around to the breakfast nook, sits on one of the high-backed oak stools and talks to her old friend, a conversation that's never really stopped since they were eight years old.

In the full dark of a late-spring night, the sky is crystal clear. In the deep black, barely lit by a waning moon, and this far from the glow of the

City, the stars are clearly drawn, the constellations are defined as a connect-the-dots puzzle. Children are tucked into bed, parents settled in for a last hour or so of television or reading. Out on Route 202, police are on the scene of an alcohol-fueled accident.

Nora sits on the ground, with her fourth cup of keg beer half full, listening to Kathleen tell some joke, something lewd and witty about the feared and ugly geometry teacher. The group around them titters and someone turns off the boom-box that's been blasting REM's *Document* and U2's *The Joshua Tree* off and on all night. One of the kids back from college for the summer, from Sean's class she thinks, and sort of a dork then, but looking cool now with his hair long over his eyes and his ear pierced, pulls out an acoustic guitar and starts to strum "Blackbird." Some people sing along. But, Nora and Kathleen's group start playing a game of "I Never" and as the secrets start to spill, as friends backstab friends by bringing out embarrassing things only they know about each other, as Nora turns to Kathleen and asks, "Can we go someplace for a minute?" Kathleen's ex-boyfriend appears from the trees and sits on the ground next to her. Eyes scan from Kathleen to her ex and back again, waiting to see what's going to happen, waiting to see a fight. But the ex says, "Can we talk for a minute?" And, Kathleen, a little drunk, shrugs, "Yeah. Sure."

Nora watches them walk off from the main group and sit on the ground. Kathleen gestures angrily for a moment in the face of the boy's pleading. Then the talk grows quiet and more serious. Nora thinks, but can't quite be sure, she sees them holding hands. Then, and this she is sure of, they're kissing. Kissing briefly and standing to walk down one of the thin paths leading to the river, holding hands as they go.

Shocked and more than a little jealous, Nora wanders over to the keg, pumps the pump, refills her glass and sits down on the edge of the clearing, alone. Over near the keg, Doug Kenworthy nudges one of his friends, "Check this out," and walks over to where Nora's sitting. "May I?" he asks, sweeping his arm at the ground next to her. "It's a free country."

They sit for a while, making small talk. She doesn't really like this guy, thinks he's full of himself, but at least he's smart, not totally boring. After a few minutes, she realizes he's coming on to her. A finger touching the wisp of hair spilling out of her pony tail, he's sitting just a bit too much in her space. She remembers his girlfriend is a year older, probably not back from U-Mass yet. But what does she care? So when he leans in and kisses her, she kisses back. Odd, she thinks, she hasn't so much as kissed anyone since she was thirteen or fourteen. And, it's sort of nice. Not earthshaking, but all right. She finds herself liking the feel of his hands on her neck, liking his lips when they press softly. Liking it more when she closes her eyes and imagines he's Kathleen. So, when he pulls back and says, "Wanna go for a walk?" she shrugs her shoulders and thinks, This will get people off my back. "Sure, what the hell."

The father pulls into the driveway and parks next to Sean's hatchback. Killing the engine, he tries to smell his clothes, tries to see if that slutty dancer left any odor on him. Guiltily, he walks into the house and finds his wife in the kitchen, talking on the phone, "Sorry I'm so late." "I'm on the phone," she says and goes back to laughing. Must be Anna he thinks. He goes into the bedroom, changes from his suit into a pair of old gray sweatpants and a T-shirt and wanders back into the kitchen. Seeing the dishes in the sink, he realizes they ate without him. Goddamn it, he thinks, she could have waited. Wrenching open the fridge, he pulls out the rye bread, mustard, ham and Swiss, and makes himself a sandwich. His wife is still chattering away on the phone. He grabs a bottle of Heineken and heads into the family room with his makeshift dinner. Settling into his recliner, he turns on the reading lamp and opens his book. About four and a half pages later, he's distracted by the feel of the sweatpants without underwear, thinks, I'm still turned on. He hasn't felt this randy in years. He realizes he wants to sleep with his wife. Realizes it's been a while.

He hears her hanging up the phone, padding into the family room. "Where the hell were you?" Thinking quickly, he answers, "Bob and I took some clients for a beer. It couldn't be helped." "You knew Sean was coming home tonight, you could've called." "I said I was sorry." "For Christ's sake, Patrick." "I know," his voice softens. "Come here." He pulls her into his lap, rubs her shoulders. "I'm sorry. Let me make it up to you. We're all alone here." He can feel himself hard again, knows she can feel him as well, and he thinks, If we do this, everything will be fine.

Kate, naked on the couch, the credits of the Friday-night movie rolling on the television, guides Brian into her and wraps her arms around his neck. Not bad, she thinks, just not what it should be. But she subsumes her thoughts, arching up to meet him, quietly gasping at the occasional touch of his body that manages to reach her.

Sean can hear the faint hum of the party in the distance, fancies he can already smell the wood smoke of the fire; the ground is springy and soft under his feet. Eager to get to his destination, he picks up his pace a bit, anticipating the twists and turns from all the times he's been this way before—as a kid, exploring with Patty, plucking crayfish and salamanders from under rocks in the little creeks feeding the river. Later, walking this way with Amy, a blanket tucked under her arm, searching for a spot to picnic and make out. And high school nights, sneaking out his window after everyone was in bed and coming this way, as he is tonight, to a party already under way.

. . .

The mother, feeling the father pushing himself at her, doesn't really want to do this. She's not finished with being angry. But he's kissing her neck now, and she thinks, Well, maybe it will help. Resigned, she moves her hand down into his lap.

Patty, naked from the waist down, her shirt and bra bunched up at her neck, kneels on the stairs in front of the grungy bartender, his pants around his ankles. Holding him steady with one hand, keeping the other beside her to hold her balance, she takes him into her mouth, using her tongue as she goes. She feels powerful when she hears his intake of breath, the little moaning, "Oh yes" that comes from his mouth. He puts one hand on the back of her head, she looks up and sees his head thrown back, his mouth slack and open. She thrills at her power over him, and goes to work.

Nora is bored. Lying on the ground, still mildly damp from April showers, the weight of state wrestling champion Doug Kenworthy, 181 pounds if he's been cutting weight, pressing down on top of her. On her back, her legs spread, Doug Kenworthy's grinding and pressing against the cotton of her pants, pushing his tongue in and out of her mouth. She thinks she can feel the mud seeping into her back, seeping in the way water leeches into your clothes when you sit on a wet picnic bench. Ceci my playmate come out and play with me . . .

Rough, clumsy hands, push under her tank top, maul along her waist, trace over the cotton of her sports bra. Fumbling hands move to her back, looking for a clasp, then around to the front, still searching. Giving up, the hands push the material up, up near her neck, the elastic cutting into tops of her breasts. How long is long enough? she wonders. When can she get back to the party? . . . and bring your dollies three.

Suddenly those hands are down around her belly button, his weight lifted some from her, the hands try to work open the button at the top of her pants, the fingers play along her zipper. Enough is enough, she thinks and says, "Stop." Doug Kenworthy rolls over onto his side, "Come on baby, what's wrong?" His voice is husky with pleading, "You'll like it." "Let's get back, Doug," she says. "My brother's on his way." Those hands, off of her finally, move to the front of his jeans, pop open the buttons on the fly, haul himself out. "You can't leave me like this, you gotta help me out." "Oh, fuck you."

She stands and turns her back on him, adjusting her clothes, brushing twigs and damp leaves from her hair and, as best she can, from her back. She starts to walk away, but feels those rough hands clamp on her shoulder from behind and spin her around. Before she's had time to think, she's down on the ground again, on her knees. A hand moving up to clench her throat. A hand squeezing, just hard enough to point out the danger, to point out who is in charge here. The other hand holding that cock, rubbing its moist head against her lips. "No," comes Doug Kenworthy's voice, husky still but not with pleading, "Fuck you. Open wide." A hand squeezing tighter, squeezing and the fog in Nora's head from all that keg beer grows thicker, and she's got the spins, and, not thinking, she opens her mouth. He pushes into her, releases his grip on her neck some, pistoning his hips, in and out, choking her air . . . Climb up my apple tree. Slide down my rainbow, and through my cellar door.

Faster, in and out, he scrapes along her teeth, shoves hard against her face. Leaves the taste of him trailing along the length of her tongue, sags a bit and the pressure eases off her neck. It can't have been more than twenty seconds . . . And we'll be jolly friends forever more.

He starts to ease away from her, "Hot damn. That was great." And feeling him slide back, feeling him scrape along her teeth, aware suddenly that she has teeth, Nora bites down hard. Bites and tastes blood welling and mingling with the taste of him on her tongue. Bites once, hard, and he's backing away from her, "Fucking cunt," he's more surprised at first than angry, "You fucking cunt." Nora still on the ground, scrambling away from him, trying to get traction to get up, to run away, to run back towards the people and the light of the fire, is shocked to feel the snap of his fist against her right eye. Shocked, after everything, to be hit. She's never been hit before, not punched in the face, and the singe of that blow spreads out, into her forehead and cheeks, and, for the first time this whole night, she starts to cry.

Climbing to her feet, sobbing now, she trudges up the path back towards the party, comes into the area of gaiety lit by the fire. She sees Sean's old girlfriend Amy-Beth sitting by herself on the edge of the circle and stumbles up to her, sobbing. Amy-Beth, not asking anything, takes Sean's little sister into a hug and cradles her head while she cries.

Princeton-bound Doug Kenworthy comes back to his friends, pulls one into a neck-lock, gives him a noogie. "You're not going to believe this," he says, "but Nora Mahoney just sucked me off."

Kate and Brian pad into Kate's bedroom, naked, leaving their clothes until tomorrow. Brian gets under the covers on the left side of the bed, turning the sheets down to his right, making room. Kate detours into the bathroom, sits on the toilet and mops up the semen slipping down into the crack of her buttocks. She runs some water over her fingers, splashes her face, and opens the medicine cabinet. Pulling out the dial of her birth control pills, she pushes today's from its foil crust and pops it down her throat like a Tic Tac. Just as she goes to click off the light, she sees the time on the old clock radio on top of the toilet tank, sees that she missed a med sometime during the movie or their lovemaking and heads out into the living room for her purse. She pops open the child-proof lid like a veteran, slides a pill into her hand and pads back into the bathroom. "Coming to bed?" Brian calls from the other room. "In a minute," she answers, "I just need to take my meds."

She puts the pill onto her tongue, feels the gelatin of this brand start to dissolve. Staring at her reflection in the mirror, she tastes the first bitter hint of the powder concealed by the capsule coating. Turning on the cold-water tap, tilting her head to the side, she gulps from the pulsing stream of water, cleansing the acrid burn from her tongue.

Patty sits alone at the bar, swirling another extra-dry gin martini on the rocks with a twist around in her mouth. The day-shift bartender's gone now; this drink his parting courtesy. She's at that terrible place of being drunk, when other patrons slide their stools an additional six inches out of her space, when she looks neither right nor left, but only down at the drink in her hands and up at her reflection in the mirror behind the shelves of liquor.

She doesn't like what she sees there, not anymore, and it takes less effort to stare at her drink. Less effort, and it's easier to lift it to her mouth if she's staring down at the liquor. The room is spinning some, she puts her head into the folded crook of her arms on the bar top and dozes. In and out of consciousness, she is still aware of the conversations running around her, and she thinks with pride, If I can keep track, I must not be that drunk.

Raising her head, she holds her glass up with rubber arms, and slurs to the new bartender, "I need more gin please." "I think you're done Doc." This one isn't all that pretty she thinks. "I just wanna another gin extra-dry martini on the mother-fucking rocks with a mother-fucking twist." "Not tonight Doc. Go home."

Giving up, Patty collects her things and heads out into the street. She weaves down Avenue B until she finds herself in front of her building. Fumbles with her keys trying to get inside her little slice of tenement. Finally, she works the door open, nearly falling as it swings in, manages to get it closed and latched, the chain on and dead-bolt set. Manages to stagger to bed and, still fighting the spins, pass out. In the morning, she won't remember much past some guy in a wife-beater plopping a Master Lock into his back pocket.

. . .

Sean comes into the clearing, looking for faces he knows, looking for
Nora, looking, mostly, for Amy-Beth. Doug Kenworthy's story has
moved around the party, spreading quickly like a blush, until even
Amy-Beth, off on her own with Nora, has gotten the gist of Nora's
tears. There's an odd little hush that comes over different groups as Sean
arrives, a brief hesitation until someone greets him, shakes his hand or
slaps him five. A slight quiet he wouldn't have noticed if it didn't happen more than once, but it eats at him as he walks between the knots
of people gathered here and there around the fire.

He spots Amy-Beth on the edge of the clearing, just outside the full
force of the firelight, some bundle of a person curled in her lap.
Walking over, he raises his hand in greeting, but she just sucks on a cigarette, her face glowing jack-o'-lantern orange in the dim. "Hey," he
leans down and kisses her cheek hello, "Sorry I took so long." Amy-
Beth just points down at the bundle in her lap, he sees first it's someone crying, then sees it's Nora. "What happened?" he asks. Pulling
Nora up, gripping her hard on the shoulders, "What happened?"

She cries harder, her sobs deepening into gasps, "He made me."
Cradling Nora into his chest, he looks over his shoulder at Amy and
mouths, "Who?" She shakes her head, as if that's not important, that's
not what matters. "Who," he mouths again. "Who?" Amy-Beth drops
her smoke to the soil and grinds it out methodically with the chunky
heel of her Doc Martens. Looking back up at Sean, she jerks her head
across the clearing and mouths, "Doug Kenworthy."

Sean pushes Nora back into Amy-Beth's arms and stalks towards the
keg where Doug Kenworthy and his friends are funneling beers. On his
way, he passes a stack of wood ready for the fire, finds a tree limb, almost worn smooth like a walking stick, about the length and weight
of a baseball bat. He's not aware of people turning to watch him pass,
not aware of people sensing his destination and turning with expectant
faces towards a fight. He's not aware of Doug Kenworthy's forty-pound
weight advantage or better coordination.

Walking across the clearing, he's aware only of the feel of the tree limb against the fingertips and palm of his left hand and the rage focusing his vision. He can't see anything except for the blond back of Doug Kenworthy's perfectly shaped head as he laughs with his friends around a keg.

The father nestles with his wife on the floor of the family room, clothes half off, and they trade nips from a warm bottle of Heineken. The father's ham and Swiss on rye sits on its plate half-eaten. "I'm sorry," he says again. "I'm used to it," she answers, draining his beer. "I'm sorry about that too," he says. And, right now he is sorry, sorry for a lot of things he normally feels he shouldn't be sorry about—sorry for the hours that have bought this house, their cars and vacations. Right now he wonders if all that stuff is worth it. He's sorry too for his interlude with Tyna, but that's not really cheating he thinks, and tries to put it out of his mind. But in the dim light of his reading lamp, he can see the places where his wife once had curves and angles like that dancer's, and he thinks, But Christ, she was beautiful.

Kate lies with her back spooned into Brian's chest, at peace, comfortable as he snores gently into her neck. She sometimes has trouble sleeping, but she can feel herself drifting off to the rhythms of his breath, and tonight, she doesn't worry.

Sean slows as he nears Doug Kenworthy's little enclave, faltering in his resolve for an instant. But he hears Doug's voice call out, "No shit man, she swallowed every fucking drop," just as someone in the group sees Sean and motions for Doug to turn around. And as that sculpted Nordic face pivots towards him, saying something about "No hard feelings," Sean just swings his branch, swinging for the bleachers. Years of his father's hopeless coaching on the Little League field suddenly make sense as he turns from his hips, extends his arms and uses his weight to follow through.

The first blow strikes across Doug's cheek, snapping his head back, but doesn't knock him over. He raises his arms to his head and the second snaps something in his wrist. Sean swings again, lower this time, catching an elbow, and following through until the branch sinks into Doug's side. The state wrestling champion falls to the ground and Sean pulls back for another swing, raising the limb like a club, but someone has grabbed his arms, and he stops.

Though there is no such thing as total silence, though the fire still crackles and "Red Hill Mining Town" still jangles from the boom-box, no one at this entire party speaks for a minute. Doug's friends think about coming after Sean, but an older guy, a former high school God himself, steps up beside Sean, someone, he's not sure who yet, still holding his arms as he trembles with adrenaline, "The guy fucking deserved it." Pointing at Sean, he adds, "If I were you, I'd take your sister and get the hell out of here."

The mother gathers her clothes and walks into the bedroom to change into the sweat suit she'll sleep in that night. She can hear the father moving behind her, and guesses he's bolting down his sandwich before coming into bed. Yes, she can hear him plopping the dish into the water in the sink, and now his feet move towards the bedroom door. The sex was nice, she thinks as she gets under the covers, it always is. Things could be worse. Her husband climbs into the bed next to her, kisses her goodnight, and rolls onto his side, facing away from her.

Leaving the reading lamp lit on her nightstand, she reaches for a book. With absurd quickness, her husband's breathing is regular and deep. She's struck by a wave of tenderness; his day must have been tough. And though she's always claimed an inability to sleep when her children are out, she only turns a few more pages before the book falls limply out of her hands and she too is asleep.

. . .

Sean turns to see Amy holding his hands, Nora dry-eyed at her side, and he drops the branch. Placing himself between Amy and Nora, he guides them to the trail that leads to the parking clearing, without speaking. When they reach Nora's little truck, Nora hands him the keys and climbs into the back and lies down across the bench seat. Amy-Beth climbs up to the passenger seat and fits her hand over his as he works the stick, his left hand shaky on the wheel. He drives quickly, taking Amy home on roads he's driven hundreds of times before, and she leaves him at the top of her driveway with a quick peck on the cheek, "Call me, okay?"

Nora climbs into the front seat as he pulls away, slumps against the door, and he asks, "Are you all right?" And suddenly she's weeping again, mostly incoherent, a bit drunk, one minute yelling at him, "I can fight my own battles!" the next thanking him. One moment mumbling something about Ceci and dollies three, the next crying, "I only went off with that fucker because Kath left me alone."

Sean decides to drive until she has worked herself to sleep. Drive until she's sleeping so he doesn't have to bring her into the house like this, so that his parents will never have to know what happened unless she decides to tell them. He stops to gas up her truck, gets a take-out coffee, some ice for her eye. They drive and he lets her talk and talk, not probing or asking, just letting her vent. And, as they drive, they pass their old elementary school, the dark strip malls out on the highway, the little airport and the 4-H fairgrounds. They drive and drive, passing the familiar landmarks of their childhood, places with memories, good, bad and indifferent, and gradually, Nora slips into the claws of sleep.

Late May, spring of 1988, coming up on 4:30 in the morning. The sky over rural New Jersey lightens towards gray in preparation for dawn, fog rises from the creeks and tributaries that feed the Raritan River. The early-morning birds, mockingbirds, finches and robins with their life-mates, stir and flap off in search of food. The forecasters have promised another beautiful weekend.

The Mahoneys? With Nora tucked into her blankets and Sean lying awake, fully clothed, rationalizing his violence and feeling for all the world as if he might vomit, they're all in their beds, scattered around New Jersey and the City, each alone with their dreams or thoughts.

1 9 8 4

Kate rocks in an old rocking chair in the corner of her room, the purple glow of a black light the only illumination, the shades drawn. She wills the colors to be quiet. "Please, please," she says softly, "please." A vintage granny dress pulled over her thighs, fingers tracing fine old scars and cuts still fresh in their dressing of crusty scabs. Her back aches. With a nail painted in garish, lusty red, chipped, she flicks a scab to the floor. Flicks it with a practiced movement and presses the edges of the reopened slash together, welling blood to the surface, pressing down hard with a handful of nails. She focuses on the pain, a burn, an itch, the pain. The colors screaming in her head dim but don't turn off.

. . .

In her kitchen, the mother lines up cheddar cheese, mushrooms, green and red bell peppers, onions, garlic and broccoli on a cutting board. Selects a knife, a cleaver, from the wooden rack along the wall by the sink. Placing the onion on the cutting board, she whacks, whacks. Drawing on the strength of routine, she chops to not think, cuts the vegetables to keep strong, to not think, My oldest child is crazy. She cries from the onion fumes.

Sean lopes across the front lawn, newly seventeen, shorts and T-shirt dusty from a day of landscaping. Lean and brown, backpack slung across his shoulder, he's hungry from working in the sun. There's one day left of lawn cutting and shrub trimming before the family leaves for a weekend at the beach. He wonders, Will I have time to sneak up to my room for a cigarette before dinner? Will Mom be making something with vegetables so Kate and I can eat?

Across the street, Nora sits in her best friend Kathleen's pink bedroom, head attached to a pink Princess phone. Kathleen has her own line, and they're calling boys, flipping through those glossy magazines of middle-school girls, those *Tiger Beats* and *Teens,* laughing, excited that Nora is spending the night. Tonight they'll smoke cigarettes Nora has stolen from Kate. And though they have never said anything about it, they know also that when the lights have been turned out, when they've climbed into bed together, their hands will trace each other's bodies in a ritual they have perfected over the last two years when they developed the pretense of practicing and took turns being the boy. Now, they feign sleep, slowly curl around each other spoon fashion, and touch and kiss until feigning sleep is no longer necessary.

. . .

The father sits in his study, ice melting into a tumbler of Glenlivet sitting by his hand. His shades are drawn too, the dying light of this summer night barred, but through the open windows he can hear the neighborhood kids in a game down the street. Is it freeze tag or capture the flag? Or some other game, some new game they have now, a game he never knew? And into these thoughts breaks the thought, My daughter is nuts. Then quickly, Is this my fault?

Patty and a local surfer leisurely clean the beach house after a full week of partying. They pluck cigarette butts from the house plants, try to obscure beer stains in the rugs, stow the feathered roach clips and the bong in the hiding place she and Kate created in the closet of the room they share down here. Checking under the sofa, she finds a vial of blow someone has lost, hails the boy, and cuts some lines on the coffee table with a no-postage-necessary reply card from some magazine. Covering a nostril, she snorts and leans back against the couch. The boy sniffs, leans in next to her. Their faces turn towards one another, lips meet, tongues lock. Patty's hand works its way under the hem of his short corduroy shorts, feels him stiffening, feels alive.

Sean comes in the back door and finds his mother whacking vegetables with determination. Says, "What's for dinner?" Then, hearing the quiet, the absence of the family's usual hum around the house—Kate's music booming through the kitchen ceiling, the father's fingers clicking on the IBM PC in his study, Nora's rough-housing with the dog in the backyard, Patty's shower in preparation for a night out—he asks, "Where is everyone?" The mother, not in the mood for this conversation, gives the bare bones. "Nora's at Kathleen's, Kate's in her room,

Dad's in his study, don't bother him. We're having a cheese and vegetable casserole." Sean's startled that his and Kate's vegetarianism has been acknowledged with a family meal. "Everyone knows vegetables are a side dish" is his father's mantra. "Don't tell Dad there's no flesh. He won't eat." "Your father's not eating tonight," the mother replies, too brightly.

His father only locks himself in his study when he's arguing with the mother and here she is, beating vegetables to within an inch of edibility. He wonders if perhaps it's him, something he has done, some transgression against the rules of this house. Have they found his stash or the rubbers in his dresser drawer, smelled the tobacco stench lingering on his shirts, heard through the town grapevine of him driving a little drunk the other night? "Mom," his voice teeters on the quavering edge of panic, "what's going on?" "Kate," she answers, flatly, as if that one word could explain everything.

Outside, lightning bugs blink on and off. The sun is down, but night will not fall, not the true dark of night, until a few more hours have ticked off the clock. Around the neighborhood, mothers call children into dinner, Wiffle ball games are halted, the summer night on pause. Fathers work the grills, taking over part of the cooking for a season. The older kids will gather again after wolfing down burgers and wiping off milk mustaches. There will be games in the dark, someone will have beer and someone else will have gone into the City to buy some pot. Couples will grope in the long grass around the abandoned barn at the end of the street where the new houses are going in—a month and a half before school starts again, and the world is a sure and constant place.

Kate feels under the pillows on her bed, wrapping her hand around the little carved wooden box she keeps there. She traces its lines with her fingertips, then slides it out, pops open the lid, pulls an antique straight razor from its depths, works open the blade. Without looking down, she draws a quick, shallow line on her left thigh, then the right. Waits for a second, feels the blood welling up, then the rush of pain, the silencing of the colors.

Knock raps a fist on her door. Knock again in the four-rap code that means Sean. Her reverie broken, she wraps her herself in some blankets, the quilt from her bed. So cold. But she presses her hands against the new cuts on her legs, feels that burn, calls, "Come in."

She invites him in because, of all the people living under this roof, he is her friend, and he needs an explanation. Invites him in because, now, today, she feels her fuses popping, glowing fiercely in her head, and she's afraid. Afraid she is going to be sent away, but knowing somewhere, she needs to go away.

As he swings open her bedroom door, the ambient light from the hallway spills in an acute angle across the floor of her bedroom, sounding to her like breaks squealing just before a car smashes into a guardrail.

Nora, polite as instructed, eats with Kathleen, her parents, and her annoying older brother with the jacked-up, tricked-out Trans-Am. She remembers her pleases and thank you's, keeps her elbows off the table, her napkin in her lap. Kathleen and her brother, at home, are not so encumbered. They talk with their mouths full, the brother burps, they don't ask to be excused when they've finished. Kathleen's parents think, Why can't we have kids like the Mahoneys?

Patty arches her back to draw the surfer deeper inside her, one hand on the small of his back, in the hollow at the base of his spine that she loves, the other behind her own head, lightly running her fingers over the nape of her neck just because she can. Because it feels good to touch herself there. She thinks, Thank God for the coke. It keeps him from getting off too soon. Then, she closes her eyes and thinks of nothing as she reaches for a rhythm that works.

She'd decided at the last minute to get out of New York for the summer. Decided that the Upper West Side was not a place she wanted to spend July and August, and she knew her parents would let her stay down at the shore, only disturbing her solitude when they came down on weekends. She needed to think. For two years, she'd been moving on autopilot through the Barnard philosophy department and she found herself chafing at the thought of being anyone's protégée, of a life in that stale and tweedy discipline. With Kate at home again and fooling everyone but Patty into believing she was fine, she'd been doing some side reading in psychology, but found its rigid theories and slots of behavior limiting. And didn't they treat their serious cases with drugs, an agent of the body?

She'd decided, the day she met this boy, after an afternoon of solitary drinking in the dim, ceiling-fanned cool of a Belmar boardwalk bar, to switch over to pre-med. She'd have to hustle to finish on time, but checking the catalogue, she felt like she could do it. She'd taken some of the biology and chemistry anyway, for kicks, and done well, as she has always done well in everything at school. So, she'd decided, settled her tab and slammed out into the sun, running smack into this boy sporting only red, knee-length trunks, tracing a hand absently through the happy trail of blond hair fuzzing around his navel, squinting out at the waves. Apologizing, she realized he was stunning. Realized too that she hadn't had any human contact beyond her family, store clerks and bartenders since she'd been down here. She thought, apologizing again, He'll do fine for a while.

Now, after a couple of weeks, she thought him dumb and pretty, not someone she'd give the time of day in the City, her real life, but decent enough for summer nights.

He's thrusting too fast now, the movement not right for her, and

Patty rolls them over, sitting on his hips and grinding against his pelvic bone.

The mother slides a casserole dish into the oven, preheated to 425, then wanders around her house. Passes the closed door concealing her husband, the door shut the way it is when they're fighting. No music tonight, no Vivaldi or jazz saxophone from that tinny little stereo he keeps in there. No sound of him rustling papers or turning pages of depositions, no click-click of his fingers on the computer keyboard. Night is falling outside, but she eschews lights. Upstairs, on the hallway walls, if she just flicked that switch, her family would grin back at her. Smiling together in neon parkas at the top of one of Killington's peaks, with cartoon characters in Orlando, clustered together on the porch of the beach house each Labor Day weekend. But, there are no windows here, she doesn't flick the switch, and the pictures reflect back at her, mirror-black. The silence grates. No hint of Kate's screeching stereo, none of Nora's rowdy laughter, nothing. She stops at the base of the stairs leading to the third floor. Thinks of going up, of explaining things to Sean, but she turns back towards her husband in his sanctuary. The time has come for them to make arrangements.

Sean takes a moment to let his eyes adjust to the gloom of Kate's room. Takes stock of a blank, stretched canvas sitting on the easel, glowing luminous purple in the corner. He sees Kate now, rocking, rocking in that chair they pulled from a neighbor's garbage last spring, shivering in the humid air of the house, shivering under a mound of blankets. "Katy-did?" he asks. "What's going on?" "It's over," she says. "They're going to send me away." "Run," he says, "go away again." Rocking in that chair, back and forth, rocking, she says, quietly, again and again, "It's over, it's over."

. . .

Several hours earlier. The racket in Kate's head, the cacophony of light and color grown too loud, her fears pressing down on her. The fear of little things like buttons on the collars of shirts, the fear of larger things like crossing the street, the fear that she is, after all, crazy. She's home alone. Tries her cuts, the little slices that always pulled her back before. They don't work. Wandering the house, she finds a lunge whip among the clutter of Nora's tack trunk and cracks it in the air, likes the sharp swish of its sound. Cracks it again, the tail this time catching her, just slightly, on the thigh. A brief, blissful second of silence. Delicious. With each little touch, each moment of contact, she feels herself coming back. In the living room now, she spies her reflection in the big, antique mirror. Crack. Shedding her clothes, naked in the living room, eyes on the mirror, harder, faster, crack, crack. The image in the glass broken by her mother's face, lips in scabby vermilion flakes of summer-school lipstick, wide in a scream. In the glass the mother grips the wrist of the hand working the whip, a lash falls uselessly on a left shoulder, falls without force, more of a brush than a caress. Kate sees her mother crying, sees herself naked, holding a whip, sees her mother gesturing wildly at the scars on her thighs, the blood seeping from her back. Hears her mother's "Whats . . ." and "Whys . . ." And falling into her mother's arms, she thinks, Help me, help me, I'm crazy.

Sean stares at Kate rocking, rocking in that chair. Hears her repeating, "It's over, it's over." He backs out of the room, closes the door and stands there facing its blank wood, more afraid than he's ever been in his entire life.

Patty, sweaty but still wired, pulls on her T-shirt and shorts, encourages the surfer to get dressed and get lost. Lies to him, "I think they're com-ing down tonight, you'd better leave." Alone in the beach house, she does another line, finishing the coke, and walks, flicking lights on and off, checking to make sure all is in order. Restlessly, she tries to read, tries three or four of the books stacked on the table next to her bed, but can't lose herself in the pages. After a time she thinks, Fuck it. I'm going for a swim.

Nora and Kathleen sneak out and head to the new development. There, in the half-finished houses, kids gather in future kitchens and rec-rooms to smoke, to drink, to plot, to hang out. In what will be the master bedroom of a big Colonial they've claimed for their own, Nora produces the crumpled Dunhill pack from deep in the pocket of her shorts. She plucks one of three worn, stale cigarettes from under the gold foil and, after three tries, touches a lit match to its end. They pass the smoke back and forth, inhaling, pretending to inhale, trying and failing not to cough.

They stub out the first cigarette, woozy, and lie on the floor, head to head. Nora feels the sweep of Kathleen's longer hair falling across her own pixie cut. It brushes now, as Kathleen shifts her weight, across Nora's forehead. Nora talks about her horseback-riding day camp, the afternoons in the dusty ring, round and round, soaring over jumps, leaning in against the withers of her pony, mornings cleaning stalls and brushing dirt and grime from those strong flanks.

Her instructor, a college girl, Dawn, wants her to show this summer. "She says," Nora tells Kathleen, "that I have promise." Nora has gone with Dawn to one of her own shows, "As her groom," she says proudly to anyone who will listen, and stood on the rail in jeans and worn paddock boots, her white tank top dusted with brown just like Dawn's during camp days. Standing on the rail, her hip bones pressed into a fence post, she watched Dawn's so serious face as she whipped her thoroughbred around the jumper course, cutting corners fast and soaring over the massive hurdles. And then, the course completed, Dawn's face broke into a smile as she leaned over to pat and rub her gelding's neck.

Opening the gate, Nora took the reins, helped Dawn dismount and was engulfed by Dawn's jubilant hug when her time and no-fault score was posted.

"She thinks you're pretty good then?" Kathleen asks. "Yeah," Nora says and, with an odd rush of feeling, adds, "But she's great."

The mother and father argue in the study. "We have to," the mother says. "No," the father says, "we'll lose her again, Liz." "God-damn it," the mother says, "this isn't just Kate being Kate. This isn't just her being *an eccentric artist,* she was naked and beating herself with a whip in the living room. She's not a kid, she's twenty-one years old. Her legs are covered in scars and cuts. She's hurting herself, Patrick. Hurting herself." The father, not able to see his daughter that way, not able to wrap his mind around all this, his little girl, naked, *beating herself,* says, "She's always been intense." The mother kneels down on the floor next to the father's chair, takes his cheeks in her hands, tears beginning to flow freely down her face, and says, "This isn't the first time."

A year and a half earlier, the middle of winter. Patty comes home, finds Kate perched, nude, in the upper branches of the big oak tree in the backyard. "Bad trip," she thinks as she climbs the lower branches, carefully, quietly, so as not to startle Kate into jumping or falling. But Kate hears her, breaks her gaze away from whatever has grabbed her attention, says, "Hey there. Just getting a bird's perspective for a painting." Patty says, "For fuck's sake, Kate, it's fucking freezing, what the fuck were you thinking?" As they go down together, there in the gray afternoon, Patty sees the first, thin lines on Kate's legs. Inside, Kate dressed again, they move warily in separate spheres of the house until the parents arrive home. Patty, thinking hard, decides, The tree, but not the legs, and tells the mother. Tells her in a matter-of-fact way, as if to say, "Listen to what Katy-did's done now." But the mother knows. Knows that the breaking of sister/sister confidentiality means something is really wrong. She tells the father, and the father, in the dark of his study, calls a friend from

the Club, Dr. Richardson the psychotherapist. An appointment is made, Kate is
dragged along; there is the first discussion of medication options, hospitalization.

Back at home that night, Kate does a runner. Cleans out her bank account and
drives off in her car. She'll sell it out in the Midwest, hitch all the way to Montana.
She's gone for months, sending word of her safety only to Sean, sending him a box
full of buttons, a pastel drawing, a couple of brief notes. When she returns, she's
strong for a time, good, and the worry eases. Even the mother starts to think, A
phase. Just a phase.

Now this.

Sean eavesdrops outside his father's study. Hears his mother say,
"Patrick, she's gone off. If you don't call Phil Richardson, I'm going to
do it. I want your blessing." Silence. Then the mother again, "Your father was a bastard, Pat. He was violent, he hurt you, and you ran. But
the problem was with him, not with you. Kate's hurting herself. There
was blood on her back, scars on her legs. Remember what they said last
time, borderline suicidal. Suicidal, Pat. And she's worse this time.
Worse." "Call Phil," his father says finally, Sean imagining his head
slumping into his hands.

He hears his mother phone Dr. Richardson at home, tell the story.
He starts to run upstairs to warn Kate, tell her they're coming for her.
But slowly, it sinks in. His thoughts linger on the word "blood," his gait
slows. Reaching the top of the stairs, he sees Kate's door open, sees her
sitting in that chair, rocking. His mother passes him, stops for a moment, just looks at him for the briefest of seconds and he can see the
tears drying on her cheeks. "Go find Nora, bring her home," she says
to him, "Check down in the new development. I know she and
Kathleen go there. Your father and I are . . ." The words stop there as
her composure threatens to crack and she wills herself not to weaken.
Not to break because she is the mother.

She enters Kate's room, but refuses to turn her attention to her daughter. She pulls a suitcase from the closet, opens drawers, and from the rumpled mess of their contents, pulls a nightgown, underwear, socks, assorted pants and shirts. Who knows what Kate will need there?

Patty's on the way out the door, her bikini under her shorts and T-shirt, a towel thrown over her shoulder, when the phone rings. Shit, she thinks and answers, "Hello?" Her father tells the story, quickly, leaving out many details. Patty doesn't interrupt. Says, "Fuck. Sorry," once, then "Uh-huh. Oh." When the father has finished, when he's said, "We're leaving shortly for the hospital," there's a long pause. "Should I come home?" Patty finally asks, not wanting to drive the hour north, but feeling she should be willing. "Not tonight," the father says. "There's nothing you can do. Sean will watch Nora. They probably won't kill each other. Come in the morning." They hang up and Patty stands holding the receiver in one hand, the other cutting off the dial tone. She's not thinking of anything at all. Placing the handset in the cradle, she grabs her towel again and heads for the beach. Not until she's moved with the powerful strokes of her father out beyond the breakers, not until she stops for a moment and treads water looking north towards where the Berkeley Carteret building is the last glow on Asbury Park's once proud skyline, does she realize, Now, nothing will ever be the same.

Kate has been her shield, the problem child. Wild when she was younger, willing to try anything once. Patty idolized her, wished she could be like her. When she started to taste life for herself, she was careful. She'd seen the worry etched on her parents' faces as Kate came in late or carelessly left a dime bag of pot on her dresser for someone to find, and she vowed, "Not me." And she got her straight A's, she got to Barnard. And she never got caught. All the while sneaking around, booze and boys and drugs. When Kate ran away, she'd overheard her mother tell her father one night, "At least we don't have to worry about Patty."

Treading black water on a moonless Jersey Shore night, small waves rolling her up and down as they head inexorably towards shore, she thinks, I'll have to be more careful. They won't ever be disappointed in me.

Nora is sick to her stomach, lying on the plywood floor, her head spinning. Kathleen stubs out the last third of the last cigarette, not feeling very well herself. The plywood splinters poke their legs and arms as Kathleen says, "I let Billy Parker go to second at the fair last night." Nora squeals, "You did what?" spinning around so she's sitting and looking down at her friend. The rush of her thoughts is so loud, she barely hears Kathleen's reply, "We went off to the woods and we were frenching and he wanted to. It felt sort of good. I made him promise not to tell."

Trying to be excited for her friend, trying not to think about Kathleen's body under her own hands, wondering why her friend is so excited about the fumbles of *some boy* after all they've done together, Nora manages to ask, "Under the bra?" "Yeah," Kathleen says, "but he couldn't get it open, so he just pushed his hands under." "Are you gonna go further?" Nora asks, desperately wanting to hear Kathleen say "No." "Maybe. Not right away."

Swooping down on her friend as if she's staking her claim, Nora tickles her and they roll around the floor, laughing, each trying to get the upper hand. But Nora is stronger, more solid from her days mucking stalls and controlling horses. She pins her friend on her back, rolls on top of her, sits on her hips, pressing her down with the new horseback riding muscles in her thighs. They're breathing hard, Nora staring down at Kathleen's flushed face streaked with laughter tears. Kathleen's hands move to Nora's arms, as if she's looking to push Nora off, but a sudden, black quiet has come into the not-finished house in the aftermath of their play, and they just stare at each other, breath becoming more regular with each passing second. A long strand of Kathleen's hair sticks to her cheek, and Nora's just reaching down to brush it behind her friend's ear when she hears someone snooping around the lower floor of the Colonial.

Nora hears Sean yell, "NORA JANE MAHONEY!" Quickly, she rolls off Kathleen, tosses the cigarette butts out the frame of a window and scatters the ashes with a breath. "What do you want, Sean?" she yells. Sometimes she fucking hates him. By way of an answer, Sean climbs the stairs, comes into the room and says, "Mom and Dad want you to come home." "But we weren't doing anything," Nora whines, "I'm spending the night." "Just come, Nora." "Why?" "Later. Just come."

Kate watches as the mother closes the suitcase, carts it down the stairs. She hears the front door open and close, catches the sound of the Cadillac's trunk clicking shut. Presses her hands onto her legs, shivers.

I don't want to be a nuisance, she thinks. Suddenly, lucidly, she's sorry for the worry she has caused. I have to do better, she thinks, I have to manage. And in that moment of lucidity comes the knowledge that maybe she can't manage, maybe she does need help. That, just maybe, there's something really wrong in her head, and that going away might sort things out.

The father finalizes the arrangements, takes notes on the names of people to speak with, the directions to the facility. He brews a pot of coffee. Waits to be told when to get behind the wheel, when to drive. Waiting, he opens mail, pays a few bills. He considers the whisky still resting on the table, but thinks, I'm driving. Finally, he picks up the book he's been reading, opens to the marked page and forgets everything for a time, forgets his family, this trouble, and just reads. As he turns the pages, his hand reaches out to his glass, lifts it to his mouth, and he sips. Swirls the single malt around his mouth and swallows. Again and again until the glass is empty and he's chewing up little slivers of Scotch-flavored ice.

Nora walks with Sean up their dark street. No street lamps, no traffic, nothing disturbs the night. "Sean," Nora asks, "what's going on?" Unable to decide what Nora's old enough to handle, seeing her still as a little girl, Sean, like his mother, just says, "Kate." "But, what?" Nora asks. "She's sick," Sean answers, "she has to go to the hospital."

Flushed with anger, Nora stomps a few feet ahead of Sean on the street. She's tired of everything the rest of them do getting in her way. Tired of them not telling her anything. Tired of having her life shaped by their whims. Kate was supposed to pick her up at Kathleen's in the morning and drive her to the barn before she went to work. She supposes she won't get to go now, and Dawn was supposed to teach her how to braid manes and tails for her show this weekend, and this all just sucks. She hears Sean call, "Nora, wait up" and she stops in the street, kicking at the ground until he arrives beside her. "Listen," he says, "take it easy. Mom and Dad need you to chill." Whatever condescension was in his voice before has vanished and the shift in tone rattles her. "Sean, this isn't like getting her tonsils out sick, this is like when she ran away, right?" "Yeah." Her anger replaced suddenly by worry, for Kate, for herself—could this happen to her too?—she asks her brother because he's there and because he might tell her the truth, "Is it bad?" Sean, matching her stride as they head the short distance left back to the house, just shrugs and lies, "Who knows, you know?"

Patty walks back to the beach house. Gathers some things, drops into her car, still up just a bit from the coke. Wheeling out to the Parkway, she turns north and heads home, thinking, I should be there. . . . How could she do this? . . . It's a good thing I cleaned up the house before Dad called.

The heavy traffic is all moving the other way, people heading to the beach for a long weekend, and she has the northbound lanes mostly to herself. Foot heavy on the accelerator, she focuses on the tail lights of a lone pickup in the right lane, falls a few car lengths back and stays behind those lights in a steady line as if they were a beacon leading her home. "Katy-did," she mutters, "you've done it now." Poor Sean, she thinks, first me going away, now her.

The high halogen lamps lighting the road flash like strobes as she drives, bringing pictures and memories of Kate. Her little-girl excitement when she won some art competition at school. Older, a high school senior to Patty's sophomore, lying stoned in Kate's room talking about whatever party they'd come from and playing one of their father's classical or jazz records softly on her stereo. Or younger, very small, and Patty's envy of Kate's coloring books, so beautiful placed next to Patty's slapdash crayon scrawls, is palpable. Oh, I envied you, she thinks, I wanted to *be* you. Seeing something you wanted and just going up and tasting it. Never a worry about consequences or what others might think. "Kate," she says aloud, "how could you do this? You fucking bitch."

Kate allows the mother to slip a pair of sneakers on her feet. Insists on a cardigan sweater to keep warm. Permits herself to be steered down the stairs and into the backseat of the car. Thinks, I hope she packed enough. Pressing her hands into her legs, she searches for a spot that still aches, tries to focus on the raw scratch of her back.

As her mother looks in at her in the backseat, her face a monstrosity of concern, Kate says, "I'm supposed to work lunch tomorrow at the restaurant. Can you call them for me? Tell them I won't be in?" The mother reaches in and lifts a strand of Kate's gaudily dyed hair behind her ear, strokes her cheek as she pulls away. "Sure, honey," she says, "I'll take care of that." "This is going to be good, isn't it?" Kate asks, "This is going to be all right? The insurance will cover this?"

She suddenly needs to know. Needs her mother the way she hasn't for years. Needs her mother to reach out to her, pull her close and whisper to her the way she did waking from childhood nightmares, "Shhh. Everything's okay. It's okay, love. It's okay." The mother's hand touches her cheek again, caressing, and she looks at her daughter. Willing the wetness in her eyes not to be tears, hoping she's telling the truth, the mother says, "It's going to be fine. Don't worry about the money. You're going to work this out."

Satisfied, Kate leans back against the seat, feels the raw of her back butting against the supple leather, "I just wish the world would shut up sometimes. I'm tired of all this God-damned racket all the time. I don't want to be afraid anymore." The mother, those lines of not-tears rolling across her cheeks and over her lips, kisses her daughter's forehead, "It's going to be okay, love. It's going to be okay." Stepping back from the car and clicking the door shut, the mother watches Kate staring at the headrests of the front seat for a moment, the tears rolling freely in the dark where no one can see, and she prays in the church of her nighttime driveway. Offers a quick prayer to St. Jude and St. Christopher, wipes the tears from her face, and stares at the front door, waiting for her husband to emerge.

Sean and Nora are greeted in the driveway by their parents. The father tells them that they'll be home in the morning. The mother tells Nora to listen to Sean. They assure them both not to worry, that everything will be all right. Sean nods, mute. Nora looks into the rear window, knocks, motions for Kate to roll it down. She kisses Kate's cheek, "Feel better." Kate touches Nora's face, finds the right words in her head, finds the right words by pressing hard on her thighs, pressing her back hard against the leather of the seat, "Thanks," she tells her little sister. "I'll be fine." Sean goes into the house, climbs the stairs to his room, crawls out onto the eaves of the roof outside his bedroom window and lights a cigarette. Nora stands just inside the front door, face pressed to the glass. The car pulls out of the driveway, its tail lights glowing soft crimson in the night.

Patty drives, faster than she should as she gets closer to home, cursing the traffic clustered around the stoplights on the rural highway, crunching hard on the brakes with each squeal of her radar detector.

Sean sits in the dark, smoking one cigarette after another until he feels woozy. Thinks, She's fine. She's fine. He thinks about all the hours they spent out here smoking, talking. All the nights down at the Broadway Diner on 22, eating omelets at three in the morning. The crazy fun they had cruising this dull, little town in her fishbowl-shaped car, smoking weed, laughing, plotting their futures. He remembers her running away and the secret pride of being the one she kept in touch with while she was gone. She's the only one who knows I want to go to cooking school and not college, he thinks, she'll be back tomorrow. We'll laugh about this. Fine, she's fine. Kate is fine.

For him, she must be fine. She's the only one who treats him like an adult, the only one who listens to him, who believes what he has to say is important. His world, his likes and dislikes, are tempered by her opinions. His records, his clothes, shaped by Kate. When he goes out to the mall with her, when she drives them down to New Hope and they poke around the head shops and funky thrift stores, he always keeps half an eye on her reactions. At times he thinks she's his only friend, the only person besides Amy-Beth who really knows who he is. She shows him her new paintings first, she sometimes lets him and Amy tag along to her art school parties, but she's never throwing him bones of attention, she cares what he thinks. And if she's odd, a little strange, that's just Katy-did doing her thing. Kate being Kate.

If she's not fine, he thinks, dragging on a cigarette on the roof of his parents' house, what does that say about me?

Nora pokes around Kate's room, looking for clues. They all tried to keep her from knowing the last time, the time Kate ran away. But she listened, kept her ears cocked when they thought she was sleeping in the car, and she heard words. Some she didn't really understand: "Temporal-lobe disorder," "Possible manifestations of Dostoyevsky seizures," "Severe synesthesia"and "Borderline schizophrenic." Some she did: "Drugs," "Troubled," "Possible suicide."

She watched her mother while Kate was gone, sniffing around Kate's room, reading Kate's diary, sitting for whole Sunday afternoons in the window seat of Kate's bedroom just staring out at the day. Nora snooped too, popping open the lock on that diary for a look of her own, trying to get a sense of her sister, trying to figure out how the person who drove her to riding lessons, who made Sean be nice to her, who gave her little pastel drawings of horses for her wall, how that sister who seemed so nice could possibly, maybe, be crazy.

She didn't know what to make of the things she found then, doesn't know what to make of those things she sees now. The casual tumult of Kate's bedroom yields little. The big, thick art books with their thrilling and dangerous nudes offer no clues. The voluptuous comfort of the strewn-about quilts and blankets provides no hints. The easel and scattered brushes in a mason jar of smelly turpentine don't yield any secrets.

In the drawers are the lace and vibrant silk colors of Kate's underthings, so different to touch than her own plain cotton. The endless spill of mostly black clothes. The Tampax and makeup scattered with coins on top of the dresser. In the bottom of her sock drawer, the little metal marijuana pipe with its lingering odor of sweet charcoal. All of this *stuff,* and nothing pointing towards any sense of the truth.

Under the bed, there's the diary, but she won't read from it again, not wanting to face how weird it is. Also, a pretty wooden box. In the box is an old, bone-handled razor. Nora works open the blade, seeing tiny, rust-colored smudges scattered around the bright metal, lightly runs her thumb across its sharpness, not feeling its pinch until the thin line of blood wells up on her thumb. "Shit," she pops her thumb into her mouth, the taste of her blood like aluminum foil.

Hastily stowing everything back under the bed, she beats a retreat from the room, wanting, more than ever, an answer. She's tired of them hiding things from her. She never asked last time because she wasn't supposed to know. This time, she's going to find out.

The father drives, negotiates the turns of the roads leading to the highway. Setting the cruise control, he twirls the radio to his favorite jazz station, but keeps the volume low. Even on this night, on this drive, his fingers tap time on the steering wheel, he can't help it. In the break between songs, the DJ with his sultry night-jazz show voice gives the particulars of the players behind Coleman Hawkins' saxophone and he introduces Miles Davis next, from the *Bitches Brew* sessions. And as the chaotic tear of those riffs, the screeching of that trumpet come into the car, he catches sight of his daughter's shape in the rearview mirror. Sees her slumped into the backseat, the vague blank stare on her face as she gazes out the window, and he remembers catching sight of his own face when he was about her age. After another session on the rice-strewn basement floor, forced there by his father to do penance for some teenaged transgression. His knees raw from the torture created by his father, his spirit breaking, his face blank in the mirror. And he remembers this too: Kate's wild energy as a child, her genuine love for life, the way she could never hide her feelings, the way her face betrayed her sadness or excitement or fear. Looking back at her in the rearview mirror, seeing her face empty as the smooth surface of the highway stretching before him in the headlights, he thinks, What did we do to you? How did we do this to you?

The mother rustles papers in the glow of the map light, rereading the fine print of their insurance policies, calculating distance and time of arrival in her head. All business now, the mother again, in charge. Doing what she has to do to make this all right. Later she'll take the time to be sad. Maybe she and her husband will be able to sit and talk this over, grieve together. But for now, she must make herself brave. And she must will herself to be strong in front of Sean and Patty and Nora. Nora's going to need some explanations, she thinks, we can't protect her from this any longer. And, Sean. She knows Sean is going to need comforting. Patty, she thinks, won't want my help at all, but she'll have it.

Clicking off the map light and leaning back in her seat, she thinks, What a terrible price Kate is paying for her talent. And, that talent has been undeniable. The praise heaped on her all through public school, her shows at art school. Her life defined by the ability and desire to translate what she sees in her head in swaths of paint and crushes of color. What will she do, the mother wonders, if she cannot paint? How will we know her without little smudges of acrylics or oils above her cheekbones from rubbing her eyes when she works late into the night? How will we know ourselves without her the way she has been? She sees the father's hand reach down to fiddle with the radio and she reaches for it, searching for an anchor in the uncharted waters they're traveling. Their fingers come together, he glances quickly from the road, gives her hand a squeeze, and lets their hands sink together to the seat between them.

· · ·

Slumping in the backseat, Kate watches the highway lights flash by at seventy-three miles per hour. She tries to close her eyes, but that rhythmic flash pulls them open, and she thinks, Just like a snare drum. Tap, tap, tap.

Sean calls Nora into the forbidden realm of his room, invites her to sit with him on the roof. Offers her a cigarette. She hesitates, but takes it. "Is Kate going to be okay?" she asks. Now that the question is hung out there, now that it has been asked, by Nora who's not supposed to know the truth, Sean has to find an answer. For himself and for Nora, pain-in-the-ass Nora who's sitting out here with him, pretending to smoke. Nora who he realizes is not a kid anymore, Nora who will be coming to the high school with him in the fall. "I don't think so," he says.

In the dark, sharing a pack of cigarettes, Sean fills her in on what he knows. When Kate was working, Kate told him she heard sounds coming from the colors. Kate is afraid the buttons on her shirts choke the life out of her lungs. He has seen Kate walk all the way around a block, or stand immobile on the corner waiting for something, a signal from someplace that tells her it is time to cross. Patty found Kate naked in the big tree in the backyard back before she ran away, trying to see what it is birds see. And their mother found her today, using Nora's lunge whip to cut chunks out of her back. He tells Nora that Kate has been hurting herself to try and silence the noise in her head. Tells her all he knows, what he overheard their parents saying that afternoon, and some things guessed at on his own.

In the middle of the telling, Patty pulls into the driveway. She sees them on the roof, the orange glow of their smokes, and climbs up and out to sit with them. Sean and Nora talk, dissecting the problem, trying to work it out. Patty, the one who's known longer than anyone that Kate's "just being Kate" was something deeper, something darker, adds little, just the weight of her presence. But she does say, "It's been going on for a while, since we were in high school. She cuts her legs. When it was bad back then, she drank or got high until she passed out. But, man, when it was good, she was a good time."

After a while, they've exhausted the subject of Kate and what is wrong with her. That question is to be handled by others now, though when Kate returns from her stay in the hospital, medicated and docile, a creature of her pills, they will all have misgivings. When Kate is back, they might search for hints of the person who left them tonight, but a chapter has been closed for all of them, only to be echoed by small events or brief moments in the future. Tonight, in the dark, on a small slab of roof big enough to seat four, sit three.

1 9 8 2

Nora wanders into Kate's room, bored. Her friend Kathleen is at her grandmother's house in Vermont for the weekend, leaving Nora with nothing to do. She drags her fingers across the thick dust layer settled on the dresser top, moodily settles in the window seat for a moment, then with one ear cocked for the sound of a car in the driveway, the front door opening, she snoops. Digging in the drawers, running her hands through the clothes left behind, the bras with the under wire sticking through, the old nightgowns Kate never wore, she looks for clues that might explain where Kate went and what she is doing. Nora Mahoney, Girl Detective, opens books, looking for photographs that might be tucked between the leaves of a coffee-table Klimt, between the tissue-thin pages of the Bible all the children were given at birth by their grandparents. Under the bed, she finds a small wooden box, rattling. Inside are stray buttons of all shapes and sizes; wood buttons, plastic buttons, bone, round, square, medium, small and large. Also, a small diary with one of those flimsy locks that begs to be popped open. It pops. Nora settles on the floor. She reads.

Patty, ensconced at the counter of Tom's Restaurant, sips her black coffee, smokes, copies into her notebook from Aquinas and Descartes. Jots notes in the margins about the mind/body problem, wonders about the soul and if she has one. At any moment, she feels she might vomit. She looks up with the arrival of her food, sees men and women pass by the window dressed in their finery. She realizes suddenly that it is Sunday, and she feels a sudden longing for the familiar Catholic rituals of her youth. The Sunday best, the growling stomach near the end of mass, Father Anthony's limp handshake on the church steps, the after-church drive to buy those little danish at the Italian bakery. Then, the short trip home to find her father still settled around the dining-room table, drinking his coffee in that worn, navy robe, working through the Sunday paper.

The father has escaped into his office for a quiet Sunday of work. Flipping through depositions, memorandums of case law, he sees suddenly the answer that will win the case for his client. "Guerin v. Polstar, Inc., 1979," he says into his Dictaphone. "The Plaintiff does not have standing if he cannot show injury as direct result of defendant's alleged negligent and/or criminal action." He fills in the forms that measure the value of his time, puts the file on his secretary's desk and leaves a note to himself to begin the brief on Monday with the history of Guerin. Strolling the perimeter of his corner office, two walls of windows the marker of his professional ascent, he stands for a moment and surveys

the new leaves greening the trees, marking the creeping spring, and realizes Kate has been gone now for almost four months. Digging in the
bottom drawer of his desk, he pulls the private investigator's file from
its hiding place and flips through the pages. Once again, he reads.

Sean stalks the mall with a crew from school. In the arcade, they swap
cigarettes and work the joysticks that move Pac Men, the track-balls
that shoot Centipedes. He hangs out with his friends, Charlie, John and
Brad, making plans for later that night, wondering how he can get out
to go to that beer blast down by the river without having his parents
deny him permission? *This is a school night.* Not for a moment does he
think of his missing sister.

John nudges him, "Amy-Beth coming out tonight? You finally
gonna make a move?" "We're just friends," Sean says. But he's thinking,
I want to kiss her so fucking much. And then suddenly, there she is
again, in his head, Kate, he thinks, would tell me what to do. His friends
laugh, "Yeah. Sure you are."

The mother sits in the quiet of the parish church, her knees stiff on the
kneeler. The last Mass ended an hour ago; she did not grace the as-
sembly with her presence. She's missed church for twenty-three weeks,
not gone to confession, not tasted the communion wafer melting on
her tongue. She prays first by rote, working the rosary beads under finger, "Hail Mary full of grace . . . Our Father who art in Heaven . . . I
believe in God, the Father Almighty, creator of Heaven and Earth . . ."
After a few cycles, she plops the beads into her pocket, feeling empty,
and turns to the statue of Mary standing near the sanctuary, her blue-
robed arms held wide, as if she's waiting to pull the mother into an
embrace, "Mother of God, I offer a prayer so you might bring my
daughter home safely, to fix my family. I pray to you as one mother to
another. As a mother who has lost her hope."

. . .

Mary stands, silent, near the sanctuary, her blue-robed arms held wide, as if she's waiting to pull the mother into an embrace.

Kate rides out onto the plain with four old ranch hands, silent in the rising sun. Their breath spills out of their mouths in wisps of steam, the horses steady and snorting under their burdens. At the fence line, they swing down and Kate takes her place with the post hole digger, scooping half frozen earth out in giant plugs. The snow's mostly melted, only islands of once-giant drifts remain in the face of spring, and this fence must go in before the warmer air brings its bustle back to the ranch. There's little chatter, and as Kate works, she moves ahead of the hand with the posts, gets herself a little space. Looking out at the world stretching off as far as she can see, the buttes rising on the horizon, she feels a pleasant ache along her back and arms. She takes comfort in the working of her muscles, in this foreign landscape. I've never seen colors like this before, she thinks, these reds and tans and browns.

The father reads: "Katherine Mahoney, 19, missing since January 5. Parents listed missing-person report with New Jersey State Police on January 7 (attached). Family worried that subject may be mentally unstable, though they did not share fears with the police. Subject closed checking account at United Jersey Bank, Hillsboro Branch, 8:02 am January 5. Funds received: $614.92. Her car, 1979 AMC Pacer, orange, sold to Beyer Used Cars, Iowa City, Iowa for $325 on January 9. Subject appears to have continued further west."

Patty heads down Broadway, weaving around the clusters of people moving slowly, talking, checking shop windows. With speed, she thinks, she can fight back the nausea, the pounding in her head. Trying to walk faster than the crowd, she chafes when her progress is slowed by families stretched across the width of the sidewalk. Against her will, she checks the faces of strangers, the shapes sleeping under blankets in side street doorways. She is certain Kate has made her way here, to this city where she could lose herself in the clutter of its streets, where she would seem normal. On her own excursions downtown, on those threatening streets east of First Avenue, coming out of after-hours clubs into the sunlight, Patty has begun to check the sidewalk and building murals, looking for the flourish of Kate's signature in the corner, wondering when she will appear in the gossip column of the *Voice* alongside Basquiat and Haring.

When Kate first left—Patty getting ready to head back to school for the start of her first spring semester—the raw worry clear in her mother's voice sent Patty reeling. She had known, known since at least her sophomore year of high school that something was wrong—horribly wrong—with Kate. All those things the parents laughed off as eccentricity born of Kate's talent, her mood shifts, the hours Kate spent just looking at a blade of grass or the light reflecting off a parked car's windshield, Patty knew were markers. She knew because Kate confided in her for a while, told her stories about how the buttons on her shirts were pressing on her windpipe, stealing her air. And, in brighter moods, sober, Kate spoke of color the way Patty had only experienced it under the influence of window pane and mushrooms. Spoke to her of color and its language as if she heard it, heard it and listened to it the way other people listened to music. But Patty kept silent until the afternoon before Kate left, when Kate naked in that tree and the cuts on her legs added too many pounds to the weight of the secret.

And even the things that worried the parents: Kate's drinking, the pot they saw, the other drugs they suspected though they couldn't have named—the ludes and acid—Patty began to understand as self-medication. Still, she held her tongue. Held it because Kate's careless indiscretions shielded Patty from prying parental eyes. Held it because she didn't want to believe it could be that bad and because, most of the time, Kate was up and when she was up, she was the life of the party even when no party was raging.

Nora reads, "Lush, dense green croons in a deep bass. Its sound so deep it lands in the middle of my shoulder blades and I want to add harmony in mold colored, scat singing brown to level out the sound. Black is not the color of death. Black, in natural light, bursts with life. It swirls and eddies and dips like swing. In physics they taught me that black was the absence of light. But take a young girl, layering crayon over crayon and she makes black. Stare at black. Looking at it hard, I catch a blue there, a red here, a vibrant purple bursting in the corner."

Kate slams the post hole digger into the ground, works it deep, feels it crush through the layer of frost to the soft earth underneath. She closes the craw of its metal jaws and lifts. The muscles in her back ache. A drop of sweat runs from her armpit down her side and, for a moment, she can feel only its progress as it traces a path to where her jeans hang low on her hips. Her arms are strong, her legs powerful. She digs. She's well rested. At night, after a full day's work, after gathering around a meal with the other hands, she retires to her bunk, writes in her diary for a moment, then sleeps. It's the hard, deep sleep of physical exhaustion. And when she wakes before the sun with the others and drinks her coffee before heading out, she thinks, I am normal.

She hasn't heard the colors' voices since she started working here. Her workshirts have most of their buttons; she has not had the energy or time to be afraid. Not once has she forced herself to sleep with the bottle of blackberry brandy tucked amongst her things or thought about opening the bottle with the last of her Quaaludes.

.   .   .

Sean separates from his friends, walking the bright fluorescent corridors of the mall. He dodges shoppers laden with bags, nods at Patty's old, high school boyfriend selling loose joints near the food court. He looks at faces, not realizing he's doing it, staring so hard that people turn away and hurry past him. Slipping outside, he sits on the curb and lights a cigarette. From inside of his jacket he pulls out a letter. The envelope is soft as fabric, worn from foldings and unfoldings, readings and rereadings. In fading green ink, the slight scratch of Kate's pen. He thinks her voice is there in the curve of the S starting his name. Slipping the note out, he unwraps it, careful to keep it from tearing along fold lines. He reads.

In the half-heat of an early New Jersey spring, tulips tentatively poke their way up from the shelter of their bulbs. Daffodils unfurled their yellow blooms two weeks prior, as if nature were joining the Church calender in marking Easter. And though the last of the winter snow, pushed in heaping mounds by the public work's plows, lingers on roadsides, crusted with grime, each day feels a touch warmer, the resurrection of spring on schedule, as promised.

The mother walks towards the front door of the church, hoping Father Anthony isn't in the Sacristy waiting to waylay her with questions about her absence from Mass. She absently dips her hand into the holy water font and makes a haphazard sign of the cross. Slipping into the front seat of her car, she turns the key, and starts towards the mall where she has to pick up Sean. As she drives, out of her way, not in the direction of home, she feels anger perking up her chest, spreading out over her arms, leaving her face hot. Kate should be doing this. How dare her. It was part of the deal when we bought that car for her.

More and more angry, she drives. The traffic pisses her off. God-damn her, she thinks, God, God-damn her. The wait at a light makes her punch the steering wheel. As she turns in to the mall parking lot, the circling cars and exiting shoppers, some mothers and daughters together on a normal Sunday afternoon, lets loose the anguish from under her anger. She finds herself saying under her breath in the incantation of prayer, "Please come home, please let the doctors be wrong, please be okay, please come home."

The father flips through the pages of the report, "Two weeks after disappearing, the subject makes contact with her younger brother, Sean Mahoney, in the form of a letter postmarked Bozeman, Montana. Letter indicates she is safe, does not want to be found, and is earning enough money to survive. It does not specify her whereabouts."

At 72nd Street, Patty hops a downtown bus. Snarled in the crush of Sunday shopping traffic, the bus plods through Columbus Circle, skirts the edge of Central Park, and hangs a right on Seventh Avenue. Patty looks at the faces passing out on the street, ponders the night before, piecing together how, exactly, she made it home. She recalls being in a club, drinking gin and tonics, getting wired from blow in the ladies' room. Someone slipped her a pill, late, told her it would bring her down. She remembers the horse pill, remembers thinking, "A lude! Kate's favorite. Don't see these much anymore," and washing it down with the last of the gin.

This morning, the pressure of a hangover waking her early in her dorm room. Suddenly, she remembers, the cab home, slumped against the door, trying to keep up with the driver's conversation just to stay awake. The bus driver calls "Fiftieth Street," Patty hops off on a whim, and feels that miraculous moment when under the influence of coffee, time and fried food, a hangover lifts.

.   .   .

Kate digs her last hole, watches as the post is wedged into place, the razor wire stretched taut, the fence finished. The hands gather around, pass a thermos of coffee. Their talk is minimal, thank you's and nice work. This silence, Kate thinks, this space. This vast, vast space. They all slip back into their down vests to keep the sweat from cooling on their bodies, to keep their own bodies from bringing on sickness. The others don't know what to make of her, this girl from the East who has come here and worked herself to exhaustion. After these months, they respect her, she has kept to herself, done the work asked of her, never complained. Standing with them, after a hard morning of work, Kate thinks, These people, this work, this life, is peace.

But in the silence, she also misses her family. Misses Patty and her skill at fooling adults, all adults, into thinking she's never broken a rule. Wishes she could have fooled them all herself, wishes she could have kept a lid on things that way. But bitter too about Patty's betrayal when she found her in the tree. She just wanted to see, that was all. It wasn't a problem.

She even misses Nora, Nora who seems to think that Kate is her chauffeur and regards that sold-off Pacer as the limousine that should take her to the barn or the mall whenever she wants. And of course, Sean. Sean who idolizes her, she knows that, she likes basking in the reflection of his admiration. But she also genuinely likes him; she can see him growing up into a guy so unlike the guys from her high school days. A guy who thinks he wants to cook for Christ's sake, she thinks, laughing out loud on a Montana ranch.

Sean reads: "Favorite brother, Alive and well. Found work. A cold here like you'd never guess. A cold that makes me aware I have bones. So beautiful. No one told me, ever, that dirt could be purple. Hope you are well. Tell Mom and Dad *I'm living*. I'll be in touch. Love, Katy-did."

.   .   .

The mother drives up to the place she's agreed to meet Sean. Sees him fold that damn letter from Kate back into its worn origami, tuck it in his back pocket. Sees him try to casually drop a cigarette to the curb as her car comes into view. Her anger rising again as he stands to open the door, she thinks, Coward.

When he gets into the car, slouching, all akimbo arms and awkward legs bumbling around until he's seated and buckled in, she suddenly wants to hurt him the way she's been hurt, not thinking for a moment that he might already be hurting, that his sullenness around the house has as much to do with his missing Kate as it does with his being fifteen. Glancing at him as she pulls out of the parking lot, she says, harshly, "You know, she just walked out on you too," and then immediately wishes she could pull the words back. Sean, stung, having thought this himself lying awake in bed at night, but knowing too that she chose to write to *him* and not to anyone else, calmly says, "She left because she couldn't stand your *shit.*" There's a sarcastic chill in his voice the mother has never heard before, and she smashes the brakes, stopping the car dead in the middle of the road, and turns to him, furious, "Don't you dare talk to me with that sort of language or that tone. I'm still your mother."

Nora, confused and bored, reads on, "The pastels are not spring. They sing sad showtunes of old women wilting, of a prime past. They set me on edge. Red is not love or hate or anger. Seeing red is a poor choice of words. Red is death. Hard reds, vermilion and crimson, play funeral marches. Burgundy sounds bag pipes. Yellow is hate. Nora's old kindergarten drawings crackling on the fridge—those harsh yellow suns seething in the corner. Green is love, torch songs in the deeper shades, the hunters and sages. They are close with blue. The longing of blue. Navy is Billie singing about Paris and April. As it fades towards gray, it's an old Irish tenor beerily singing along to 'Danny Boy.' The gray of Dad's eyes."

. . .

The father stares at the family pictures on the edges of his desk with-
out seeing. Looks at his diplomas on the wall. Harvard, Columbia Law.
Glances down at the report in his lap. We were happy, he thinks. A good
family. Kate helped around the house, drove Nora and Sean around.
The kids fought. All kids fight. Good grades. Patty got into Barnard.
But. Looking at the pictures on his desk, studying them now for hints
in their faces that things could possibly be different than they appear.
His eyes fall back on the last paragraph of the report, "The New Jersey
State Police concluded their investigation when it became apparent that
the subject, a legal adult who posed no threat to herself or others, was
gone of her own volition. The subject is findable, it is my belief she has
found transient work someplace in Montana, perhaps as a waitress,
paid in cash. There is no record of her income being reported by any
business. At the request of the family, my investigation has been halted."

*The investigator calls the father at his office a few days after the mother has
steamed open the letter to Sean, read its contents and resealed it. The mother and
the father argue long into the night, the mother wanting to press on, the father saying, "No. She's gone. If we push her, she'll never come back." The mother insist-
ing, "She's in danger." The father, recalling the violent bluster of his own father
pushing him out of the house, his desire when he went away to school to never, ever
come back, tells the mother, "Give her time. Wait. She'll keep writing Sean, she'll
come home." When the investigator calls, the father says, "We've decided to stop."*

Months later, no new news, no word to Sean, and the father thinks,
Did I do the right thing?

Sean, riding in the car with his mother, sees the anger etched on her
face. He tries to figure out how to soothe the damage he's wrought, but
is afraid of *that tone* creeping into his voice again. Finally, after the silence has grown too strong, his voice drips with *that tone,* "I'm sorry."

The mother glances away from the road for a moment and wrinkles her nose, "You smell like an ashtray." Christ, Sean thinks, ever since Dad quit she smells everything, but he doesn't say anything. She knows anyway. "At least have the guts to do it openly," the mother says.

Patty stands on Fifth Avenue in front of the grand facade of Saint Patrick's Cathedral, hesitates for a moment, then pushes inside. The gloom, cool stone and dark wood, patches of brilliant stained-glass light, the lingering scent of the morning Mass' incense, feels like a sort of home. Kneeling in a pew, she prays, "Bless me father for I have sinned." Silently she recites her confessional litany of deception, lies, lust, missed Sundays and Holy Days of Obligation. She finishes, looks up at the high ceiling, realizes she is sorry for none of it, thinks, I don't need forgiveness.

What does she want then? Why is she here? She has everything she could possibly need. Her life, at last, under her own control, no one to answer to but herself. She is young, smart, her options are wide open; her future glitters before her. She has friends, she takes lovers. When she enters the smoking section in the dining hall or comes into a party, the room reconfigures itself so she's at the center. Even mere acquaintances will tell her their darkest secrets; she's heard about thefts, listened to tails of unrequited love, heard confessions of closeted homosexuality. It's always been this way for her, easy, but it secretly embarrasses her, this neediness of her peers. Why can't they manage on their own?

Flipping ahead in Kate's diary, Nora reads, "Bad day. In class, working with collage, the clutter got to me. Without realizing, I popped the buttons off the collar of my shirt. I knew they would choke me. The racket of all those scraps, slicing them with that mat knife, trying to arrange them to quiet the noise. It sounded like screams when I sliced with the mat knife. I tried to concentrate on the music from the stereo. Too much, I couldn't concentrate, and cut my hand. That quieted things."

The father stares out his office window, filled with a sudden desperate wish to understand his children, to speak with each one of them and learn what he's done wrong. What he can do to fix things for all of them. Nora is too young, her world still thankfully safe. Sean he can't speak to, not now, and not about this. He's never been able to get through to that boy, and Sean's vision is cloudy about all things Kate. He sees her going as somehow *heroic*. So he turns, as he's always done when trying to learn his children, to Patty, the only one who speaks with him as if he were a person and not just a father. He dials her dorm room at Barnard, gets her roommate and leaves a message for her to call him at home. Gathering his coat, his briefcase, he decides he might as well head off.

The mother turns the car into the driveway, cuts the engine and looks at her only son. He stares out the window, tapping his fingers on the door handle in time to some tune playing in his head. She softens, re-alizes she can't afford to lose another one, thinks, I'll give it to him when we get inside.

Two days earlier. The mother arrives home first because of a district-wide half day and flips through the mail. Bill, bill, bill, catalog, Sports Illustrated, *letter from Nora's school, bill, small package addressed to Sean. Looking closer, she sees the pre-cise curves of Kate's handwriting, reads the Bozeman, Montana, postmark, shakes the box. Rattle, rattle. Holds it up to the light, hefts it, puts her fingers into the creases of its wrapping, as if she's going to open this package not addressed to her. But she doesn't. Not this time. She knows it won't hold any clues, that what's in*

here is meant for Sean. She remembers the dirty feeling last time, holding the let-
ter over steam pouring from the kettle. But because she's jealous that Kate is turn-
ing to Sean and not to her, because she's angry that her daughter doesn't trust her
to understand, she takes the small box and stows it in her dresser, decides, I'll wait.

Nora hears the car in the driveway, the opening creak of the front
door. Quickly, she stows the diary in the box, pushes the box back
under the bed, and slips out of Kate's room. Down the stairs, her heart
pounding, guilt spreads like sunburn up her neck and into her cheeks.
"Hey, Mom. Hi, Sean. What's going on?"

Patty, back uptown, finds her roommate blissfully not at home. She
gathers up some books, slips them into her backpack, then finds the
note pinned to her desk. "Your father called. Call back at home." She
looks at the phone, sees the flashing light blinking on the answering
machine, the luxury of her roommate's wealth, and presses PLAY. Beep.
Hang-up. Beep. Hang-up. Beep. "Hey Patty, it's Bob from Identity and
the Self, we're having a study party tonight. Gimme a call." Beep. Hang-
up. Beep. "Patty, it's Jason from the other night. Wondering if you
wanted to get together? Six, six, seven, nineteen fifty-four." Beep.
Settling on her bed, she picks up the phone, starts to dial home, then
sets the phone back in its receiver, thinks, Kate's in those hang-ups. And
who the fuck is Jason?

The father puts his car in PARK, leaves the engine running, stares at his
house, notes that the mother's car is in the driveway, turns the stereo up
louder. For a moment there, in the closing riffs of a Coltrane solo, he
closes his eyes, descends into the slight comfort to be found in the
depths of the music, and, in his own way, he remembers and prays that
Kate is all right.

. . .

1957. The father, not yet the father, but Patrick Mahoney, high school senior. A star athlete and good student; he's entertaining scholarship offers, considering the enticements of the Baltimore Orioles A Ball farm team, pondering the future offered by his acceptance into the pantheon of the Ivy Leagues. There are things he doesn't know: he has not heard the rumbling of the Beats, not yet found the rhythms of jazz, not learned all the secrets concealed by his girlfriend's Catholic will. There are also things he knows: the feel of a baseball's seams spinning off the fingers of his left hand when he breaks off a great curve, the story of his parents coming over to America from Galway to find the United States in the belly of a depression, the hard work that got them where they are today, the giddy, bloated drunk of Pabst Blue Ribbon, the violent, unreadable bends of his father's moods.

He knows this. He knows when his father is "tired" and has locked himself in his dark study with that heavy green bottle, when he hasn't ventured from his bed for days at a time, and his mother tiptoes around the house, that his father is close to breaking and he must do anything to avoid setting him off. To avoid raising his Irish and hearing his lingering brogue break with anger. The sting of a belt has become, after years and years, bearable. His father seems to know this. And Patrick has grown bigger and stronger than his father, both father and son know the time for beatings has stopped. Now there's the new torture. Patrick made to kneel on uncooked rice strewn on the cement floor of the basement. Made to kneel until his knees, bleeding and raw, stain the grains under him, while his father sits in the dark in the corner, smoking Lucky Strike after Lucky Strike, cradling a shotgun.

Not until November 1963, Patrick's mother dead for almost a year, Patrick himself a father for the first time, does his own father, bathed in the flicker of a black-and-white television broadcasting the shooting of that young, Irish Catholic President, turn that shotgun on himself. At the funeral, next to his veiled wife cradling their first daughter, Katherine, Patrick recites the prayers by rote until the time comes to kneel. There in church, at his father's funeral Mass, the soft leather of the kneeler seems to dig into his knees like a million knife points, and he vows, "Never again, except when my children marry, will I darken the door of a church."

. . .

Sitting in his car, in the spring of 1982, the father thinks, Did that bastard put something in me that I've given to my children?

Sean takes a small box from his mother as she explains, "This came on Friday." He sees that it is addressed to him in Kate's hand, "How long were you going to wait to give this to me?" The mother doesn't answer for a moment, just shrugs and says simply, "I'm sorry." Sean stares at her, shakes the box, hears its intriguing rattle and starts to work it open. Inside there is a pastel sketch that looks like the plains rising off into a butte. On the back, he can hear Kate's voice in the inscription, "This is where I live." He lays it flat on the breakfast-nook counter, studying the sure lines and the way the deft smudges lend depth and texture. Over his shoulder, he can feel his mother come to stand behind him, can hear her sharp intake of breath. "It's beautiful," she says, mirroring his own thoughts.

Turning back to the box, he also finds a package of Dunhills, a battered Zippo, extra flints, and a bottle of lighter fluid. He tries the lighter, it spits out a small flame. Looking up at his mother, he opens the Dunhills, pulls off the gold foil and wedges a cigarette into the corner of his mouth. He works the lighter, touches its flame to the tobacco, draws a deep drag, and exhales through his nose. It tastes like gas stations smell. He watches as his mother shakes her head, turns and leaves the room. Looking over at Nora sitting at the dining-room table, he sees her shocked look, "What?" "Nice going, Sean." "Oh, fuck you." Feeling ridiculous, holding a burning cigarette in the family dining room, he looks for a place to put it out. In the hutch, he finds an ashtray left over from his father's smoking days.

Carrying the ashtray over to the kitchen garbage can to empty it out, to erase the tangible evidence of this transgression, he's exhilarated and ashamed all at once. Exhilarated knowing once again that she sent something to *him* and not to anyone else. Ashamed of snapping at his mother in the car. Exhilarated by showing her *he is an adult* and can smoke if he wants to smoke.

Patty dials the number she has known for her entire life, for as long as she can remember. She waits for the phone to ring.

The mother stands in the hall, not sure where she should go or what she should do. She can't yell at Sean, can't take him to task for smoking—she *dared him* to do it. What is happening to her children? Kate gone, the ever-present gnawing of that knowledge even in the moments when she's happy and not really brooding on it. How long it's been since her father's castoff oxford shirts became smocks streaked with flat tempera colors. Patty, not calling, up to God-knows-what in that city, but at least keeping her grades up. Is that girl with her nose buried in those yellow Nancy Drew books still there someplace? Nora, who seems to have no friends except for Kathleen, is changing so fast, seeming to lose some of her joy as she grows. How can it feel like just yesterday that she was gurgling happily in Pat's arms? And Sean a moody teenager, cursing at her, smoking in the house, sulking around and coming home with beer on his breath on Friday nights. What has happened to her brood? Where have they gone? Can they ever be returned to her?

The father comes in the front door and smells the lingering cigarette smoke in the air, thinks, Huh. Feeling a craving coming over him, he reaches into his pockets for a hard candy to suck on. "Hello?" he calls, "Where's everyone?" He finds Nora sitting at the dining-room table, swinging her legs aimlessly. Kissing the top of her head, he only half minds when she squirms away, "Anybody else home?" "Mom's around someplace," she says, "Sean's in his room, probably smoking a cigarette." "No one likes a tattletale, Nora," the father says as he heads towards his study.

The safety of his study reassures him: the dark wall paneling, the orderly file cabinet, the row of law books on the shelf. In here, he has music from the cheap little stereo he bought just for this room, the work he brings home, a decanter of good Scotch. In here, he doesn't have to deal with the mess of their lives conjured by the other parts of the house. In here, there is no hint of Kate's absence. With the door shut and a glass of single malt in hand, he doesn't have to worry that his son is not the strapping athlete of his dreams, doesn't have to think about Sean's pierced ear or awkward skinny limbs that will never catch a winning touchdown pass or stroke a double to center field. He doesn't have to remember that Nora isn't six years old anymore, doesn't have to see the surprise of her growing up each time he bumps into her around the house. In here, he doesn't have to deal with his wife's despair. He can read and work in peace and, when he *chooses,* his thoughts can linger on the problems of their lives. But, when he's in here, they all know not to bother him, that when the door is closed, *he is busy.* And for hours, he can sit undisturbed and not think about any of it all.

The phone rings. Sean stows his bong in the closet, the smoke still heavy in his room. He reaches for the extension under a pile of laundry on his floor. The mother, startled from her reverie, heads for the phone on the table at the end of the hallway. Nora leaps up to grab the line in the kitchen. The father stretches his hand towards the chirping phone on his desk. "Hello?" "Hello!" "Hello." "Hello—"

In the bunk house of a Montana ranch, Kate, overwhelmed by four voices at once, presses two fingers down on the pay phone's disconnect button, the dial tone interrupted by a small symphony of loose change spilling into the phone's bowels.

Patty, trying to call her father, gets a busy signal.

Nora, Sean, the mother and the father listen to silence on four separate phone extensions. "Hello?" the father tries one more time. No answer. Sean says, "Crank call." The mother says, "Since everyone's here, dinner in half an hour."

Sean rummages through the pile of records he's carted up from Kate's room, drops *Dark Side of the Moon* onto his turntable, turns the volume down low. He lies back on his bed and fires up a Dunhill, careful to blow the smoke out the open window above his head. He plots his escape that night. A pile of pillows under the covers, the fire ladder down to the ground, then the walk through the woods to the river. A walk he knows by heart from when he was younger, eight or nine, and he used to go down there with Patty to see the debris left by the last generation of high school parties. He's going to kiss Amy-Beth tonight. Before Kate left, he'd told her about this crush he had, this crush on a dark, brooding girl with all-black clothes, a Nikon camera always slung around her neck. Kate had given him tips, and they'd sort of worked. He and Amy-Beth were friends now, they talked for hours on the phone, hung out at lunch, went out with groups of people. She took pictures of him, black-and-white shots that had him smoking, long hair over his face, pictures he thought *were really him*. But he didn't know how to make the leap from friends to something else. Friday night, they'd been out at some party, drunk, stoned, whatever, sitting together on a beanbag chair as the party raged around them. She'd been pressed up against him, all he could feel was her leg against his, and she'd said, "Sean, you're my best friend, like a brother," and put her head on his shoulder. And though his heart was breaking, though he already had three fucking sisters and wanted a girlfriend, he ruffled her hair, lightly kissed a spot he knew she wouldn't feel, and said, "You too." He was thinking, I'll take what I can get.

The mother trudges up the stairs to the third floor and knocks on Sean's door. Hears him call, "Just a minute." She pictures him, crushing out the cigarette, trying to clear the air of smoke, and she almost laughs. When he pulls open the door, she can feel the cooler blast of air from the open window, smell the sweet cloying remnants of marijuana in the air, a smell she has laundered out of Kate's and Patty's clothes and now Sean's. She sits on his bed, motions for him to join her and says, "If Kate gets in touch with you and she sounds weird, will you tell me, please?" "Not necessarily." "Jesus Christ, Sean." "Everything she does is weird to you." The mother, exasperated, says, "You know what I mean."

Sean, at this moment, has no idea what his mother means.

Nora passes the mother coming down the stairs as she slowly heads up. She walks past the grand mess spilling out of her own bedroom, up the second flight of stairs. As she goes, she checks the flat white of the walls, the patterned reds and blues and golds of the worn Oriental rug running the length of the hallway, straining to hear the sounds, thinking on the words in Kate's diary, "Colors sing to me." Nothing.

On the third-floor landing, Sean's door is shut, the KEEP OUT! sign hanging at an uneasy angle. Underneath, with a thick black Sharpie he has clawed, "THIS MEANS YOU NORA!!!" She stands for a moment, shifting her weight back and forth, thinking, Forget it. Ask him. Forget it. She swings open the door without knocking, sees her brother sprawled out on his bed, nodding his head to Pink Floyd, trying and failing to blow smoke rings. Some motion, some noise she has made, breaks his reverie. "Get the fuck out of here Nora," he says. But he says it wearily, without punch. A year ago, he would've sprung from the bed and chased her down the stairs, caught her from behind and hit her, hard, in the kidneys. Always fighting, they've not yet noticed a sort of cease-fire that's come into effect these last few months.

A cease-fire brokered mainly by Kate who always gets angry with Sean when he hits Nora. When Sean and Nora get into it, whether Nora has taunted Sean until his quiet temper is unleashed or Sean has snapped at Nora without provocation, Kate sides with Nora, ignoring Sean, sometimes yelling at him, once or twice punching him on the arm the way he's punched Nora. The threat of her distance from him, the unwieldy weight of her anger, has tamed him. Caused him to re-think his reactions, cool his temper. Though Nora wouldn't say it or see it, though Sean would never admit it, the justice meted out by Kate over their disputes is causing them both to grow up, causing them to mature. The justice meted out by Kate is building a frame that will someday let them grow into friends.

The father picks up the phone in his study, flips through his Rolodex, finds the card he's looking for. He dials, squinting at the small numbers, reading, "Investigator" in bold print under the man's name. The phone rings. Once, twice, five times. An answering service picks up. The father demurs when asked to leave a message and hangs up the phone.

Patty calls home again. Again, the line is busy.

. . .

Kate finishes a late-afternoon meal with the other hands. The day's work is done, the free hours lurking ahead fill her with anticipation settling like weights on the scale of her head. She takes a cup of coffee out on to the porch and just stares at the colors of this barren, beautiful place. Suddenly, softly, she can hear them singing to her. Back in her room, she pulls a sack from under her bed. Produces pens and pastels and the big drawing pad she's mostly ignored. Back on the porch, she sits in a chair, stares off at the horizon and listens, then begins to scratch quick, frantic lines onto the page.

The early-evening air picks up a slight chill, a reminder that it's not yet summer. It will be warm-sweater and light-jacket weather tonight. But after the long drag of February and after March's indecision, when the thermometer holds its descent at fifty-three degrees this evening, those lucky enough to be outside will consider it warm. In the front yards of neighborhoods like the Mahoneys', husband-and-wife teams finish an afternoon of mulching and arranging new plots of annual flowers, tossing dirt-crusted garden gloves and trowels into the garage before heading inside to wash up. Vegetable gardens have been re-tilled and seeded; with all the recent rain, the ground is yielding, the air loamy. Newly returned songbirds flutter back to their nests and a lone cricket chirps its call, singing to the approaching dark.

Sean stares at Nora standing in his doorway, surprised to find himself not angry. She used to come up, open the door, wrap her hands around the inside and outside knobs, lift her legs from the floor and swing. Just her feet touching the ground in his room caused him to rage, to chase her, to hit her. And he wasn't sorry, ever. She deserved it, she asked for it, she sometimes tormented him just to get him in trouble. "What?" he asks now. "Is Kate coming back?" "How the fuck should I know?" He doesn't want to talk about this, he wants to think about Amy–Beth, and what the hell is Nora doing in his room anyway? "I read her diary," he hears Nora blurt, "It was weird." Those words cause that old anger to rise again. He gets off the bed, chases her halfway down the stairs and grabs her collar, his left hand balling into a fist. Nora flinches, curling up around herself in feeble protection. Then suddenly, he pushes her away, "You're an asshole. Don't you respect anyone's privacy?" But, as he turns up the stairs, he thinks, I've read it too.

Patty gives up on the phone, slips her flask into her pocket and heads down to the dining hall. Making her selections, she watches the jovial black women spooning out heaps of food onto her plate. Beige, she thinks, I'm eating beige food. In the dining room, she ambles to her regular table in the smoking section and makes her way to an empty seat. She arches her eyebrows as she sits, cracking a joke, reveling in the laughter. Pulling the flask from her jacket, she sings, "A spoonful of sugar helps the medicine go down," and pours a healthy shot into her grape juice. She offers the flask around, caps it after two of her friends have poured out small measures and takes a slug of her drink. The hum of conversation flows around her. A girl from her hall swings by their table on her way out, leans in next to Patty whispering, "You going to be home later? I need to talk." "Going to the library. Come by later." Someone from her Philosophy course wonders, "You solid on the Aquinas stuff?" "Piece of cake."

But, as she eats the overly salty food, as she sips from her doctored glass of juice, as she jokes and joshes and dispenses advice, she pities them all. Pities these people because of their reliance on the advice and affection of others. I, she thinks, make my own way, on my terms. None of this needy crap for me.

. . .

The mother sets the table, laying out the plates, the silver, the napkins. She finds herself holding, as she has at least once a week since Kate left, an extra setting she has to put away unused. "DINNER'S READY," she calls. From their places in the house the family clambers to the table. As they sit, the father looks to the mother, waiting for her to say grace. As she has done for these last months, she holds his eyes for a moment, shakes her head, and starts to ladle food onto her plate. Nora, fussy, picks. The father pours a glass of wine for the mother and one for himself. Sean spoons big helpings of the vegetables onto his plate, a portion of salad, some noodles in butter. When the roast comes his way, he passes it to his father without taking even a slice. The father looks at him, at his skinny frame, for a moment the word "wimp" forms on his tongue but he chokes it down. Thinking of his own time on the gridiron, the shutouts pitched back in his day, and then his own son's dismal attempts at sports, that sissy game soccer and his yearly stint as a Little League right fielder, he says, "You need to eat protein to grow. Everyone knows vegetables are a side dish." "Whatever Dad." There's some small talk, some questions about homework, but mostly in silence, they eat.

Kate sketches, smudges pastels, listens. From time to time, someone from the ranch pokes his head out, looks, decides not to ask her questions, not to bother her. Paper piles near her feet, sheets ripped from the sketchbook. The housekeeper, one of the few other women around, comes out and lowers herself down beside Kate, rocking her weight on her heels. "Everything okay, honey?" Kate likes this woman, the quiet efficiency of her movements and the kind way she takes care of all these people like a mother. Taking a break, Kate turns to her, "Fine," she says, "Just remembering what something is like."

It's all been coming back to her—the thrill of working with her hands to make images on paper that do more than just look like something, creating pictures that *are something.* Finding the emotions lurking in objects or nature and drawing them out so they can be seen by others. She feels the desire to see again. To look closely at color and texture, to hear the joyous callings of the shifting patterns of sunlight on breeze-blown leaves. But as she's been drawing, she feels as if she's failing. Failing to capture what's in this place because it isn't part of her— she's coming to realize she's a spectator here, a visitor. And with that knowledge comes also the knowledge that her material, the landscapes and portraits and still lifes that make her who she is, are back East, back with the family she's been missing. With the subtle failures of her shadings, visible only to her, comes the knowledge that soon she must be heading home.

"Anything I can do for you?" asks the housekeeper. "No," Kate says, "but thank you. I've got some thinking to do."

Sean finishes his food, asks to be excused, races upstairs to get his homework out of the way. Sort of like Patty, he thinks, getting the school work finished so they don't suspect.

Nora goes to her room, pulls the phone in from the hall and dials Kathleen, hoping to catch her back already from her trip. She is and they make plans on what to wear tomorrow and Nora agrees to ask Billy Parker if he likes Kathleen. She hangs up the phone, drafts the note she'll give to Billy, then copies it out, meticulously, onto pink paper, drawing and shading the boxes he's supposed to check, one for if he likes Kathleen, one for if he doesn't. As she folds the note into the required hall-passing shape, a little square with neatly tucked in edges, she thinks, Billy Parker is a stupid, pimply jerk. But I'd do anything for Kathleen.

She changes into her nightgown, locks the door and lies back on her bed remembering last weekend. The night of the big balloon festival she slept over at Kathleen's house. Chattering late into the night as they lay in her pink canopy bed, wearing only underwear and old white undershirts stolen from their fathers' drawers. Together they poured over *Seventeen, Cosmopolitan* and Kathleen's parents' copy of *The Joy of Sex*. Lingering over the line drawings in that book, working from the advice found in those magazines, they practice kissing on one of Kathleen's stuffed bears. They do that for a while, filled with a mixture of curiosity and embarrassment, until Kathleen leans back on her bed and says, "But the bear doesn't kiss back."

In the silence that follows, Nora sees the obvious solution, they could kiss one another to see what it's like. But raising that prospect seems somehow wrong though also palpably exciting. Her palms have gone sweaty and the pulse in her head thumps quickly in time to the ticking of Kathleen's Mickey Mouse alarm clock. Finally, shyly, stumbling around the words, she says, "What if we pretend one of us is the boy?" Right away, as if the thought has been in her head as well, Kathleen agrees, "You go first."

So Nora presses her mouth to her friend's mouth, and they push closed lips against closed lips until Nora pulls away. Kathleen giggles, "That wasn't so great. I think we should open our mouths, and you're supposed to get on top of me." Rolling on top of her friend, wedging one leg between Kathleen's, one on the outside, making a four-legged creature, Nora lowers her mouth to her friend's mouth again. She watches Kathleen close her eyes and closes her own. Working on instinct, Nora dances her tongue into Kathleen's mouth, touches the tip of her friend's tongue, traces over the rough ridges of her molars. Breaking the kiss, lifting her head and opening her eyes, she stares down at Kathleen's face, shining under the 60-watt glow of the night-table lamp until Kathleen opens her eyes. "That," Kathleen says, "was better."

Nora, feeling her body is somehow both soft and taut—that new feeling she's felt from the jets in the YMCA pool and in the shower when it's okay to touch herself—leans in and they kiss again. Establishing a rhythm that's half play, half desire, getting their hands into the act as they're rolling now, tickling, giggling around the edges of their kissing, blowing raspberries onto each other's neck. Those T-shirts are pushed higher by tracing hands, baby-fat stomachs sticking together with sweat, and Nora is kissing little flea-bite kisses on Kathleen's neck and looping her tongue around the conch of her ear and they are bolder with each passing second. Pausing, they push off the T-shirts and are back at it. Nora, rolled onto her back with Kathleen pressing as much of her body into her as she can, rocking against her, hears Kathleen say, "I'm going to get that good feeling." Nora, not sure what she means, watches as Kathleen's face grimaces in what looks like hurt and then, suddenly, Nora's face reflects that grimace.

When it's over, they sleep. And though they do it again in the morning, starting with Kathleen waking sleepy-eyed Nora by blowing a raspberry on her stomach, they play the rest of that Sunday the way they always have, never saying a word about it, but each knowing they're going to do that, whatever that was, again.

A week later, playing all that over in her head, in flashes like film strip frames, Nora moves her hands around her body under her nightgown, learning it, and after she gets that good feeling, she sleeps.

The father and mother sit in the family room. The television's tuned to the Sunday Night Movie, but neither watches. The mother sleeps on the couch, her mouth open as she snores. The father's head is buried in a thick spy novel, he's away from home now, plotting intrigue in the Kremlin. Eventually, his eyes tire. He finishes a chapter, closes the cover, rouses the mother. She wakes with a start, sitting up, eyes darting quickly, "Huh? Kate?" The father settles next to her on the couch, pulls her into his chest, "Shhh. You were dreaming." Slowly, her eyes focus, her mother's armor weakened by grogginess, "Oh, Pat. I saw her leaning over me. I thought I heard her waking me like she used to when she came in at night."

The father holds her close, no idea how to make this right, worried she blames him, worried his force in suggesting they call off the search has imperiled their daughter. "What if she's hurt herself?" the mother asks, bringing his deepest fear into the open. He knows it would be his fault if she's out there somewhere destitute or worse, and he wonders how, if any of that is true, he will be able to shoulder that shame.

The mother's eyes and nose leak onto his shoulder while he strokes her back. All the months of worry well up in him suddenly. There is fear for Kate, yes, but also fear for him and the mother. How can they possibly endure it if Kate fails to return to them soon? Will his wife be able to bear the sight of him if their darkest suspicions prove true?

He feels his own eyes pool, and everything he's kept battened down, the thought that Kate's condition, whatever it is, is somehow a result of his faulty chromosomes, the thought that his hours away from the family prevented him from noticing the changes that marked her descent, presses on his chest until he sobs, "I'm sorry," into the top of his wife's head.

She pulls back from him, grips his face firmly in cupped hands, "This is not your fault." His head is shaking, no, no. "It's an illness, Pat," she says, trying to still the shaking of his head with her hands, "An illness. Nothing you or I did can change that. This is not our fault."

Though he does not entirely believe her, he calms himself and they sit in an embrace shaped by shared grief, crying freely together for the first time since Kate left. After a while, he stands and offers the mother his hand. Heading slowly upstairs to their bedroom, they check on Nora, and find her sleeping with the light burning in her room, wrapped fitfully in her sheets. The father reaches into her doorway, and clicks off the light. At the base of the third-floor stairs, they call up to Sean, "Goodnight," and hear his answering, "'Night," come down to them. Knowing that their two youngest at least are home and safe, they head into their bedroom, both doubting they'll find sleep quickly, but grateful for each other's presence.

Patty sits in the study lounge of the library, taking occasional nips from her flask of Beefeater's, absorbing a text on the Problems of the Self.

Sean shimmies down the fire ladder dangling from the window of his room. He makes his way through the woods and as he gets closer to the river, he can hear the ebb of conversation, the crackle of the small fire. Someone has brought out a guitar, and the strumming blends with the night noises. Just before he breaks out of the trees, he stops for a moment and takes in the faces, letting his eyes adjust. He spots Amy-Beth sitting off by herself, staring at the flames, flipping the end of a cigarette into the fire. Coming out into the party, he says a couple of hellos, grabs two beers from the cooler and slides down onto the ground next to her. "Hey," he hands her a beer. She tilts her head back, takes a long swallow from the long neck Bud and snuggles in next to him.

Kate stands in the open doorway of the ranch foreman's office. Knocking on the solid door frame, she shifts her weight as he looks up, "What can I do for you, Kate?" "I've been thinking," she begins, "that it's about time I start thinking of heading back East." "You're leaving then?" Suddenly unsure, not believing she's ready to go back to whatever is facing her there, she says, "I'll give you two weeks' notice." "This isn't the real world. You can go whenever you like. You've got some wages accumulated. After room and board, it should be more than enough to get you home. I'm sure you can catch a ride to the bus station in town with the cook after breakfast."

Awed again by what she thinks of as the quiet perception of these ranch people, by the way their quiet force has bolstered her when she's doubted her ability to perform certain tasks, she simply says, "Thank you."

The foreman returns to his books, but Kate stands in the doorway, waiting, she's not sure for what. He lifts his head again and smiles at her. "You've worked hard here," he says, "and you're welcome to come back. But it seems you've quieted whatever it was drove you this way. Give thanks you can go home." She feels the smile creasing her own face as she answers, "Yes, sir. Goodnight."

Back in her room, she packs her things, falls into a fitful sleep, and just as she begins to doze, she begins to believe that whatever is waiting for her when she gets home, whatever trouble her running has caused, when she gets back there, everything just might go on being all right for her.

Patty slams closed the cover of her textbook, tucks her study notes between the leaves, and as she rises to head back to her dorm, she is confident she has the theories and case histories down. Even a little drunk, she knows she's going to ace this exam. Ace it because it's expected of her. Ace it because she can.

Nora dreams. Kate's face meshed with Kathleen's at the Spring Dance, Kate/Kathleen french-kissing Billy Parker, no music, just colors screeching off the disco ball hung in the gym. Nora hears herself yelling over a piercing shade of blue, "STOP, KATHY! I TAUGHT YOU HOW TO DO THAT. STOP!"

The mother and father sleep, snoring in unison.

. . .

Some time later, Sean climbs the ladder back into his room, the smell of wood smoke and Amy-Beth's hair in his sweater. What a great fucking night! he thinks. Somewhere in the evening, as the fire died, the beer ran low, and cigarette packets moved towards empty, he and Amy-Beth found themselves holding hands, not talking. He loved the press of her fingers against the sides of his hand, the small callous on the end of her thumb. Her ride called out, "Amy B., we're leaving." "That's my cue," she said, turning to him, and without the expected awkwardness, without bumping noses or clicking teeth, she left him with the soft brush of a kiss on his lips, just the very tip of her tongue touching his. "I've been waiting for you to get around to that," she said. And, with a squeeze of his hand, she was off, walking backwards, looking at him, then turning with a wave. Home now, in his room, he peels off his clothes, climbs under the sheets, touches one hand to his lips. The other traces down his body to where he's still half hard, and like that, without finishing, he drifts into sleep.

The family sleeps. Separated by geography, by the solid walls of an old house, by different dreams. They sleep, and in that shadowy place, at some point during the night, each of them has no knowledge that they are apart.

1 9 8 0

Patty leans forward into the mirror, squinting through the lingering fog from her shower. She puckers her lips in the shadowy glass, precisely dragging a deep red lipstick over those plump curves. Stepping back a moment, she admires the effect, but catches sight of a small blemish on her chin, leans in, manipulates the skin around the budding zit. Decides it's not quite ready for squeezing. Rummaging through the clutter scattered on the counter, she comes up with eyeliner, frosty blue, and a tube of clumping mascara. She goes to work. Ready for her on the countertop: the industrial pink can of Aquanet, the curling iron already heating, the massive gun of the hair dryer. Sixteen years old, putting her face together; she's going out tonight.

. . .

Kate sits in the window seat of her bedroom, her eyes riveted on the stalactites of ice spilling off the bare branches in the back yard. The bright play of a winter's sunset bounces off the crusted snow piled almost a foot deep on the hill, the forlorn wave of a tattered yellow ribbon flaps around the trunk of a maple. Wrapped in a towel, another curled turbanlike around her head, she idly wonders if she's still on restriction. Wonders if the stupid furor over that little dime bag of grass she accidentally left on her dresser when she came in on New Year's Eve is still raging. The duration of her sentence was never outlined; it's been a month and a half. And though her parents have softened towards her in the last week, she wants to get out of this house. Too much time locked in her room, playing the same Joan Jett record over and over again, has given her too much time to think. In all this quiet time on her own, her brain races, turns up thoughts that frighten her, and she wants, she needs, to get out of this house.

Nora, bundled in her stiff, hand-me-down, navy snowsuit, pom-pom hat, and bulky mittens, drags her fire-engine-red toboggan up the hill behind the house. She positions it at the top of the icy track she's worn since the snow fell last week, canceling school for two days and replacing math and spelling with snow angels and sledding with Kathleen. She gives a small leap, landing on her belly in the center of the sled, races down the hill, catches some air on the small jump shoveled into place by Sean and his friends yesterday, careens off the track and slows to a stop as the sled cracks through the snow's fragile icy crust in the flat portion of the yard.

The mother lifts the lid of a pot simmering on the back burner and examines the broth bubbling around the carcass of last night's roast chicken dinner. Dipping a ladle into the liquid, spooning off a taste, she raises it to her lips. Blows across the surface, dulling the heat a bit. Tastes. It's not quite ready for straining, the full flavor of the chicken not yet infused into the water. Replacing the lid, she turns to Sean at her side, still a gangly little boy with bony knees, standing only at breast height, even at twelve. "All right," she says, "let's start cutting up the vegetables." Looking out the window, she can see Nora running back up the hill for another trip down on her sled. Listening, she can hear the faint hum of Patty's hair dryer running upstairs, the bass and drums from Kate's stereo thumping through the ceiling, the dull roar of a basketball game in the family room, her husband's encouraging murmurs or groans of disgust at the television. But it's Sean who is with her, on the cusp of his teen years. She's teaching him how to make soup, and though some traditional part of her brain tells her that it should be one of the girls in here, she's pleased it's Sean. Pleased that he still wants to be here with her. The older girls were mostly lost to her now, and as they all get older, she has a desire to see them unchanged from moment to moment. To freeze them, to keep them as they appear in the family albums, without the added worries that come with their growing up.

The father polishes off a can of Bud as a guard from the University of Houston snatches a wayward pass from the Villanova back court, and that break is on again. The guard lobs an alley-oop pass towards the basket. From just outside the lane, one of the big men launches himself towards the rim and stuffs the ball with a crashing two-handed dunk. "God-damn it!" he says, Nova's suddenly down by six with just over five minutes to play, and forced to take a time-out just to slow things down, get some breathing room from Houston's relentless press.

As the commercials come on, he heaves himself out of his chair and ambles into the kitchen. Liz is seated at the breakfast nook with Sean, both of them bent over a cutting board lined with carrots, celery, parsnips and turnips. Something smells terrific, but why Sean should be doing this on a Saturday afternoon baffles him. When he was his age, in snow like this, he and his friends would have gone down to the park, gone sledding, thrown snowballs at cars, ran like hell from irate drivers slamming on their brakes. He could at least be interested in the game, watching and asking questions, cheering or mourning as Villanova's fortunes change. Peering into the fridge, poking around for a possible snack, he settles for pulling another Bud from the plastic rings holding the last four cans together. Pulling the top, turning to head back towards his game, he eyes Sean and Liz for a moment. Sees Liz's hand guiding Sean's as those winter vegetables are cut into symmetric pieces. "The game's pretty exciting," he ventures, "Want to catch the end with me?" "Nah," Sean says, voice not yet breaking, "I'm doing this." "Suit yourself," he says, heading back towards his chair just as the television comes back to a live shot from the arena. As he settles in, as Villanova starts things back up with their inbound pass, he briefly feels rejected, hurt somehow by Sean's refusal. But as Nova's players begin to whip the ball around, Houston shifted into a zone, Nova looking for a shot, he's back in the game, and the small forward is open at the top of the key, a tight bounce pass finds him. Fluidly, he drills the jumper. "Yes!" he slops a bit of beer onto his shirt in his excitement. Down by four, four and a half minutes to play.

Sean, often a bit clumsy, not particularly coordinated in sports, feels a rhythm suddenly as he works the heavy, sharp knife through a carrot. His mother removes her guiding hand and perfect little circles of orange continue to fall away from his blade. He glances up at her, sees her benevolent half-smile, grabs the next carrot. His hands work together, one hand briskly pistoning the knife up and down, the other pushing the vegetable under the rocking blade, those perfect little pieces, all the same thickness, pile up on the wood of the cutting board. He realizes, I'm good at this. The carrots finished, he moves on to the celery, learns from his mother the parts to use and the parts to discard, works the knife, this time creating perfect little translucent green *U*'s. When he's finished, when he's done the parsnips and the turnips too, his mother shows him how to strain out the chicken bones from the broth, and together they shred the remaining meat from the carcass, keeping it in the pot. He watches as she uses the blade of the knife to push the vegetables into the broth, as she adds a couple shakes of salt, a few more of pepper, and puts the lid back on the pot. "How do you know how much to use?" he asks. "You learn it," she says, "You just know." "Now what?" "Now," she says, "we wait. The longer it cooks, the better it gets. Right before dinner time, we'll cook some noodles, and strain the fat off the top of the pot before we put them in." He sees her smiling down at him, thinks, I've got a handle on this soup thing. Wants to do more. Watches her walk to the sink, turn the water on, and start washing up the cutting board and the knife. He pulls the foot stool over to the stove. Stepping up, he reaches over to the pot, pulls the lid off, breathes in the warmly scented steam, dips the wooden spoon into the broth, stirs. "Sean," his mother says, "you have to let it be for it to cook." "Okay," he says, the slight exasperation in his voice at the intrusion of instruction a clue that he's growing older.

The sun is down. It's not dark, not quite, the snow holding some of the bright glare of the day. Children gathered together on drainage ditch and backyard slopes, bundled against the cold, say their good-byes and walk off towards home. Over in White Oak Park, the sulfur lights on leaning wood poles ease to life around the pond, thinly illuminating the last pairs of skaters navigating the ridged surface. The high school–aged hockey players pack in their pick-up game, the black puck beginning to get lost in the dark patches of ice. Clustered around their cars, the odd cigarette flaring in the coming dark, the players hurriedly remove their skates and slide wool-sock covered feet into boots, lacing them tight against the cold. The wind is beginning to pick up, further chill-

ing the already frigid air, conversation and breath visible in steam rising from mouths, spilling from nostrils.

Still in her room, dressed now in artfully ripped jeans with a designer
label, a T-shirt advertising CBGB'S, a flannel workshirt unbuttoned because it has no buttons, Kate works with dark-colored pencils in her
sketchbook, blacks and grays, hints of deep greens, slashes of moldy
browns, a small scratch of yellow, drawing the scene from her window.
She has no thoughts as she works. As if all that time staring out at the
yard, all the tumble of her mind, is stilled by the infinite patience required to get light onto paper. As she works the colors on the page sing
to her, the green a resounding bass, tempered by the up-tempo swing
of the black, the jazzy scat of the brown. As she works, the needle lifts
from her Joan Jett record, and there's silence in the room, but she barely
notices. Going deeper, filling in the silent blank space more carefully,
pausing to set the light of the afternoon in her head as she stares out
at the yard, flattened out into gray tones without the sun, she thinks,
This still works.

She can still quiet her mind through concentration, can still ease
back into the cadences of the world through the manipulation of color.
Sometimes it's the only thing available to her that makes sense.

Things are getting worse. The previous Sunday, in the hollows of
the early morning, while the house slept around her, she dragged all her
button-down shirts, the blouses, her school uniform tops, from her
closet and went to work on the buttons with a nail scissor. She popped
the top buttons off all of them, only denuding the entire placket on the
worn shirts her mother might not notice. For weeks those collars had
chafed her, driving her crazy, making her unable to concentrate on anything beyond the itch of her neck. But then those buttons, even out of
their holes, became a threat. They cut off her air, threatened to suffo-
cate her as she sat in class or at the dinner table. She tried to ignore the
danger, to push it from her mind, but it just grew worse. Even the loose

man's pajama top she wore to bed, its neck hole huge, its first button down near her breasts, clawed at her windpipe. For days she lay awake at night, terrified by her clothing, dreading the morning when she'd have to get dressed again. Quaaludes helped, they let her slip into a jumbled sleep, and when the ludes were unavailable, she could rely on window-cracked, pin-thick joints. But still, it was all too much, and fueled last week by pot paranoia, she set to work with her tiny scissors, and though she feels better wearing her shirts, she knows the problem hasn't gone away.

Patty, cloaked in towels that match Kate's earlier ensemble, scans the rows of clothes lining her closet. From the recesses of that space, untouched by parental hands, she pulls a lacy, black bodysuit, bought impulsively from a small shop in New Hope when she rode down there with Kate to do some Christmas shopping. She fingers the delicate weave of its pattern, looser around the part that would cover her stomach, affording flashes of skin, more densely woven to obscure crucial areas, the slight frill of its daring neckline. They'd never let me out of the house in this, she thinks.

Dropping the towel from her torso, she steps into the suit, secures its snaps, straightens the straps on her shoulders. Admires her reflection in the mirror. Feels amazed at the effect. The angles and planes of her body, the sharp jut of her hips, those vestiges of her girlhood, seem smoothed somehow. As if this article of clothing adds a few crucial years to her age. Turning to her dresser, she pulls out a pair of jeans. Her mother may grumble that they're too tight, but they were a Christmas gift, and she knows she'll get away with them. Sitting on her bed, she undoes the zippers around the ankles, pulls them over her legs, sucks in her stomach, and pulls with force on the zipper until it eases all the way up. She goes to the mirror again, checks her look from all angles.

Thinks, Not bad. With my leather coat and black go-go boots, not bad at all.

Now, digging in her cedar-scented sweater drawer, she comes up with a green monogrammed sweater in soft, virgin wool. Pulls it over her head. In the mirror now, just a teenaged girl, her jeans maybe too tight, but that's the fashion of the season, her sweater all bulky innocence with it's small "p," large "M" and small "e." One last look in the mirror and she thinks, Christ, it's almost too fucking easy.

Sean wanders upstairs, slowly traverses the picture-lined hallway of the second floor, past Kate's closed door, angling towards Patty's room. He doesn't understand what's happening to her. *She doesn't seem to like him anymore.* Her door is ajar, the light clicked off. She must be in Kate's room. He stands on the threshold, this a place he was once welcome to visit, even unsupervised, but now he's not sure. In the shadows, he can see her mess—stacks of books piled on shelves, the floor, her night table, dirty laundry heaped in the corner.

He takes a step into the room, right hand wandering automatically towards the light switch, still guarded by a pink plate from the days when this was a room belonging to a little girl. He flips the switch, the room comes into sharp focus, and he takes another step forward, dodging a pair of school uniform loafers kicked off just inside the door. He begins to notice the smell. A vague hint of mildew, her perfume, the lingering fumes of a burned-out incense stick not quite masking the odor of old cigarette smoke. It all seems so foreign to him. It seems as if his sister has disappeared somehow. The sister who looked after him, whose company thrilled him, gone. Replaced by the person who lives in this room. A stranger who looks and sounds like Patty, but isn't Patty at all.

From down the hall, he catches the faint murmur of Kate's stereo coming to life again, and he quickly peeks out the door. Kate's room still closed off, he has a few minutes at least, and he's seized by an urge to snoop. Quickly, he opens the top drawer of her dresser, roots around among the socks and feels something hard and small. It's a metal pipe, the bowl blackened from use. Instinctively, from school-bus gossip and talks with his friends, he knows what this is. She's doing drugs. Rooting further, he finds a small plastic bag, full of clumpy green stuff. Stuff that looks vaguely like the spices lining the shelf of the cabinet next to the stove. Pot, he thinks, holding the bag to the light. Impulsively, he opens it and breaks off a piece of one of the clumps, drops it into the pocket of his jeans and stows the pipe and the bag back in the drawer.

Moving to her nightstand, he slides open the slightly skewed drawer. Inside the shallow space is a pack of Marlboro Lights, half empty. Also, her locked diary. He pulls out the book, bent on working open the lock, scanning the pages, but stops when he sees what's underneath. A strip of blue foil squares, each marked TROJAN. Rubbers, he thinks, Patty's got rubbers. She's having sex.

He quickly replaces the book on top of the Trojans, plucks a Marlboro from the pack, and pushes closed the drawer, careful to keep it on the same angle he found it.

Clicking off the light as he goes past the switch, he climbs the second flight of stairs to his own room. He closes the door behind him, pushes the lock into place. Dropping the small nugget of marijuana and the cigarette into his desk drawer, he flops onto his bed, amazed. She's having sex and smoking grass, he thinks, badly wanting to be grown-up and cool about the whole thing, but he's scared. Kate makes sense, she's weird enough to do drugs. But not Patty. All his teachers always ask him about her, "How's that sister of yours doing in high school? She's a smart kid."

Gradually, as he worries over the things he's found, he finds himself growing curious. He's found a vague discomfort in his own body these last few weeks. The backs of his knees aching at night, painful erections as he daydreams in class, staring at the wispy hair curled on the neck of the girl who sits in front of him in math. All the guys ribbing each other about jerking off as they pore over the stash of porno magazines thcy found out in the woods, the first small tendrils growing around his penis. He knows the technical details from his father's terribly vague talk and a book left on his bed by his mother. Not even thinking of Patty's secret stashes anymore, caught somehow on the image of the hair on Sandy Leary's neck, he manipulates his hard-on through his pants, trying to ease the pressure of the thing, but his hands stay in his lap, until it's all too much. Not really giving any thought to what it is he's doing, he slides his jeans down to his knees and begins to touch himself.

Nora, at the bottom of the hill, finds that she's freezing. The cold numbing her face, her mittens soaked through, the tips of her earlobes throbbing with a dull, repetitive ache. One last time for the day, she trudges up the hill. Leaning her sled against the back of the garage, she trudges to the back door and stamps her feet to loosen the snow crusted around the tread of her ridiculously huge boots.

The door's window looks in on the kitchen, and steam from the central heat, from whatever her mother is cooking, limits her view, but the light is bright and she can see inside. Her mother lifting the lid from a pot on the stove, stirring with a wooden spoon, lifting a taste to her lips. Her father padding in, dropping a can into the garbage under the sink, opening the fridge, grabbing another beer. It's almost like watching television with the sound off—she doesn't really believe that they can see her. Doesn't believe that if they turned their gaze in her direction, they would spy her out here. I'm invisible, she thinks.

She watches as her father moves to the stove, stands behind her mother and wraps his arms around her. His lips move. What is he saying, she wonders, imagining romantic whispers, the stupid things men say to women in movies. Her mother lowers the spoon into the pot, turns with a taste for her father, left hand held under the spoon to catch any drips that might fall from its shallow bowl. Watching, Nora sees her father's neck move as he swallows, sees him smile, nod his head, say something else. Watching, she sees her mother answer, her father brush a brief a kiss on her mother's lips, turn and walk away.

She's freezing, and it looks so warm inside. She's been outside, alone, for hours. Enjoying herself, enjoying the games she's made up, pretending she's an Olympic luge champion or bobsled driver as she hurtled down the hill. Racing up the hill for another run, loving the sharp stab of her breath, the blinding reflection of the afternoon sun on the snow. Happy to be outside, fond of the cold, the way it makes her feel sharp and alive as she plays.

But it's time to go inside, into the place where she's not an Olympic champion, where she's the baby, always the youngest, without power. Where things happen all around her she's not meant to understand, where she's left out of what's going on. Inside, she feels invisible, and it's not the same as the secret invisibility of watching them through a foggy window.

Opening the door, she trudges into the kitchen. Her mother, rooting around in one of the high cabinets over the breakfast nook, turns to the noise of her entrance. "Have fun?" she asks. "Yeah," Nora pulls off her boots, leaving them next to the door with five other pairs. "Go on upstairs and get changed, dinner's in half an hour or so." As she walks past her mother, her feet cold now in damp socks on linoleum, her mother places a hand on her head, ruffles her hair. Nora stops for a moment and stands by her mother's side, comforted and welcome. Forgetting in an instant, before she heads up to her room to shed her play clothes, all those things that made her wait outside the door and stare in at the lit kitchen as if she was unwelcome in its glow.

Kate and Patty sit side by side on Kate's bed, their backs propped against the wall, blowing the smoke from a shared pre-dinner cigarette towards the cracked window over their heads, flicking ashes into an empty Coke bottle. "Think you can get out tonight?" Patty asks. "Dunno. Gonna try." "You want me to ask? There's a big party over at the

McNallys'. Parents are out of town." "Jimmy's the only one at home, right?" Kate remembers Jimmy McNally. How before she knew anything about sex, before she had ever fallen in love, the sight of him in the hallways of St. Anne's Middle School between classes was enough to send the blood to her face, set her belly aflutter. The sweep of that white blond hair, the way his skin seemed almost clear, his painting every day in the art classroom during lunch. He'd kissed her at a dance one fall. Her first real kiss as they swayed tightly pressed together to the last few bars of "Stairway to Heaven," her arms wrapped around his neck, his hands linked around her waist. By the time the next dance rolled around, it must've been the Holiday Dance in December, they'd broken up, over something she can't even recall. In the larger crowds of Immaculate Conception High School, he'd disappeared to her. She caught rumors, passed him in the hallway, saw his work at the student art shows, but they didn't run in the same crowd. He graduated last year, she knows that, and enrolled at Rutgers, she thinks probably in the art school at Mason Gross, and commutes from home to save money.

"I heard his sister Ann is home for the weekend with a bunch of her friends from school," Patty interrupts Kate's reverie. "It should be wild." "Ask for me," Kate says. "I need to get out of this fucking room." She takes the cigarette from Patty's proffered hand, pulls the last drag into her lungs, drops the butt into the bottle, exhales over her head and is momentarily mesmerized by the pattern of the smoke as the draft from the cracked window sucks it outside. Turning to Patty she raises her voice into a parody of shocked incredulity, "And you're wearing that?" "You know me better than that," Patty says, jumping from the bed and pulling the sweater over her head, spinning slowly around, giving Kate a look from all sides. Stunning, Kate thinks, slutty but weirdly beautiful. Too much for a party in fucking New Jersey. She wolf-whistles at her little sister, grinning, "It's a bit risqué, no?"

"Darling," Patty says, grabbing her sweater and pulling it back on, "I'm nothing if not a bit risqué. Let's see if I can spring you from this joint." She pulls open the door, theatrically tosses her hair, and *makes an exit*. Heading towards the stairs, she considers her approach and decides to try her father first. He'd been the most angry back at New Year's, but she's got some pull there. She has to do this. She needs Kate tonight, needs a protecting shield, because she's feeling crazy in her hidden black lace, and she can't wait to cut loose.

The mother sets a large pot of salted water on a burner and twists a dial until the pilot catches and the gas flame springs to life. Sets the level to high. She wanders into the family room and flops on the couch. Picks up a magazine from the coffee table, flips through the pages. Pat has flipped the channel to the network news, some reporter with solid, unmoving hair and a heavy parka broadcasting from outside a clapboard New England meetinghouse, droning about the Presidential primaries. "Fucking Reagan," her husband mutters. "I can't believe people are taking this jackass seriously." "It'll pass," she says. "There's no way." But she can almost see the appeal. Everything has been so shoddy lately, the world, her family seeming to falter.

There are moments when things seem right. Just a few minutes back, she and Pat in the kitchen, a quiet, shared moment. A second of tenderness. But though she doesn't doubt its sincerity, doesn't doubt how good she felt, tipping a sip of soup into her husband's mouth, she also felt outside the moment somehow. As if she were watching a movie about a happy marriage, a good family. There would have been something soft, perhaps pianos, on the soundtrack. The final scene in a feel-good domestic drama, a closing moment to show that the family will endure.

But below the surface, in real life, she knows there are troubles. Kate slipping out of control, her grades slipping a bit, coming in boozy or on who knows what. The marijuana she found on her dresser New Year's Day morning. The sneaking around, the lying. She knows some of it is just a case of senioritis, just normal rebellion. Some just Kate being Kate, her natural enthusiasm for sampling life leading her down potentially dangerous paths. But she's worried.

Then there is Sean and Nora always at each other's throats, fighting relentlessly about anything at all, about nothing most of the time. They really seem to hate one another some days, Sean lashing out at her with his fists, Nora antagonizing him. Sean is old enough to know better. At least there's nothing with Patty. Always high honors, the perfect PSAT scores, all those club meetings, the phone always ringing with her friends on the other end. And if she's private, always locking her door, never mentioning boyfriends, barely alluding to her plans when she heads out with friends on weekend nights, she feels it's her right. Feels that as long as she's doing well, not giving her any cause to suspect illicit behavior, that they're probably right in granting her the space she needs to grow into whatever success she'll eventually become.

And, she and Pat. He's home more often now. His work week settled into what, by most standards, would still be long hours, but in terms of what they've been used to are distinctly not. She sees more of him, and there's been no increase in friction between them, no resentment of the other's presence. He's been good with the kids, all the kids, though she sees his struggle with Sean; she wishes they could be closer, father and son. And, she secretly finds it contemptible that he so obviously favors Patty. They're so much alike, she thinks, but it should be his son, it should be Sean, who draws all that paternal regard.

And here she is, Patty wandering into the living room, prettily preppy in her stocking feet and monogrammed sweater over jeans that flatter her legs, flopping onto the floor close by her father's chair, her attention on the television news. "What's for dinner?" she asks, looking up at her mother. "Chicken soup, grilled-cheese sandwiches. Speaking of which—"

She hauls herself off the couch and pads back into the kitchen. Her pot of water has tiny bubbles along the sides and bottom, clinging to the iron surface for a few more moments before bursting into a boil.

She opens a cabinet, pulls out a box of egg noodles and leaves it next to the stove. She grabs a loaf of bread, the butter dish, a package of American singles, a couple of hothouse tomatoes from the fridge. Nothing is all that bad, she thinks, laying out a dozen slices of bread, everything will pass. And she sets to work, finishing dinner for her family.

The sky is starkly clear against the bright shine of a nearly full moon. The temperature eases downward even further, any snow softened by car tires, snow boots or the bright shine of this afternoon's sun coalesces, hardening into a crust, treacherous and slippery. Lights glow in the windows of every house in this neighborhood, smoke slips from chimney tops. If anyone stood outside, gazing inside at the unfolding lives, feeling the cold bite of this night, they'd see everyone looking warm and comfortable. Safe in their homes, protected, preparing dinner or already settled around a table, eating. A silent movie, a fairytale of the American family, unfolding as expected.

Patty watches the news for a moment, seeking the precise moment to launch her query. The screen switches to a commercial break, and while Madge is soaking in it, her father turns to her, "Hey, how's school?" "Pretty much the same. We're doing *Taming of the Shrew* in English." "What do you think?" What do I think? she wonders. At school, she cruises through, anticipating questions and answers, reading ahead, knowing somehow that her understanding of the material, whatever material, has more depth than most of her classmates. She knocks off most of her homework quickly, during study hall or in a quick hour in her room, aces anything they put in front of her. Some of it she loves. She loves the order of geometry and chemistry this year, the ways the small things learned first apply to the larger concepts as they move into deeper, more difficult work. And there's always that

soaring, solitary pleasure of her reading. Whether it's the books as-
signed for her English class or the ones she takes out of the library or
picks up at the inadequate store on Main Street in Somerville. Just a few
pages and the world is gone, the same way it disappeared when she was
a little girl and read on the beach or curled up on the floor of this
room. It's not unlike the slipping away she's found in a few drinks, a
couple of bong hits, a pair of hands tracing her body.

But she's also aware that whatever it is that makes her instinctively
understand the way the principles of science and math build on each
other, whatever it is that makes her love the feel of a book's pages on
her fingertips, separates her from most of her peers. So she compensates
on the weekends. She runs wild enough to make them forget she's
smart, but not wild enough so that news of her activities will land at
her parents' feet. It's a delicate balance, but Kate's propensity for fucking up has helped keep her out of the gaze of suspicion.

"I like it, Dad. How can you not? It's Shakespeare, you know?"
"What's everyone else think?" "Everyone grumbled when the books
were handed out, but it's kind of racy, and they're starting to get that, so
they're more interested. But most of them want Holden Caulfield all the
time." "I thought you liked *Catcher in the Rye.*" "I did. But when I read
it again, it bugged me. I love *Franny and Zooey.*" "Me too," her father
says, "who do you like more?" Quickly, empathically, with a feeling she
didn't know she had, "Franny." "Yes, me too. There's something . . ."
"There is." It's moments like this that can almost make her feel bad
about deceiving her father. These moments when he treats her like a
friend, like an adult, like a peer who has valid, intelligent thoughts on
the subject at hand. When he treats her in a way he never treats Kate or
Sean or Nora, she has sudden, fleeting urges to tell him about some ex-
ploit, diving off the Neshanic railroad bridge into the river, boozing it
up out in the woods last spring, something that would be part of the
novel of her life. But she doesn't. She cannot spoil the treasured image
he holds of her, cannot damage the regard in which she is held.

The television comes back to the news, a warmhearted feature to end the Saturday broadcast. "Going out tonight?" her father asks. "Yeah. There's this thing over at the McNallys' house." "They live down in the Hillsboro part of Neshanic right, that big farmhouse? There's about five hundred kids?" "That's them—they used to fill a whole pew at church. Ann's home from Brown with some friends, and we're just going to hang out for a while." She knows her father, who only sees Mass on Christmas morning and Easter Sunday, won't know that Ann is a fifth-year senior, won't know that the youngest McNally is already in college, won't ask if the parents are home. Knows that the magic word, "Brown," will quell any concerns that might bubble into his head. "Sounds like fun." "It should be." Almost time, she thinks, get the right weight into the pause, let him think the next words out of her mouth are a bit uncomfortable. The television begins broadcasting promos for tonight's prime-time episodes and her father picks up his book from the table by his chair. Now. "Dad?" "Hmm?" "Well." "Yes?" "Katy-did really wants to go tonight." "I don't know, honey. She hasn't proved to us she can be trusted." "It's been almost two months." "You'll have to check with your mother," he says, burying his head back in his God-damned book. "I'll keep an eye on her." His eyes come up over the cover, "Ask your mother." "Dad, I need a ride from her." "Listen. You've got my vote. But check with your mom."

It's in the bag, she thinks. Bouncing to her feet, she kisses the top of her father's head, "Thanks, Dad," and heads for the kitchen. She finds her mother, stirring egg noodles in a pot of boiling water and suddenly feels the tight rise of hunger in her gut as the scent of homemade chicken stock hits her nose. "Mom?" she says, "There's this thing tonight at the McNallys', and Kate really wants to go, but she won't ask. Dad said he's all right with taking her off restriction if it's okay with you." A moment's pause in the rotation of the wooden spoon, her mother looks over at her, weight all leaning on her left side, right index finger twirling a strand of her hair, round and round. "Fine," her mother says finally, "she can go tonight. But tell her she's on probation. Even a hint of drinking or drugs when she gets home, and she's stuck here for the rest of the school year." Patty takes the few steps towards her mother, gives her a quick hug, and is briefly amazed as she has been for almost a year, that she's several inches taller than her own mother, "Thanks, Mom," she smiles, "I'll go tell her."

She takes the stairs, two at a time, heading for Kate's room, thinking, Damn, I'm good. She knocks on Kate's closed door, turns the handle before she gets a response, pokes her head inside. Kate's just as she left her, sitting against the wall on her messy bed, staring vacantly into space, "You're free," she says, "Let's leave around eight-thirty." Pulling the door closed again, she skips down the hall to her own room, with the uncomplicated thrill of a child who has gotten what she wanted.

The mother feels bile rising in her throat as she flips a grilled cheese-and-tomato sandwich with her spatula. That weakling, she thinks, her feelings for her husband suddenly harsh, shrill. How could Pat do that? she wonders. How could he just tell Patty it was okay with him? It's not that he *thought* it all right to end Kate's punishment, she would have agreed, probably. But he didn't come to her. He left the decision at her feet without talking it over. *He abstained.*

What do I want? she thinks. What would I have done differently? She flips two sandwiches from the frying pan onto a waiting plate and drops the next two into the pan, three more to go after these. Thinks, I would have made Kate ask herself, the three of us would've sat down, hashed out some rules, arrived at the same place probably, but arrived there together. And Patty played him like a virtuoso. Again. If it were Sean or Nora, or even Kate herself making this sort of request, he'd have done things differently, she is sure. It isn't Patty's fault; she plays the cards she's been handed. It's not her fault her father's stacked the deck in her favor.

She's getting more angry, using the flat bottom of the spatula to mash the sandwiches down, the buttered bread crisping too soon, the cheese not melting all the way through. Smoke comes from the no-stick bottom of the pan. "Shit," she flips them over, lowering the flame, trying to correct the damage, keep them from burning, keep her anger from delaying their meal.

Sean, cleaned up and redressed, bounces down the stairs and pauses outside Patty's room. From the crack between the jamb and slightly ajar door, he can see a light burning. He knocks. "Who is it?" "Your favorite brother." He pushes the door open, spies Patty sprawled out on her bed, a paperback book open in front of her, "You're my only brother," she says, smiling slightly. Warming to that smile, he asks, "What are you doing?" "Homework," she says, "Reading for English class." "Any good?" "Yeah." She turns back to her book, leaving him standing on the threshold, shifting his weight back and forth. To him, the time passing seems like minutes, hours. All these things happening, Kate in trouble, the stuff in Patty's drawers, and he doesn't have anyone to talk to about any of it.

Finally, he walks into the room, slips down to the floor, sits with his back to her bed. "Are you going out tonight?" Peering over the top of her book, she answers, and he thinks he can hear the tone of her voice telling him to go away, "Yeah, Katy-did and I are going out." "She's not grounded anymore?" "Nah, she's free." "What are you gonna do?"

He looks up, over his head at her, as she lays the book down, spine up, her page propped open, "Nothing." And her voice dismisses him, keeps him feeling like a child out of the loop of what's going on, "We're just meeting some friends, hanging out. I've got some home-work to finish. Do you mind?"

He wants to cry, but he's doing his best to keep his eyes dry these days, at any cost. He wants to ask her why she doesn't like him any-more, he wants to still be her friend. But he just says, "Yeah. Okay," and hauls himself to his feet, throwing one last look over his shoulder as he dawdles out the door. He pulls the door closed behind him, and slowly

walks the length of the snapshot-lined hall, past Nora's closed door decorated with horse pictures and the open door to the darkened bathroom, until he finds himself outside Kate's room. He can hear music
playing inside. Not knowing why, he knocks. "Who is it?" "Sean." "Just
a second." He hears her scuttling about inside, doing whatever it is she
does behind locked doors, and suddenly the door opens and she's there,
filling his view, blocking the room. "What's up, favorite brother?" she
asks. "Something wrong?" "Nothing. What are you doing?" "Getting
ready to go out. Patty sprung me from jail. Come on in."

He goes into the room, perches tentatively on the bed. There's a
draft from a cracked-open window. The curtain's lower edge sucks into
the bottom of the window frame, and the fine blond hairs on his arms
stand straight as gooseflesh pops out. Her sketchbook is there, and he
idly plays with its cover, riffling the pages without opening and looking. "You drawing?" "Earlier. Have a look." He flips through pages of
smudgy faces, human torsos, what looks like it might be the backyard.
"I like this one," he says, stopping at something abstract, blue and green
pastel colors, everything angular, "What is it?"

She comes and sits on the bed with him, picks up the book and
stares at the page he's opened. "I'm not sure," she says, "something I've
obsessed on for a while. I can't seem to get it right." "It sort of looks
like tile," he says, "but alive and wet." She looks some more, neither of
them speaking as she eyes her own work. Then her voice is surprised,
"Yeah. You're right."

The needle lifts from the record and she crosses the room to her
stereo, flips to side B and sets the needle back in the groove. Sean listens. He doesn't know this song, but the low sounds of one of the instruments hits his spine, the drums snap, and he bobs his head along,
"What record is this?" "The Police," she says, "You like it?" "Yeah." "I'll
make you a copy if you want. For your tape deck." "Thanks."

He doesn't understand why she's being so nice to him. She's never
been mean exactly, just older and not interested. He goes on flipping
through her book, pictures of flower arrangements, a half-finished

horse thing she must have started for Nora. Out of the corner of his eye, he watches as she rifles through her closet, her drawers. "I haven't been out in so long," she says finally, "I don't know what to wear." Without thinking, he asks, "What's wrong with what you have on? It's like what you always wear." She turns around, her face slowly moving to a smile, "You're right," she says, and starts to laugh. Sits on the bed next to him, watching him flip through her drawings, still laughing, "You're absolutely fucking right. Why should I get all dolled up for some party in Hillsboro where the parents are away and the house is going to get trashed?" She reaches into her nightstand, pulls a pack of Dunhills and a lighter from inside. From under her bed, she pulls out an old Coke bottle with some brown-looking water and a few butts at the bottom. She lights the smoke, and he knows his eyes are wide. He's surprised, a bit uncomfortable, but he also feels suddenly blessed. She trusts him.

She exhales over her head, sings along to the new song on the stereo and winks at him, "You won't tell that I'm smoking?" "Nope." "Good." She takes the book from his hand, flips back to that page with the blue and green angles and rips it free from the spiral binding. "For your wall," she says, "A Katy-did original." "Thanks."

He watches her smoke a bit, clutching his drawing, until their mother calls from the base of the stairs, "Kids! Dinner's ready!" She drops the butt into the bottle, swishes everything around to make sure it's out, and they head downstairs together to take their places at the table, Sean leaving his picture on top of her dresser, a subconscious excuse to come by her room later.

From their separate corners of the house, they move towards the kitchen. The father, from his seat in the family room, arrives first, finds the bowls and plates and spoons all laid out on the counter. He ladles himself a bowlful of soup, grabs a sandwich. Rips off a paper towel from the holder and takes his place at the head of the table in the dining room. "Smells great, Liz," he says. He doesn't notice the slight chill in her "Thanks."

Nora, clad now in the sweatpants and T-shirt she'll sleep in, clumps down from her room, pulls out her chair, right next to the place her mother will sit, and waits. She can see her mother ladling out a bowl of soup, plopping a sandwich on a plate. Everything carried over and set in front of her. "You must be starving, you were out there for so long." "Uh-huh." And, she *is* hungry, her stomach a small gnashing, angry knot. But she doesn't tuck right in, she knows to wait, and she does.

Sean and Kate are next down the stairs and into the dining room. Seeing the table's not set, they head into the kitchen to fix themselves plates. Kate, ignoring the soup, actively repulsed by the shreds of chicken meat floating in the broth, grabs only a sandwich. "I made an extra one for you," her mother says, "because of the chicken." "Thanks," she says, plopping a second grilled cheese on her plate, "and thanks for tonight." "Just don't screw up," her mother says, resignation in her tone, "It's the rest of the school year at home if you screw up." "I promise." Sean moves to the table with just his bowl, full to the brim, holding both edges, desperately trying not to slop any soup onto the floor; but he manages to get to his place, opposite his father at the far end of the table, without spilling. He goes back to the kitchen for his spoon, his plate and his paper towel.

The mother ladles out her own bowl, gathers her own sandwich, the only one burned badly on one side, and settles into her seat next to Nora, at the foot of the table. They wait on Patty. Finally, they hear her slow tread down the stairs, she comes into the dining room, her face buried in her book, as she dawdles so she can finish this scene before coming to the table. In the kitchen, she folds over the top corner of a page, marking her place, and leaves her book on the counter. She quickly gathers everything together, then joins them all at the table.

They all look to the mother, and as she begins a sign of the cross, they follow suit. "Father, we thank you for this food we are about to

eat and ask that you bless us this night and beg forgiveness for any of-
fense we may have committed in your eyes. Amen." Five answers,
"Amen," and six more signs of the cross, and spoons are dipped into
bowls, sandwiches lifted to lips.

Sean watches as everyone but Kate tastes the soup, blowing cooling
breaths across spoonfuls. "Excellent soup, Liz," his father says. "Really
good, Mom," from Nora. "Don't only thank me," she says, "Sean made
the soup too." He tastes his own bowl then, a spoonful of broth, a bit
of noodle, a surprisingly soft and sweet piece of turnip. All the flavors
move around in his mouth, lingering even after he swallows, and a
surge of pride fills his body. I made this, he thinks, and it's good. Even
Patty seems to like it, "It's great Sean," she says, "Really good."

They dig in in earnest, conversation on hold as they steadily lift
spoons to mouths, take bites from sandwiches, wipe lips with a swipe
of paper toweling. Patty finishes her bowl and goes to the kitchen for
a bit more, Sean does the same, then the father. Kate chews her sandwiches, glad she's not being asked to follow any conversation in this
brightly lit room, her eyes wander too much, trying to burn the sounds
of the light onto her brain. She finishes first and asks to be excused, taking her plate to the sink and leaving it there. It's Sean and Nora's night
to take care of the dishes. She heads back up to her room for a clan-
destine, post-meal smoke. Patty follows her soon after. Then the father
heads back to his book and the low hum of the television. Finally, it's
just Nora and Sean eating, the mother seated with them, waiting. They
finish almost at the same time, "Get started on the dishes before any television. You can leave the soup pot on the stove for now, just cover it
up," she says, helping them clear the table, putting everything into the
sink. "And no fighting," she adds as she heads into the family room to
join Pat.

Sean and Nora stand together in front of the sink, confronted with a
pile of bowls and plates, the dirty frying pan. He hates doing the dishes

with her, prefers the nights he gets to work with Kate or Patty. Nora does everything wrong, gets in the way, and it makes him angry. But, he's trying not to fight with her, trying to keep his cool. She's just such a pain in the ass.

"I'll load and dry, you wash," she says. "I washed last time." "Did not." "Did too." Her voice rises, "Did not." He tops hers, "I *did too.*" When it's out, he realizes he was too loud, that Mom probably heard. Sure enough, "Kids, what's the problem?" comes her voice. "It's Nora's turn to wash," Sean calls out, "and she won't do it." "It's not my turn," Nora whines, loud enough for her voice to be heard in the other room too.

Suddenly their mother is back in the kitchen, her face level the way it is when she's just starting to get angry, "I don't care whose turn it is to do what," she says, "Sean, you're older, you wash tonight, Nora will do it next time you have to do it together. I'm keeping track now." And she's gone back to the family room.

Sean slams on the tap, starts to rinse the bowls and plates and hand them to Nora without looking at her standing in front of the dishwasher, waiting to load everything in. The injustice burns at him. Wednesday night they did the dishes together, dinner was lasagna, and the serving pan was crusted with burned cheese and sauce along its edges. It took forever to get the damn thing clean, he knows he washed it, and Nora knows too, she always gets her way. When he's finished his rinsing, the last dish handed to that little snot, he turns to the heavy, fancy French cast-iron skillet, all speckled with burned butter marks and spots of congealing cheese. Struggling to hold the pan with one hand, he slams at its surface with a Brillo pad, loosening the grime. When it's all clean and rinsed, he turns to hand it to Nora for drying, looking at her for the first time since their mother left the room. Her face is all smug satisfaction, and as she works with her dish towel, the pan resting on the counter because she can't hold it up with one hand, he gets even angrier. She finishes, uses two hands to return the pan to the cabinet. When everything's put away, she walks past Sean drying his hands, sticks her tongue out at him and pinches his arm, "Too bad, sucker."

That does it. He doesn't hesitate as his fist clenches, his arm raises, and he lands a blow on her bicep. Doesn't feel remorse as she balls up and turns away from him and he punches her low on the back as hard as he can. "Mommmy!" she's screaming, "Sean hit me!" and all he wants to do is get away, because he knows no matter what, this will be his fault in their eyes. But his mother is there, blocking his exit from the kitchen—he can just make out the dining room behind her, leading to the stairs, but there's no escape. Backing away from her, his hands raised, "She started it," he offers, "she pinched me." "I don't care, you're older and bigger and you should know better." Still backing away, he wants to protest, "I'm not really bigger. We're almost the same size," but he can't get it out. She gets him by the door, and spins him roughly around, landing one, two, three sharp swats on his butt. They don't really hurt, not badly. Rather, it is the anticipation, the possibility that *this time* it might really hurt, that this time she might snap the way he does when Nora taunts him, that brings the tears to his eyes, the runny mucus to his nose. "To your room," his mother says, "for the rest of the night. No television, no Atari. No nothing." From behind the tears, he snuffles, "What about her?" "Sean. Don't start. To your room. Now."

He heads towards the stairs, starts slowly up, sucking snot back, trying to get everything under control. At the top of the stairs, he looks down and sees his mother crouched next to Nora, wiping *her* nose and drying *her* eyes. Jerk off, he thinks, I hate her. *It's* Dukes of Hazzard *night* and I don't get to watch because of her.

Patty slides a pair of ankle-length, spiky heeled black leather boots over her feet. Minutely adjusts the tight fit of the leg where it disappears into her shoes. Pulls open her nightstand drawer, grabs her smokes and her rubbers, flips them into her purse. She opens her top dresser drawer, fishes out what's left of her last pot purchase, adds it to her bag.

Grabbing her leather bomber jacket from its spot strewn on the floor, she tosses it over her shoulder and heads out the door, clicking off the light as she goes.

Outside Kate's room, she knocks and pushes the door open. Kate swings around to face her sister, her features panicked. "It's just me." "Shit. I'm rolling a joint here. Close the door." She bumps the door closed with her hip, watching Kate crumble buds into the crease of a Bamboo paper, expertly spread out her weed, lift the paper up by its ends and roll it up. Raising the glue strip to her tongue, twisting the ends to prevent spillage, she tucks the joint inside the protection of the cardboard Dunhill box. "Ready?" "Let's go."

Downstairs, Kate and Patty both shrug into jackets, head into the family room to wish goodnights. "We're on our way out," Patty says. "See you later." She brushes a kiss across her father's forehead. "Have fun," he says. Kate follows her over, bestows a forehead kiss of her own. Moving to her mother snuggled on the sofa with Nora, " 'Night, Mom," Patty says, leaning down to buss her too. "Thanks," Kate adds when it's her turn. "In by one," the mother says, "not a second later. Ten-fifteen Mass in the morning. You know the rules." "We know," Patty says, smiling, "Don't worry." "I can't help it," the mother smiles now, "it's my job."

Out in the driveway, the frigid air slams into their faces, their chests where unzipped jackets flap open. "Fucking-A," Kate bends down to unlock the passenger door on her Pacer, "It's freezing." Patty scoots in, slams the heavy door shut, reaches over to unlock the driver's side as Kate walks around back. Hurriedly, she settles into the seat and twists the key in the ignition. The cold engine hesitates, a few seconds of a brutal whine, before catching and turning over. The windows are covered with a sheen of ice, they need scraping, but Kate'll be damned if she's going out there again. She clicks the button that arms the ineffectual rear defroster, twists the heat dial to High. A rush of cold air pours into the car. "Brrrrr," Patty says. Gradually, the air from the vents gets warmer, the bottom edge of the windshield clears, and Kate can

see enough to drive if she squints through the narrow opening, hunch-
ing low in her seat, using her side mirror until the rear window finally
clears up.

She punches the automatic gear shifter into *R,* pushes her right foot
down on the gas, too hard, the car lurching up the steep slope of the
driveway. At the top she cuts the wheel, pops the car into drive, turns
the volume on the radio as high it will go, and heedless of ice or slippery road-salt deposits, speeds in the direction of their party.

"I can't handle it, Pat," the mother says from her reclined perch on the
couch, "He's got to stop, this fighting is driving me crazy." "It'll pass,"
he says, turning back towards his book, "kids fight." She glances over
at Nora, curled at her feet, half asleep, the edge of their shared blanket
curled tight in a fist held up around her mouth. Maybe he's right, she
thinks, maybe I come down too hard on Sean. But this hitting. She
doesn't like herself when she strikes out in anger at one of the kids, it
doesn't happen often, just the occasional spanking like tonight. Usually
when she feels her anger rising, she counts, "One, two . . ." leaving a
pause before hitting three, the unspecified violence of three, to give
them a moment to stop whatever behavior has pissed her off. But she
almost understands, almost knows what makes him take his frustrations
into his fists. He's so like her.

She recalls herself as a good-natured child, quick to laugh, but given
to an unpredictable temper. The quickest girl fists in Newark, she
bloodied noses in her day. She was small for her age, like Sean, and her
temper got her noticed, got her what she thought was the respect of
her friends. It wasn't until later, when she was older, that she saw it
might be fear. She was arguing with Anna, the worst fight they'd ever
had, about what? Something to do with some boy maybe, they went
to the same all-girls high school then and dated boys from Seton Hall
Prep. But it was summer, they must have been about fifteen. Her parents had gone away for a week, cruising to Bermuda, and left her and

Anna alone at the beach house. It was early evening and they were slumped on the porch, waiting to head down to some party, sharing a quart bottle of Schlitz. It was early evening on their fourth or fifth day together, they'd been grumpy all afternoon with one another, and it was an argument over something stupid and inconsequential, of that she's sure. She raised her arm to make her point, gesticulating to accent her words, but Anna flinched away from that raised hand. It gave her pause, that movement away from her by the person she valued most. And though the argument continued for a while before they made up, though Anna's flinching went without comment, it made her think. And she worked at controlling her temper, measuring her responses, until she found she didn't have to work, not resorting to her fists first was natural, she wasn't thought of as a person who *could* hit anymore. But she's seen Nora flinch as Sean's anger builds. And although she knows Nora probably provokes him, wants him to strike because she knows he'll be punished, her provocation an exercise of her limited power, she doesn't want him to have that inclination or her to have that fear. But what can I do, she thinks, what more can I do but discipline and hope for him to grow up and out of this stage?

Nora, tuckered out from her day of sledding, sleepily watches the television. A car chase, the Duke brothers coming to Daisy's rescue and Rosco P. Coltrane bumbling Boss Hogg's plans. Daisy's her favorite. I wish I was her, she thinks. Sean's not as nice a brother as Bo or Luke. But she feels a little guilty, Sean loves this show, and she knows it was her night to wash. She's not sure why she did it, she knew he'd eventually hit her, she was counting on it, she *wanted it.*

She feels a little bad, but also a little hungry, and she wonders about dessert. There's ice cream, heavenly hash, her favorite, it was her week to pick at the grocery store. During the commercials, she rouses herself from the couch. Her mother looks over, "What're you doing?" "I'm gonna get some ice cream." "I can get it for you." "S'okay. I'll get it."

In the kitchen, she pulls open the freezer, pokes around for the half-gallon container, plops it onto the counter. She drags the stool over to the dish cabinet, climbs up, grabs a bowl. From the silverware drawer, she takes the ice-cream scoop. At first she's not strong enough to dig the scoop through the freezer burn, whoever last had ice cream didn't close it right. But, she turns the sink tap to hot, runs the scoop under the water, and is able to cut through the frozen surface. Slowly, she fills her bowl. She still feels bad about Sean. All his friends watch *Dukes* too, and he knows they're going to talk about it in school on Monday. And he's not getting any dessert. Suddenly, she makes a decision. She gets back on her stool and gets down another bowl. Dishes out a portion for Sean. She can just make out the commercials still playing on the television. Grabbing a second spoon, she races up the two flights of stairs, clutching her offering. Outside Sean's closed door, she can faintly hear music playing, it sounds like one of Katy's records. She hesitates before knocking, decides against asking to come in. Placing the bowl on the floor, she sticks the spoon into the mound of ice cream, knocks twice quickly, ignores his "Who is it?" and races back down the stairs. Her father's coming out of the powder room off the kitchen as she goes to grab her own dessert. He sees her, flushed from her running, but says nothing, just smiles and heads back to the family room.

She takes her bowl back to the television and settles in next to her mom as the show comes back on, feeling better, sucking a chocolate ice cream–covered nut from the end of her spoon.

Sean waits a minute, wondering if he imagined that quiet knock on his door. Lying on his bed, back propped up on the headboard, nodding his head to one of Kate's new records, some Irish band no one's ever heard of, he's over feeling burned. He's missing *Dukes of Hazzard,* and that sucks. But he's got books in here, no one can hear his record player from downstairs, and he's starting to like having this place, his room, and time alone. And, the rationalizations he's always used after popping Nora aren't holding up as well anymore. She had it coming, sure, but maybe he hit her too hard, maybe he hurt her. He doesn't mean to do it, doesn't want the problems it causes, but he can't help himself sometimes. She's such a pain in the ass. But I'm not a kid anymore, he thinks, I'm in seventh grade, I've got to stop.

He heaves himself to his feet, convinced someone was at the door, propelled to the threshold by the snap of a snare drum and the singer's reedy, rapid-fire vocals, "Walk away, walk away, walk away, walk away. I will follow." Opening the door a crack, he peers into the darkened landing at the top of the stairs. No one. He opens the door wider, taking a half-step out of his room. I must have imagined it, he thinks, shrugging and turning to close himself back inside his room. But his foot nudges something on the floor. Crouching down, he retrieves the bowl of ice cream, a spoon stuck in the top like some explorer's flagpole.

It's heavenly hash, one of his least favorite flavors and melted around the edges, but he's happy to find it all the same, a correction of one of the injustices visited upon him this night. Settling back on to his bed, ears tuned to the music from the stereo, I like this record, he thinks, I like it a lot, he raises the spoon to his lips and starts to eat. He doesn't have to wonder hard about where the ice cream came from. Kate and Patty are at that party, his father would never think of doing something like that, his mother might, but she'd come in, and they'd have to talk about Nora and all that bullshit. Nora brought me this, he thinks, but why?

He scrapes the last bits of chunky ice cream from the bowl, running the spoon around the surface to scoop up some of the melt before setting the bowl aside and resuming his propped-up posture on the bed. He feels bad all of a sudden, for swatting Nora, for stirring up trouble. He wants to apologize to Nora, catch a little television before he goes to bed, but he can't leave his room, the terms of his sentence are clear enough, so he tries to shrug it all off, thinking, The hell with it.

. . .

A front pushing down from Canada moves into the area. Most of the moisture it gathered as it crossed the Great Lakes gone by the time it reaches New Jersey, dumped in a few inches of lake effect snow on Chicago, Cleveland and Buffalo. But it brings clouds, whipping in streaks across the moon, blocking the stars. It brings clouds and flurries, buffeted about by the wind, giving the appearance of a blizzard because the snow doesn't seem to land. It eddies about on the gusts, joined by any loose snow the wind can whip off the ground, obscuring visibility, stinging exposed cheeks, pushing drifts against the bases of trees, along the lines of snow fences strung beside these country roads.

Kate sits on the third-to-last step leading down into the basement of the McNally house, watching shadowy bodies moving together in tight quarters, listening to the low roar of a thousand conversations competing with the music. The lights are dimmed, but someone's hooked up a strobe, a police light, and a mirror ball. Colors flash all around her, pulsing in time to a Pink Floyd record so loud her fillings seem to hum, the flashes of red and thin shards of spinning prisms adding to the cacophony in her head. She's too high from the joint she and Patty shared on the ride over, her mouth bone dry, the warming half-filled cup of keg beer in her hand sweating from the heat of all those people.

Patty's in there someplace, the center of attention, Kate's sure, her outfit almost assures fawning admirers tonight. Around the edges of her skull, in the tips of her fingers, she can feel the speedy beginnings of the half tab of blotter she dissolved on her tongue just after arriving. It makes her both eager and afraid. Some guy was stationed by the door with a full sheet and scissors, his pupils swollen so large she could barely make out the thin circle of deep blue. She did a quick calculation, eight hours from now puts her after four in the morning, but half a hit would probably be all right. She loves acid, so strange and unpredictable, it makes sense to her. Other trippers suddenly see the world the way she does, assign sounds to colors, colors to sounds. The guy at the door had snipped off a hit and clipped it in half after trying to convince her a whole hit would be better, promising her it's good stuff, strong, he dipped the sheet himself. That tiny piece of paper dropped in her palm, so small, so powerful. "Cheers!" she'd said, laying it down on her tongue, tasting something vaguely metallic as it moistened. And pupil boy smiled a "Cheers!" right back at her, and popped the other half into his mouth.

She feels a drop of sweat rolling down the side of her face, creeping towards her cheekbones, and raises a finger to swipe it away. As her hands move in front of her eyes, her fingers are followed by bright strings of flesh-colored light and she's captivated, running her hands in front of her face for a few hour-long moments. But she's distracted by the weight of someone settling down on the step above hers. Turning her head up, her fingers still waving idly in front of the space where eyes used to be focused, she sees spiky white-blond hair and pale skin glowing against the dark. This head is ringed with a halo of light and it's speaking. The voice seems to hold the mysteries of music, "I see you met Tommy at the door. I'm tripping my face off." "Never caught his name." "You're Kate Mahoney, right?" "Yeah." "You don't remember me?" "It's tough to see you. You're glowing." "It's Jimmy. Jimmy McNally." "Jimmy," she murmurs, "I was just thinking about you this afternoon." "Come on," he says, standing and offering down both of his hands. "Where?" "Just come on." She reaches up and allows herself to be pulled to her feet. He's stomping up the stairs, she follows, and they're tooling through the main part of the house, the music only a dim memory after the door to the basement is pulled shut. They pass a few people crashed out on the couch and on the living-room floor. She thinks she sees Patty playing quarters in the kitchen, but she's not sure because she's following the light spilling off Jimmy through the laundry room, out a door and it's cold concrete working its way through the soles of her boots from the floor of the garage, then they're out another door into another world.

Freezing, the wind buffeting, howling, whistling through bare trees. It's snowing again. The sky is full of crystals, moving horizontally, getting tossed back into the air when they manage to settle for a moment on the ground. She watches and she feels herself lifting, joining the snow in its pas de deux with the wind, until she tears her head down and sees her feet, her cold, cold feet, planted on the ground.

A flash of flame to her side, and she slowly swivels her head to see Jimmy cupping his hand around a Zippo, getting a cigarette lit. "Gimme," she says, suddenly needing to feel anchored. He hands it to her and goes to work on another for himself. As she takes her first drag, she can feel the smoke working past her teeth, spilling down her throat, filling each of the thousands of cilia in her lungs, expanding her chest, and slowly slipping back out of her again. Each drag settles her back a bit more firmly into her body. She can watch the snow now, wonderfully, amazingly pretty, without getting sucked away from herself. She starts to shiver, and feels warm arms wrapped around her. Leaning back into that warmth she asks, "Why did you bring me here?" "It's so beautiful," comes that music-tinged voice, "I had to show someone."

Turning in those arms, tossing her butt hissing into the snow, she tilts her face up and opens her mouth to his, trying to suck some of that light into her. Their lips meet and she touches her tongue to his, and the whole world might suddenly be contained in the pressure of lips on hers and the rough catlike brush of his tongue. They kiss. And though it lasts no longer than a kiss can last, for them they are kissing for hours and she opens and closes her eyes, mixing the pleasure of the mouth on hers with the swirling patterns of the wind-addled flurry, finding a rhythm for her mouth in the weather. Seconds or days later, they break apart, both shivering and laughing, and dart back into the garage, into the house, returning to the chaos of the party.

. . .

The father tucks the dust-jacket flap of his book between two pages, marking his place, and looks over at the couch. Nora's sleeping now, her chest rising and falling regularly. Liz's staring at him, hood-eyed, sleepy herself probably. "What?" he asks. "Are we doing something wrong?" "How do you mean?" "With the kids. Nora and Sean. Kate. Is it our fault?" "I don't think so." "No?" "They're kids, Liz. Try and remember being a kid." A long pause, wheels turning in both their heads. Finally, "I guess. Maybe you're right."

Remembering his own growing-up, he thinks his kids are blessed. They don't know what it can be like. They don't know violence, seemingly random and liable to greet you at any moment for any transgression, real or imagined, against parental authority. They're good kids, these four. Loving, generous, smart, they'll be fine. Turning back to his wife, still watching him from the couch, he says, "Nora snuck Sean a bowl of ice cream tonight." He sees her lifting her head slightly, gazing down the couch, taking in their sleeping youngest, "She did, huh?" "Yeah." "Why would she do that?" "Maybe they were both wrong and she sort of knew that." "Maybe." Still looking at Nora, she continues, "I'll get her to bed." He watches as she gently rouses Nora, leads her over to his chair to bestow a goodnight peck, and guides her up the stairs for her tucking-in.

Alone for a few minutes, he reaches for his book again, but pauses, wondering suddenly himself, *are* we doing all right here? Kate. She's odd, no doubt. Her clothes strange, those razor-cut jeans and decorative safety pins. That noise she calls music. The occasional friend that stops by sporting a purple mohawk. But she works so hard at her art stuff. He can't understand why, though he respects the dedication that makes her spend hours in front of an easel. Relates to her successes. And, she's so kind, bestowing drawings on Nora, driving Sean to soccer practice without complaint. He's not all that concerned with the marijuana. He supposes most of the high school kids dabble; he's sure that's the extent of things. They'd know if she was doing something harder, they'd see the warning signs. And Patty, his joy, he never ceases to marvel at her ability to please him. It's not intentional, he thinks, she doesn't set out to do things she knows I'll like. She's simply like him, keeping her own counsel, quietly driven.

He has some guilt over Sean. So small, he seems frail, unsure, unsteady. The father hasn't got a handle on him. He's not the boy he envisioned when the hospital doctors proudly slapped his back and informed him of his first son after two daughters. He loves him, sure. But when he takes the time to think about Sean, he feels a thin shard of guilt. He hasn't tried to meet Sean on his own terms, hasn't tried to be the father of this boy, but rather has been the father of the boy *he* wanted. At least he hasn't been cruel, he will never be cruel to his son, not after the way his own father bestowed cruelty on him like a blessing.

And little Nora. He can't see her, not really. She'll always seem smaller than she is. She surprises him when he comes across her around the house. Exactly when did she get so reedy tall? And what goes on in that little head, who will she be? Now, hearing Liz's footsteps coming back down the stairs, he wonders if she'll get a fair shake, the same parenting they've given the others. She'll always be last, nothing she can do will surprise them. By the time she reaches each milestone of her life, they'll have seen it all before, seen it three times from three different perspectives. He realized it back with the infant triumph of her walking, the leaping joy of her first word, "Dog." Of course they were excited, but there was a sense of inevitability about it. Of course she'll walk, of course she'll talk. And now, as she gets older, moving towards the moody emotional swings of puberty, the crushing, wonderful blows of first love—they'll have been through it with each of the others and Nora's struggles will seem somehow less dramatic, less real. No matter how hard they try to treat all four of them the same, Nora may get short shrift in spite of any good intentions.

Liz is back, flopping onto the couch, absently flipping through her magazine, one eye on the *11 o'Clock News.* He's tired suddenly, the same stories recycled from earlier in the night, coupled with the late-news staple of tonight's New York murder. It's all the same, nothing changes. But he watches, he feels he must. And when the news ends, he'll put down the footrest on his recliner, kiss Liz goodnight and head to bed. She'll fall asleep there, "waiting up" for the girls, and flop into bed when they get home. Everything will be as it always is.

Patty bounces a quarter off the hard surface of a kitchen breakfast bar. It crests the lip of a shot glass, and falls clattering into the bottom. "Drink," she points at the guy to her right. She's on a roll, nicely buzzed, she can't miss. Five in a row, one drink for each of the people clustered around the counter. Bounce, clink. "Drink," pointing at the girl two people from her right. She doesn't know these people, never seen them before, they must be some of the kids down from Brown for the party. All eyes on her now, bounce, clink. "Drink," to the next girl.

All eyes on her, she can feel the malevolent glares from each of the other women at the table. Whenever they manage to land the quarter in the glass, she can count on them to order her to drink. And, covert, leaden stares from the guys, bestowing their victorious drinks on her almost wistfully, with hope. Bounce, clink. This drink to the guy two away on her left. Bounce, clink, and she points to the guy directly to her left, the one she's got her eye on. She watches as he tilts his bottle to his lips, opens his throat, and polishes off the last of his beer.

She retrieves her quarter, settles it into position between her left thumb and forefinger, her middle finger braced along the bottom, keeping it steady. She's ready to go again, another trip around the table, but one of the girls is getting up, "I'm gonna head downstairs, see what's going on. Anyone want to come?" The other girl, and, after a moment's hesitation, two of the guys who must be with them get up. She turns a hopeful glance to the guy on her left, the only one still sitting with her. "Want to keep playing?" "Sure. But I need another beer. Can I get you one?" "I'll come with you."

Their little group navigates through the house to the basement.

The party all over the house now, threatening to grow out of control. Bodies overload stressed furniture, empties left scattered where they're finished, houseplants used as ashtrays, the bathroom a dirty, sodden mess, the toilet streaked with vomit. In the basement, a bunch of tripping kids lie scattered on one end of the floor, occasionally giggling, mostly just staring at the rest of the party, stuck in the artificial repose of the second half of an acid trip.

She follows too closely to this guy, this man—he must be twenty-one or twenty-two, in the light of the kitchen, she saw his face bedecked with a thin spray of five o'clock shadow. Powerful, she keeps thinking, staring at the broad swath of his back as they wind their way through the cluster of people around the stereo, into the tighter quarters by the makeshift bar. As they get closer to the booze, she hears one of the girls she was playing with mutter, "That little slut with her eye on David," but she doesn't care, she only hears the name, thrilled to have learned it.

At the bar she hangs back a bit, watching him gather a couple of drinks, say something to one of the guys they were playing with, and come back over to her. They're slightly apart from their little group now, and he hands her a cup of foamy keg beer, raising his own in a toast. They touch plastic rim to plastic rim, and taking long swallows, she keeps her eyes on him over the top of her cup. A new record is dropped onto the turntable, scorching guitars, something a few years old, and David is nodding his head along. Peter Frampton, she realizes, as someone raises the volume even higher. It's too loud to talk, she thinks, checking her watch, and I've only got about an hour until I have to find Kate and make sure our asses are home.

She leans up until her lips are right at his ear and whispers, lightly touching her lips to the twitching of his lobe, "I've got some pot if you want to go someplace and smoke." He nods, "Sure." Moving past him, heading for the stairs, Patty offers her hand and he takes it. Up into the quieter region of the first floor, through the living room, they pass Kate sprawled out on the couch, her head in Jimmy McNally's lap, her fingers tracing the bones in his chin. Up the stairs to the second floor, all the doors closed, they try knob after knob, the first three locked. At the end of the hall, a door gives. They click the light switch up and find themselves in the master bedroom, a bit untidy, but blessedly empty. David pulls the door closed behind them, twists the lock.

Patty pats her pockets, looking for her weed, and realizes she left her purse in the car. "Shit," she says, flopping down onto the bed, on her back, hands beneath her head, "I left the weed in the car." "That's all right," he sits heavily beside her, bouncing her slightly up off the bed. "We'll think of something."

He eases himself down next to her, the weight of his head propped in one large hand. With the other he brushes a strand of hair away from her mouth, letting his fingers linger along her neck. This better be good, she thinks, better than the last two five-second wonders she's had. "What?" he asks, reacting to the frown that must have passed across her face. "Nothing. Come here." She reaches up, puts her arms around his neck and arches her back slightly to meet him as he lowers his head to her.

Sean sneaks down the stairs to Patty's room, hoping no one downstairs will hear him. Stealthily, he slips into her room and flips the bedside lamp on. Tiptoeing over to her dresser, he opens her sock drawer, digs around and comes up with that little metal pipe he found earlier. In her nightstand, wedged against the back of the drawer, he finds two books of matches, both half empty.

Quickly, he ducks out of the room, eases back up the stairs and slips back into his own bedroom. Closes and locks the door behind him. Flips open the window over his bed. From his desk drawer, he pulls out that nugget of pot, the purloined cigarette and heads back to the bed, settling himself in a sitting position, his back propped up on the head-board.

He hesitates. Scared, not at all sure he should do this, but bored.

While he's been stuck here, trying to amuse himself, he's found himself more and more curious. Kate smokes, Patty smokes, their father used to smoke. He can remember the smell of it in the car, the backseat behind the driver's side bathed in the cold air from the cracked window, the side of his father's face red in the glow of the car's cigarette lighter at night. And the pot, the marijuana. Kids smoke. Even a few burnouts in middle school talk tough about it. Not his friends, *all good kids,* feigning disinterest, disgust even. In school, over and over again, the message, drugs make you stupid, a loser.

But. Patty's not a loser. She gets straight A's. Kate's going to art school next year. And they both smoke. Sitting there, with the weight of that small pipe heavy in his hand, the deep green lump of pot on the bed, he wonders, If I get high, will Patty like me again? Will she stop hiding from me? Resolved, he breaks a small piece off the bud and crams it into the pipe. Raising it to his lips, he practices sucking in, feeling foolish.

He holds the pipe between his teeth, fumbles with one of his matchbooks, finally extracting a match. Clumsily rubbing the sulfur along the striking strip, he drops the match onto the bed as it roars to life, the flame startling him. Quickly, he snuffs out the flame. Checks for damage to his bedspread and is relieved to find only a small brown mark, he's sure it will go unnoticed. Still with the pipe clenched between his teeth, he manages to get a second match lit. He raises it to just above the pipe and lets out a breath he didn't even realize he'd been holding. He knows you're supposed to suck in the smoke and hold it for as long as you can. But how long is enough? How long until it works?

He lowers the match flame to the bowl, sucks in a huge breath. His chest is filled with pain, bright searing pain from his throat down into his lungs. Briefly he's aware for the first time he can remember that he has lungs, but then he's coughing. Deep racking coughs, one after the other, hacking, he can't breathe, he's afraid he's going to puke. As he struggles to regain his breath, keep his dinner and ice cream down, the match, still lit somehow, burns down to his fingertips. The tiny burn manages to quell his coughing, and holding the pipe in one hand, the burned-out match in the other, he looks for a place to put the burned-out match. Nothing.

"Shit," he murmurs, catching his breath, still a bit shallow. His eyes fall on his empty ice-cream dish, and he drops the match in there. Taking a few deep breaths, regaining himself, he decides, one more try. He gets the match lit, touches it to the pot and breathes in lightly, feeling the heat of the smoke in his mouth. He tries to breathe in again, and this time he manages, he can feel it in his throat, in his chest. Tight. He holds it in—one, two, three—and blows back out again. Okay, he thinks, that wasn't so bad. He drops the match in the bowl and fires up another. Repeating his experiment, he manages to hold the smoke for a bit longer. Again and again, one of the matchbooks empty, until he's smoked all the pot, emptying the pipe into his dish and re-filling it three times. Every so often, he bursts out coughing, but it's not as bad as the first time. He thinks he's getting the hang of it.

But it's finished, and he doesn't feel anything, not really. His expectations are high, fueled by health-class propaganda and bits of Cheech and Chong movies he's seen on his friend Charlie's WHT movie channel. His mouth is dry, and he's light-headed, but that could be the coughing. This is no big deal, he thinks, overrated.

He picks up the Marlboro next. This somehow is fraught with more danger, is somehow *more adult*. Lighting another match, he puts the filter into his mouth, touches the flame to the tobacco. He pulls in a drag, keeping the smoke in his mouth, blowing it out quickly. Then another drag, a bit getting into his lungs this time, he can feel it, he's smoking. Leaning back against the headboard, he blows the smoke up and over his head, out the window. Entrancing. He stares at the cherry end of his butt, the smoke spilling up in two streams, spiraling together as it's sucked towards the window. He's just read *The Outsiders* in school and he imagines that he's a greaser, tough like Dallas sucking on a

Kool. Trying another drag, sucking harder, the smoke barely has time to hit the back of his throat before he's coughing again, like the first time with the pot, but in the discomfort, there's suddenly something funny, something that makes him giggle around his heaving chest until he's crying.

"Shit, shit, shit," he laughs, stubbing the cigarette out in the bowl, lying back on the bed, running his tongue over the parchment that seems to have grown on the roof of his mouth, "I wish I had something to drink." But this is funny too, and he's gonna bust a gut he's laughing so hard, rolling on the bed, wondering between giggles why the marijuana didn't work.

Kate happens to glance down at her watch. Lying on the floor of Jimmy McNally's bedroom, flipping through his sketchbooks, old and new, something about the time seems important. Something. Jimmy's gone off somewhere, he's nice, Kate thinks, full of the ability granted by her trip to see through people's facades, *get a look at them as they really are.* But the time. What about the time?

She stares at her watch, her body still speedy, everything around her tinted slightly red, but the intensity of the dose slipping away. The hands form a perfect line bisecting the watch face, little hand on the twelve, big hand on the six. 12:30, she thinks, pleased. She stands and wanders around the room, touching the spines of the books on this boy's shelves, glancing her fingers over old ribbons tacked to the wall, a trophy on top of the dresser. This room, she thinks, has something from every part of his life, from little boy to now. She's sure her seventh-grade class picture is here somewhere, in a box with urgent notes she passed him in the hallway, old drawings she gave him. At the bottom of a desk drawer maybe, with notes from the other girls through the years, maybe letters now from someone at college, someone who missed him during Christmas break.

Something about the time . . . she checks her watch again, a few more minutes clicked off the face. Twenty-five to one. To one. "Shit," she says aloud, "I've gotta find Patty and get home."

Quickly she's out the door, down the stairs. She scans the living room, a mess of empty bottles and burn marks on the carpet. A broken chair. A few crashed-out bodies, but no Patty. Down into the basement, checking her watch every few steps, the minutes slipping away. Still no Patty. Fuck, fuck, fuck, where the hell is she? Maybe twenty people still linger, drinking the end of the keg, the dregs of the bottles. She looks for a face she knows, one of Patty's friends, someone from school. There, propped against the wall, sitting on the floor, is the guy she sometimes dates, the one who sells pot. "Hey, you seen my sister?" she asks. "Not for a while. You need any weed?"

Back up both flights of stairs, she's growing frantic, it'll take at least ten minutes to get back to the house, and they've only got about seventeen left. Down the hall she tries door after door, all locked. She ducks into the bathroom and flicks on the light, no one. Her reflection in the mirror is ghastly pale, the light still tinged pink. She can't afford to get sucked in, not now. Ducking out again, the last door ahead of her swings open, and Patty steps out, hair and makeup mussed.

"I've been looking all over for you. Come on, we gotta go." Behind her is a guy Kate's never seen before. He's older, strong-looking. "Gimme a second," Patty says, turning to him, reaching up on her tiptoes, and mashing her mouth against his. "Thanks," she says to him, "that was fun." Then turning to Kate, "Let's roll. We gotta hustle."

Down the stairs as quick as they can, Patty's steps are a bit unsteady, she's weaving as they get into the yard and head towards the car. Rushing, the car's started, and they're on the road, Kate concentrating hard, trying to drive fast enough to make curfew but still be careful. She doesn't really have to worry about cops, this town doesn't have its own force, but the roads are slick, coated with a dusting from the earlier flurry.

Patty's writhing in the passenger seat, getting her sweater back on, digging in her purse for a couple of breath mints for them. "Relax," she grins, "we're going to make it." Kate wants to be angry with her, but it's Patty, and she's more curious than anything. She glances at the dashboard clock. Patty's right, they're cutting it close, but they're going to make curfew. Relaxing her white-knuckle grip on the wheel, she fumbles around on the seat beside her for one last cigarette. Patty lights one of hers for her and hands it over. "Who was that dude?" Kate asks around her first drag. "Just some guy. David something." "Did you do him?" "Yeah." "And?" "It was okay. We didn't have rubbers though. I forgot mine in the car." "Patty . . ." "It's all right. He pulled out." "Christ." "Spare me the lecture, okay? What about you? I saw you and Jimmy in the living room." "Made out some, nothing major." "Why not? He's cute." "Dunno. Didn't feel like it." Kate glances over, sees Patty smiling at her, "I feel like it most of the time."

They're almost home, Kate hanging the right onto their street, Patty flipping down the visor, checking her reflection in the mirror, making some minute adjustments to her hair, holding a hand in front of her mouth, checking her breath. Kate cuts the wheel again, a broad turn into the driveway, and the whole house is lit for a moment by the flash of her headlights. The clock on the dashboard gives them three minutes to spare. She cuts the engine and they both lean back for a moment, catching their breath before heading inside. Braced against the cold, they dash to the front door. As Kate grips the knob, Patty says, "Deal with Mom, okay? I'm a little drunk." And I'm tripping, Kate thinks, but she agrees because she knows her mother might smell booze on Patty's breath, but she'd never think to check her pupils.

They push inside and Patty dashes for the stairs. Kate walks into the family room and sees her mother snoring on the couch, her mouth open, a thin stream of drool connecting her to the pillow. She looks younger, Kate thinks, more like she used to look when I was little. Almost beautiful as she rests.

She crouches down next to the couch, lightly shakes her mother's arm. Waits for her startled eyes to focus, "Mom, Patty and I are home."

"Huh?" "We're home, Mom. Go in to bed." Sleepy, touching, her mother says, "I was waiting up." "I know. Go in to bed. We'll see you in the morning." "Okay." Kate stands, offers her mother a hand and helps her to her feet. She kisses her softly on the forehead and watches as she stumbles off towards the parents' bedroom. Slowly, she heads up herself, running her fingers along the wall of the staircase, clicking off the few lights that have been left on, glancing at the family portraits lining the walls of the hallway before ducking into her bedroom.

Sean dashes back into his room. Just a few minutes before, his room briefly lit with the headlights of a car turning into the driveway, he remembered he had to return Patty's pipe to her drawer. A quick run down the stairs, the pipe tucked back amongst her socks, and he was just halfway back up to the third floor when he heard her on the stairs. He feels incredibly sleepy as he changes for bed, he's not used to being up this late, everything feels sluggish.

Pulling his comforter up to his chin, he sticks his other hand down under the bed, feels around for a moment, and comes up with the stuffed rabbit he keeps down there during the day, too embarrassed to have it on his bed when others might see it. As he's drifting off, he remembers the bowl with the ashes and stubbed-out cigarette, and he's suddenly wide awake again. Tiptoeing out of his room, quietly all the way into the bathroom. He scrapes the residue from the bowl into the toilet, flushes it away, rinses the bowl clean under the tap, then sticks his mouth into the flow, swallowing greedily. Sneaking down the stairs, he heads into the kitchen. Quietly, he slips open the dishwasher door, fits the bowl between the row of spokes, and tiptoes back upstairs. Kate's door opens as he passes, and he steps up short, startled. "Hey," she says, giving him a kind smile, "What are you still doing up?" "Nothing. Couldn't sleep." And then Patty is in the hall with them. "The gang's all here," her words are too loud and sound somehow distorted or thick to Sean. "We were just going to have a last cigarette before bed,"

Kate whispers, "wanna come in with us?" Sean sees Patty shoot a look at Kate, but he doesn't care. "Okay."

He follows Kate into her room, Patty right behind. Kate puts one of their father's jazz records on her turntable, turns the volume down low, lowers the needle. Almost too quiet to hear, riffing saxophones and trumpets float into his ears. He takes a seat on the floor against the wall. Kate cracks a window, lies back on her bed and Patty slips onto the floor with her back against Kate's feet hanging off the mattress. He's very tired again, almost drifting off to the music, but he can't believe he's here, with them. They both fire up smokes, the familiar and comforting smell taking him deeper into his reverie. Smoking, they chat about the party, what happened to who, but carefully, not implicating themselves in front of Sean. He tries to listen, to learn, maybe catch a glimpse of what's ahead, but his eyes flutter closed, and his breath goes deep and regular. When he wakes in his own bed in the morning, cranky, overtired, he won't remember getting there, and he won't be sure if sitting here was real or a dream.

Patty leans forward and gazes at Sean, "He's out." Kate sits up a moment, looks over at him slumped against the wall and lies back down, "Yup." They both drop their smoldering butts into the bottle under Kate's bed, and Patty asks, "Want to smoke a quick bowl? It'll help you sleep." Kate knows there's no sleep coming to her anytime soon, she's got to ride out the last few waves of the acid before her body and mind quiet, but she's willing. She pulls her bag of pot and her pipe from her nightstand drawer, packs the bowl, hits it with her lighter and passes it to Patty. When it's done and they're both more mellow and sleepy, Patty rouses herself. "Thanks for getting me out tonight," Kate tells her, "I needed it." "My pleasure," Patty says, thinking, I needed you there too. "I'll get him upstairs," she continues, "Goodnight." " 'Night. Flip the light off on your way out, would you?"

Patty gently shakes Sean awake, gets him to his feet and leads him up to the base of the stairs. As he trudges up, she imagines him falling into bed and curling himself around that battered stuffed animal he tries to hide, and she thinks, I forget what a good kid he can be.

She heads back to her own room, flops into bed, and with all that beer and a few hits of pot, she's quickly slipping into a dreamless, heavy slumber.

Eventually, just before the end of the last solo on the record spinning on her player, Kate drifts off too. In the morning, they'll wake, all of them more or less on time to get them to 10:15 Mass. They'll pull out together, four well-dressed children and their mother crammed into the station wagon. The father will sit at home, wrapped in his blue terry-cloth robe, sipping coffee and reading the Sunday paper. It will look like it has looked for hundreds of earlier Sundays. But things are changing, there's nothing to be done about it, and no one, even with the reassurance of that morning's Catholic ritual and the familial love which has bound them together for all these years, no one can say for sure how they will survive what might be coming.

1 9 7 5

Kate hops down from the school bus, crosses the street in the protection of its flashing red lights and dashes across the lawn towards home.
Along the way she scuffs her feet through a scattered carpet of fallen
leaves, watches them lift in swirling patterns of red and yellow and
crunchy brown until they settle around her saddle shoes again. Her
shuffling progress across the wide swath of lawn is a curious mixture of
play and embarrassment. As if she's free to still be a child here and
now, without the eyes of St. Anne's Middle School on her back. And
though she's not sure she still feels like a child, the kicking of leaves into
the air on a bright, after-school autumn afternoon is both silly and fun.
Half-girl, half-woman; the age of molting, her body's beginning to

curve out from its years of lankiness, but is still encased in that little-girl uniform of plaid, pleated skirt, knee socks, and white, ruffled blouse. Just before she goes around the back to let herself in through the always unlocked kitchen door, she gives in completely and scoops up a big heap of leaves, throws them over her head and feels them settle around her, sticking to her hair, the wool of her skirt. Skipping around the garage, plucking leaves from the static pull of bangs and wool, she pulls open the door of the house and feels older as she remembers the house is empty. Her mother is still at work, and getting the dog out, keeping an eye on Patty and Sean when they get home is *her responsibility now* with her mother working again.

The mother collects the spelling tests her charges are finishing up at the end of their last period. She hands out the notices about parent-teacher conferences and the dittoed permission slips for next week's class trip to the Statue of Liberty. The bell rings. The throng of third-graders pushes out of their seats and rushes to the coat closet at the back of the classroom. She watches as they shrug into coats and struggle to get their backpacks over their shoulders, and, for a moment, thinks of Patty and Sean. In their separate classrooms at Immaculate Conception Elementary across town, waiting eagerly for their bell to ring, fifteen minutes later than the public school. She doesn't know how the nuns manage to hold their attention any longer on days like today when it's warm, bright as summer, and the kids just want to get outside and jump in the leaves.

She has bus duty this year, a royal pain in the ass she has to bear with the youngest teachers in the district because of all the years she spent waiting to go back to work until her children went to school. Over a decade of lost time, many friends and colleagues from those early, idealistic years turned bitter, retired, or moved away. The theories of learning and discipline changed or changing, the sureness she once felt in front of a room filled with young, eager, sometimes unruly faces occasionally lost. She's not sorry, not exactly. She wouldn't trade those years at home, those years when her children changed almost minute by minute and she was there to chronicle those moments of growth for herself and for her husband. But. She's thrilled to be earning an income again, the extra money a pittance compared to what Pat brings home, but allowing for luxuries, additions to the kids' college funds. She's thrilled to be out of the house for a while each day, away from the dependence of grabbing little hands solely her responsibility, in a place where she's not a mother at all, where she's merely Mrs. Mahoney.

She gets the last of her students zipped up and waiting in line out in the hall for their bus number to be called and quickly gathers her own things. Outside, she takes her place beside the young teachers on the sidewalk as they make sure no one gets on the wrong bus. Stealing glances at their faces, it feels like she should be teaching them—they are impossibly young. She wishes she was in the faculty room with her friend Anna, counting the minutes until they can leave, sucking down a shared can of Tab and gossiping about these young teacher-kids and how much has changed.

Patty's hand me down uniform shirt, smudged around the collar with a year of Kate's dirt, chafes at her neck as the clock clicks another three-minute lurch towards the end of the day. Three more lurches, she thinks, and we're out of here. From her seat in the front of the room, she keeps one eye and ear on Sister Eugene as she details the history homework for tomorrow, the rest of her body clamoring to be released into the beautiful afternoon, the sun-warmed vinyl of the seat on the bus home. Maybe she'll run through the worn paths down into the woods with Sean or read in the window seat of Kate's bedroom while Kate draws. She is bored, bored the way she often is at school, the lessons too slow, the work too easy. I've already read that chapter, she thinks as Sister Gene completes her assignment, and the one after it.

. . .

Nora, sticky with splotches of paste and spotted with little shreds of cotton, clutches a piece of construction paper covered with a mass of fluffy balls. Looking carefully, with the doting, indulgent eye of a parent, it might just be a sheep. She waits while Miss Kim helps her classmates into their windbreakers and matches the right book bags with the right kids. Her mother will be here soon. Since Nora started school, her mother comes in at the end of the day with Aunt Anna, and she walks with the two of them and Miss Kim to the parking lot. Driving home, her mother and Anna ask her about her day, and she tells them. About what she had at snack time, who played with who, who cried and what Miss Kim did or said. She loves school, she loves Miss Kim and she loves driving home with her mother when everyone else, Kate and Patty and Sean, has to ride a bus.

The father sits in his firm's law library surrounded by green copies of *New Jersey Statutes Annotated* and the red faux leather of the *Shepard's* books. Pulling his eyes away from his yellow pad of notes, he leans back in his chair and stretches his arms over his head, working the cricks from his neck. Checking his watch, he sees that it's after three o'clock. He's going to need to stay late again. Eleven years since law-school graduation, ten since the prestigious clerkship with the Appellate Judge in Trenton, nearly a decade at this firm. He expects to make partner within a year, but he can't slack off now. If anything, the pressure's greater than it's ever been—the pressure to do good work, but more the pressure to bill. To come in early and work late, to grind out the hours, *to generate revenue for the firm.* It wasn't supposed to be like this. He's making more money than he ever dreamed he would and he doesn't mind the work. He likes procedure and case law, the piecing together of rulings and arguments from different cases to benefit his clients, assuring their trust in him and this firm. What goads him is the sheer accumulation of hours spent here, away from his wife and his children, the sixty or eighty hours he dedicates to Eastman Kodak or Pillsbury each week. Hours torn away from his marriage. Hours when his kids seem to grow taller, barely an echo of the toddling children who once mobbed him at the door when he came home to a dinner kept warm on low heat in the oven. When he came home to the sympathetic ear of a wife who, to his mind, had only the burden of a family and wasn't dogged with his extreme fatigue. A wife who would sit with him and talk while he ate, filling him in on the small ways his children were being carved into distinct shape by their growing experience of the world. A wife who would coax him into making love after the children were tucked in and sleeping.

Sean saves a seat for Patty on parochial bus #12. The second-graders are herded out of the building before the fifth-graders, and the bus is full of excited, high-pitched chatter. Sean's friend John from down the street is one seat ahead of him, twisted around and looking over the seat top, asking, "You wanna come over and play?" Sean isn't sure. It might be fun to go to John's house, kick a soccer ball around in the backyard, and John's mother always has good snacks. But he and Patty might go into the woods and explore, catch crayfish in the creek, poke under the rocks and hold squiggly salamanders up by their shiny black, yellow speckled tails. And there she is, coming out of the building with a gaggle of girls clustered around her, the center of attention. They push ahead of her onto the bus, heading towards the back, staking out seats so that Patty might slide in next to them. Sean sits alone in his two-seater right in the middle, waiting for her to spot him, and one of the girls is calling, "Patty? Over here!" But she sees Sean, gives them a wave and calls over her shoulder, eleven years old and world-weary, "I told my mom I'd watch out for Sean." Sean, for a moment, feels small. Sensitive tears threaten his eyes as she settles on the seat next to him, but they're gone in an instant as she says, "Hey, you wanna go down to the creek?" He smiles his gap-toothed smile and nods his head up and down, up and down, "How about all the way to the magic clearing you told me about?" "Maybe," she says, "but it's far."

The mother watches as the last bus pulls out of the school's circular driveway, the driver giving a little toot of the horn as she heads out towards the highway. Turning back into the building, she walks the suddenly silent, almost chilly hallway towards the faculty room. In the only realm of adulthood in this building, the only place protected from the susceptible eyes and ears of children, she finds a couple of her older colleagues sitting around the cigarette-scarred folding table, talking about their students, "That Kenworthy kid is pure, fucking, unadulterated evil." Scanning the room for Anna, she looks them over; the men with their wide-lapeled, brilliant-hued polyester suits and mutton-chops sideburns, the women with their iron-straight, center-parted hair and hip-huggers. She holds them in contempt, but nods her greetings. Their attempts to meet this year's fashion land them squarely in the midst of three years ago, they produce clumsily rolled joints at faculty parties. She sees their desire to be happening and wonders, How can they be teachers? They're just holding on for their pensions, their twenty-five years. Coasting.

She spots Anna in an orange-vinyl chair by the soda machine, flipping through a copy of *Time* decorated with Brezhnev's fleshy face, one of her Salems dangling from the corner of her mouth, her fingers drumming impatiently on some faculty member's no-longer-needed end table. She plucks the cigarette from her friend's mouth and takes a drag, marveling at how good it still feels to have smoke spiraling down her throat and into her lungs even though she gave them up back in '62 when she was carrying Kate and decided, in that first flush of maternal instinct, to do it for the baby. Handing the cigarette back, she perches on the chair's arm, "Haven't you heard? Those are bad for you." "So it says on the package. How was your day?" "Same as always.

Yours?" "Ditto." Anna hands her the dregs of her Tab, gathers her canvas tote bag, stands and says, "Let's get Nora and get the fuck out of
here." The mother tilts the last swallow down her throat, wincing
slightly at the cloying bite of the saccharine. As they head towards the
door together, she pitches the can towards the garbage bin, "Is keeping our figures worth that taste?"

Kate steps into the warm flow of the shower in the kids' bathroom, lux-
uriating in the play of water around her body. This, her second shower
of the day, is just for the pleasure of it, the rush of water over her head,
streaming down her back; the massaging showerhead twisted to coarse,
tattooing a rhythm on her shoulders. It hasn't been that long since she
had to be coaxed into the tub or shower a few times each week by the
demands of her mother. But now she loves being here. Loves being
alone under the endless deluge, loves soaping her body and washing and
conditioning her hair, squeezing the ends of those tresses to coax the
last of the soap out into a sudsy spiral down the drain.

The tile is a rich royal blue and dull green, separated by wire-thin
strips of grayish-white grout in a pattern that separates and swims before her eyes if she stares at it long enough. There's something to see
in there, some sort of music to the arrangement. She could draw it if
she just sat and looked long enough. So, she's taken to sitting on the
floor while the water flows around her, watching the walls closely, *taking forever* in the shower so that *she's going to make everyone late* on week-
day mornings. Her mother, finding Kate's plain cotton underwear
spotted blood-brown in the laundry, that undeniable sign of her
coming-of-age, pulled her aside one night and, both of them excruci-
atingly embarrassed, they had a talk. In keeping with the enlightened
times and the work of Dr. Spock, she assured Kate masturbation was
okay, that most people did it, but told her to be "considerate of everyone's time in the morning." Bordeaux-faced, Kate nodded, "I know
that stuff." Satisfied, her mother left her alone. But Kate knew it wasn't

that. She was no stranger to the pleasures of water rushing from the tub's tap, all her friends at school giggled knowingly about taking long showers. Besides, it didn't take that long. She wanted to tell her mother about the pattern and the way it shifts and moves under her gaze to suggest something. But if she could explain the tile, she wouldn't have to look it at, she wouldn't want to figure out the tune of its lines, she wouldn't have to draw it.

So she's been forcing her eyes closed in the morning, willing herself not to get caught up in those shifting shapes, but when she gets home to the empty house in the afternoon, she has a half hour or so to herself, and lately, she has found herself showering a second time. Now, she's plopped on the floor, staring at the blue and green and gray-white, watching the shower's wall through a curtain of water, and trying to put her finger on just what, exactly, compels her gaze.

Patty swings her legs out into the bus aisle as it wheels towards her house. Looks towards the back where Jason Post from next door sits in the very last seat, his fringed buckskin jacket thrown across the lap of his black uniform pants. He's a bad kid. A sixth-grader for the second time, greasy hair hanging past his shoulders, his early maturing bulk putting him a full head taller than most of his grade, making him something of a bully. He's neat, Patty thinks. He doesn't speak to her in school; not pretty, popular Patty Mahoney, teacher's favorite and ringleader of that privileged crowd that falls between the geeks and the bad seeds. Away from school, it can be different.

Near the end of summer, back from the shore for a few days before Labor Day weekend, the whole family, everyone but Patty who opted out and the father who had to work, had gone off to the county college for a student summer art show. A show where Kate was honored, again, for her drawing. This time it was for things she'd done at the college's Creative Youth program, the program where Kate was the only one not in high school. Sullen, bored with her own company in the centrally air-conditioned cool of the house, Patty'd gone for a walk in the woods. Aimless, trudging down deer paths towards the river, she'd come into a clearing and found a burned-out ring of an old fire, the unmistakable debris of a party. Hundreds of cigarette butts and crumpled beer cans, the thin, cruel shards of pull-tops, piles of broken glass. She immediately thought of the book she'd just finished, with its wood elves who partied in the dark of night and vanished at the first sound of anyone approaching. For a time, she sat against a tree, still, hoping they might come back, but her lively imagination faded, and she saw it then as just a place where some of the older kids from town came at night.

Curious, she poked in the remains of something that was just a few years from her grasp, until she heard someone crackling down the path toward her. Jason Post came into the clearing, kicking a can towards the charcoal ring. She startled him when she softly called, "Hey," but he composed himself quickly, already figuring out what it means to be cool, and reached into the pocket of his Wrangler cutoffs. Pulling out a packet of Kent cigarettes, he tucked one between his lips, struck a match on one of the rivets and, holding those greasy strands from his face, got it lit. "Hey," he answered. Feeling suddenly as if she wanted to stake a claim to something for herself, not to be just Kate's little sister, she asked, "Got an extra smoke?" "You're too little," he said, "Fifth grade, right?" "I know how to smoke." "Sure you do," he said, tapping a cigarette out of the crumpled pack, "Show me." She got it going, pulled smoke into her mouth, and eyes watering and head swimming from her first taste of illicit, adult pleasures, she managed to convince him she did know. They sat for a while, talking about summer and the school year to come, and she asked where he got the cigarettes. He said he stole them from his dad, and look what else, two airplane bottles of booze, one peppermint schnapps, one blackberry brandy. Walking towards the river, they took nips from those miniature bottles, Patty flinching from the burn, but liking the sweet taste and how she suddenly was giggly and brave. At the river, she felt hot, and wished aloud they had bathing suits, and he, brave as well, said, "Who needs 'em?" Shucking down to his white Fruit-Of-The-Looms with a blue stripe, he ran into the river. Patty, briefly hesitating, stripped down to her flowered undies and the training bra she didn't need but insisted her mother buy for her, and followed him into the mud-brown water. They splashed and paddled and dunked one another, like innocents from another age. After, lying on the bank, *everything see-through,* she stole glances at him and he at her, but that was all as they slowly dried and sweated out the last of the sweet drinks until they realized it was getting late, put their clothes back on and headed through the woods towards home.

But now, even though Patty had fun that day, even though he wasn't anything like what she had expected, she couldn't talk to him. She wasn't supposed to even know anything about him. In the strict social code of school, all she could do was look back at him as he ruled the backseats of the bus, teasing one of her school friends, and hope to catch his eye before the bus stopped in front of her house.

Nora jumps up and runs into her mother's arms as she and Anna come into Miss Kim's classroom. "Mommy, I made you a sheep!" she calls out. "Miss Kim showed us how, we used cotton balls." "It's beautiful, honey," the mother tells her. "Thanks for waiting, Kim. Good day?" "No problem, Liz, the same." As the teachers make small talk, Nora rushes to the big closet at the back of the room, gathers her Speed Racer backpack, and scampers back. "Aunt Anna," she asks as her mother and Miss Kim continue to chat, "is it time to leave yet?" Miss Kim looks over at her, smiles her pretty smile, and says, "Well, I'm ready." They walk towards the teachers' parking lot, Nora holding on to her mother's hand as the grown-ups talk, spelling out words when they don't want Nora to get the gist of their conversation. At the woody station wagon, Nora waits until her mother unlocks the front door and reaches around to pull up the lock in the backseat and open her door. Scooting across that vinyl bench, she cranks down the window and waves as Miss Kim gets her little green car unlocked, "Bye, Miss Kim!"

She leans between the gap in the front seats as her mother turns the ignition and pops a Jim Croce tape into the 8-Track. "Nora," her mother says, "Miss Kim says you got a one hundred on your test today." "I got them all, Mommy. Nobody else got them all." Pausing, but not stopping at the top of the driveway, the mother turns left and, as she accelerates up to just above the speed limit, she says, "I think that might just call for an ice-cream cone. What do you think, Anna?" "I think it might," Anna says, "What do you think, Nora?" Leaning her head as far as she can into the front, Nora agrees, "I think so." "Okay, then," the mother says, "sit back, and we'll stop at Hid-E-Ho."

Nora leans back against the seat, the mother turns up the volume on the tape deck, and Nora sings along with "Leroy Brown," loving this song because it's got junkyard dogs in it, and she gets to say "damn" each time it comes up and doesn't even get in trouble. It's just part of the song.

The father loosens his tie and undoes the top button on his Brooks Brothers shirt as he walks towards his little office with the window looking out on the parking lot. Near the kitchenette, he spots a gaggle of secretaries gossiping, their work mostly finished for the day, waiting eagerly for the magic hour of five o'clock so they can head home. Glancing at the legs on one of the pool secretaries he, as an associate, has occasion to use, seeing them go up and up until they disappear into the hem of her miniskirt, then that smooth, tight fabric unblemished by panty lines, the father thinks, God I love the seventies.

He passes the open doors of the partners' bigger offices, they sit behind their desks, speaking on the phone, their papers all around them in neat order. Small client tables with the occasional coffee service set out wait in the corners. They look relaxed. How different from the tiny offices he and the other associates use, overflowing with file folders and old Styrofoam coffee cups, mold-flecked drecks lingering near the bottom. One of the senior partners, his name on the door of this firm, cups a hand over the phone receiver and calls to the father as he passes, "Pat, could you come in here for a moment?" Nervous; this sort of summons from George Riker could mean anything—a reprimand, praise, a heaping on of more work—the father sits down in his boss' client chair, facing him across the big, delicate antique desk, and waits. Riker finishes his conversation, making a notation on the calendar portion of his desk blotter, and hangs up. "Cigarette?" he asks, reaching into the inner pocket of his black suit jacket. "Sure," the father says, "I'm trying to quit, but—" He accepts the smoke and a light and watches his boss press the button on his desk that summons his personal secretary, "Mandy, could you bring in some coffee please," then lean back in his chair and blow smoke rings towards the ceiling.

Mandy, older than the pool group—she's been here since before the father—comes in with a silver service, places it on the end table, and pours out two china cups. She hands one, black, to her boss, then turns to the father, "Milk or sugar, Mr. Mahoney?" "Both please." She doctors the coffee, hands cup and saucer to the father, "Anything else, Mr. Riker?" "That will be all, Mandy, please close the door on your way out."

Riker stubs out his cigarette, pushes the ashtray towards the father and waits for him to do likewise. "So, Patrick," he begins, "you've been here almost ten years now? Are you happy with your work, with the firm?" Not sure where these questions are leading, thinking, something like this from Riker is never good, feeling as if that cigarette may have been the last smoke of a condemned man, but pretty sure he *has* done good work, the father says, "Yes, sir. On all counts." "Well, Patrick, I just spoke to opposing counsel on the Meyerson case." Meyerson. The case that's been eating most of the father's billable time for these past months, his evenings too, sometimes his weekends. It's a liability case, murky in its details, with Kodak, one of this firm's major clients, seemingly on the hook for a lot of money. A loser if there ever was one. But last week, late one night, the father thought he'd stumbled on a loophole, a vaguely worded ruling in one of the plaintiff's key precedent cases. Working past midnight, he prepared a memorandum of law for Riker and left it on his desk before leaving. The next morning, the father's in-box held a terse memo from Riker instructing him to put his work on Meyerson on hold until further notice, and the father feared he had blown it. "Yes sir?" the father asks now.

"I filed a Motion to Dismiss based on your memo. The ruling was scheduled for Monday, but they've offered a settlement for about a quarter of initial damages. The in-house boys over at Kodak are very, very pleased. Nice work." "Thank you, sir." "Please, George." Reaching into his desk, George pulls out a bottle of expensive Scotch, an old single malt, and two Waterford crystal rocks glasses. He pours two fingers for each of them and hands the father one across the desk. "We've got a partnership meeting at the end of the month. I have a feeling your name's going to come up." Relief has been spreading across the father's features since he heard the word "dismiss," and his face spreads now into a comfortable smile as he leans back into the chair, "Thank you, sir." Raising his glass at the father from behind the desk, George says, "I told you, it's George, and congratulations, you've earned it."

The father sips his Scotch, marvels as the texture of the whisky spreads across his tongue and fills his mouth with its soft flavor of heather and peat. Slowly, as he chats amiably with *George* about both their families, the case he's been researching this afternoon, the legs of that pool secretary, as he chats the small talk of equals, he begins to think with satisfaction, I belong here. The crystal, this Scotch, this office, I belong *here*.

As the sun slants lower in the sky, a breeze begins to stir. Ruffling first the top layers of trees, spinning helicopter seed pods from their fragile moorings on maple branches, it releases another round of brilliant-

hued leaves to the ground where they mingle with those already fallen
in a carpet of dying festivity. The air temperature drops from the still,
false heat of an Indian summer afternoon towards something that could
be called crisp. At the end of the Mahoneys' street, the apple trees in
the orchard of one of the last working farms in this town are laden with
fruit. Fat wasps and stealthy hornets buzz around the windfalls, lured
out of hiding by the promise of the sun and a last taste of sweet juice
before winter. The cows cluster around the gate of their pasture, low-
ing occasionally under the burden of full udders, waiting to be driven
towards the barn and their afternoon milking. As the sun slants lower
in the sky, it glances through the thinning branches of trees, bounces
off the river, and lends this afternoon, in this part of rural New Jersey,
something of a golden shine.

Parochial bus #12 pulls up in front of the Mahoney house and the
driver throws the heavy lever that accordions open the door. Sean
bounds out of the bus behind his friend John and waits until Patty and
Jason Post climb from the steps. He walks a little way up the street with
John, the bus blowing them with a warm, exhaust-scented breeze as it
staggers forward to complete the rest of its route. "I don't think I can
play today," he tells John, "but we've got the soccer game tomorrow afternoon." "Okay, see you," John says, shouldering his backpack and
starting up the street towards his house where they both know his
mom will be waiting with homemade brownies or cookies or chocolate cake. Sean watches him for a moment, a little hungry and knowing there's not much snack-wise around the house these days. But he'll
grab something, maybe a piece of fruit or a few Oreos, before heading
out into the woods. He turns towards Patty and sees her talking to
Jason, their mother has told them not to talk to him, "Come on, Patty."
"Go inside, Sean, I'll be there in a minute." "Patty," he draws the vow-
els out into a little whine this time. "Just go, Sean. I'm coming in a
minute."

Sulky, taking his time, he shuffles across the front lawn, kicking his feet through dead leaves, turning around a few times to look at the two of them sitting on the curb, Patty hugging her knees to her chest and Jason's legs sprawled out in a V-shape into the road. When he gets to the point where he has to go around the back to let himself into the house, he looks back one last time—they're still sitting there. "Kate!" he yells, opening the kitchen door, "I'm home." From somewhere upstairs, he hears her call, "I'm in my room." He kicks off his shoes by the door, pops off his clip-on tie, tosses it on the hutch in the dining room, and scuffs his socks through the shag carpeting, up the stairs to the second floor. He scuffs through the shorter nap on the stairs and along the run of the hallway to Kate's room. He sees her in there, perched on the window seat, drawing in her sketch pad, wearing shorts and a loose white V-neck undershirt stolen from their father's drawer, her hair done up in a towel twisted to look like a genie's turban. Scuffing across the forbidden threshold of her doorway, he picks his way through the debris-strewn rug of her room, skirting clothes and album covers to where she sits in the window. He leans over her shoulder, sees the vaguely square-shaped blobs of colored pencil lines, blue and green, smudged by her thumb. She's barely registered his presence, and when he reaches out a finger and pops her bare arm with a static shock, she jumps back. "Shit, Sean," she pushes him away, "You know you're not allowed in here." "I'm telling Mom you used a bad word." "Grow up. Where's Patty?" "Outside with Jason Post." Kate looks up at him, a funny little smile on her face, "Really?" she says, holding on to the middle point of the word with curiosity in her voice. "Yup. Mom told us to stay away from him." Quickly, she answers him using her firm, I'm-in-charge voice, "Don't worry about it. Go change out of your uniform," and turns back to her pad.

Wandering out of her room, scuffing through the carpet once again, he pauses, grabs hold of the knobs on either side of the door, giving himself a small shock, and swings. "What're you drawing?" he asks. "What?" "What're you drawing?" "Nothing, just messing around." As

he leaves and heads towards the stairs, he hears Patty thumping in the
back door, tossing her things aside, and bounding up the stairs. But she
doesn't follow him up that second flight, she must have turned into
Kate's room, and just to make sure she hears, he slams his door, hard.
He strips down, leaves his uniform pants and shirt in a heap on the floor
and rummages in the drawers for something to put on, still hoping
they're going to the place where Patty told him that elves had parties.

The mother cuts the wheel of the family station wagon and turns off
Route 202 into the parking lot of Hid-E-Ho, and Nora scrambles to
open her door as soon as the car stops. "Whoa there," her Aunt Anna
calls, "The ice cream's not going anyplace." Nora pulls up short. Waits
while her mother takes her by the hand, all the while continuing her
conversation with Anna about contract negotiations and the way the
NJEA representative, a blocky woman who teaches history in the middle school, has been calling them both at night, speaking to them about
the possibility of a strike, drawing out the word "solidarity" and looking at the two of them at union meetings as if the three of them share
some secret complicity. Coding their words for the benefit of Nora, the
mother reverts to the lingo of the fifties, "I think she's an invert," and
Anna nods her head, "Wouldn't be surprised." "What's invert mean?"
Nora asks. "Nothing," her mother answers, "she's just backwards sometimes."

As they come around to the side of the building where the take-out
window yawns open, they spot a man at one of the picnic tables, filthy
hair spilling down past his shoulders. His green Army jacket tattered,
his eyes darting wildly, a brown bag bottle clutched in one hand. The
mother pulls up short, jerking Nora's arm hard. Her daughter gasps,
"Ow, Mommy," but her gaze takes in the man, and she points and says,
too loudly, "Look! A hippie!" The mother wheels Nora around, hush-
ing her, "Shhh. We'll eat inside today," and pulls her towards the front
door. But Nora's fascinated, swiveling her head around for another

look, taking in the Army jacket, the long hair, her mother's apprehension. "Was that hippie in the army, Mommy? Why can't we sit out here?" The mother glances back, sees the wild-eyed man staggering up from the picnic table, ambling in their direction. She can practically smell him *all the way from here.* Moving faster towards the entrance to the restaurant, saying under her breath, "Shhh. Come on Nora. Keep it down," the mother hustles them inside, pushing Nora ahead of her, watching as Anna looks over her shoulder just as the man passes the door. Anna's body flinches as the man says something in passing and she gives him the finger. Wondering what provoked her friend, the mother thinks, What are we coming to when that can intrude on us here, an ice-cream stand for Christ's sake, where people bring their kids.

Kate gives up on her sketch as Patty flops down on her bed and tosses her book into the mess on the floor. Patty sprawls on her back, hands behind her head, staring up at the ceiling, her uniform skirt billowed around her skinny thighs. Tossing a throw pillow at her sister, Kate teases, "I hear you've got a boyfriend." "What?" "Sean said you were out there with Jason Post." "Gimme a break, he's a creep-o." "So, what were you doing?" "Being polite. He asked a question." "Sure." "I was. What about you? You going to the Harvest Dance? All the sixth-graders are talking about it."

Of course Kate's going to the Harvest Dance: the school gym dark on a Friday night, stalks of wheat and arrangements of gourds for decoration, a high school dee-jay playing records, the nuns watching anxiously from the sides, making sure a flash light can shine through the space between dancers on the slow numbers . . . Of course she's going, it's the only thing talked about in the hall between classes, the girls in the hairspray cloud of the second-floor bathroom gossiping about who was going with who. It's the biggest social event of the fall, and she wants to go with Jimmy McNally, an eighth-grader. He's the youngest of a large family that takes up a whole pew at church, mother and father, then a line of children each a head shorter than the rest, nine in all. His older brother Kenny was killed years ago in the War when Kate was in fourth grade and Jimmy wears his dog-tags all the time, braving the wrath of the Phys-Ed teacher, taking the demerits for wearing jewelry during gym class. He's quiet, not part of any of the cliques, but floats among all of them at will, and his features are so delicately sharp with his pale skin, and chin-length white-blond hair. Kate feels like she's looking right through him. That he's not even there as she stares at him from across the art room during lunch when they both go there to paint with a handful of students who've found themselves favorites of the lay teacher. His paintings are all harsh acrylic strokes. Kate has stolen glances at his canvases and suffered from odd little rushes and tumblings in her belly, the strange, unnameable queasiness of a first crush. He has secrets, she thinks, and no one to tell them to. He could tell me. He could tell me.

"Yeah, I'm going," she leans against the window as if it's no big deal. "Who with?" "Nobody." "You gonna ask anybody?" She mulls her answer, wondering if she should share this, wondering if Patty will blab to the rest of the family, but dying to tell someone. To tell anyone, because her friends all think Jimmy's strange. It's really only cool to like guys from St. Anne's if they play on the basketball team or end up in regular trouble with the nuns. Jimmy just sort of floats by all of that, making the honor roll, never joining any of the teams. "Keep a secret?" she asks Patty. "Okay." "Promise?" "Promise." "Cross your heart and hope to die?" "Cross my heart and hope to die." Leaning forward and lowering her voice, Kate confides in her sister, the first of hundreds of similar confidences they will share over the coming years, "I want to go with Jimmy McNally." Patty sits up on the bed and stares over at her, her face aging as it takes on a serious expression and Kate fancies for a moment she can see what Patty will look like when they are both grown-up. "From church, right?" she asks, "The one whose brother died?" Shy now, with the revelation out in the open, Kate just nods, and

Patty leaps up from the bed, swoops down on her in the window, making kissy noises, puckering her lips up like a fish, "Oh, Jimmy. Kiss me, Jimmy. I wuv you, Jimmy." Dancing away from Kate, she singsongs, "Katy-did's got a boyfriend. Katy-did's got a boyfriend. Kate and Jim sitting in the tree, K-I-S-S-I-N-G," and Kate is up from the seat, pushing her, gathering her into a headlock and dragging her from the room, Patty laughing all the way, "First comes love, then comes the marriage——" Kate shoves Patty into the hall, eyes moist with tears, "You promised. Cross your heart." And Patty, choking back her laughter, coughing, but sensing, even at eleven years old, that something she can't quite put her finger on, something bigger than the short-term fun of teasing Kate, something about what it means to be sisters, might be at stake at this moment, says, "I won't tell." Kate nods, and using her I'm-in-charge voice again, says, "Go change," around the closing door. She moves back into the room and grabs her book bag, where she has a notebook page covered with Jimmy's name and the phone number she got from the church directory. As she flips the pages back and forth, she hears Patty skipping down the hall into her room, humming "Katy-did loves Jimmy, Katy-did loves Jimmy" indistinctly as she goes.

Nora stares at the garish pictures of various ice-cream desserts tacked along Hid-E-Ho's walls, trying to decide what she should have. The Banana Boat, with its special blue plastic container, the mounds of whipped cream, the blazing red cherry and three different colors of sauce, captivates her. She points at it, "I want that, Mommy," tugging on her mother's arm as they wait, her mother chatting in a low voice with Aunt Anna. "It's too big, you'll spoil your dinner." Her mother turns back towards Aunt Anna, and Nora hears Anna say, "He said, 'Swallow my vet C-O-C-K B-I-T-C-H'." Interested, because it maybe has to do with the hippie from out front, but not able to follow the spelling, she tries to listen and turns away from the posters, concentrating. Suddenly they're at the front, and her mother asks her, "Chocolate or vanilla?" Realizing she won't be getting the Banana Boat this afternoon, accepting that without injury because she's still getting something, Nora answers, "Vanilla. With rainbow sprinkles?" Her mother says to the man behind the counter, "One small vanilla cake cone with rainbow sprinkles and one large root beer float with vanilla and two spoons."

The man behind the counter swirls Nora's little cone, rolls it in the bin of brightly colored jimmies and hands it across the counter and down into her outstretched hand. Immediately, she dives in, pushing at the top of the cone with her mouth, sucking in the crunch of the sprinkles. "What do you say, Nora?" her mother prompts. From around a mouthful of her treat, she mumbles, "Thank you," and waits while her mother collects her float, balances the spoons and straws on top of the cup and jams change back into her pocket.

They make their way to a booth in the rear of the restaurant, Nora on the outside of the bench seat, next to her mother, Anna across the table, and they all dig in. Nora, focused only on her cone, licks quickly, spinning it around in her hand, trying to keep it from going lopsided and falling over onto the floor. Her mother and Aunt Anna work more slowly, languorously sucking small spoonfuls from those long-handled white plastic spoons, pausing to sip liquid from the straws, talking all the time. In just a few short minutes, Nora's down to the cone, crunching at it, trying to work the last bit of ice cream out from the flat bottom. At the jingle of the bell that signals the opening of the door, she looks up and sees her friend Kathleen from school and across the street come in with her mother. Bored with the adults who aren't really paying any attention to her, she stands and waves, "Hi Kathy. Hi Mrs. Wallack."

Kathy and her mother come over, Nora hears her mother and Mrs. Wallack saying hello, her mother introducing Aunt Anna, but only vaguely. She and Kathy move to the booth behind them, giggling, and as soon as they sit down, they're playing a game that Miss Kim taught them during play time. Reaching across the table to slap hands in a sloppy pattern, they sing, "Ceci my playmate, come out and play with me." It barely registers on them when Mrs. Wallack plops a small cup of chocolate-and-vanilla swirl in front of Kathleen and joins the other adults at their table. Kathy produces a loop of string from the pocket of her overalls, and Nora twists the beginnings of cat's cradle as Kathleen starts to eat. Between Kathleen's spoonfuls of ice cream, they pluck at the strings, change the shapes it makes, pass it back and forth between them in an ever-changing array of geometric patterns. Suddenly, it's time for both of them to leave. As they're climbing back into her mother's car, Nora says, proudly, "Kathy's my best friend in the whole world."

The father, a bit foggy from a second two fingers with George, checks his watch and decides he'll finish his work at home tonight. Five forty-five is an okay time to head home. Not right at the stroke of five, but still earlier than usual. Maintaining the illusion that he's working hard. A little later than the traffic spilling out onto the highway from the John Manville plant. Home by 6:30. Home in time for dinner.

But that leaves him with just over an hour to kill. He pushes his office door closed and pops the little lock into place. Easing back into his chair, he leans back and locks his hands behind his head. Gazing at the cramped space, the cluttered desk, the stacks of papers, Redweld folders and file boxes on the floor, he thinks, Not much longer. Soon, I'll be working in one of those big offices with a little table, my own secretary and a good bottle of aged whisky in my bottom desk drawer.

He pulls his hand-tooled, once-beautiful but now old and battered, trial bag out from under his desk. His wife presented it to him after law-school graduation; this bag that held his Bar Exam study materials during that first post-graduate summer, carried him from clerkship to associate and now, soon, up to partner. Running his fingers over the leather, working open the clasps, he sees the way time and use have aged and softened the fine details of the outsized briefcase. He remembers how proud he was once lugging that stiff case into the courthouse, feeling it marked him as a lawyer to any who saw him, and he wonders how it could've come to look so shabby. He doesn't feel much different from that kid smiling from the law-school graduation photograph on his desk, beaming and shaking hands with the dean. And though his face has settled some, there's a hint of gray streaked in his hair, his belly a bit rounder with each passing year, he *doesn't feel any older.* But if he's the same, how come the bag looks so bad?

He loads it up with the papers he'll need to lug home later, and takes out the Bobby Kennedy biography he's been reading on those rare lunch hours he can steal away and late at night when he's still keyed up from work, his wife sleeping next to him. Filled with the guilty pleasure of doing something else while he's supposed to be on the job, he thinks, I should call home and let them know I won't be that late, but he puts it off in favor of some time with his book. Digging in, he finds himself transported to Bobby's tour of Appalachia and his growing indignation over rural poverty.

Sean wanders down from his bedroom, changed into jeans and a T-shirt, the sneakers he had to have or he'd just be humiliated at the outlet store in Flemington where they did their back-to-school shopping. He clicks on the television and flips the dial aimlessly through the channels, stopping on 11 and a *Tom and Jerry* rerun. Padding into the kitchen, he pokes around for something sweet and has to settle for an apple from the bowl on the counter and a swig of milk right from the carton. He plops onto the floor in front of the television and munches on the fruit, grinning at the predictable antics of cartoon cat and mouse; he hasn't seen this one before. Soon, the mangled cat is restored to shape and the episode is over. 4:30. After a commercial break aimed at impressionable after-school viewers—Lawn Darts, Toys-"R"-Us, you-put-your-chocolate-in-my-peanut butter—Magilla Gorilla is for sale, and Sean, bored but without much else to do, just some home-work, watches.

Without meaning to, he becomes engrossed in his cartoons. He doesn't even hear when Patty comes into the room and sits on his back. "I thought we were going to the woods, lazy-boy," she says. "If you still want to," Sean answers, petulant. "Let's go. If we're going to get to the elves' magic clearing, we've got to go now." He clicks off the tel-evision and yells up the stairs to Kate, "Patty and I are going explor-ing." Her answer comes down, "Be back by five-thirty for dinner or Mom'll kill you."

They set off, scampering through the backyard, almost falling as the slope of the hill carries them down. At the edge of the property, they duck under a barbed wire fence, careful not to catch their clothes on the rusting points, and are off across the old pasture bought from the farmer by a developer a few years ago and gone to seed while the de-veloper waits for more funding. The grass, almost as tall as Sean at its seedy tips, crackles underfoot and springs back up around them. From the house, if anyone was looking, they'd be obscured from view, their path traced only by the movements of the high stalks.

At the other end, another ring of barbed wire separates the pasture from the woods, and they dip under. Walking along the tree line, they keep their eyes peeled for the almost concealed opening of the path, and finding it, they gently pry the pricker bush branches aside and step into the cool cover of the trees. They wind down to the creek, and Sean watches as Patty nimbly hops across the strewn rocks, keeping her sneakers dry. Just at the water's edge, he lifts a crumbling piece of red shale and a salamander darts out, just faster than his grabbing hand. "I almost got one!" he yells to Patty. "We don't have time," she says, "If we're going to get to the magic place, we've got to hurry." So Sean fol-lows her path across the rocks, getting the toe of his left sneaker soaked when he misjudges a leap, but not caring one little bit. We're going to a magic place, he thinks, and we might even see an elf. Patty said they were there.

Running down the path now, skipping then, and galloping like a horse next, they make good time, Patty's memory of the way to the clearing unfaltering at the various forks they encounter. Sean, right at her heels the whole way, out of breath, almost slams into her when she stops short suddenly. "We're almost there," she says, "we have to be quiet in case they're out." So they creep, creep along the path, freezing when someone steps on a twig and its snap seems ominously loud against the quiet noises of the woods. Then Patty raises a hand for him to stop behind her, ducks into the denser cover of branches to one side of the trail, and motions him to follow. She pulls aside the softly bending branches of a sapling, peers ahead for a moment and gently eases them back into place. "They're there," she whispers right into his ear, "They're having a party. If they hear or see you, they'll vanish without a trace, the fire will go cold, and they'll be off safe in their secret tunnels under the river. If you listen, carefully, you can hear the music." He strains his ears, the rush of the river reaches him and he believes. Believes maybe it could be elfin music, and Patty's read about them, so she would know. "Do you want to see?" she whispers. Solemnly nodding, trusting her entirely, he quietly works his way in front of her, and she starts to peel back the branches for him. Just before he can see into the clearing, a branch snaps with a loud crunch and Patty says, "Rats" in her normal speaking voice. "That was too loud. Sorry." But as the clearing comes into his line of sight, he sees the black ring of an old fire, the rusting cans, the broken glass, the empty wine bottles, and is certain. With everything he is, he believes Patty has brought him to a special, magic place where elves gather, and that but for the unlucky snap of a tree branch, he might've seen them too. Pushing into the clearing, he investigates, holds his hands over the fire ring, feels no heat from its surface, and sits down on one of the fallen logs, hoping they might come back, and maybe a little disappointed he missed them.

Patty joins him there, "Sorry you missed them. I wanted my favorite brother to see them too." "I'm your only brother." "I know, but you're my favorite too." "Tell me more about the elves?" "Sure."

He listens, rapt, glancing around the clearing as she spins him a tale, and he's sure, without a doubt, that his sister is the best, that she likes him better than she could ever like anybody. Sure she knows more than anyone else and sure too she will always share what she knows with him.

The sun lingers on the edge of the horizon, brilliant orange, perfectly round. Teasing with its light and heat for just a short while as it prepares to dip down and out of sight. And in a quirk of this time of year, the moon, heavy and full, is already visible on the opposite end of the sky. Rush-hour traffic builds up on the two-lane, stoplight-dotted rural highways that carry people to and from this part of New Jersey. The road crews working on the new interstate designed to relieve this congestion cut the engines on their machines, hop down onto the new tarmac they've been working on, and fire up Marlboros, minds already focused on whatever they have planned for this night. It will be light for a while still, even after the sun goes down. The days still hold lengthy hours of afternoon light, though the nights are growing longer, and if anyone turned their mind to the possibility, they'd see that the cruelly short afternoons of December are just around the corner.

Patty winds up her tale, her sources that Tolkien classic she read over the summer, the C. S. Lewis she's picked up at the school library. But it's her own imagination and the eager look on Sean's face that allow her to take the details of the clearing—the rusting Bud cans and the decomposing cigarette ends—and work in how the elves, grown wary of the treachery of human beings, have taken to stealing people's garbage and scattering it around their magic places to trick people who try to find them. When she's done, he asks questions, and she gives answers, making most of them up on the spot. "What's mead?" "A drink they make from gold and spiderwebs that tastes like sunlight." "What happened to the dwarfs and the wizards?" "Remember when you learned about the coal mines in Pennsylvania in school? The dwarfs moved into those mines. The wizards are still here, but they've made themselves look like regular people until the time comes for them to take over again. We might even know one. You'd never know because they're so powerful."

Sean takes it all in, quiet with his thoughts, and Patty notices that the sky above the clearing has lost its shine. It's not dark, but it's not daytime either, and if they don't start back soon, they're going to be caught in the woods in the gloom. I wouldn't be scared, she thinks, but Sean would, and Mom will be mad at me. "Come on," she says, "we need to get going." "All right."

She leads him down the path, trusting behind her, and she realizes he's forgotten all about her talking to Jason after school. That Kate's probably forgotten as well, too busy thinking about Jimmy McNally. That no one would ever suspect she had smoked cigarettes and drunk alcohol and practically gone skinny-dipping with him in the river. And though she doesn't yet think of things in these terms, though it will be a few years before her transgressions against her own image get serious enough for her to actively conspire to keep them hidden, she begins to realize she can get away with some things. That the rules ordering her behavior most of the time are flexible as long as people don't find out.

The mother leans across the front seat, gives Anna a peck on the cheek, a quick squeeze about the shoulders that's not quite a hug. "See you tomorrow," she says. "Sean's got a soccer game after school. We'll have to go separately." "All right," Anna answers. Opening the door and stepping out into her driveway, she pokes her head in to finish, "See you in the faculty room. My love to Pat." For the first time in many hours, maybe since he left for work before seven this morning, she thinks of her husband, and with a touch of bitterness, she says, "Yeah, if I'm awake when he gets home." Suddenly surprised, she hasn't heard herself use this tone before, thinking all along that the hours didn't really bother her, that she'd accepted them as a necessary evil at this point in their lives, she wishes Anna could slip back into the car, that they could hash this out in her driveway with the engine running. Turn it over the way they've turned over everything major in their lives from the time they were little girls, but of course Nora's bobbing along in the backseat to "Don't Mess Around with Jim," and Anna's husband Jack's waiting for her inside. So, seeing the level-mouthed concern on Anna's face, she nods her head in Nora's direction, "I'll talk to you tomorrow." "You sure?" "Yeah." "Okay then."

Anna slams the heavy door into place; the mother watches as she walks to the front door, fits the key in the lock, and gets it open. Before disappearing inside, Anna turns and gives a fleeting wave. Working the automatic transmission into reverse, the mother wishes for a moment that things were the way they once were, she and Anna the durable duo of their youth. No husbands, no kids, the unfaltering sense every day that their bond was sacred, blood sisters, and as long as that remained constant, through the relative innocence of a 1950s childhood, the chaos of adolescence, the growing responsibility of adulthood, nothing else really mattered. The bond is still there, still sacred, but seeing Nora happily singing in the backseat, feeling her irritation at Pat, praying her other children are behaving and safe at home, she thinks, Other things matter now and there's not a damn thing I can do about it.

All this spins in her head as she navigates the residential streets back to her heavily mortgaged house, and turning into the driveway, twilight descending, she attempts to push them out of her mind. There's dinner to be made, homework to be helped with, Nora needs a bath before bed. She cuts the engine and Nora pops out of the backseat, running around to the kitchen door, the mother following more slowly.

When she gets around back, Nora is down on the ground, rolling with the mutt who favors her above all the other family members, the back door wide open. She feels too tired to be angry about Nora getting grass stains on her school clothes, too tired to take issue with the open door and the flies that are undoubtedly streaming into the house. "Come on Nora, come on Lucky," is all she says. And the two of them, a girl and her dog, bop off the ground and run into the family room, continuing their game.

The mother sinks onto a dining-room chair and drops her heavy purse onto the table, "Hello? I'm home! Kate? Patty, Sean?" From somewhere upstairs, Kate calls, "I'm on the phone! Sean and Patty are in the woods. I told them to be back by now." Wondering how she could possibly have a teenager with the phone surgically attached to her ear, the mother heaves herself to her feet. Pulling a whistle from the key rack hanging by the back door, she opens the door again, and calls over her shoulder to Kate, "Finish your call and come down and set the table." Out on the back porch, she raises the whistle to her lips, and blows three long blasts, a signal she knows will travel down to the creek where Sean and Patty are probably getting covered in mud as they chase after salamanders they'll cart home, put in homemade milk-bottle terrariums and unintentionally murder. If their butts aren't back in ten minutes I'll murder them, she thinks and comes back into the kitchen. Checking the wall calendar—she's been putting her weekly dinner menu there since she's been working so she won't forget things at the grocery store on Saturdays—she sees tonight is spaghetti and meatballs. She gets out the ground beef she transferred from the freezer to the fridge before leaving this morning, the saltines, the blue Ronzoni box, and family-size bottle of Ragú from the cabinet. As she sets to work, her spirits lift because she knows everyone likes spaghetti, no one will complain or refuse to eat, and that the dinner hour, at least, should pass without fuss or excitement.

·   ·   ·

Kate, cross-legged on the floor of the hallway, the phone tucked into place on her left shoulder, the pointer finger of her right hand twisting around a clutch of slightly split ends, says, "See you tomorrow?" Pauses, listens, "Yeah." Listens a moment longer, "Okay. Bye." Releasing those tortured strands of hair, she reaches up to the table, pushes the disconnect button on the phone's base, and holding her finger there, feeling nothing but pure happiness, feeling, if she thought that way, giddy. Wow, she thinks, standing and putting the phone in its cradle, he likes me. Jimmy McNally likes me, and we're going to the dance, and we're meeting for lunch in the art room, and. Wow.

It hadn't been, at first, an easy conversation. Palms sweaty and stomach clenched, she'd carried her scrap of paper to the phone, dialed six numbers and hung-up. Gathering her courage, she'd picked up the phone again, dialed all seven. Four rings and just as she was overcome with relief that no one, after all, was home, someone, his mother or one of his two older sisters, answered, and Kate managed to strangle out, "May I please speak to Jimmy?" The muffled, hand cupped over the speaker yell came through the line, "Jimmmmmy phone," then the singsong, "It's a girl!" One of the sisters then. Another line picked up, another muffled yell, Jimmy's "Got it," the click of the sister disconnecting, then Jimmy again, his morphing baritone softer, maybe surprised, "Hello?" "Hi. It's Kate Mahoney." "Hi."

Panic. This wasn't at all like talking to her girlfriends on the phone, when they pick up and blab and blab for hours about anything, boys from school, gossip about other girls, how much they love the new Pink Floyd record, trading answers to the math homework, ways they can get away with altering their uniforms. Silence. The only sound on the phone her breathing and his, and she slowly tried to match his exhalations and inhalations, to make up for having nothing to say by synchronizing their moments of breath. Worrying that scrap of paper into folded shapes. Finally, he says, "So, what's up?" "Nothing, I was just calling to say, 'Hi.'" "So, hi." "Hi yourself." And, for some reason, this got them laughing, she stuffed the scrap of paper into her pocket, and they were able to talk about their shared lunchtimes in the art room. He told her—perhaps he was sincere, perhaps it was an instinctual compliment—that he liked the thing she'd been doing, a charcoal still-life of classroom objects arranged on a table that the teacher left in place for her during the rest of the day. She said his paintings were "Bold, powerful," and immediately felt like she'd said the dumbest thing imaginable. Yet, he thanked her, and the conversation turned towards the weekend and the Harvest Dance, and he said, "Yeah, I guess I'm going," and she quickly added, "Me too." They talked around the dance for a while, and he offered his eighth-grade knowledge, "They're not as much fun if you don't have anyone to go with." "Yeah, I know." Ask me, she was thinking, willing his request into being through the phone, ask me. But now they were talking about how cool the new art teacher was, not stuffy like the nuns, but *really happening,* even letting them sketch nudes from pictures in art books. But then that silence again, just the sound of breath matching breath, until his voice blurted through the thickness on the line, "Maybe we could go together. To the dance, I mean." "Okay. Yeah. Sure." Then, too soon, she thought, her mother was home, calling her downstairs. "My mom just got home. I gotta go." "Okay." "See you tomorrow?" "Coming to lunch in the art room?" "Yeah." "See you then, bye." "Bye."

Walking the length of the hallway, heading down the stairs, she starts to half hum, half sing an Eagles' song that's been stuck in her head since it came on the art room radio at lunch, "Runnin' down the road, tryin' to loosen my load . . ." Distracted by thoughts of the phone call, she dance-walks across the kitchen and kisses her mother on the cheek. Singing, humming, she gathers the plates, silver, and napkins to set the table. Her mother looks at her curiously, "You're awfully chipper tonight. Good day?" "Not bad. Not bad at all." "Did you get that math test back?" Pulled from her reverie, thinking, Who cares about some stupid math test and she's not going to like that I didn't get an A, her mood shifts suddenly to surly. She lies, the change in her feelings obvious in her tone of voice, "No, Sister Mary-Elizabeth was out sick. We had a sub." But before the mother can react to the change, Nora comes barreling into the room, charges into Kate, wraps her arms around Kate's waist. Pressing against Kate's legs, she almost knocks her off balance as she lays the last knife to the right of the last plate. Allowing herself to be pulled into the family room, Kate feels her good mood coming back as Nora chatters away, "Katy-did, come color with me. Draw me a horse while I color. I wish I could draw like you."

They sit side by side on the couch, Nora rips a blank sheet from the back of her coloring book and hands it to Kate. Very serious, "I want one jumping. What color do you need?" "Black." Kate watches as Nora peers into her Crayola box of 64, plucks out the black, and says, "Remember, jumping." Nora goes back to work, struggling to keep her colors in the lines, and Kate drawing, doing what most makes sense to her, tucks the tip of her tongue in the hinge of her lips. Humming that song again, working on the horse for Nora, she thinks some more about Jimmy, what to say at lunch tomorrow, what she might wear to the dance on Friday night.

Sean and Patty had been crouching together over the creek bank, prying up rocks in a little sheltered pool, trying to grab hold of scuttling crayfish by their backs, out of reach of those little lobster claws, when the first whistle toot reached their ears. They both strained to listen, caught the last two blasts, recognized the call of their mother. They looked at one another, "Mom's home," then started to look for a way to cross the banks.

Now, having found some larger rocks suitable for hopping across and keeping dry, they're galloping together, side by side, through the tall grass, keeping an eye out for the barbed-wire boundary. When they're safely under, they run together up the hill, racing, Patty allowing Sean a slight advantage at this early stage, 'til Sean calls over his shoulder, "Last one home's a rotten egg." When the hill gets a bit steeper, Patty pours on the speed and they reach the back patio simultaneously, playfully trying to push one another out of the way, trying to get in the door first.

Inside, they're out of breath, their sneakers tracking mud, and their mother greets them, "Have fun? Take off your shoes." "Patty took me to a magic place where elves have their parties," Sean gasps as he kicks off his shoes, "She told me all about it, and I almost saw them, but a branch snapped and they disappeared, but she saw them, and, Mom, they were there! What's for dinner?" The mother looks at Patty, feeling overwhelmed with pride for her, feeling, momentarily, blessed by her children. She gives Patty a wink Sean can't see, "Wow. That must have been something. Was it far Patty? You'll have to show me. We're having spaghetti and meatballs." Patty, catches the wink and sends it back at her mother, "No, not that far. I'll take you sometime." "Okay, both of you go wash up and work on your homework, dinner will be ready in about forty-five minutes. No television if your homework's not done."

Patty trudges up to the kids' bathroom on the second floor, twists the tap, soaps up her hands, and when she's cleaned up, gathers her books and heads into her father's den. Sean joins his other sisters in the family room, "Patty and I went and saw where the elves go," he says to Kate and Nora. "What's an elves?" Nora asks. "An *elf*," Sean corrects, "is a magic creature that lives in the woods and drinks cobweb drinks and shoots bows and arrows. They have pointy ears like Mr. Spock on *Star Trek*, right Kate?" "I don't know Sean, if you say so." "I wanna see them too," Nora says. "You're too little, you couldn't go that far," Sean says, superiority ringing in his voice. "Could too." "Could not." Their voices rise. "Could." "Couldn't." "Jesus, you two," Kate whispers, "keep it down." "COULD NOT!" "COULD TOO!"

Sean gets up to leave, to wash up and do his homework before dinner as instructed, but as he walks by Nora, he can't resist grotesquely twisting his features, popping out his eyes, bulging his cheeks, and pushing his tongue out at her, "Could not, because you're too ugly, your face'd scare them away." She shoves him, close to tears, "Yes, I could. I even saw a mean hippie today." Thinking her push has given him license, Sean shoves her back, fairly hard, bouncing her head off the couch cushions, "You probably scared him away too, fart-face." But Nora's crying now, working up to a scream, and Kate's angry, pinching Sean's shoulder as hard she can, muttering, "Nice work, shithead," as she strides from the room. Suddenly, Nora stands up and heads towards the kitchen, howling, "MOMMY! SEAN HIT ME!"

"SEAN MAHONEY," his mother bellows from the kitchen, "GET IN HERE!" Dawdling, he goes into the kitchen to face his mother. "She hit me first—" "—It doesn't matter," the mother says, "you're bigger and you should know better. Go to your room until dinner and do your homework." "But, Mom, she—" "No buts. Go, or you'll have to deal with your father when he gets home."

Sean goes, slowly, pouting. He gets to his room, flops on his bed, tears in his own eyes, thinking, It's not fair. Nora started it. I always get in trouble, even if she starts it. It's not fair.

The father, stuck at a light not far from the house, his resolve to stay until 5:45 gone by 5:20, realizes he's forgotten to call home to let Liz know he'll be home for dinner tonight. A surprise, he thinks, I'll surprise her. With that thought spinning in his head, he keeps his eyes peeled for the almost squalid strip of shops that houses the only liquor store and florist in this little town. They're overpriced, normally if he was going to pick something up on the way home, he'd stop in Somerville or Morristown, but what the hell, he thinks, we're going to celebrate tonight. Turning off, he fairly hops out of the car, a bit of a swagger in his step as he goes into the florist's and selects a dozen long-stemmed roses for Liz. "Big date?" asks the attractive young woman behind the counter, her voice heavy with suggestion. "With my wife," the father laughs, thinking, I've still got it, and holding up his gold band-wrapped finger. "Well then," the girl says, a bit peevishly, "we'll make them up nice for her." Clutching his bouquet, he walks over to the liquor store, feeling like a much younger man as he thinks, The hell with the work, I'll go in early in the morning.

He wanders the shelves wondering what to buy, the taste of Scotch still lingering somewhere near his molars as he pokes among the wine, wishing he knew more about what was good, which ones were steals, which ones were just priced by the label. Scanning the racks, he thinks hard, trying to remember what the calendar said they were having for dinner. Should he pick white or red? Unsure, he impulsively selects two mid-priced bottles, one of each shade, and hopes for the best. At the register, Old Jack behind the counter gives him a raised eyebrow. His normal purchase here is a six-pack and a pack of Winstons. "Anything else, Mr. Mahoney?" "Nope. Trying to quit smoking," the father says, but behind the register he sees the carefully arranged, more expensive bottles of liquor, the ones not trusted to clumsy hands on the floor. "Tell you what, Jack," he adds, "Give me a bottle of that Glenlivet as well." More surprise on Jack's features as he shuffles over to the rack and pulls down the pricey Scotch, "Celebrating tonight?" "Something like that. Things are looking up at work." He slides his MasterCard across the counter, signs the receipt. Is back in his car lickety-split, and thinking, I've got to learn about wine and good whisky if I'm going to be a partner. I'll have to entertain clients soon. I'll have to get my golf game in shape.

Soon, he's heading up his own street, turning into his driveway. It is the dappled light time of dusk, and he can't remember the last time he saw his house in this light. Gathering his trial bag and his purchases, he knocks the car door shut with his hip, and stands for a moment, savoring the air of the evening. One of his neighbors is burning leaves and the purely autumnal smell wafts around him, filling him with something that feels like a promise. He can hear calls from around the neighborhood, what sounds like a father and son tossing a football around, the boy's cry "TOUCHDOWN!" and the lower rumbles of the father's, "Good grab, I didn't think you'd get to that one." Those sounds make him think of his own son, how he doesn't get home all that often when it's still light enough to toss a ball around. Anyway, Sean would rather kick a soccer ball than toss a football. The few times he's been able to get off work to see his son's games, he's been unable to understand what the hell was going on anyway. And Sean's so small and skinny, the father thinks, that boy worries me. I'll have to spend more time with him. But, not tonight. Tonight, we celebrate. He walks around to the back door and sees his pretty wife through the screen door as she works on dinner. Taking a deep breath, he tucks the flowers behind his back, pushes the door in, "Alice, I'm home," he says in his best Ralph Kramden voice, "When's dinner?"

The mother, deep in thought, wondering why she'd threatened Sean with his father when all the discipline seems to be her bailiwick, is startled by his unlikely appearance. But she stifles her surprised irritation, trying hard to be happy to see him, and after the briefest of moments, she in fact is. "Well," she says, "this is a surprise. What've you got there?" "Just some wine and a bottle of Scotch," placing his trial bag on the kitchen floor and plopping the liquor store bag on the counter. "Oh yes," he produces the roses, "And these. For you." She looks at him carefully, trying to remember the last time he brought her roses or grabbed some wine without being asked. And Scotch? But she sees the look on his face, open and soft, that eager, delicate look that coats his features when he's hungry for her. "Thank you, they're beautiful," she takes the flowers and nestles herself into his waiting hug, marveling at how, even with the way their bodies have softened and settled over the years, even with the way she often feels completely separate from him during the day, when they finally come together, they still fit as closely and perfectly together as they did on the night they first met. "To what do we owe this pleasure?" she murmurs. "Riker basically told me I'd be a partner by the end of the month. I thought a celebration might be in order." Rocking against him, she says, "That means more money, right?" "Yes. And shorter hours after a while," he answers, tracing an enthusiastic hand along her side, around the curve of her hips, down and around to the hollow of her back, fingers reaching down and playing near her ass. She feels desire bubbling slowly forth in her, feels him aroused, pushing against his suit pants, and she licks a tiny playful lick on his neck, "A celebration indeed."

Then Nora's bounding into the kitchen, intruding on their embrace, working herself into their hug. "Daddy," she squeals, "You're home! I got a hundred today, and Mommy took me to get ice cream, and I played with Kathy, and there was this mean hippie there. I made you and Mommy a sheep in school, and Miss Kim told me it was really good, and we're having scgetti and meatballs for dinner!" Disentangling themselves, the mother pulling a vase from the cabinet over the fridge and filling it with water, the father asks, "Where are the other kids?" "Kate's doing whatever it is she does in her room all afternoon with the door locked. Hopefully her math homework, but she's probably doodling or mooning over some boy. Patty's in your den doing her homework on the coffee table without a word of protest. Sean's in his room until dinner." "What now?" Nodding her head in Nora's direction, the mother says, "The usual."

Feeling his anger rise, the father thinks, Christ, that boy needs a swift kick in the pants. But his wife puts a gentle hand on his shoulder, "Why don't you put the white in the freezer so it's cold in time for dinner? I know I'm supposed to have red with pasta, but it kills my head." He puts the wine in to chill, leaves the red on the counter, and puts the bottle of Scotch in the liquor cabinet with the cast-off bottles of cheap booze that lie untouched between New Year's Eve parties. Gathering up his trial bag, he heads towards the den and his favorite child.

As he comes into his personal sanctum, he sees Patty's school books scattered on the coffee table, but she's curled on the floor with an old Modern Library book from the basement. Taking note of her avidly scanning eyes, he says, "Hey," his affection clear in his voice, "is that homework?" "You're home?" she asks, rising and skipping over to hug her dad. He drops the bag at his feet and welcomes her jumping embrace. "What're you reading?" *"Tom Sawyer,"* she says. Their hug released, she sits and takes up the book again. "How is it?" "Not bad," she says, "I like Becky Thatcher. She should've gotten her own book." "And your homework?" "It's done." "You sure?" he prods, not really caring, thinking whatever it is she's supposed to do for school is probably not as valuable as Twain, but play-acting the role of concerned parent. "Daaaad," she answers, telling the truth, it hadn't taken long at all, "please. It was easy, and it's done." "Okay, then. Go back to your book. I'll join you in a minute."

He goes through the connecting door to the master bedroom, kicks off his brogues, pulls off his tie, tosses his oxford shirt into the hamper and carefully hangs his suit back in the closet. Standing in the master bathroom, he catches his jockey-shorts-clad reflection in the mirror. Trying to suck in his gut, he takes stock, thinks, Not too bad for an old guy, then pulls a pair of jeans and a rugby shirt from the floor, slips them on and heads back into his den. Patty flicks him a glance from her spot on the floor. He grabs his own book from the trial bag, kicks back on the love seat and, as obsessively as his daughter, starts to read.

In his room, Sean tucks into his homework. Finished, for now, with feeling sorry for himself, he wants to get it finished so he can watch the Muppets after dinner.

Kate smuggles a battered copy of *Fear of Flying* all the girls have been surreptitiously passing around at school into the bathroom, sits herself on the toilet, and thumbs through the pages looking for the folded over corners marking "the good parts." She feels a rising flush as she starts to read, putting Jimmy's head on the stranger in a train in her imagination.

. . .

The mother drains the spaghetti, slides it into a big bowl and stirs in some sauce. She spoons the meatballs from the pot into a Corning Ware dish, sets a trivet on the table, puts out the serving dishes, two wine glasses and both open bottles. Finished tossing the salad, she checks the garlic bread in the oven. Almost ready. She grabs her glass off the table, pours out some of the white and as she takes a sip, she thinks, Only a few hours until bedtime for the kids. Only a few hours until bedtime for us.

Dinner is ready. The mother calls to the various places in the house, "DINNER!" and everyone makes their way to the table. Sean's first, knowing the call is his release from unjust bondage in his room. Then Nora. The father and Patty are a few moments behind, both delayed by the quest to finish a chapter or paragraph. They all wait for Kate. Finally, the mother stands, exasperated. "Katy-did!" she hollers from the base of the stairs, "Dinner's ready. Come on." "Just a minute, I'm in the bathroom." "Of course she is," the father mutters. She always seems to be in the bathroom these days when it's time for something else. After a few moments, they hear the toilet flush and she joins them. Surprised at seeing her father in the usually vacant place at the head of the table, she says, "You're home," in her new blasé, teenaged voice. But she walks over and gives him a kiss on the top of his head before settling into her place. The mother says grace, plates are handed around, filled. They dig in, making conversation between bites, Kate politely asking Sean to please pass the cheese, Sean asking if his father will come to his game tomorrow, boasting, "I'm gonna play forward this week." "I'll try my best," the father tells him, "but work's pretty busy." The mother tries not to be irritated, at least he's home tonight, "It'd be nice if you could make it." All of the children are quizzed about what's going on at school. Kate serving notice that she'd like to attend a dance on Friday night, stoically bears some ribbing from her father and the two younger kids about whether or not she has a boyfriend to go with, though on another night, this sort of teasing might send her crying up to her room. Patty fills them in on her latest academic success, trying to wrest some of the attention from Kate onto herself. All in all a successful family dinner, and soon they're finished. Dutifully, the children file to the garbage, scrape their plates, load them into the dishwasher.

The father wanders to the liquor cabinet, gets his new bottle and pours two small, after-dinner measures for him and the mother. Without a fuss, Sean and Kate take up tonight's drying-and-washing positions at the sink and go to work on the dirty pots. The mother covers up the leftovers and loads them in the fridge. In the family room, the father calls up CBS on the television just in time to catch Walter Cronkite's nightly dispatch. The mother stretches out on the couch and sips at her little whisky, trying to decide if she likes it. Nora and Patty settle on the floor, Patty with her book, Nora playing with the dog. When Walter declares, "And that's the way it is, October 1, 1975. Thank you, and good night," Sean wanders in to catch the opening strains of *The Muppet Show* theme and Kate heads back upstairs to the phone, where she's got some business to conduct with a couple of girls from school, arranging tomorrow's details.

The night moves on. Nora's shepherded to bed after John Denver signs off the Muppets for the night, Sean's tucked in soon after, raising only a minor fuss about having to go to bed before Kate and Patty. The programs on the television move from half-hour comedies to the nine o'clock hour-long dramas, the mother feels herself dozing off on the couch, but tonight she manages to keep herself awake until Patty's sent to bed at 9:30, Kate at 10:00. They go up on their own, kissing their mother on the cheek, leaning over the recliner to brush a goodnight peck on the top of their father's head.

. . .

Sean and Nora are slack-jawed, and steadily, regularly breathing as they sleep the uncomplicated sleep of youth. Patty stealthily turns the pages of *Tom Sawyer* by the light of an under-the-covers flashlight until her eyes are so sleep-heavy, she drifts off, the light shining until its batteries weaken and die in the hollow hours of the morning. Kate lies awake for a time, her thoughts flashing—trying to recall the shower's pattern in her head one moment, thoughts of Jimmy McNally muddling up with the guilty pleasures of the illicit words in that book the next—until, without realizing she was heading in that direction, she slips into sleep lying on her side with one hand wedged between her legs, cupped over her underwear.

With Kate at last gone to bed, the father snuggles himself onto the couch with the mother. For a time they just cuddle there in case one of the children comes down, unable to sleep, in search of a glass of water, troubled by nightmares. But not for long, their mild drunkenness usurping any caution, and with both tenderness and eagerness, they set about making up for a lot of nights when they've both been too tired for this sort of thing. When they both are naked, a moment of reality sets in, *one of the kids could come down at any moment,* and giggling at the possibility, they quickly gather their clothes and chase each other to the master bedroom, locking the door, and taking up where they left off.

Some time later, everyone under this roof sleeps soundly. They have a few years, at least, before the mother will lie awake at this hour, waiting with nauseous worry for one of her children to come in. A few years until they'll feel the need to confront anything as treacherous as drugs or emerging sexuality or beer binges or the growing distress of

a marriage that might just possibly be fraying at the seams or a daughter whose moody oddities might have gone too far. They are a few
years away from the sort of problems that will keep them up at night.
And so tonight, on a lovely autumn evening in the mid-1970s, the
Mahoney family sleeps untroubled.

1 9 7 2

Nora wakes first and toddles to the television hulking silently in the living room. Pulling the knob, she quickly lowers the volume to a bare murmur; mustn't wake anyone yet. Kneeling on the floor, inches from the images coming into focus, she spins the dial around to 13. Today's show is dedicated to the letter P.

Sean sleeps the deep, hard sleep he will always sleep. His features, soft now even when he's awake, will only find this easy comfort in the hollows of the morning as he grows older. A smile plays on his lips as he dreams. He'll be going to the beach later. There will be birds and waves. The bridge will open, spitting out lines of large boats to the clink-clacking of the warning bell.

Kate and Patty open their eyes in matching twin beds separated by a strip of carpet worn from good night walks. Rough sleep grit is rubbed from their eyes, and they turn to face each other with smiles. At ten and eight, they're still in synchronicity. Climbing out of bed, they slip right into still damp bathing suits. There's no time to waste, summer is ending.

The father, holding on to sleep with the tenacity of his son, presses against the mother as she wakes, knowing with certainty that her children are stirring and will need to be fed. She allows herself a moment of unfocused pleasure as the father slips an arm around her waist and pulls her tightly against the taut roundness of his growing belly. Sighing, she plants her feet on the hardwood floor, her thoughts shifting to a pot of coffee and how many eggs are left in the refrigerator.

Nora, hearing the others moving over the soft voices of Bert and Ernie, raises the volume. People are up now; it's okay.

The mother drifts into the living room, kisses her baby on the top of her head, and continues into the kitchen. She starts the coffee perking, opens the door of the fridge, peers inside. Raising her arms over her head, she stretches out her back, little cricks moving over her spine. Kate and Patty come into the kitchen and see their mother with her body raised like a dancer's, the dark outline of her limbs just visible through her nightgown, and they think, Our mother is beautiful. The mother hears her oldest girls behind her, turns with a smile, "Good morning, morning glories. Bacon and eggs?"

. . .

The men of the house finally stir. The father picks up the rich wake-up scent of coffee and senses an empty space next to him. He feels the sun playing warmly along the sheets and knows the time's come to shake off sleep and greet the day. Sean too smells the coffee, but it's the clank of the heavy, black frying pan on the stove, the hiss of bacon, the almost maple scent of the fat popping into grease that lets the day seep in. We'll go to the beach, he thinks as he throws the covers off his skinny limbs and heads towards the food. He's just five and not yet coltish, though if you look, you can tell he will be soon. As he comes into the kitchen, the light from the window catches the downy hair on his spindly legs, and his mother sees him, sees his older sisters sitting around the table with their tall glasses of orange juice, and she thinks, Remember this, remember the blessed feeling of this summer, because look at them, they are growing so fast.

Nora, distracted from Oscar by a rumbling in her little stomach, heads into the kitchen. The television plays on. Her mother's back is to her, tending to the stove. Nora sees this and knows it means food is coming, "Brekfst?" she asks. "Soon, darling," the mother hands her a wooden spoon and a metal mixing bowl. Nora plops down on the faux brick linoleum, happily scraping the sides of the bowl, pretending to stir her favorite foods, marshmallow and peanut butter and noodles, then offering tastes to Kate and Patty and Sean. They eat the air on the spoon, say, "Mmmmm."

The father slips on cutoffs and a T-shirt and walks out onto the porch to pick up the paper. He scowls at the headlines on the front page, but flipping to the sports section, he nods with satisfaction. The Yankees have won again. On his way to the kitchen, he flips off the television. The sound goes first, quickly. The picture collapses in on itself to a line of shrinking color, then disappears with a rush that looks as if it sounds like "Pop!"

Everyone's in the kitchen now. The mother hums an off-key melody under her breath as she portions out bacon and eggs onto four plates and sets them before her children. The eldest three dig in. Nora is lifted from the floor, strapped into the highchair worn by three other bottoms. She holds a fork in a tight fist, shovels eggs towards her mouth, bursts into laughter as she smears bits of breakfast on her lips, her cheeks.

The father pours a cup of coffee, stirs in swirls of milk and grains of sugar and sips. Just right; the color of sand with just a hint of sweet over the dark roast.

Sean eats quickly, barely tasting, thinking only, When we finish eating, we'll go to the beach.

The mother nibbles on a corner of toast as she helps Nora guide her fork to her mouth and snatches bites from her baby's plate. "One for you," she sings softly, "one for me." Nora laughs at this game, takes the fork and directs a mouthful at her mother's face.

Kate finishes, dumps her plate in the sink, runs to her room to grab a set of schoolgirl colored pencils and construction paper. She carries her bundle to the front porch and perches on one of the wicker chairs. The sun shines in under the eaves; the porch basks in the morning sun. She pulls pencils carefully from her box, mulling her choices, and layers lines onto the paper.

Patty, a bit slower, scrapes her plate and rinses it under the tap. She too heads to their room, grabs a book, a book meant for older children, and joins her sister on the porch. She climbs in the hammock and begins to turn the pages. Her face is serious, eager. Looking carefully, you can see she sometimes stops and stares at what Kate is drawing.

The father, changed into his bathing suit, brings a fresh cup of coffee out on to the porch to finish the paper. The station wagon is still loaded with the beach things from yesterday; he's ready. Three-quarters of a Churchill biography promises to fill most of his day.

The mother leaves Nora in the high chair as she cleans the remains of breakfast from the kitchen. Finishing, she swoops down and cleans the baby's face with kisses and a wet towel. Sean comes into the kitchen holding a pail and shovel, "Are we going soon?" "Soon," the mother says. "As soon as I put on my suit and change the baby."

Then everyone is in the car. Sun has already warmed the interior to smoking. Legs suck onto the cracking vinyl seats. Nora is buckled tight into a car seat although it's only four blocks to the beach. Before the children, when the parents visited Liz's mother here during the summer, they would have walked, hand in hand, towels slung across their shoulders, books tucked into folding chairs dangling from their other hands. But, now. Now, there's the beach pen and the umbrella to keep the sun off the baby's head and the pails, shovels, and Frisbee. The cooler full of snacks and lunch, sun lotion and zinc oxide for Sean's per-

manently peeling nose. The blanket to sit on, six towels for after swimming, the small first-aid kit should anyone cut a foot on a beer pull-top
or a finger on a razor clamshell. The baby's inflatable arm floats and
Styrofoam back bubble as added insurance should a wave sweep her
from a parent's protective arm.

Patty never put her book down as she was moved from the porch to
the car. Now, she just keeps turning the pages as the car slowly rolls towards Ocean Avenue looking for a good parking place.

Kate stares at the big trees lining the streets leading to the beach, noticing the way the soft ocean breeze stirs the leaves and shifts the pattern
of sunlight on the sidewalk.

Sean, in the way-back surrounded by beach things, faces away from
their destination. As the car turns onto Ocean, he swivels around to see
the stretch of sea leading off forever. Something in him, something he
will never understand, leaps with joy as the car rolls to a stop, and he
can hear the slow grind of the swells, the high shriek of the gulls
swooping over the fishermen on the jetty.

Nora turns her head as far as it will go in the confines of her car seat,
naming off each of them in turn, "Ma, Da, Tat, Kay, Shoon."

The father sits still as the car shivers into stillness, wishing for a moment, just for a moment, that it was just him and the mother going to
the beach today. But he catches sight of his children in the rearview
mirror and smiles. Looking at them, at Kate who's grown all gangly in

the last six months, at Patty's serious face as she reads, at skinny little Sean, and the baby humming to herself in the car seat, he wonders sentimentally how long this can last, this going together as a family, in peace.

The sand already seethes with heat as they kick off flip-flops and quick-step the dance of beachgoers. "Oh!" "Ouch, Ouch!" The father picks a spot a few feet off from the lifeguard stand, plops down his portion of the bundle and plants the umbrella into the sand with a fierce thrust. A round, dark circle of shade spreads at their feet, and the mother spreads the blanket and unfolds the baby's beach pen, the wood creaking around its hinges. She plops Nora inside, hands her some toys, a picture book. Nora sits quietly, raising fistfuls of sand to her mouth, making patty cakes around her feet.

Kate and Patty run right to the water's edge, shrieking as they run back towards the sunbathers as waves lap around their feet, then, as the water retreats, they chase it back. Another wave, another shriek, another retreat, another chase.

The mother settles into her chair, checks the baby, shields her eyes from the sun with the flat of her hand, and watches her eldest daughters play by the water. Her light heart is tinged with worry. All this, she thinks, is too vast for them.

The father stands, checks to make sure all is arranged, wipes a glistening line from his forehead. Glancing over at his son, he sees him taking it all in, smiling at the pigeons and the gulls, the sparkles on the sun-dappled water, the old clam-diggers in overalls casting for blues from the end of the jetty. "Go for a swim, Champ?" but Sean shakes his head no. The father shrugs, runs off towards the water, gathering speed, spraying water from his feet as he hits the shallows. Then with an old athlete's lingering grace, he launches a dive into a cresting wave, surfaces, and swims far out into the swells with easy, powerful strokes.

Kate watches her father swim, sees the bright red of his suit against the churning green of the water, catches the flash of his arms as he slides over the top of the waves. France is that way, she thinks, he could swim all the way to France.

Nora feels the heat, but not the bright pull of the sun. Feels herself growing sleepy, slides into a nap.

Sean sits on the edge of the blanket, nibbling a cookie, pushing sand around with his feet, building shifting hillocks and crumbling mountains. The birds, fat with a summer of beach scraps, gather nearby as he tosses crumbs. A big old gull, feathers mottled with the scars of a hundred summers, comes almost close enough to take portions from Sean's fingers. He's dying to touch them. Patty told him they had hollow bones, she read that, and he wants to feel them light and eager, feel what it is to fly.

The wind is from the south, bringing heat. The mother is glad for this. For days, it's blown from the west, carrying small, stinging bugs and heavy air that made everyone slack and irritable. The forecast calls for a shift later, the air growing cooler by late afternoon, the wind whipping in from off the water as the tide rises, the possibility of a storm, the first breath of autumn. Summer is ending.

. . .

Patty builds sand castles, intricate cities of different-shaped pails and kitchen containers, dribbling wet sand to make turrets like candle wax on a bottle in an Italian trattoria she will discover on a left-over New York street during college and think, I love this place.

The father bodysurfs in on the biggest wave of the morning, and dripping, makes his way to the blanket. He kisses the mother on the top of her head, shaking beads of seawater on her body. "Stop, you're getting me all wet," she says, but she's smiling and her eyes, just for a moment, see the young man she met here years ago.

Kate scootches in against her mother's chair and looks out at the horizon, searching for boats. Sailboats are her favorite—big, open ocean yachts with large and painfully white mainsails taut in the wind, leaning almost into the water as they race along.

Sean, his cookie finished, slowly stands so as not to frighten the small flock gathered near him. Creeping towards the birds, he looks old. But as they hop and skitter away from him, he bursts into a wild, slanting run, chasing, trying to grab their wings, their feet, kicking sand on neighboring blankets, and he's young again. A child with waking dreams of flight.

The father, toweled off, water shaken from his ears, hair growing stiff with salt as it dries, plops into his chair and opens his book. He listens for a moment to a transistor on another blanket tuned to the Yankees' pre-game show, then begins to read and is gone.

. . .

Up on Ocean Avenue, the warning bell of the drawbridge begins to clang, the light turns red and the traffic barriers lower. "Can I?" Sean dances from foot to foot. The mother thinks, weighs her answer, and Kate says, "I'll take him." So, hand in hand, they start for the jetty as the bridge slowly creeps open.

The sun moves higher in the sky and the mother shifts the umbrella to keep Nora covered. Sensing movement or maybe the subtle change in brightness, Nora wakes, says, "Hungry." The mother rummages in the cooler and hands her a plum. Nora takes it, pushes it at her mouth, chews and sucks at the skin, staining her lips and cheeks with the soft patina of a bruise.

A line of boats, evenly, carefully spaced, emerges from the shadows under the bridge. First a sailboat, the sail gathered in a roll along the mast, moving under the power of the motor. Then a big Chris-Craft chafing at the slow progress out of the harbor, weaving slightly from side to side in repressed speed, its passengers with eyes only for the last channel marker buoy, the place where the throttle can be thrown down, the boat rearing up and racing off. Finally, the boats Sean loves, the party fishing boats out for a half day after fluke or blues or the dwindling striped bass. The boats his father has promised they will go out on before this summer has ended. The men cluster along the rail, downing sodas and cold beers, thinking, Tonight, we'll eat fish, Goddamn it.

The mother eases her chair back as far as it will go, closes her eyes and drifts into a shady half-sleep.

. . .

Patty, finished with her castle, comes up to the blanket and finds her own plum. Taking a bite, she turns her head up and down the beach, watching for the blond boy who has kicked down her castles all summer long. Satisfied he's not there, she picks up her book. Quickly, like her father, she is off the beach, visiting someplace else.

Sean waves his arms as the boats pass. Some of the men wave back. The last boat has passed under the bridge, the chime starts its "dinka, dinka, dinka" song, and the bridge moves downward. Out on the road, engines rev as drivers wait impatiently to continue their journeys.

Nora feels a wetness creeping around her diaper, fusses. The mother stirs, clucks her tongue, "What is it honey-bunches?" Nora stands, holds the rails of her pen and giggles. "Okay, I'll take you out." The mother lifts Nora under the arms, swoops her a bit through the air, then cradles her for a moment, feeling the laden Pampers. "Let's get this off and go for a swim." Quickly, Nora is released from her suit, the diaper removed and rolled into a sodden mass. Wipes are pulled from the bag and just before the mother pulls the suit back on, she plants raspberries around Nora's tummy, drawing squeals of laughter.

The father falls asleep, his book propped open on the hump of his belly.

Kate and Sean wander farther out on the jetty, peering into buckets. They see bluefish lazily swooping their tails, moving in lax circles, struggling for breath. Farther on, a doormat fluke lies flat at the bottom of an old paint can, its tail halfway up the side. Its eyes, clustered together, two black globes in the mottled brown body, are slowly losing their luster.

The tide is coming in, the waves growing larger. The green, "open swimming" flag atop the lifeguard stand whips faster with a steady crack from the wind, blowing now from the northeast, chilling the air.

Nora and the mother walk along the water's edge, down to the place where the jetty juts out at an angle, forming an artificial cove to limit the waves, the spot the locals call "diaper beach."

Patty reads, more slowly now, she knows the end is coming and wants to delay that moment. She's forgotten to bring a second book.

Kate and Sean are almost at the end of the jetty, they are careful to walk on the rougher rocks that feel like cement. The granite slabs are slick with water from the waves, the footing treacherous. Back in June, their feet still tender from a winter's worth of shoes, they couldn't bear the rough texture, but they step easily now, soles hardened in just a few months.

The mother wades in up to her waist, holding Nora aloft, then dunking her. First just her feet, then halfway up her legs, then to the spot where she will someday grow hips, then to her neck. The mother supports Nora's thighs and chest, proud to see her little girl hold her head above water on her own, her face turned into a wide open smile. And those legs: they kick, kick, kick.

. . .

The father wakes, feeling it's grown chilly. He has a moment of panic when he spies only Patty, but smiles to see her buried in a book, "Where's everyone?" Patty, distracted, hasn't heard him, "What, Daddy?" "Where's everyone?" "Mom and Nora are swimming, Kate and Sean are out on the jetty." Satisfied, they both go back to their reading.

The wind grows stronger. The temperature is falling quickly, the water emptying, people packing up to go home for the day. The lifeguard zips a windbreaker over his shoulders.

Kate and Sean try to stay out of the way as the fishermen suddenly begin a sudden frenzy of casting and retrieving. The incoming tide has brought in a school of bait fish and the blues are running. Breaking the surface, feeding on the darting killies, they flash out of the water in an orgy of instinctual hunger. Kate points as the fish crash through the surface, drawing rainbows as sun meets the water shaken from their backs. "Sean," she yells, "flying fish!" "Flying fish?" he says. Then he spots them, clapping, he points as a bluefish crashes through the water's surface, "Flying fish!"

The mother, feeling gooseflesh break out on her arms, leads Nora out of the water back to the blanket. Grabbing a towel, she holds Nora tightly and briskly rubs her dry, pulls her dripping suit off, slaps a clean diaper on, then covers her in an old, red windbreaker of Kate's that Nora wears like a dress. She does all this first, then tends to herself. Dries herself with Nora's damp towel and pulls on a wrap with a little shiver.

Out on the horizon, the sky darkens. The storm, miles away still, is coming. Boats pull up anchor and turn towards the harbor. On a neighboring blanket, the transistor Yankee game is interrupted by a thunderstorm warning for coastal New Jersey and Long Island.

The father, suddenly noticing from the depths of his reading that he's cold, looks at the mother and asks, "Should we pack up?" "Yes," the mother says. "What about Kate and Sean?" "Load up the car and we'll all walk out and get them."

The fishing frenzy has ended. The bait fish feel the power of a storm still rising in the hidden currents and retreat further inland, down river, towards the bay. The blues follow, gnashing their thin, sharp teeth, still feeding, not fearful of hooks or weather.

Kate stares out at the deep ocean, notices the swells have grown larger still, thinks, We should get back. But her eye catches on the line of the storm, the inky black sky roiling the water, making it darker out near the end of where she can see as it slowly engulfs the green and blue sea still speckled with the sun.

Sean shivers in his short-sleeved yellow shirt and realizes the weather means they will be leaving soon. But then the bridge sings out its song again, "dinka, dinka, dinka." His first thought is on what boat will come out first, but then he sees them lined up beyond the buoy, waiting to get home before the storm breaks.

The father packs the car in three trips. Only the mother's small sack remains, and he knows she'll hold on to that because it almost always can produce what is needed: candy, a Band-Aid, a pacifier, a nail file.

. . .

The beach is nearly empty. The lifeguards drag their rowboats up to the shelter of the boardwalk, lower their stands and blow their whistles to wave in the last couple of surfers waiting on the waves the storm is drumming up.

Patty holds Nora's hand as they walk along the water line towards the jetty to fetch Kate and Sean. The mother and father linger a few steps behind, arms wrapped around the other's waist. The mother, a long afternoon and evening ahead, thinks, We'll eat the sandwiches from the cooler on the porch, then Kate will draw, Patty will read, the baby will nap and Sean can help me make cookies. Maybe later we'll go out for pizza.

Kate and Sean sit at the end of the jetty. Sean watches the boats, so many boats racing in, then looks up at the foghorn, at the gulls huddled there, heads tucked into their wings, bracing. Then there are those who haven't landed yet, still out over the water, wings spread wide, soaring higher and higher on the air rushing ahead of the storm.

Patty and Nora reach the jetty and walk out a bit. Nora finds a small piece of driftwood, a stick really, worn smooth by the water. About three-quarters of the way to where Kate and Sean sit, Nora is distracted by a small crab marooned in a tidal pool. She stops, points and says, "Ouch." Patty laughs, crouches next to her, "Crab." Nora, poking at the crab with her stick, says, "Cwab?"

. . .

Most of the fishermen have called it a day, packed up their gear and headed towards wherever home is. The storm comes closer, thin strips of lightning flash out over the water in widely spaced intervals.

The parents walk out on the jetty. It's almost empty, just the family there now, Kate and Sean with their backs to the land, facing the sea, Kate's arm raised to something on the horizon. Patty and Nora crouched over something, Nora poking at whatever it is with a stick too large for her chubby, little hands. She touches the father on his arm, stopping him from calling out to their children, and pulls his camera out of her bag. He takes it, raises the viewfinder to his eye, fiddles with the focus and f-stop, then quickly snaps a picture.

A photograph has been taken. The first heavy, fat drops of rain hit the water not far from the beach. Summer is ending. As the mother calls, "Come on, kids! Time to go!" her voice is partly obscured by the wind. But they hear her, and they turn and walk towards her and the father. The whole family makes it to the car just as it starts to pour. Drops pelt the windshield as they settle in and the father starts the ignition. The mother, doing a mental inventory of all their things, satisfied that everyone and everything is in the car, safe, leans back in her seat, and says, "I guess we should head on home."